GREAT AND PRECIOUS THINGS

REBECCA YARROS

GREAT
AND
PRECIOUS
THINGS

Copyright © 2020 by Rebecca Yarros.

All rights reserved, including the right to reproduce, distribute, or transmit in any form or by any means. For information regarding subsidiary rights, please contact the Publisher.
Preview of *Full Measures* copyright © 2023 by Rebecca Yarros.

Excerpt(s) from EAST OF EDEN by John Steinbeck, copyright © 1952 by John Steinbeck; copyright renewed © 1980 by Elaine Steinbeck, Thom Steinbeck, and John Steinbeck IV. Used by permission of Viking Books, an imprint of Penguin Publishing Group, a division of Penguin Random House LLC. All rights reserved.

Entangled Publishing, LLC
644 Shrewsbury Commons Ave., STE 181
Shrewsbury, PA 17361
rights@entangledpublishing.com
Visit our website at www.entangledpublishing.com.

Amara is an imprint of Entangled Publishing, LLC.

Edited by Liz Pelletier
Cover design by Bree Archer
Cover images by
Marc Andreu/GettyImages and
Michael Lane/Gettyimages
Interior design by Heather Howland

Print ISBN 978-1-64063-816-7
ebook ISBN 978-1-64063-817-4

Manufactured in the United States of America

First Edition February 2020

10 9 8 7 6 5 4 3

To my father,
whose hands never let me fall.
I love you, Daddy.

CHAPTER ONE

Camden

My lungs burned as I drew a deep breath, seeking oxygen that wasn't there, and my fingers itched to hold the cigarette I'd thrown away six years ago. Altitude did that to me every time—at least the breathing part.

The craving for a smoke? That was courtesy of Alba, Colorado, population 649. Or so the sign I'd passed about a mile back proclaimed. Then again, I wasn't about to trust a sign that hadn't been updated since before I'd been born—which was par for the course in my hometown.

Nothing about it had changed since I'd left, which was pretty much the point of the whole town. Just past the paved roads, Alba was the best-preserved ghost town in Colorado, and the tourists who flooded her streets in the summer kept the tiny town alive all winter long.

The total on the gas pump climbed as I stretched my hands toward the late-afternoon sun and the snowcapped peaks above me, willing life back into muscles I'd kept cramped for far too long during the drive from North Carolina. The bite in the March breeze cut through my exhaustion, and I welcomed its icy fingers on my exposed skin. It definitely wasn't T-shirt weather up here at ten thousand feet.

A gasp caught my attention, and I turned toward the minivan that had pulled up behind my Jeep a minute ago. A blonde wearing sunglasses too big for her face and a puffy winter coat gawked with one foot on the concrete and one inside her vehicle, as if someone had pushed pause during her exit.

I lowered my arms, and my shirt slid back into place, covering the inked strip of stomach she'd no doubt gotten an eyeful of.

She shook her head quickly and started to pump her gas.

At least she didn't make the sign of the cross and back away.

Either she'd moved to Alba in the last ten years or my reputation had softened some since I'd joined the army. Hell, maybe the population of Alba had forgotten all about me.

I finished filling my tank and headed inside the small convenience store to grab a drink. God only knew what Dad would have in his fridge.

A set of bells chimed as the door closed behind me, and I nodded in greeting to the older man leaning on the counter. Looked like Mr. Williamson still owned the gas station. His bushy silver brows rose with a quick smile. Then he did a double take, both his brows and smile falling as he blinked in confusion. And then his eyes narrowed in recognition.

Looks like that rep is alive and well.

I quickly chose a few bottles of water from the slim selection and carried them to the counter.

The old man's eyes darted between my hands and the bottles as he rang them up, like I was going to steal them or something. I'd been a lot of things, but a thief wasn't one of them.

The bells chimed again, and Williamson visibly relaxed. "Afternoon, Lieutenant Hall," he greeted his newest patron.

Awesome.

I didn't bother looking. That stubborn, old, judgmental piece of work hated my—

"Holy shit. Cam?"

That wasn't Tim Hall wearing a badge—it was his son, Gideon.

Gid's mouth hung slack, his light-brown eyes wide in shock. It was a similar expression to the one he'd worn that time Xander had shoved us into the girls' locker room the fall of our freshman year. I'd never found a way to properly thank my brother for his attempt at hazing—not that anyone would believe Xander would stoop so low. After all, he was the good son.

"I didn't think police officers were supposed to swear in uniform." I gave him a quick once-over. Unlike his dad, Gid was still too trim to sport a belly over his belt.

"As opposed to soldiers?" he countered.

"Actually, that earns us bonus points, and besides, I'm not in a uniform anymore." I hadn't been for seventeen days. "Does your dad know you stole his badge?"

"Anymore? Does your…" He sighed. "Crap, I've got nothing!" His laughter unleashed my own. "It's good to see you!" He pulled me into a fierce, back-pounding hug, his badge digging into my chest.

"You too." I grinned as we broke apart. "In fact, you might be the only person I'm happy to see."

"Oh, come on. Not Mr. Williamson here?" Gid looked over my shoulder and cringed at whatever expression he saw on Williamson's face. "Okay, maybe not him."

"He's never really cared for me." I shrugged, well aware that he could hear me.

"You did throw someone through that window the last time you were here." Gid motioned toward the glass that had long since been replaced. "Man, how long ago was that? Four years?"

"Six," I answered automatically. Of the few things I remembered about that night, the date was still crystal clear.

"Six. Right." Gideon's expression fell—no doubt remembering why I'd been in Alba last.

Sullivan's funeral.

Grief threatened to rise up and steal what was left of the oxygen in my lungs, but I beat it back for the millionth time since we put Sully in the ground.

God, I could still hear his laughter—

"You going to pay for these waters, Camden?" Mr. Williamson asked.

"Yes, sir," I responded, thankful for the interruption, and turned back to the counter to finish the transaction. I didn't miss the flash of surprise on Williamson's face at my tone or when I thanked him as I took the bag and moved aside.

"That stuff will kill you," I told Gideon as he purchased a six-pack of soda.

"You and Julie, man," he muttered under his breath as he handed over his debit card. "Can't a guy drink in peace?"

Funny. This was more than I'd smiled in the entire last month. "How are Julie and the kids?"

"Driving me to drink." He lifted his soda in the air. "No, really, they're great. Julie's a nurse now, which you would know if you ever joined the social media world."

"No, thank you. What's the point?"

Gideon thanked Mr. Williamson, and we headed outside. "What's the point? I don't know. To keep in contact with your best friend?"

"No, that's why we have email. Social media is for people who need to compare their lives. Their houses, their vacations, their accomplishments. I see no reason to stand on my front porch with a bullhorn to broadcast what I had for dinner, either."

"Speaking of dinner, how long are you in town for?" he asked as we paused between my Jeep and his faded squad car. "I know Julie would love to have you over."

"For good," I replied before I could choke on the words.

He blinked.

"Yeah, it's taking me a little time to process, too." I glanced up at the mountains Alba slept between. Mountains I'd sworn I'd never see again.

"You got out? I figured you'd be career."

So had I. Just another thing to mourn.

"Officer Malone?" a scratchy feminine voice called over the radio.

"Marilyn Lakewood still calls out dispatch? What is she, seventy?"

"Seventy-seven," Gideon corrected. "And before you ask, Scott Malone is twenty-five and a giant pain in my ass."

"What did you expect from the mayor's kid?"

"Mayor's kid? When's the last time you talked to—"

"Officer Malone?" Marilyn repeated, her annoyance pitching her voice higher.

"Do you need to get that?" I motioned toward the radio on his shoulder.

"Malone needs to get that," he muttered with a shake of his head. "It's probably Genevieve Dawson whining about the Livingstons' cat in her yard again. If it's serious, Marilyn will call me. Now, fill me in. When did you get here? You're back for good? As in you've moved back here? The place you called Satan's as—"

"Xander called." I cut him off with the half-truth before he could remind me of yet another reason I'd sworn I'd never come back here. "Since it had been six years, I answered."

"Your dad," Gideon said softly.

"My dad."

A quiet moment of understanding passed between us.

"Gideon Hall!" Marilyn snapped through the radio.

"Lieutenant," he whispered to the sky before responding. "Yes, Marilyn?"

"Since Boy Wonder isn't answering the call, it seems that Dorothy Powers has lost Arthur Daniels again. She woke up from her nap, and he was gone."

My stomach dropped, and my gaze drifted up the mountain. According to Xander, Dad ditched his home nurse a few times a week but never wandered far from the house. It didn't help that Dorothy Powers was older than Dad and probably in need of her own nurse.

"On my way. Call up the usual searchers." Gideon caught my eye, then dropped his hand from the radio.

"My dad." How far could he have gotten?

"Second time this month." His lips flattened. "I'm going to head to the station to grab the four-wheel drive. I won't make it to your place in the cruiser."

"Just hop in with me. I'll take you up," I more ordered than offered, unwilling to wait. My Jeep was lifted and sported massive tires, a V-8 engine, and more than enough four-wheeling capability to survive the apocalypse. Even the road to Dad's wasn't that bad this time of year.

He agreed, and a minute later, we pulled onto Gold Creek Drive, which served as the town's main artery—no stoplights needed but snowmobiles optional.

"How long have you been gone?"

"Six years." I shot him a look. Hadn't I just answered that?

"No, I mean today. When did you leave the house? Was Dorothy awake? Was your dad?" He was already thumbing through his cell phone.

"I wish I could help you with a timeline, but I haven't been home yet." I motioned toward the back seat of the four-door Rubicon.

"You literally just pulled into town?" He took in the bags and boxes that had been my only companions on the two-thousand-mile drive.

"Yep," I replied as we passed the last post-fifties building in Alba. We crossed the bridge that spanned all thirty feet of Rowan Creek, and the snow-packed pavement ended, marking our entrance into the time capsule that kept Alba alive. "Figured it was a good idea to gas up. Someone told me once that it's easier to run from the cops on a full tank."

Main Street opened up on my left. Wooden buildings with metal roofs lined both sides of the dirt road that would fill with tourists in the next few months, all looking to experience a real 1890s old west mining town.

"Someone grew up. Also, please don't make me chase you.

This thing is a beast. I might have to tell Julie I've found the perfect birthday present."

"Sure, if you get it with a ladder." We turned at the Hamilton place, where the grant money for preservation had run dry. Snow sat piled in the shade against structures that had long since lost their roofs, windows, or walls.

"Shut up. Not all of us are six foot four."

"It's all in the genetics. At least it should make Dad easier to spot."

"He's been easy to find, but Cam… It's gotten pretty bad," Gideon told me as we pulled onto Rose Rowan Road and started to climb in elevation. "The last couple times I've seen him, he either hasn't known who I am or he thinks I'm Dad."

My hands flexed on the wheel. "Xander's reached his limit. He basically told me to get back here or Dad was getting shipped to a home in Buena Vista, which would screw Dad's whole 'your mother died in this house and I will, too' vow."

"Hold that thought." He held the phone to his face. "Hey, Mrs. Powers. Yep, it's Gideon." He paused, rubbing the skin just above his nose. "I know you are. I know you do. We're going to find him, and we've got some searchers on their— Oh, she is? Good. That will help. We're about four minutes out."

I took the final turn onto Dad's property and cursed at the conditions. Spring runoff was always hard on the drive, but it looked like it hadn't been maintained in years. Washboarding, which was no doubt under the packed snow, was easy enough to fix, but the deep, canyon-like trenches carved out by the mini river currently eating away the right side of the drive were going to take some effort to repair.

Not that I hadn't seen shittier roads in Afghanistan or any of the other places I was never supposed to be, but this was my fucking driveway.

Gideon hung up as I came to a stop and put the Jeep into four-wheel drive.

"How does Dorothy get up here every day?" I asked as we started the ascent. The Jeep rocked with enough force to jostle the boxes in the back, and Gideon braced himself on the roll bar as we made it around a shady, iced curve. That particular spot was always the last to melt.

"She cuts over from the Bradley property. You know the judge keeps his drive paved and clear."

The land was adjacent to ours, but it would have added ten minutes, and I wasn't in the mood for sightseeing...or Bradleys.

God, if there was anyone in the world who had the right to hate me more than I hated myself, it was—

A flash of blue in my rearview caught my attention.

Gideon glanced back. "Xander," he said, answering my unspoken question. "That's his truck."

"Well, this should be fun."

"Welcome home?" he offered.

I blatantly ignored him as we rounded the final switchback and came into the clearing. I'd been back only once in the last decade, but I'd seen this view nearly every night in my dreams.

The setting sun reflected off the windows of the two-story structure I'd grown up in, painting it with a picturesque light that matched the majesty of the bare peak that loomed just behind it.

Dad had always joked that it was safer to raise his family at the tree line, where the wildfires weren't as big of a threat.

Personally, I thought he took a perverse pleasure in living at the edge, where there was barely enough oxygen for anything to grow.

I threw the Jeep into park, killed the engine, and then grabbed my coat from where it had fallen to the floor behind me.

By the time Xander pulled in next to me, I was out of the Jeep and had the black North Face on and zipped, wishing it was my Kevlar. I would rather have been dodging bullets than facing him—or Dad, for that matter.

"I'll...uh...not be here," Gideon said awkwardly before leaving me in the yard. I heard the house door open and shut right around the same time Xander's car door did.

He came around the front of his polished, brand-new truck and stopped suddenly, his hands pausing mid-zip on his coat.

A lifetime of memories assaulted me—the good, the bad, and the worst. Pretty much in that order.

He raked a hand through his Ken doll–perfect blond hair and sucked in a breath. "Camden."

"Alexander." I shaped the brim of my ball cap.

Guess we both had our nervous tells.

He hadn't changed much. Same blue eyes. Same lean frame. Still Dad's obvious genetic gift to the world. Still my opposite in every way.

He shook his head as if struggling for words, and instead of reciting every way I'd failed our family, he crossed the decomposed granite of the drive and threw his arms around me.

"I'm so glad you're home."

His words sliced deeper than any insult could have. An insult I could handle—I'd been prepared for that.

But the way he pulled back, clasped my slack arms, and smiled at me—all tight lipped and furrowed brow, fighting back emotions I no longer felt capable of—wasn't anything I could have built a defense against.

He laughed, the sound thick with six years of absence. "You're huge. What do they feed you Delta boys? And what is this?" He motioned to my light beard as he stepped back.

"Green Beret, not Delta," I corrected him with the decade-old joke and a forced smile as my stomach sickened.

"Yeah, yeah. Guys like me who never saw action can't ever tell the difference." His eyes skittered over my features, as if he were trying to memorize them before I disappeared...again. "God, Cam. I'm just..."

Nausea churned as the pit in my stomach deepened to a gaping chasm of regret and guilt.

He smiled, boasting even white teeth and a happiness I wasn't sure I'd ever experienced. "I'm just really glad you're home."

"You said that." I was going to vomit. How could he be so nice to me?

"Well, it's true." He clapped me on the shoulder. "What do you say we go find Dad?"

"You don't seem too worried."

"I am, but for every time he's forgotten my name, he's never gotten lost on the land. We just need to spot him before the temps drop."

I nodded, and he turned toward the house. It was in the high twenties right now, but we'd hit single digits within an hour of the sun retiring.

"Nice Jeep, by the way. It suits you," he called back over his shoulder.

My eyes slammed shut as I sucked in breath after breath through my nose, willing the bile to slide back down my throat. It was like my body couldn't physically handle the emotions.

Of course he forgave me. Of course he welcomed me with open arms. Of course there was no malice in his eyes, just open, raw love. He didn't need to blast me with all my flaws. He'd always lived as an example, showing me every single way I'd never measure up by simply being him.

Just as I got myself under control, he turned back.

"You okay?" His voice dropped in concern.

"Yeah," I lied. Because it was one of the things I excelled at.

"Altitude?"

"Something like that."

"Just make sure you're drinking enough water," he reminded me, arching an eyebrow until I nodded my consent, and then headed up the steps to the front porch.

An eyebrow that was bisected by the first flaw I'd ever seen on Xander—a scar that hadn't been there the last time I'd seen him. A thin, short scar that had me fighting back the urge to throw up my lunch all over the driveway.

The scar I'd put there when I'd thrown him through Mr. Williamson's window.

Xander was halfway up the stairs when the front door flew open and Gideon ran from the house.

"He has a gun!" he shouted.

Xander froze, pivoting to watch Gideon race down the steps toward me.

"I'm sorry?" I pinned Gid with a stare, hoping he'd correct that asinine statement.

"He has the shotgun! Dorothy just told me. We have a couple search parties coming in from the Bradley side." Gid strode past me, already talking into the radio on his shoulder.

"How the hell does Dad have access to the shotgun?" I growled at Xander.

"I…" He shook his head. "I thought I had them all locked in the safe. I hid the key and everything."

"In the laundry room?" Dorothy asked as she walked onto the porch, holding a familiar, faded bottle of fabric softener. Time had apparently decided it was done with Mrs. Powers, because she hadn't changed in the ten years that had passed since I'd enlisted. Her hair was the same shade of silver in the same chin-length cut. She even wore the same green winter coat.

"Yeah, right above—" Xander sighed, his eyes sliding shut. "Right above the fabric softener he refuses to use."

"This fabric softener that I found in the entry hall?" she asked, giving him one hell of a "mom" look.

"That would be it." A muscle flexed in his jaw.

"Tell me you stored the ammo separately." *Tell me you at least remembered that much from serving your three years.*

Xander blanched. Awesome.

"Let's find him before he kills someone." I turned on my heel and headed back to the Jeep. Oddly enough, I was more comfortable with guns than I was with mushy reunions.

I dropped my coat, climbed up the Jeep, and popped the lock on the cargo carrier I'd anchored to the roof for the cross-country trip. Selling off just about everything I owned had seemed the logical choice at the time, but I'd held on to a few things for reasons I didn't have time to examine.

"What are we going to do?" Xander asked, peering up at me.

"What do you mean?" I found what I was looking for and closed the carrier. Then I jumped to the ground, landing in front of Xander, whose eyes were bigger than my headlights.

Two more trucks and the APD pulled up the drive and parked.

"I mean…" Xander eyed the newcomers as they talked to Gideon and then lowered his voice as he turned back to me. "What are we going to do? He has the shotgun and doesn't know who I am about seventy-five percent of the time."

A comforting weight settled on my chest as I dressed for the occasion before zipping my jacket and tying my boots. "I figured we'd go find Dad."

I rustled through my glove box, quickly grabbing my headlamp and a flashlight, then stuffed them in my pockets, pausing only long enough to tuck in the little white onyx bishop next to my driver's manual so the chess piece didn't get lost. We probably had another hour of good light, but if I was wrong, it was going to take more than that to cover the hundred acres Dad owned, and that was if he'd stayed on the property.

"Don't you think we should let Gideon and the PD handle this now?" Xander asked quietly.

I looked back to where Gideon stood with the other four officers who made up the Alba Police Department. They all had sidearms strapped on. I was on the receiving end of more than a couple of glares. Not that I could blame them. At least three of those guys had put cuffs on me at one time or another.

"You mean, am I going to let the men with the guns find our dad, who has his own gun?" I didn't wait for Xander's response, turning toward the northern section of the property.

"Wait!" Xander gripped my elbow, and I tensed, reminding myself at least a dozen times not to beat the crap out of him for touching me without warning.

"Let go of me."

My tone must have gotten through to him, because he dropped his hand.

"There are rules, Cam. Regulations. They know how to handle this kind of thing. The last thing we need is you flying off the handle."

Ah, there it was, the butter knife–soft condescension Xander used when he thought the twenty-five months he had on me age-wise gave him the right to issue orders. He'd never make a quick, clean cut to get his way. He'd simply saw with that lightly serrated edge until you were too raw from the friction to object.

I preferred the more direct butcher's-knife approach.

"You and your rules. You're telling me that if he points that shotgun at them, they won't pull the trigger?"

Xander scoffed. "Come on, it's the guys."

"You willing to bet Dad's life on that twenty-five-year-old bully who doesn't bother to answer his radio and has flicked open the holster on his weapon at least four times since they started talking? I'm not. I know where he is, and I'm getting there before they do."

Xander's head snapped toward the little meeting Gideon was holding, and I started off after a faint set of tracks I knew would disappear as soon as we hit the mountain grass. They were more than enough to tell where he was headed. I muttered a curse at the altitude. It would take me only a few days to adjust, but I didn't exactly have a few days.

"Where are you going?" Gideon called out.

"To find our dad!" Xander responded, radiating confidence.

I rolled my eyes at his public facade but kept going.

He caught up quickly, falling into step next to me as we stuck to the areas where the snow had already melted. Our strides were equal. They always had been. We were equal in height, but I had a good forty pounds of muscle on him.

"I hope you know what you're doing," he said as the tracks disappeared.

"Yep." My gaze raked the terrain, looking for any sign that Dad had come this way.

"Seriously, you think you know where he is?"

"How long has he had that bottle of fabric softener?" I asked as the granite crunched beneath my feet. At least it wasn't snowing.

"Years." Xander shrugged.

"Right. At least a decade. Paula Bradley brought it over when he was sick that year, remember? Tried to help out with laundry."

"How the hell do you remember that?"

"I'm cursed with an excellent memory." I turned toward the part of the property where Sullivan was buried. "Trust me, there's shit I would love to forget. Do you remember why he wouldn't use it?" We crested one slope and started back down toward the tree line, keeping the peak on our right as we trekked through a snow-covered section.

"I barely remember Mrs. Bradley bringing it over."

"He wouldn't let her use it, but he refused to throw it away," I tried to remind him.

Xander threw me a clueless look.

"It's lavender scented," I said, answering my own question.

Xander sucked in a breath. "Mom."

"Mom," I confirmed as we reached the tree line and started to hike through the pines. In the shade, the temperature dropped to an uncomfortable level.

"But she's buried at the other end of the property with—"

"That's not where he goes when he misses her. Not that he'd ever admit that he misses her." Admitting that would be tantamount to broadcasting a weakness, and Arthur Daniels was anything but weak.

"The ravine."

"Yep."

We pushed through the finger of forest that covered this strip of the property and came out into a clearing I knew all too well.

I cursed under my breath as it came into view.

"Oh no," Xander whispered.

Oh no didn't quite cover this. My heart paused mid-beat, then slammed, pumping adrenaline through my system.

Dad stood about thirty yards to our left, in the middle of the clearing, shotgun raised at the one person I'd hoped to never see again.

I'd know that frame, that thick braid of chestnut hair, that profile with a slight bump in her nose anywhere. Hell, I'd been there the day she'd broken it when we were kids. I'd been the one to carry her out of that mine.

She stood about fifteen yards in front of us with her hands out and open, but she wasn't retreating from the double-barreled reaper pointed straight at her chest. Backing down had never been in her nature, and while I'd always been intrigued by her tenacity, right now I was cursing her stupid stubborn streak.

Willow Bradley was going to get herself shot.

Sullivan's Willow.

You gotta help me here, Sully. I sent the thought rather than spoke it, knowing Xander wouldn't understand.

"Walk through the trees until you can come up behind him. As soon as I give you the signal, get that gun away from him," I whispered to Xander, leaving zero room for argument.

"What signal?"

"Trust me, you'll know."

"He won't recognize you. He'll shoot you," he hissed.

"Better me than her." Death had never scared me. We'd played a game of cat and mouse for as long as I could remember, and one day I would lose. It was that simple.

If I died today, then so be it.

I moved.

CHAPTER TWO

Willow

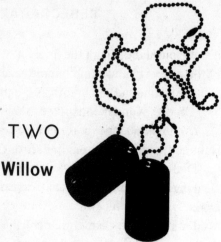

Think, Willow. Think.

This was Mr. Daniels. I'd known him my entire life. Alzheimer's or not, there was no way he was really going to shoot me, right?

Except there was this one troubling factor: he had no idea who I was. Oh, and he had a shotgun pointed at my chest. That was troubling, too.

"Mr. Daniels," I tried again, keeping my voice soft. "It's me. It's Willow. I live next door, remember?" If you considered a mile away next door.

The breeze whipped a loose strand of my hair across my face, but I didn't dare tuck it back beneath my hat. The sun had set precious minutes earlier, and it was already getting dark. What if he just couldn't see me?

"Be quiet!" he shouted, jerking the shotgun. His eyes were wide and wild but not evil. He simply didn't know me or the circumstances that had led him here.

I gasped in reaction, my heart jumping into my throat. What if he pulled the trigger? What if it went off the next time he jostled it like that? We were half a mile away from the Danielses' place and three-quarters of one above my parents'. My cell phone was in my pocket, but I had a feeling he'd shoot me if I reached for it. At this range, I'd be dead before they could get me to a hospital...

if they found me.

At least there were other search parties out right now. They'd come at the sound of gunfire.

"There are cougars out here, you know," he snapped.

Like the one that had mauled his wife fifteen years ago on this very field.

"What are you doing here? You're trespassing!"

I didn't bother arguing the trespassing point, since technically, I was. But Dorothy had called in a panic, and I'd immediately headed out to look for Mr. Daniels just like I had a few times in the last month. The gun... Now that had been unexpected.

"I know there are cougars," I told him with a slight quiver in my voice. "You taught me what to do if I ever ran into one." I'd been seven years old when he'd pulled aside Sullivan and me for lessons. Naturally, Cam had played the cougar while Alexander watched in quiet judgment.

Cam. My chest tightened in that same physical ache it always did whenever he crossed my mind, even with the present danger. Heck, maybe because of the danger.

"I don't know you! Stop lying! What do you want here? Why are you on my land? Get out!" He jabbed the gun toward me.

"Okay," I said with a nod and backed up a step.

"Stop moving!" he screamed, his voice pitching high in alarm. "Don't speak!"

I halted immediately. He was slipping further and further into the episode, and my mind stopped fighting the possibility that he might shoot me, my muscles locking in paralyzing acceptance.

Movement to my left caught my eye, and I turned my head a fraction of an inch to see the shape of a man only a few arm lengths away, approaching with hands up, palms out. Who was it? Where had he come from?

I couldn't make out his face beneath the baseball hat, but he was massive, dwarfing my five-foot-four frame as he put himself between Mr. Daniels and me. The broad expanse of his back blocked my entire view.

I didn't recognize him—which was odd, considering there were only about a dozen of us who usually came to search for Mr. Daniels—but there was something familiar in the way he held himself, the way his posture advertised submission but his energy felt 100 percent aggressive. I had the utterly illogical impression that this guy was more dangerous than the loaded gun pointed at him. At least, I assumed it was loaded. If it wasn't, at least it would be a not-so-hilarious story to tell Charity later.

For all that Dad accused my sister of being impetuous, Charity had certainly never had a shotgun held on her.

"What is this? Who the hell are you? How many of you are there?" Mr. Daniels questioned, panic rising. The shoulders in front of me rose as if he were preparing to— "No, don't speak! All lies! You claim jumpers are all full of lies!"

Well, that story changed quickly.

The man reached back, hooked his hand around my waist, and tugged me closer. I tensed, even though the violation of my personal space was nothing compared to the shotgun pointed at us. His arm was a vise, locking me in place with casual strength. Just like freshman year when— I cut myself right off. *There's no way.*

"Be careful," I said softly to the stranger. "He has Alzheimer's. He doesn't know what he's doing."

He pulled me tighter against his back, and the scent of mint and pine filled my nose as he started to shift in tiny movements so my back was to the trees and not the ravine. God, that smell... I knew it.

"We're just hikers," he said to Mr. Daniels, low and slow.

Certainty slammed into me with the force of an avalanche, knocking the breath from my lungs. My eyes fluttered shut as I swam through the flood of memories, desperately hoping I wasn't the one hallucinating right now.

"Cam," I whispered, letting my forehead rest against his back as I gripped a fistful of his coat.

"Are you okay, Willow?" he asked, so softly that I would have gone with the hallucination theory if I hadn't felt his deep voice rumble through his chest.

I nodded, the fabric of his coat soft against my skin. Maybe Mr. Daniels had already pulled the trigger. Maybe I'd never felt the impact. Maybe he'd killed me instantly. That was the only logical explanation for Cam's presence.

Because Camden Daniels had sworn the only way he'd ever come back to Alba was to be buried here. But he felt so real. So solid. Smelled exactly like I remembered. And if I were really dead, wouldn't it be Sullivan's arms around me? Not Cam's. It could never be Cam. Not for me.

I followed Cam's almost-imperceptible lead as he backed us away from his father.

Cam couldn't be here. He hadn't been here in years. And he definitely couldn't stop a bullet. But a feeling of safety drenched me anyway. It never mattered if the rest of the world saw him as a menace—Cam had always been my unlikely refuge, even when he earned every last bit of his reputation. He'd protected me for the simple reason that I'd been theirs all my life.

The girl who tagged along with the Daniels boys.

The naive teenager who stayed behind when three brothers went to war.

The woman who shattered when only two came home.

Cam might be here now, but one misstep, and we'd both be buried next to Sullivan.

"Stop moving or I'll shoot!" Mr. Daniels shouted, and Cam obeyed. "Empty your pockets! You'd better not be stealing from me!"

"I'm going to let you go, and I want you to slowly back into the woods and then get the hell away from here," Cam ordered me softly.

I vaguely heard Mr. Daniels's agitated muttering in the distance.

"I can't leave you here," I protested.

"For once in your life, listen to me, Pika. I'm trying to save your neck. Alexander is coming up behind Dad, and help is on the way, but you have to go."

The nickname tightened my throat with a lump so big, I couldn't swallow it down. "He doesn't recognize you, Cam. He'll shoot. It's been six years since he's seen you. He doesn't even recognize me, and I see him almost every day."

"He'll remember me."

"Yeah, that's what I thought, too, until he pointed a shotgun at me, you stubborn idiot."

"What was that?" he whispered. "I thought I heard a squeak, but my coat must have muffled it."

I would have pinched him in retribution under any other circumstance.

"He's not going to remember you," I argued, "and you'll just agitate him even more when you try to remind him who you are."

Mr. Daniels's muttering grew louder until he was shouting again. "You trespassers, trying to steal what's mine! You can't have it! Can't have it…"

Cam's heartbeat stayed calmingly rhythmic, his breathing deep and even. If I hadn't seen Arthur Daniels myself, I'd never think there was a gun pointed at us.

"You can't have it!"

A shot rang out, and birds scattered from the woods at my back. I froze, my grip tightening on Cam's coat.

His hand splayed wide over the small of my back.

"Cam!" I whispered as loudly as I dared. If he was hurt—if he'd come back only to be buried… I wouldn't survive burying another Daniels boy. I leaned to see around him, but Cam's grip tightened, trapping me firmly behind him.

"I'm okay," he replied just as quietly. "He aimed at the sky."

"I guess at least we know it's loaded." My heart slammed against my ribs, fear coating my tongue with a bitter, metallic taste.

"Way to find the silver lining."

A corner of my lips lifted slightly.

"There's one more in the barrel. Remember what I said. Back toward the woods slowly."

"No," I argued.

"Yes," he countered, and his hand disappeared from my back. "Now, Willow."

Ice rippled through my veins.

He stepped forward, and I let the fabric of his coat slide through my grasp, leaving me precious inches away from Cam.

"Dad," Cam called out. "I could have sworn you told me never to point a gun at a pretty girl."

I stood paralyzed, watching Cam walk forward like his dad didn't have a gun pointed at his chest.

"What?" Mr. Daniels called out. "I'm not your… Who are you? What do you want?"

There it was—a softening in his tone. If Cam could get through to him, they both might live through this. But the odds of that happening were so small, they almost weren't worth mentioning.

"It's me, Dad. Camden. And you looked about ready to shoot Willow, so I figured I should step in. You don't want to hurt Willow, do you? Little Willow? Our neighbor?"

"Willow? Who's…"

The farther Camden walked, the more his dad came into sight. I needed to move, needed to get back into the woods so this all wouldn't have been in vain, but the idea of leaving him here to face his dad alone was simply unfathomable.

Sullivan had been alone. I couldn't reach him. Couldn't hold him. Couldn't brush his hair out of his eyes one last time.

I wasn't leaving Cam.

"Come on, Dad. Put the gun down. We'll go back to the house, and I'll cook you up some chicken exactly how Mom made it, okay?" Cam kept his arms outstretched, his palms facing his dad.

"Get off my land! You can't have it!"

Another shot fired, and I screamed as Cam's body flew backward, landing in the field with a sickening *thud*.

"No!" The denial ripped from my throat as I sprinted across the uneven ground to where Cam lay on a patch of winter-brown grass.

"Willow!" Xander shouted from behind his father, already gripping the shotgun.

"Call 911!" I didn't spare more than a cursory glance as my knees slammed into the unforgiving ground next to Cam. How the hell were we going to get him down the mountain? Could a helicopter land up here?

His jacket was shredded, tiny feathers spilling free all over his chest and blowing away in the wind.

But they weren't red. Yet. Neither was the grass beside him, right? But it was already so dark.

I reached for his coat, but his back arched, and I scanned up to his pained face—God, I'd missed this face—then took the scruff-softened angles between my palms without thinking. Motion in my peripherals told me that the other searchers had arrived. Too late. Too late. Always too late.

"I'm here," I told him, looking into eyes so dark, they swallowed me whole. "We've got this," I promised when I had no right to, forcing optimism into my tone with an exaggerated nod and a shaky smile. "Help is coming."

His eyes were wide as he struggled for a breath that wouldn't come, his fear palpable as his gaze dropped down my frame and over my white coat, frantically searching.

"I'm okay. I'm not hit. You are," I assured him. Idiot. Like that would comfort him. "I need to see how bad it is."

His hands reached between us, fumbling at his coat.

I jolted back, gently brushing his hands out of the way. "Let me."

He's okay. He's okay. He's okay. You can't take him, too. Do you understand? You took Sullivan. You can't have Cam.

Cam's lungs wheezed as the first stream of air made its way in. My eyes flew to his, finding them already on me, his brow slightly furrowed as he struggled for more air.

I unzipped his coat in one long pull and steeled myself for whatever lay underneath.

"Jesus, Cam!" Gideon cursed as he hit his knees on Cam's other side.

"Arthur shot him." My shaking hands opened his coat, revealing an expanse of dark fabric with several holes ripping apart the weave where the buckshot hit him. Where was the blood? "It's too dark! I can't see!"

"I'm. Fine," Cam forced out with a rasp of breath.

A *click* sounded as Gideon powered on his flashlight.

"Shut up," I ordered. "Stupid man can't even tell when he's been—" Light shone on Cam's chest and reflected back on tiny bits of shiny metal like a lone constellation in an otherwise dark sky. "Wait. What?"

"Son of a bitch!" Gideon laughed, shaking the flashlight with heaving breaths as he looked over his shoulder. "He's fine!"

"I. Said. I'm fine," Cam growled.

"How? You're shot..." And I could see the bullets—buckshot. Defying all logical thought, I dipped my finger into a tiny hole and felt cool metal pressing back. I let my fingers trail down Cam's hard—too hard—chest.

"Pika, stop." Cam captured my hand, then flattened it, pressing my palm against the unnaturally hard surface of his chest. "I'm okay. Just had the wind knocked out of me." He let go of my hand and unsnapped a clip up by his shoulder and another at his side. Velcro ripped. A giant piece of... *What the heck is that?*

"Nice. What's that rated?" Gideon asked, nodding toward a slab of armor as it fell to the side, baring Cam's Black Flag T-shirt.

His very clean, very white, very intact T-shirt.

I blinked, then blinked again, convincing my brain that my eyes told the truth and this wasn't something I dreamed up out of desperation. There was no bullet hole. No blood. No damage.

"It's a four," Cam said, his voice returning to full strength. He ran his hand over his chest and abdomen, then gave a sigh of relief, letting his head fall back to rest on the ground.

"Nice. And you carry it around?"

"Funny thing about having all your belongings in your car," Cam answered with a wry grin.

"You're prepared for your dad to randomly shoot you?" Gid scoffed.

"Something like that." Cam winced as he sat up.

"You're okay." My butt hit the unforgiving soles of my hiking boots as I rocked back, sitting on my heels. The voices behind me registered as white noise even as they became louder, everything buzzing in my head except the fact that Cam wasn't shot, or bleeding, or dying.

"I already said I'm fine." He pulled back his shirt and glanced down his collar. "I'll probably have a nasty bruise, but it's too dark to see."

"I'm just saying it's a good thing you were here," a voice said at my left. "The way you got that gun away from him was...that was heroic, Xander."

Sgt. Acosta stepped into my view, patting Xander on the back. The two were the same age, but Acosta looked way more comfortable with his sidearm than Xander did holding Arthur's shotgun.

"No, I didn't do anything," Xander argued, dropping down to Cam's eye level. "Cam took the brunt of it. Are you okay?" he asked after glancing at the body armor.

Cam nodded and got to his feet.

"Yeah, if the brunt means aggravating your dad into shooting him." Acosta laughed, and my fingernails bit into my palms.

My mouth opened to tell Acosta that Cam had most likely

saved my life, but a swift shake of Cam's head in my direction had me shutting it. He'd always been content to let others think the worst of him, and I guess nothing had changed.

"Let's just get him home," Cam said to no one in particular, clipping the vest back in place and staring straight ahead. His tone was one I'd heard often growing up—shutting down the conversation, letting me know he'd disengaged from whatever would have had the chance to touch him emotionally.

With the danger passed, I greedily drank in the sight of him. He was bigger—not taller, of course, but thicker, harder—and the same went for his presence. He had an edge to him that had been missing when he'd left Alba a decade ago, and those impenetrable walls he'd always kept felt even more impossible to breach. But his eyes— Those carried the same grief that had echoed in mine when I'd seen him last.

He and Xander walked forward, pausing to no doubt discuss what was going on with their father as Art stood with Captain Hall, getting a quick field exam. Mr. Daniels was shaking his head, as if trying to explain the situation.

It had been tragic when Mrs. Daniels had died. Heartbreaking to bury Sullivan nine years later. But watching Arthur Daniels these last two years felt like burying a piece of him at a time, and it was torturous.

"Don't see much of you around town, Willow. You still playing with your paints?" Robbie Acosta asked, smirking down at me as Gideon joined the Daniels brothers.

"You still pretending there's enough crime here to warrant your job?" I retorted, my voice saccharine sweet. My graphic design business kept me more than financially comfortable, but no one ever took note of that. It was always the painting—or lack thereof—that people wanted to bring up.

Guess it was more fun for them to pick at my scabs than examine their own.

"Whoa." Robbie held his hands up like he was under arrest—

like Cam had when he'd appeared in the field ahead of me. "Put your claws away, Willow. I'm just teasing."

"Yeah. Not in the mood." I kept my focus entirely on Cam's back. An all-too-familiar ache invaded my chest. When had he gotten home? How long was he here for? What—or rather whom—was he going to break this time?

"You need to get out more, especially if the only time you're social includes a man with dementia and a loaded gun," Robbie said, his voice pitching higher than I'd ever heard in high school as he rubbed the back of his neck. "You know, maybe I could take you to dinner?"

"I'm sorry?" I asked him, my head tilted to the side in genuine confusion. "You want to take me to dinner?"

"Yeah." He shrugged with a sheepish smile.

"You...you don't like me," I said slowly, shaking my head.

He'd always gone for the prom queens—the girls who had perfected their makeup by middle school. The ones in Buena Vista, where we'd gone to school, who were styled and Instagrammed. I was twenty-five and didn't even have a personal Instagram account...or any interest in Robbie.

"I mean, you're single. I'm single. Makes sense, right?"

"Sure, if humans were an endangered species or something." I immediately regretted my brash words when he looked away. "You know there's life outside Alba, Robbie. You don't have to date within town limits just because you're all grown-up now."

"True," he admitted with a cringe. "Oh man, I bet you're not ready yet, huh? Shit, that was a dick move."

"What, asking me out after Art Daniels pulled a gun on me?"

He blinked. "No, I mean, maybe you're not ready to date yet..." His eyebrows rose.

Seriously.

"Oh. I'm okay, really. Not that I don't miss Sullivan, but it's been six years." Time moved slower in small towns, I supposed. I'd healed my heart in the years I'd spent at college, but everyone here acted like we'd buried him last week.

Guess I was still supposed to be traumatized.

"Right. Good for you, keeping strong," he said with a nod and a pat on my back before answering a summons from the group at the edge of the tree line.

It was too dark to make out who they were, but my bet was the usual suspects—sans Dad. Had Dad been here, he would have gone ballistic.

Xander headed for Mr. Daniels, and I found myself drawn to Cam's side just like a million times before.

"I still can't believe you're here," I said before I thought better of it. *Mouth, engage filter.*

"Me either." His eyes stayed locked on Xander and his dad. "What were you doing out here?" he snapped.

"Looking for your father." I bristled at his tone.

"Well, you sure as hell found him."

"I help search all the time. It's no big deal."

A muscle in his jaw ticked.

"And how many times has he pulled a gun on you?" His gaze swung slowly to mine, and the darkness was suddenly more of a blessing than ever. I saw enough in those eyes to know he was pissed.

"Never. And I'm sure Xander will lock up the guns and it won't happen again."

Cam scoffed. "Yeah, okay. He could have shot you."

"Well, he did shoot you." I poked his armor-plated vest.

A ghost of a smile passed over his lips, and I nearly crowed in victory.

"Looks like he's about ready to go," Cam noted as Mr. Daniels shook off Gideon's offered arm to help him across the uneven terrain. "Still stubborn as ever," he muttered as his father approached.

"Must run in the genes, or did you not remember me warning you that he wasn't going to remember you?" I teased, trying to lighten the mood. Cam had always done better if he could turn the hurt into something laughable. Not that this was.

"Remember him?" Mr. Daniels answered instead, stopping just in front of Cam. He was only a couple of inches shorter than his son but had the kind of presence that made him larger than life. "I shot you."

"You did." Other than the clenching of his right fist, Cam showed no emotion. Guess that hadn't changed, either.

"Art," Captain Hall said as he clapped Mr. Daniels on the shoulder. "Not sure if you can see in all this dark, but this is—"

"I know exactly who it is," Mr. Daniels seethed.

I mentally prepared myself for what this episode of dementia was going to gift us with.

Cam cocked an eyebrow as Mr. Daniels glared.

"This is the son of a bitch who killed my Sullivan."

I gasped, sucking in air as I reflexively stepped close enough to Cam to brush my arm against his. He may as well have been a statue for all the reaction he showed. "Mr. Daniels—"

"I don't know why the hell you're here, but you can see yourself right back out." He cut me off, effectively dismissing the son he hadn't seen in six years.

Then he turned his back on Cam and walked toward the tree line, Captain Hall at his side.

"Cam," Xander called softly. Whatever he saw in Cam's eyes led him to shake his head and walk away, following his father.

"I'm so sorry. He doesn't know what he's saying," I whispered around the lump clogging my throat.

"Sure he does. And he's right." He looked down at me with a vacant-eyed smirk that sent me straight back to high school. He'd always been able to put a million miles of distance between us— between anyone—with a single look. "Told you he'd remember me."

He walked off toward his family.

"Cam!" I shouted in a desperate attempt to keep him here just a little longer—the Camden who had stepped out in front of his father's gun to shield me. But his transformation into cold, zero-fucks-given Camden was already underway.

"Go home, Willow."

And now complete.

I watched him disappear into the trees and battled the bone-deep urge to follow. So much for the idyllic homecoming I'd foolishly let myself fantasize about over the years.

But he was here. He was home.

And I desperately wanted to know why.

CHAPTER THREE

Camden

It had been naive of me to think I might make it a day, or even two, before someone mentioned Sullivan's death—or my role in it.

I'd made it roughly twenty minutes in my father's company, and he'd already shot me and accused me of fratricide. Welcome home.

Silence kept me company as we hiked back down to the house, our flashlights and headlamps bobbing along the way. There were eleven of us, since Acosta had walked Willow home.

Willow. I shut that shit down in my head. Nope, not going there.

God, but the relief in her voice when she'd whispered my name and leaned closer... She didn't hate me. I deserved her hatred, her absolute loathing, and instead she'd trusted me like the last six years had never happened.

"I think he's pretty close to lucid right now," Gideon said as he fell into step next to me. "You could go talk to him."

"I think he was pretty close to lucid up by the ravine, and no, thank you. He's doing just fine with Xander up there." I jumped the three-foot ditch that currently housed a stream of spring runoff. How easily it all came back, muscle memory guiding me where the light failed. Now if only I'd remembered to exchange my Avs hat for one that covered my ears before heading out after Dad.

"You honestly think he would have shot—" Gideon grunted, then scrambled by the sound of it. "Jesus, hold on. Still part mountain goat, aren't you?" He huffed, jogging to catch up.

"No, I don't think he would have shot me if he'd recognized me in that moment," I answered his question—and mine. "He definitely would have considered it, though. Hell, I bet he's pictured it in his head a few times while he's been perfectly lucid."

"Some homecoming," Gideon muttered as the house came into view across the clearing.

"Why do you think I stayed away so long?"

"Because you knew he'd shoot you on sight?" He rammed his shoulder into me, and I tensed for a millisecond. It was a familiar enough move from Gid, but no one got that close to me anymore without a direct invitation.

"Something like that." My eyes drifted north, as if they could cut through the dark and forested ridge to the little grove of aspens where Sullivan lay at rest next to Mom and Uncle Cal.

"You'll settle in. Hey, you can always come work with me at APD!" His teeth flashed in the dim lighting.

"Last time I checked, there are already five of you for our little town, and my name isn't Hall, so the chances of me advancing are pretty much zero."

"Dick," Gideon muttered between fake coughs.

"Never pretended to be anything else." Maybe I wasn't popular. Maybe I was the unlikable son. The bad penny. The black sheep. Every fucking cliché there was when compared to Xander's annoying perfection. I'd stopped caring about that twenty years ago and simply decided to embrace it. There was power in not giving a fuck.

The lights of the house shone from the windows as we came to what used to be the gardens Mom spent her mornings in. The once-lush plants were all but gone—surviving only as volunteers that grew from the seeds in the leftover rot of the previous year—or had been overrun by the mountain grass.

Dad had called it folly to garden this close to the tree line. Mom had rolled her eyes and done it anyway.

We rounded the side of the house, and I made note of the places where the siding had peeled back. The gutters drooped, and the drainage system was in shambles, if the small canyons that began at the drain spouts were any indication.

Dorothy met Dad on the front porch, and the two disappeared into the house while Captain Hall and Xander spoke at the base of the steps.

"That doesn't look pleasant," Gideon noted as we approached my Jeep.

I opened the passenger side and stripped down to my T-shirt, ignoring the bite of temperature as I threw the armored vest onto the seat. When I'd decided to keep my personal gear, it had been out of an unexplainable sense of attachment, not because I thought I'd still need to use the damn thing.

I put on my ruined coat as we headed for Xander.

"This can't happen again," Captain Hall lectured my brother, which immediately set me on edge.

"It won't. I never thought he'd locate the key. You have my most sincere apology." Xander's mouth was set in a firm line, which was pretty much as upset as he'd ever get in front of an authority figure.

I took my place next to him as Gideon took his by his father.

"I respect what you've done, Alexander. I really do." His forehead puckered in what would have been a worried expression had the porch light not thrown half his face into shadows that painted him an old-west villain.

Guy seriously needed to lose the cowboy hat.

"Thank you," Xander replied. "Now, we're going to go check on our—"

"But the time has come for you to put him in that assisted living facility in Buena Vista," Captain Hall interrupted in that morally superior voice that had always led me to the opposite of what he demanded.

"That's why I'm here." I folded my arms over my chest.

"And it's nice to see you, Camden. Really, it is. Been boring around here without you destroying everything. What do you know about caring for your father? How long are you here on leave? What's going to happen when you go back to wherever it is you live?"

Gideon swallowed, his gaze darting between his dad and me, but he didn't move or respond like he once would have. Guess some things had changed.

"I'm not on leave. I'm here for good. Xander called, and I came." *Hence my packed-to-the-hilt Jeep, jackass.*

"Okay, you've been back all of five minutes and your father shot you. Does that sound like he should be living on his own?" His eyebrows rose, and he leaned forward a little.

That intimidation shit hadn't worked on me in a good decade and sure as hell wasn't doing it now. But I wasn't going to let him taunt me into a reaction, either.

"It sounded like Xander needed me to come home, and I did. We're going to make some changes that make it safer for Dad, and we'll do it as a family. We appreciate the search party more than you know. Thank you for helping us bring him home. We can take it from here."

His eyes narrowed.

"Listen here, son. You have no clue what it's been like—"

"I'm not your son." My voice dropped into that deadly, calm little space I reserved for moments I needed to keep my finger off the trigger. "And you're right. I don't know, but Xander does. So if you'll excuse us, we're going to head inside. Gid, are you good to catch a ride?"

"Yeah, no problem. Captain, let's get out of here."

Making sure Xander was with me, I started up the porch steps.

"Camden," Captain Hall called out.

We both turned.

"Do me a favor and keep yourself out of trouble while you're here? Hate to see anyone else get thrown through a window."

Xander stiffened beside me.

I'd killed lesser men in my career. Better ones, too. His comment had his intended effect—rage coiled in my muscles, ready to spring.

"You have yourself a good night, Captain," Xander said as he rested one hand on my shoulder, the shotgun still gripped by the other.

Of course he appeased the asshole. Of course he backed down to the place he was supposed to be, the place where everything was safe and everyone knew their roles.

Xander's place was to make peace. Mine had always been to bring war.

"Will do, Mayor Daniels," Hall responded.

I clenched my jaw to keep it from dropping.

The two Halls gave us nods that meant different things and climbed into their SUV.

We stood there in silence, shoulder to shoulder, like the unwilling sentinels we'd become, guarding the man who'd never done the same for us. A few moments later, with the searchers and police dispersed, there was only one car I didn't recognize in the driveway.

"So, Mayor Daniels, huh?" I asked my brother as we turned to climb the rest of the steps.

He shrugged.

"Seriously? You're not dishonest or power hungry enough to be a politician. Trust me—I've met my share."

"It's possible to serve without presidential ambition, you know. I'm happy where I'm at. And it's not like we're a bustling metropolis." He rolled his eyes and opened the front door.

"Until summer." I paused, my gaze drawn to the mat under my feet. I'd sworn never to cross it again.

"Yeah, those extra fifty thousand people who pop up tend to complicate things, but that income keeps the town running the rest of the year, so I'd call it an even trade. Now, were you thinking of coming in, or were you going to sleep on the porch?"

I'll never go back to Alba.

I'll never get out of the service.

I'll never listen to Dad blame me again.

I'll never again lay eyes on Willow Bradley.

Compared to breaking that last promise I'd made to myself, the act of stepping over this threshold was cake.

I walked in before my common sense could stop me. After all, how the hell was I supposed to help Dad if I wouldn't go in the house?

Xander shut the door behind me as I stood in the entryway, taking in the changes around the house I'd grown up in. Home. It had been one while Mom was alive. Little by little, the feeling had drained from the house in the way water dripped from that slow leak in the upstairs bathroom. We'd all been too distracted by other things to grab a wrench. The love had bled out in a steady trickle that we'd left unchecked out of sheer apathy.

Sullivan had cared.

Sullivan had died and taken the last sluggish heartbeats of this corpse of a house with him.

"I'm going to put this back in the safe." Xander motioned to the shotgun.

"Does he still have the key?"

"He handed it over after we left the clearing. You know, he's only lucid about fifty percent of the time anymore. You should go talk to him while he's really…him."

"Right." Because the real him was a peach.

Xander bounded up the stairs, disappearing at the landing.

I kicked off my shoes out of habit and put them against the wall.

How can I keep these floors clean when you boys insist on tracking in half the mountain?

I smiled at the memory before my eyes caught on the rug just down the hall that hid the bloodstain we'd never been able to scrub out of the hardwood. The place Dad sat, holding Mom as she'd bled out after the cougar had gotten the best of her. She'd begged him to stay with her, to let her die where they'd made a life.

He'd respected her wishes and said it was a miracle she'd lasted while he'd carried her home, that she'd never make it down the mountain to the hospital.

He'd been right.

"Oh my. Camden? Is that really you?"

I stood and faced the hallway to see Hope Bradley, Willow's mom, gawking at me.

Yet another person with a permit to loathe me. Fucking awesome.

Her lip trembled, her eyes watered, and then it took everything I had in me not to put the front door between us as she quickly walked my way.

"You…" She shook her head and gave me a watery smile. "You look exactly how I remember you. I didn't know you were in town!"

"Just got in today," I told her, stuffing my hands in my pockets.

"Oh wow! Does Willow know? I bet she'd love to see you."

That kindness in her hazel eyes—so like Willow's—was almost my undoing. There was a reason she'd been Mom's best friend.

"Yeah, I actually saw her about an hour ago." What the hell was taking Xander so long upstairs?

"Oh good! She's always the first to jump and help when Art takes one of his walks." The skin between her eyebrows furrowed as she examined my coat. White feathers poked out of the holes the buckshot left. "What on earth have you gotten into, Cam?"

"Hope, I'll be ready to go in just a second," Dorothy called as she crossed the hallway, headed for the kitchen.

"I drive her home," Mrs. Bradley explained. "Plus, it lets me check in and make sure Art has everything he needs or give Xander a little break. I'm so glad you're here! How long are you in for?"

"I'm back for good." The words tasted like bitter lemon on my tongue.

She clasped her hands. "Really? Well, that's the best thing I've heard all week!" Her eyes dropped to my coat again, and she shook her head. "You might need to get a new coat, though."

"I'm ready," Dorothy said, coming out of the kitchen. "Now, Cam, I've given your father his evening meds. Maybe you could take a shift sleeping in Art's room so Xander can sleep at his own place tonight? That boy is worn to the bone. Oh, and how are you feeling after all that...?" She acted like it hadn't been years since I'd been in this house, like I'd left mid-conversation and she was simply picking it back up.

"All that what?" Hope asked.

"Boy got himself shot saving your daughter; at least that's what Art just told me." Dorothy passed us both to retrieve her coat from the rack by the door.

"You were shot?" She focused on a hole in my jacket. "And Willow?" Her panicked gaze darted back to mine.

"She's fine," I assured her. That had been the only acceptable outcome.

"Because you were there," Xander commented as he came down the stairs.

Great, now he chose to show up. I shot him a look, but it didn't stop my brother from running his mouth.

"Cam stepped right between them, even with that gun pointed straight at his chest." Xander beamed like a proud parent.

Hell. I was in Hell. And knowing Hope, she'd see straight through me.

"You stepped... He had a..." Hope blinked quickly and then spun back toward the living room as Dad stepped into the hallway. "You aimed a gun at my daughter?"

"Claws are out," Xander murmured.

"Because you couldn't keep your mouth shut," I retorted.

"Like the whole town won't know by morning," he scoffed.

"What the hell are you doing here?" Dad shouted, jabbing his finger in my direction.

"You aimed a gun at my Willow?" Hope repeated, getting right up in Dad's face.

"I didn't know it was Willow, and you have my most sincere apology," he told her quietly, then focused his venom right back on me, as usual. "Explain yourself."

"Dad, it's Camden. Remember? He was up at the ravine with us earlier. He's home now," Xander said slowly, as if he were talking to a child...or a man who couldn't remember who he was 50 percent of the time.

"I know who the hell he is, Alexander. Why are you in my home, Camden?"

Hope gasped and stepped back.

"I'm here to help you," I told him in the calmest voice possible, gathering every emotion in my body and shoving them in a box, just like I did on missions.

"You? The boy who vowed never to darken my doorstep again? The boy who burned down the bunkhouse in a fit of boredom? The boy who's been here once in the last ten years, and only to bury his brother? You're here to help?"

The boy I'd been would have cried.

The teenager I'd grown out of would have cursed at him and walked away.

The man I was now stood there and took it because I was finally strong enough to.

"Dad!" Xander snapped, stepping forward. "Stop it! You don't know what you're saying."

"I know exactly what I'm saying. He's the reason Sullivan isn't here. He's the reason your daughter"—he looked at Hope—"buried the love of her life when she was nineteen. He's the reason everything goes to shit."

"Art, you know that's not true," Hope said quietly.

"He gave the order that killed Sullivan."

My breath caught as Dad's ice-blue eyes met mine. I couldn't deny it. Not when it was the truth.

"I didn't know—" I started.

"You got him killed! You're not sleeping under my roof. You're not welcome here. Get out."

My stomach turned to lead and plummeted to the floor.

"Dad! No!" Xander shouted.

There was zero mercy in my father's eyes, zero give, and zero chance he was going to change his mind...but he was the one who'd asked me to come here. Didn't he remember?

Screw this. Screw all of this. He was never going to listen. He'd made up his mind the moment he read the report Xander had promised not to show him.

I turned around and walked out of the house, letting the screen door slam behind me. Rocks jabbed into my feet as I hit the drive. Shit. I'd left my boots inside. Whatever. I had another ten pairs in the Jeep. I'd find a hotel—

"Cam!" Xander yelled as I reached the Jeep.

I climbed in, but he got to the door before I could close it. A set of keys jangled from his outstretched fingers, but I kept my eyes straight ahead, refusing to see the inevitable pity in his eyes.

"Go to my place. This will all blow over. I promise."

He'd made that same promise when the mood of the house hadn't lifted six months after Mom's funeral. Xander's optimism was a giant heap of lies he told himself to make swallowing the shit easier.

"No," I replied. The last place I wanted to be was in Mayor Daniels's house, getting my dirt all over his perfect life. I didn't even know where he lived.

"Come on," he pled. "I've got HBO."

"Don't watch much TV."

"You're still so damned stubborn," he muttered, digging into his pocket and retrieving another set of keys, this one with an eighties-style Broncos stallion on the key chain. "Then, at least go up to Uncle Cal's house. Well, I mean, technically he left it to you, so it's your house."

Uncle Cal. The one person I'd been able to lean on. The only guy who'd ever understood the rage that always seemed to simmer just beneath my surface.

Xander shook the keys. "Come on. Don't go to a hotel. None of the tourist places up here are open yet, and it's a forty-five-minute drive back to Buena Vista. The electricity still works up there, and the water runs. I check it every month. It's not like I've dusted or anything, and it's not the Four Seasons, but it's yours. Do it for me, please. I can't watch you drive away and wait another six years to see if you'll come back."

"I'm not leaving the state, for Christ's sake. Just Dad's house," I promised. I'd had no intention of coming back when I left last time. We'd both known it. I couldn't blame him for that touch of worry in his voice, so I took the keys, and he sighed in relief.

"I'll check on you tomorrow."

"I'll be fine. Will you?" I motioned back to the house. "I know you need a break."

"I'll take one once Dad comes to his senses."

Ha. Like that was going to happen.

"Look." His voice softened. "We all know you didn't kill Sullivan. Dad just…" He shook his head.

"I gave the order. May as well have pulled the trigger," I said quietly, staring at the front porch. Our team had been called in to support a combat outpost under fire, and when our chopper managed to land, all hell had broken loose. I'd been ordered to head toward a break in the defenses with whichever soldiers were available.

"You relayed orders. That's all."

"I chose a squad leader to reinforce the side of the outpost taking the heaviest fire," I corrected him. "That sergeant took his squad and did just that." We'd split what was left of that platoon down the middle. I could have chosen the staff sergeant on my right. Instead, I took the one on my left and headed for the wall with his soldiers. "Sullivan was in that squad."

"You didn't know that." He shook his head emphatically. "How could you have? I've read the report. There's no way you would have seen him in a mess like that."

By the time I'd recognized Sully, it was too late. My hands tightened on the wheel. He'd been shot ten feet away from me.

If I had just chosen the guy on the right, Sullivan would be alive. That was where Dad had stopped listening.

"I've got to get out of here."

"The back way is still open," he said. When it became apparent that I wasn't going to reply, he mumbled something about my stubbornness and shut the door.

I waited until he was clear, then started the engine. Instead of taking the road back to Alba, I followed the fading dirt road west, putting the Jeep into four-wheel drive and skirting the edge of the Bradley property line for a few minutes until I climbed the next ridge and turned north.

I crept through the open, rusted gate and crossed onto Uncle Cal's land. Guess it really was mine now, according to the property taxes I'd been paying. Still felt like his, though. He'd died the year before Sullivan, and I'd been deployed again, unable to bury the man I'd loved more than my own father.

A few minutes later, I put the car in park.

In the sunlight, I'd be able to see what remained of the ruins at the hot springs down the ridgeline and the tip of the abandoned Rose Rowan Mine below those. But given the sight my headlights illuminated, maybe it was a good thing it was dark.

The landscaping had overgrown the sprawling single-story home, and the roof was missing so many shingles, it looked more like a suggestion than a reality. Uncle Cal had added rooms as he'd wanted, giving the house an unsymmetrical, eclectic feel that I'd always loved as a kid. Now that I was an adult, it just meant that there was a shit ton of roof to repair. I could only hope that the solar panels had fared better.

Yeah, it was going to be a massive amount of work, but at least I wouldn't have to sleep in body armor. The same couldn't be said for the house I'd grown up in.

I got out of the Jeep and headed for the front door, pausing at the porch. My thumb dusted off the markings Uncle Cal had carved into the upright stone he'd jokingly called his address.

"Elba," I repeated, shaking my head with a little laugh at the joke no one in our family ever remarked on. Napoleon's island.

Guess I was well and truly exiled now.

How the hell was I supposed to accomplish the one thing Dad had asked of me if he wouldn't even talk to me?

CHAPTER FOUR

Willow

My cell phone flashed an alert for a front-door entry, and a video clip automatically started playing. I tugged my headphones down to rest around my neck, effectively silencing the BANNERS album I'd been listening to, and saw my best friend on the screen, juggling a carrier tray of coffee and my house key.

Another hour and this project for Vaughn Holdings would be finished, but something told me I was about to hit a major delay. Thea never popped in without a reason, and I had a sneaking suspicion that reason was Cam.

"Willow?" Thea called out.

"In the office!" I mentally kissed my productivity goodbye and set my headphones on the glass desk.

"There you are!" She gave me a smile brighter than the morning sun and a cup of coffee from Alba Perks.

I thanked her for the coffee, then took a sip of the chocolaty mocha and waited to hear why she'd dropped by so early. She liked to get to her yoga studio before nine, even in the off-season.

"I was hoping you'd be home." Her eyebrows rose over light-blue eyes.

"Ha! It's eight thirty a.m. on a Tuesday, so I'm working. Where else did you think I might be?" I took a sip and savored the mocha, wondering how long it would take for her to bring him up.

"Oh, I don't know...over at the Danielses' place?" she asked in mock innocence, blowing the steam across the lid of her cup.

Not long at all.

"Okay, what have you heard?" I leaned back in my chair as she plopped her butt right on my desk. The gossip wasn't something I'd missed while I was at college, but Thea was someone I'd longed for every day at Rutgers.

"I know that I was dropping Jacob off at preschool and some of the other moms had a few fascinating stories about a very hot, very tattooed, very Daniels-looking man stopping in at the gas station before heading up the mountain. You wouldn't happen to know anything about that, now, would you?" Her blue eyes sparkled as she tilted her head.

"Why on earth would I know who stops in for gas?"

"Oh, come on. Julie Hall was dropping off Sawyer before heading to the hospital, and she said—"

My cell phone alerted me to another entry, and a quick peek showed my mother walking in.

Work from home, they said. It'll be fun and productive, they said.

"Mom! Boundaries!" I called down the hall.

"Thea! How lovely to see you." Mom ignored my comment, her perky grin sending warning signals down my spine. What was she up to now?

"Mom, seriously? I thought we had the whole 'the key is only for emergencies' discussion?" Moving back last year had definitely challenged my mom's hovering nature, but I knew she did it out of love. She was in her element with someone to fuss over, and lately that someone was me.

"Well, you get so grouchy when I interrupt your work, so I figured I'd just let myself in and see if you were here before bugging you."

I wasn't touching the lack of logic in that statement with a ten-foot pole. "Right. Mom, what's up? I know you didn't drive all the way up here to see if I was home. You could have done that with a phone call."

She shifted an overstuffed canvas tote on her shoulder. "Is it a crime to want to see my daughter? I mean, you were gone for four years, and I feel like I'm still getting used to having you back. I love having both my girls home again." Her tone was so exaggerated that I nearly choked on the syrupy sweetness of it. "But I do need a favor from one of you."

"We both know that Charity is asleep, so out with it!" I demanded with a laugh. No doubt my older sister had gone back to bed after taking Rose to school. She usually worked the closing shift at her bar, since she lived right above it.

Mom smiled back, mirroring my own, and set the bag on the purple armchair in my office. When I'd bought what I'd lovingly called The Outpost, I'd repainted every wall and all the woodwork white, decorating in pops of bright color that I could easily change out when the mood struck. Art school had given me an appreciation of how color affected mood, and after losing Sullivan...well, I'd needed a lot of color. Now, I was good with just bits and pieces.

"So you're right, we both know Charity is still sleeping, so I was thinking that you might run a few things over to Camden for me."

"Ha! I knew you knew!" Thea jumped off my desk, making my monitor wobble.

I steadied the equipment that cost more than I'd made my first year and sighed, glancing up at the onyx rook that sat next to my monitor. That little chess piece was more valuable than any of my electronics.

"Yes, I knew," I told Thea. "Why can't you run it over yourself, Mom? The Danielses' place is way closer to your house than mine."

I'd put off thinking about Cam since the moment I'd woken up this morning. And by put off, I meant refused to acknowledge when he'd popped into my head...which had been about every minute or so. Plan was working out great.

It wasn't like I could help it. He'd basically been gone ten years.

He was bound to bring up some thoughts...some feelings.

"Because he's not at the Danielses'. He's up at Cal's place. Not that it's Cal's anymore. It's his, you know," Mom finished with a nod.

"He's at Cal's?" I asked quietly. He'd always been more comfortable there as a kid—we all had—but it wasn't like that place was really cleaned up enough to live in yet.

"Art... He was difficult last night, as you well know." Mom shot me a glare that told me she'd been filled in on what had gone down at the ravine.

God, Cam had just gotten home, and Art had kicked him out? That was the only explanation for him staying up at Cal's. My eyes were drawn to the huge picture window in my office that looked east across the ridgeline, and my heart lunged against my ribs, like it was straining to travel without me. If he was at Cal's, that meant there was only a mile between our houses. For ten years, he'd been thousands of miles away—half a world, sometimes—and now he was close enough to visit with a quick walk.

If I dared...which of course I never did. Because I was an idiot, not a masochist.

"Willow?" Mom prompted me from my thoughts. Always here but never present. That's what Dad lovingly said when I drifted off as a kid. He didn't find that same quality quite so enchanting now that I was an adult.

"Sorry," I apologized out of habit. "So why don't you just run it over to him yourself?"

Mom cringed. "Well, I grabbed his boots— It's a long story, but I was there when it all happened, so I thought he might be a bit embarrassed to see me."

"As opposed to being delighted to see me?" I tilted my head. "You know he can't stand me." Cam's loathing of me was the worst-kept secret in all of Alba, and we were known for fast gossip. Even when I'd been with Sully, Cam had barely tolerated my presence those last months before he went off to basic, and then it had been under obvious duress.

It hadn't always been that way, but it was sure where we ended up.

"Right, and that's why he stepped in front of a loaded gun for you," Mom chided. Oh yeah, she was miffed that I hadn't filled her in last night.

"He did what?" Thea shouted, the sound echoing off the bare walls.

"Calm down," I mumbled. "He had on a bulletproof vest." Not that I'd known. When I'd thought that bullets had penetrated his chest... I never wanted to feel like that again. As for what I'd felt, well, I wasn't pausing to examine that, either.

"Not on his head, he didn't," Mom retorted.

"Who had a gun?" Now it was Thea glaring at me.

"Arthur Daniels," Mom explained. "Don't worry—Xander locked it up. But you can't tell me that boy hates you when he literally put his life on the line for yours."

My mind drifted to his mint-and-pine scent. His arm locked around my waist. The way he'd ordered me to go, both before his father shot him...and after. Glad to know he was still a walking contradiction.

I sighed, letting my head rest against the high back of my chair. One thing I'd learned about Camden was that he might absolutely abhor my presence, but he'd never stand by and watch me get hurt.

"I never said hate. He no doubt did that because he loves you guys. Always has. And I'm sure he feels some weird sense of responsibility because Sullivan died."

Both Mom and Thea averted their eyes, as usual.

"I can say his name. You can, too. It won't hurt me any more than it already does." Sure, his loss still ached, but not in the way it had. That first year, it had been a sucking chest wound. I couldn't breathe, couldn't sleep. Couldn't see past the next few minutes.

Now it was like a reconstructed knee that ached when the weather changed. I knew it could flare up again at any minute when the conditions were right, but it consumed me only in rare moments. I had put myself back together years ago. Unfortunately, none of Alba had gotten the message that I was healed. They still treated me like I might dissolve into a puddle of tears at any moment.

"We know," Mom said softly with a sad smile. "We just...worry."

Thea's lips pressed into a thin line, and she nodded. Sully had been her husband's best friend, and Pat had struggled just as hard as I had.

But no one had suffered like Camden. I'd known with one look at the funeral that Cam had been irrevocably shattered by what happened to Sullivan.

"So his boots are in the bag?" I put us back on topic just to steer clear of the grief tsunami that threatened to overtake the room.

"Right. Yes. And a few other things he might need. Would you mind running them over? I'd really appreciate it. And I know you two don't particularly get along, though you most certainly used to."

Man, did she love to remind me that at one point I'd been attached to the Daniels boys at the hip. Especially Cam.

"I just..." She continued when I remained quiet. "I know he's not mine, but if Lillian were here..." She shook her head, unable to continue.

"I'll take it," I agreed, knowing it would ease her and maybe myself, too. "If I hurry, I can be back by ten and get this finished."

"Oh, I have to head to the studio!" Thea jolted as if she'd just noticed the time. "I have a class coming in at ten I need to get set up for."

"Business is good?" Mom asked.

Starting up something new was always a risk in Alba. Sure, the season—the summer months—was a gushing waterfall of business, but the fall was slow and the winter downright dead before a trickle started back up in the spring. It was one reason the younger generations kept leaving.

"Not bad! We partnered with that little resort down in Mount Princeton, so they've been sending business our way. Today is a bridal party!" Thea finished in excitement.

Mom's expression changed in a way that only I caught. It was a twinge of pain that she'd learned to camouflage quickly over the years, but it was there nonetheless.

In some ways, losing Sullivan had been harder on her than it had me. I'd lost the man I loved, the one I'd planned on spending my life with.

She'd lost her dream of holding a grandchild that she could see both herself and Lillian in. It had been like losing her best friend all over again, combined with mourning what she'd considered to be my future.

I saw it all the time around our small town—the specter of what-if. The futures parents dreamed for their children died hard around here, and laying them to rest demanded a thousand impromptu funerals over the course of a lifetime. The past could be buried and would eventually set you free. Hopes and dreams for futures that would never come to fruition? Those suckers were the real ghosts.

Mom blinked herself free of her most recent burial.

"That's just great, Thea. I'm so proud of you. How about I walk you out? You can tell me how Jacob is doing. I just love getting to see his sweet little face around town."

Thea agreed, then hugged me tight. "Call me. I mean it. I want to know everything." She pulled back and gave me the same look she'd dished out around locker doors in high school.

"I promise."

"Oh, and Willow, if you have anything you think Cam might find...useful, why don't you take that over at the same time?" Mom hinted. "He says he's back for good, so he might need it."

My face flooded with warmth.

"Yep. I'll get right on that. See you later." I forced a smile and ushered them out my front door.

Once I shut it behind them, I leaned against the oak expanse and did my best to breathe like a normal person on a normal day.

So what if he'd jump to conclusions? So what if I'd be opening myself up to a heaping dose of ridicule and that cold, cruel stare? Mom knew damn well what I had stored in my spare bedroom, so wasn't it better if I delivered it before she accidentally blurted out my secret to Cam? The only thing more embarrassing than what I was about to do would be him showing up and demanding it himself.

I was doing this now to save myself further humiliation…not because I stupidly wanted to see him. Right.

My bare feet crossed the sun-warmed hardwood of my little house, passing the open-concept living, dining, and kitchen area, then my office, and heading back to the two bedrooms, only one of which was occupied.

Mom and Dad built The Outpost the summer I'd decided not to go to college. The summer I'd decided to stay home and wait for Sullivan to return from deployment. Bed-and-breakfasts were huge up here, but little houses where families could vacation were even bigger. They'd rented it out for a couple of years before Mom decided that the rental business wasn't for her, and now it was mine. Well, in another three hundred and forty-eight mortgage payments, it would be.

I opened the spare bedroom and sighed at the contents.

"Stop being a chicken," I lectured myself.

Then I put on my shoes, tied my hair up in a messy bun, and got to work.

A half hour later, my SUV climbed the last stretch of snow-laden dirt road that led to Cal's. Camden's black Jeep sat parked in the driveway, the tires and lower portion of the paint caked in mud.

I put my car in park and killed the ignition, and before I was ready, I found myself knocking on his front door.

Only a minute passed before he flung said door open. He really was bigger than when he'd left; my mind hadn't made that up yesterday. He dwarfed me in a way that would have intimidated me if I didn't know him so well.

Camden might slice me open emotionally with a few careless words, but I was 100 percent safe with him and always had been. Oddly enough, I was probably the only person in Alba who could say that.

"What do you want, Willow? I was trying to get the Scout up and running." His voice was rougher than the scruffy beard he'd grown.

Well, that explained the grease streaks on the white shirt that draped over his heavily muscled frame and the jeans that hung sinfully well on his hips.

Enough of that. This is Cam.

"I wanted to bring you a few things," I said, motioning to the bag I had slung over my shoulder. "Can I come in for a minute?"

A debate flickered in those dark eyes momentarily before he nodded and stepped back, allowing me entrance.

The house was just as I'd remembered—an eclectic homage to the man who'd built it between visits home from wherever he'd been working. The entry's smooth hardwood led to warmly painted walls that boasted exotic artwork framed between exposed beams of reclaimed wood.

A smile lifted the corners of my lips as I glanced around.

"What?" Cam asked.

Saying "nothing" would just irk him, so I was honest about my random thoughts.

"I was thinking that Cal was years ahead of the whole reclaimed-wood trend. He would have been the ultimate hipster now."

He blinked at me, and warmth crept up my neck.

"You know, because hipsters do everything before it's cool?" I added, hoping to ease the awkwardness of my joke.

It didn't.

"Right." He looked at me with expectation, and I cleared my throat.

"My mom asked me to drop this by." When he didn't reach for the bag, I kicked off my shoes, skirted around his enormous body, and headed for the kitchen. I'd been in this house almost as often as Cam growing up, so at least I knew my way around. When I reached the well-loved handmade table, I set the bag down and emptied the contents.

Homemade cookies began the assault on table space, followed by muffins and banana bread in quantities that suggested Mom had expected a small army.

"Guess she baked last night," I muttered before setting his shoes on the floor.

His eyes dropped to the boots before meeting mine.

Tension strung between us so thick, I could have hung my laundry on it. I hated how he only spoke when he'd finally driven me bonkers from wondering what he was thinking. Hated how he'd always known exactly how to get under my skin. Hated that he made me wonder what was going on in his head when I so often blurted out whatever was in mine.

"So you're staying up here?" I asked, breaking the stare to take in the familiar lines of the kitchen. It was dusty in places, especially in the cracks of the hand-laid backsplash that depicted the mountains around us in carefully chosen pieces of granite.

"Seems like it. Tell your mom thank you for me."

I ignored the gruff answer and let my palm trail over the stonework. "I've always loved this piece."

"You should, since you did it."

My gaze flew to his. He'd remembered that? He'd barely been around that last summer.

"I just helped." I shrugged.

"Whatever you say."

"Thank you. For yesterday. You saved my life." I paused

between each sentence, hoping he'd reply. "Rumor is that you're here to stay."

"Since when do you listen to rumors?"

"Are they true?" If he was going to ignore my question, then I was ignoring his.

"Yeah, I'm sticking around." He folded his arms across his chest, drawing my attention to the ink that decorated his skin from his wrists up into his short sleeves.

His left forearm held a scene of pine and aspen trees that sheltered a twisting creek that formed a pond just above his elbow—a pond I recognized. The hot springs that straddled the property line between what had been our parents' but was now our land.

"What are you thinking about?" he asked, just like he always did. Most people were content to let me live in my head, or they tried to bring me back to the conversation. Cam had always pried my thoughts loose, and I let him, even if he'd usually mocked me for them right after.

Maybe I *was* a masochist.

"That I always figured you just left and never looked back." My finger lightly traced the outline of the hot springs, his skin smooth and warm under mine, then paused at the inked rendition of the abandoned structure we used to jump from as kids. "But you took us with you." Where had he found the drawing? Did he realize it was mine?

His scent hit me, and I realized just how close I was to him, that I was actually touching him. I jerked back and felt my cheeks heat all the way to my ears.

He didn't say anything or even move. Nope, he stood there like the brick wall he was, giving nothing away in those unreadable eyes of his, but at least he wasn't making fun of me.

"So anyway, I brought a few more things. I can just grab them from the car, and then I'll be on my way."

"Need help carrying them in?"

The thought of him seeing everything in my car had me scrambling for an out. "Oh, no. You go back to the Scout. It's only a box or two. Nothing I can't handle. I'll just let myself out when I'm done."

His eyes narrowed slightly, but he finally nodded. "Okay, suit yourself. I'll be in the garage if you change your mind."

He headed toward the garage, which opened along the east side of the house, and I put my shoes back on and went out the front door. Even if he had the garage door open, he wouldn't see the collection I was about to haul in.

Sweet, crisp air filled my lungs, and the contrast from indoors made me realize how badly the house needed to be aired out and thoroughly cleaned. How long had it been since anyone had lived here? It had been since before Sullivan died.

I made trip after trip from my car to the entry hall, first pushing boxes against the wall and then stacking them until I'd carried in everything I'd brought.

The grandfather clock chimed, and a smile tugged at my lips. I loved that clock. *Had it made in Germany*, Cal had told me before showing me how to wind it.

My feet carried me across the entry into my favorite room in the house—the library. Dust sparkled in the air as light came in the row of windows taller than I was. Books lined the walls, reaching toward the ceiling in stacks and unorganized lines. It was a riot of color, paperback and leather, but though dust covered the floor, none touched the shelves or the empty chessboard in the corner.

Camden had been in the house for only a night and had already taken down the sheets Sullivan and I had cut apart to cover the books and furniture when Cal passed away. That day with Sullivan, so close to his enlistment, should have been the memory I lingered on, should have been what sent my hands to the spines, but it wasn't.

It was the sound of Cam's voice, lighter and higher, reading aloud while I painted in the corner on the little easel Cal always left just for me. My hands had been busy and my mind quiet—full of other people's stories and Cam's voice.

I plucked a title from the shelf, noting the multicolored, highlighted passages just as Cam found me.

"Sorry, I got distracted," I told him, my nose scrunching.

"So I see." He looked around the room, and I couldn't help but wonder if he remembered the same things about it that I did.

He walked over, his boots heavy on the floor, and I cringed at my lack of manners. "Sorry, I forgot to take off my shoes after that last load."

He snorted. "That's our parents' rule. Not mine, if you can't tell." He took the book from my hand and surprised me by not putting it back but flipping it to read the cover. "*East of Eden.* Good choice."

"Steinbeck," I commented.

"So it says." He slightly lifted the corner of his mouth. "'There is more beauty in truth, even if it is dreadful beauty.'" The quote tumbled from those lips easily.

"You always did have a good memory for books." That was putting it mildly. He could remember lines and details that most people glanced over and never thought about again.

"It's one of my favorites. Besides, books are easy," he said with a shrug. "They lay out their truth in literal black and white. Probably why Dad never liked them. He'd rather make up his own stories so they conform to what he already believes."

"People are harder," I noted. "Are you really okay? I mean, he shot you." I asked the question that had plagued me since last night.

"Right as rain." He lifted his shirt with a smug little smirk, revealing miles of abs that dipped and rose to the tattoos that started along his side and covered his chest. In the center, just beneath his pecs, the skin was a livid red, peppered with a series of deep-purple bruises. "See?"

"Cam," I whispered, stepping closer.

He backed up and dropped his smirk and the shirt. "No problem here."

"I wasn't worried about you physically," I muttered to his back as he left the library, but I knew that was the only response I was going to get. Cam would tell you he was fine if he were bleeding to death.

"Holy shit, how many boxes did you bring?" he asked as he walked into the entryway.

Crap. I should've been gone by now. I really didn't want to see him realize what his father had done. What I'd done.

"Um. A few." I beelined across the entry as he opened a random box.

"This is my football jersey."

I paused with my hand on the doorknob. So close.

"Yeah," I said quietly. Cursing myself for a fool, I turned to watch him.

His eyebrows drew together in confusion as he riffled through the box. "My trophies, my foot—" His head jerked up, and his eyes found mine. "This is from my bedroom."

I nodded.

"But…" He shook his head. "But Xander said Dad boxed it all up and threw it out after…" He drifted off.

"After Sullivan died," I finished for him. "You knew?"

Now he was the one nodding.

"Xander called that night and told me what your dad had done. Said he'd left it all at the base of the drive to go out with the trash." I focused on the boxes, ripping my eyes from the stare that was always too intense to hold for long. "I waited until a little after midnight so no one would see, then drove over and took it all."

"You took it all."

"Doesn't that look like all of it?" My chest tightened with the need to get out of here, for this humiliating moment to end.

"Willow."

I shook my head and opened the door.

A large palm appeared above me, shutting the door and caging me on one side.

"Willow, look at me."

Slowly, I dragged my eyes up his shirt, over the supple lines of his throat, and past his lips until I found his dark eyes on me. Those eyes had always screwed me over. People who didn't know him well called them soulless, and I'd rolled my eyes and let them think what they would. Those eyes were so full that there simply wasn't room for any lighter colors, already saturated with every emotion he never let himself show.

"Why would you do that? Haul yourself out of bed in the middle of the night to save my stuff? Go against both our fathers?"

"Because Sullivan would have done it for you."

He backed away, a flicker of pain showing in the way his mouth tensed. "Thank you," he finally said, his voice low and deep.

I nodded, then opened the door and retreated to my car, leaving Cam in the entryway with his boxed-up, rejected childhood.

I'd never lied to Cam, not once. I'd never been capable when those eyes were on me. And I hadn't just now...not really. I'd simply given him the easiest of both truths.

Yes, Sullivan would have done it for him. That was just who he'd been.

But I hadn't done it only for Sullivan. I'd crept out of my parents' house and filled my car to the very last box for the truth that Camden would never admit.

Sullivan may have done it for Cam, but even in our worst moments, Camden would have done it for me.

I was almost home before I realized I still didn't know why Cam was here. But if he was sticking around, my safe little existence was going to get shaken up like a snow globe if I couldn't keep my feelings to myself.

CHAPTER FIVE

Camden

"Gutters," I muttered, writing the word in the notebook I'd brought with me. "Siding." I'd been standing in front of Dad's house for the last twenty minutes, making a list of all the things the house needed and procrastinating knocking, if I had to be honest.

In my defense, it had been less than forty-eight hours since he'd kicked me out. But I'd given up the life I'd made for myself to be here, which meant I couldn't exactly lick my wounds if I wanted to get shit done.

"Replace banister on front steps." Another item to the list.

The front door creaked, and my fingers paused on the last word.

"I've seen a lot of things in my life," Dorothy said from the porch, her footsteps heavy as she approached where I stood at the bottom of the steps. "But I've never seen a man so big try to hide behind a notebook so small."

"Not hiding," I corrected her as I finished. "Just avoiding."

"Uh-huh." She folded her arms and gave me a knowing look. "I see you got your shoes back."

"I did." Thanks to Willow. I had more than just my shoes thanks to her.

"Why don't you come on in? I'm sure you'll find plenty for your list."

"He kicked me out."

"And yet here you are."

I'd never won a stare-down with Dorothy Powers, and something told me today still wasn't the day it would happen.

"I don't want to upset him," I admitted. "I came home to help, not to get him all worked up."

"Well, he's not sure who he is today, so I don't think he'll care that you're here. Besides, it's Wednesday, so Walter Robinson is in there keeping him occupied. Now, get in this house." She waved me up the steps like I was eight years old.

I went.

"How is Walt?" I asked as she led me in the front door.

"Stubborn, opinionated, and loud."

"So basically the same." I kicked off my shoes and lined them up against the wall, promising myself that I'd remember them this time.

"People don't tend to change without good reason, and the Lord's never given Walter one, that's for sure. Plus he's still as good-looking as ever, which doesn't exactly seem fair. Now, let's get you something to drink and have us a little chat."

I followed Dorothy down the hallway I'd taken my first steps in, pausing when I noticed Xander's and Sullivan's senior pictures hanging in the hallway.

There was a frame-size rectangle of darker-colored paint where mine had hung. Not that I had to wonder where it had gone. I'd found it earlier today in one of the boxes Willow had salvaged from my exorcism, along with my baby box, where Mom had kept my first lock of hair, tooth, all that stuff.

Willow, who'd never broken a damned rule in her life unless I'd been the one pushing her, had rescued my childhood from destruction. A little spark of...whatever lit in my chest with that thought, and I quickly shut it down and shoved it as far away from me as possible. Willow was so untouchable that she didn't even go on the untouchable list. She went on the unthinkable one.

And yet, here I was...thinking.

"Well, are you coming?" Dorothy asked from the kitchen.

"Yes, ma'am." I glanced down the hall to the living room, where I heard Walter's boisterous laugh, then made my way into the kitchen.

Mom's cherry cabinets were faded in places from sunlight, and the apple wallpaper she'd hung peeled at the corners, but other than that, it looked exactly the same.

"Coffee?" Dorothy offered, motioning to a steaming pot under the ancient coffeemaker.

"No, thank you." I pulled out the chair closest to the wall and sat at the table.

"Suit yourself." She poured herself a cup and sat down across from me. "What happened out there with your father—and his gun—was unfortunate."

"That's putting it mildly." I set my notebook on the table, covering the unfinished splotch on the wood where I'd spilled Mom's nail polish remover twenty years ago.

"I would say that I'm sorry, but if I apologized for every inappropriate thing your father did or said, I'd never shut up." She shrugged, then sipped.

My lips turned up at the corners. "You're funnier than I remember."

"I've always been this funny. You were never mature enough to appreciate it."

"I wasn't mature enough to appreciate a lot of things." The admission was easy because I'd never hurt her with my actions. The chances of me saying that to Dad? To Xander? To Willow? I wasn't quite that mature yet.

Dorothy's eyebrows shot up. "And now you're home to help."

"I am."

She nodded slowly, assessing me in a way that made me take my elbows off the table. "Okay, then."

Tension unraveled in my chest, easing a burden I hadn't

realized I was carrying.

"Tell me what he needs." I clicked the pen and opened the notebook to a fresh page. "What I can do and what he won't let me do."

Dorothy smiled and began.

He needed a night nurse, since there was no telling if he'd kick me out at any given moment and Xander deserved to sleep at his own place. She could handle days, but hiring someone to pick up the slack was a good idea, too.

I swallowed, realizing Dad needed around-the-clock care.

"I gave Xander a list of names from Dr. Sanderson, but he said they were too expensive."

Halting my pen, I looked up at Dorothy. She had to have misspoken.

"I know." She waved me off.

Unless Dad had gone on a spending spree in the last decade, there was zero chance he couldn't afford it. We'd grown up knowing the financial worth of our family and how to spend responsibly so that worth didn't diminish.

"I'll talk to Xander," I said with a curt nod.

Dorothy continued, and my little list became not so little anymore.

"Xander does his best," she assured me. "That boy is a saint."

"Sure is." Guilt sat in my stomach like a rock, but I managed a nod. Alexander's sainthood wasn't exactly news to me.

I'd just finished writing down her last recommendation when Walter's and Dad's voices drew closer.

"Thank you," I said to Dorothy, getting to my feet quickly.

"—and you know there's no telling—" Walter's eyebrows rose toward his salt-and-pepper hairline. "Welcome home," he said softly, reaching for my hand. Dorothy was right—Walter hadn't aged much. His dark skin was unwrinkled with the exception of the laugh lines at the corners of his eyes, and his brown eyes still held a ready smile.

"Thank you," I replied, shaking his hand. He stood between the exit and me, making the kitchen window look like a good option if not for the thirty-foot drop to the ground below. Damned walkout basement.

"He looks good, doesn't he, Walt?" Dad asked, slapping his best friend on the back.

We both turned to stare at him in shock.

Dad's grin only widened as he held my gaze. "So young to be so accomplished, too. Definitely a man to be proud of."

"He is," Walt agreed.

My breath paused, as if sucking in any of the air would pop this moment like the little bubble it was.

"I'm so surprised to see you here," Dad went on.

"I just stopped by to see if you needed anything," I said carefully.

His smile softened. "Such a good kid. Dorothy, why the heck didn't you tell me Rich was home from college?"

Air gushed from my chest like a deflated balloon. Rich was ten years older than me and owned Alba's only auto body shop. Which meant not only did Dad not know who I was, he didn't know what year it was.

"Art," Walter began, his tone dropping.

I caught his eye and shook my head. It wasn't worth it.

Walter's shoulders sagged, but he nodded.

"I never quite know what the boy is up to." Dorothy patted me on the back as she walked to Dad. "He's just headed home now."

Taking the cue, I grabbed the notebook and headed for the door. I couldn't ask Dad about the voicemail now anyway. I needed him lucid and not hating me. Hell, I would have taken either at the moment.

"It really is good to see you," Dad told me with a warm smile.

For that millisecond, I let myself pretend he was actually talking to me. That he had missed me and wanted me home.

"You too."

I exited quickly, grabbed my shoes, and took them out on the porch, sitting on the steps to get them on. The door opened and shut behind me as I finished with the second one.

"That must have been tough," Walter said as he sat beside me, resting his forearms on the knees of his dress pants.

"Which part? Him not knowing who I was? Or him being happy to see me?" I looked over the driveway to the break in the pines where the mountains showed through. "It's all fine."

He looked at me and sighed. "You know, I think it doesn't matter that we're grown men. There's always a part of us that looks for our father's acceptance, his approval. Even if we don't recognize it or even fight it, it still stings when it doesn't come."

"I gave up on that a long time ago, Walt."

"Even so, I'm glad you're here, Cam."

"That makes one of you."

"Art is happy, too. He just can't always show it."

"He literally shot me the day before yesterday." My chest ached like hell.

He cringed. "Okay, well…" His eyes met mine. "Honestly, I've got nothing."

"It's okay." I stood, savoring the chill in the air as the wind kicked up. "I'd rather he treat me like he did just now. I can help him a lot more if I'm not dodging bullets."

"He's pretty hit-or-miss these days, not going to lie. Half the time I'm up here, he knows who I am but might confuse what year it is, like you just saw."

"And the other half?"

"Those days are tougher. If you'd told me a decade ago that Arthur Daniels would lose his mind to early-onset Alzheimer's, I would have laughed you off the mountain. Not as stubborn and strong-willed as he is."

There was a lot about this last decade I wouldn't have believed. Losing Sullivan was at the top of that list.

"How's Simon?" I asked, trying to remember my manners and

change the subject at the same time.

Walt grinned. "That boy is something else. He's practicing family law in Buena Vista now."

"That's great. You have a lot to be proud of." Simon had always been one of the straight shooters, from what I remembered.

"You do, too, Cam. I mean that. It took a lot to come back here."

I nodded and lifted my notebook. "I guess I'll get on this. Or at least what he'll let me do."

"Do you need anything? I doubt your dad or Alexander asked."

"I'm okay up at Cal's. Or I guess it's not Cal's anymore. It's mine." Not that it hadn't always felt like more of a home than this one, but it was weird without Cal there.

"Okay, well, if you change your mind or if you need a job or anything, just let me know. This town isn't always the easiest to come back to. Believe me, I know." He stood, tucking his thumbs into the belt loops of his jeans.

"Thank you for the offer." I had pretty good savings, so I wasn't worried just yet. But I appreciated it, knowing the fine people of Alba wouldn't support Walter offering me a job at the Rowan Inn, given that it was the largest hotel in Alba. Then again, there weren't a lot of job openings for a civil engineer around here.

"And you should come to the Historical Society meeting next week," he urged. "I know you didn't have any interest when you were younger, and of course Alexander has been exercising your dad's vote, but nothing reminds Alba that you're a local more than showing up to a Historical meeting. Just a thought."

Xander exercised Dad's vote? What else did he take care of?

I was taking a risk, opening my mouth, but Walter was Dad's best friend and had been since they were kids, so he'd find out eventually anyway.

"Does Xander oversee Dad's medical care, too?"

The skin between his eyebrows puckered. "Yes. He holds his medical power of attorney. Why?"

"Just trying to get the lay of the land. Plus, I have a couple questions." My thumb rubbed over the canvas spine of my notebook.

"Alexander takes him to all his appointments, but now that you're home, I'm sure he'd be happy to share that duty with you. Might free up his time. You are home, right? For good?"

"Seems like it. I can't really help him if I'm not here, whether he wants me or not."

"Fair enough." He glanced at my tattooed arms, bare to the elbow from where I'd pushed up the sleeves of my shirt. "One word of advice?"

I didn't answer, and I didn't have to. Walter was going to give it to me even if I didn't want it.

"I know I'm not your dad or even your uncle, but let's pretend you give a damn what I think. Keep out of trouble, Camden." If his voice hadn't been so soft, I would have scoffed.

My muscles stiffened, but I held his stare as he continued.

"I know you're a good man, not because of who you were as a teen but because that reckless boy grew into the man who came back when his family called. You knew what you were walking into, given what happened when you were here last, and that speaks volumes to your character—to who you are now. But some people in town, namely ones named Hall, aren't going to give you a fair shake. He's still counting every mark you'd racked up from a decade ago, if what he was saying this morning at Earl's was any indication. He's looking for the first reason to lock you up or throw you out."

The warning was oddly touching, even though my inner teenager wanted to throw it back in his face and tell him to mind his own business.

"You all still meet up at Earl's?" That old barbershop was on the receiving end of more gossip than Ivy's Salon.

"Haven't you noticed that nothing changes around here?" He grinned.

"Yeah, I'm beginning to catch on." I started down the steps and turned as I reached the hood of the Jeep. "And thank you. I appreciate the warning."

His eyebrows rose a fraction. "You're welcome. And if you need anything, you know where to find me. Just don't make me post bail, okay?" His lips quirked up in a failed attempt to keep a straight face.

"Hey, that was only once. Twice, if you count the time—"

"I do. Everyone does. It's good to see you, Camden."

My lips pressed into a line, and I offered a nod. Then I got the hell out of there.

"When I said 'let's get together,' I didn't mean it had to be tonight or at the bar," I said to Xander as we held down the back-corner table at Mother Lode, Alba's only bar, a few days later. "It's Saturday night. I'm sure you have better things to do than hang with your little brother."

Xander leaned back in his seat and loosened his tie, his suit coat already draped across the back of the chair. "I haven't seen you in years. Of course I'm going to jump at the chance to have dinner with you twice in a week."

"You could have jumped at Bigg's," I offered. "Man, I've missed those burgers."

"We can grab them tomorrow if you want. It's not like we're on a time line anymore, right?"

"Right." Because I was never leaving this little slice of anachronism. "Are you sure you can hang at the bar, Mr. Mayor?" I looked out from the corner and noted at least twenty people, all doing their best not to look like they were staring at us.

One of those people was Tim Hall, who didn't bother hiding his glare. At least the jukebox blared a rotating selection of eighties rock, keeping the bar loud enough that our words weren't fodder for gossip.

Xander laughed, drawing even more eyes. "It's not like I'm the mayor of New York City. Besides, it makes me approachable. At least that's what I tell myself."

I shook my head. "Born politician."

"I've been keeping the peace pretty much since you were born, so why not do it professionally?" He sipped at the bottle that held his microbrew. "You just waiting to get adjusted to the altitude?" He motioned at my water.

"Nope." I watched the ice move as I swirled my glass. "I don't drink anymore."

Xander's eyes widened. "Since when?"

"Since the day we buried Sullivan."

He flinched and set the bottle on the table. "Because..."

"Because bad things happen when I drink, and to be honest, I'm too good at killing people to lose control. Look what I did to you." I rubbed my eyebrow, and his mouth tightened. "I never told you how sorry I was. How sorry I am." How fucking sick I felt every time I saw the scar.

"No. This was not your fault." Xander shook his head and leaned forward, keeping our conversation private in the noisy bar. "I grabbed your shoulder. I knew how messed up you were from Afghanistan. I knew better. You reacted. That's on me. Not you."

"I was beating the shit out of Oscar Hudgens in the snack aisle of the gas station. You stopped me, and I threw you through a damned window." My grip tightened on my glass. "Don't excuse my fuckup."

"Oscar deserved it." He shrugged, dropping his voice low. "I heard what he said about moving in on Willow, since Sully was gone."

Rage, as unsettling as it was comfortingly familiar, locked my jaw for a moment, and I sucked a breath in through my nose, noting that Oscar held down a seat at the bar. Even all these years later, I wanted to bash his head into the bar top. Unlike all those years ago, I'd learned how to control my temper...for the most part.

Willow was the only woman I'd ever gone to blows over. That night hadn't been the first time, either.

"I don't think I would have stopped," I admitted and turned my baseball cap backward so he could see my eyes. See that I meant it.

"I know." His thumbnail pushed under the beer's label. "You know Charity owns this place now, right?"

"I didn't," I answered, thankful for the change of subject.

He nodded back toward the bar, so I leaned to the left and saw a pretty brunette talking to our waitress.

"Never thought I'd see the day that Judge Noah Bradley's daughter owned this place. Did he have a heart attack?"

"Nah," Xander replied. "Doesn't talk to her much, though. Not since Rose was born, I guess. That all happened while I was gone. You know how he gets when he feels like he holds the moral high ground."

"His daughters—and granddaughter—be damned, I guess," I muttered. The news of Charity's pregnancy hit right before I left for basic, ripping through the town like a machete, dividing the population into Team Charity and Team Noah. No one sided with Gabe, who'd abandoned both his high school sweetheart and his unborn kid for a few years.

My fingers rubbed together, as if they still rolled that little onyx rook I'd left on Willow's windowsill that night so she wouldn't miss it. Not that she'd needed me when she had Sullivan. She'd been far better off.

"Fathers." Xander sighed, tipping back his beer.

"Speaking of fathers," I jumped in, only to pause when our waitress brought two orders of eggs and bacon.

"Thanks, Jenny," Xander told the young woman, who looked to be about five years younger than I was.

She tossed me a skittish glance, and I thanked her, which earned me a shy smile.

"You in a relationship?" Xander asked as she walked away,

definitely swinging her hips.

"Nope," I said, salting my eggs. Damn, I loved breakfast for dinner. "Not looking to be, either. You?"

He smiled at his eggs. "Kind of. She lives down by the resort. Nothing serious yet, though. So, you were saying about fathers?" He shoveled a bite into his mouth.

Subject changer extraordinaire.

"Yeah, so this is going to sound like it's out of left field, but I was wondering how much Dad has talked to you about his advanced directive."

Xander paused mid-chew and then swallowed, looking at me oddly. "What do you mean?"

"I mean he asked me about a DNR." There it was, spewed on the shiny surface of the wooden table, where it sat between us as heavy as an elephant.

"A Do Not Resuscitate order?"

"Yeah."

"I thought you said he didn't know who you were when you dropped by." His brows furrowed.

"He actually left me a voicemail about a month ago."

Xander sat up straight, abandoning his food. "He left you a voicemail."

"He did. Honestly, it's what brought me here. Not that I wasn't long overdue to come home and help you, but it was the first time he'd called in six years."

His expression didn't change. Not even a muscle twitched. "And he asked you for a DNR. In a voicemail."

I took my cell phone from the back pocket of my jeans and scrolled through to my voicemail. Then I tapped the saved message and hit speakerphone, putting it between us as it played.

"Camden. It's your father. I don't even know where you are anymore. This isn't easy for me to say, but you need to come back. Alexander is overwhelmed. He takes on so much for me, for the town… You know him. I'm losing myself more every day, and it's dragging him down. Your brother needs you. He's so good but so stubborn. He sees the world in black and white, no grays. Not like you do. I want a DNR, Camden. Alexander thinks that means I'm ready to die, and that's not what this is about. I'll keep living as long as God wants, but if He calls me home to your mother, to Sullivan, then I don't want to be held here by extraordinary measures. I deserve to make that choice. You're the only one Alexander will listen to and—"

The voicemail ended.

Xander blinked and picked up my phone, no doubt looking for the second part of the message.

"That's all there is," I told him as he handed it back to me.

"He can't…" Xander hesitated, shaking his head. "He has no clue what he's asking for. He's probably not even lucid in that message." He dug back into his eggs.

"He's asking for a DNR. Does he have one?" I asked, leaning forward.

"Hell no, he doesn't," Xander snapped. "You think I want to bury our father? He's fifty-eight years old."

Shit. This was going to be way harder than I'd originally thought.

"Has he mentioned it to you?"

"Sure." He waved a fork. "In passing a few times, but it's always been while he's depressed, and I'm not helping our father kill himself." He jabbed the fork in my direction.

"That's not what he's asking for." I kept my voice as level as possible, watching the color rise in his cheeks.

"It's close enough."

"Even if it were, he's the one asking for it. It's his life. His body. His decision. The fact that you have his medical power of attorney means you're the only one who can legally do it for him." How could Xander go against what Dad clearly wanted?

"Right. I do. And I say no, Camden. He's not getting a DNR."

"How is that your choice to make?" An edge crept into my tone.

"Because Dad made it my choice the minute he signed that damned power of attorney." The fork hit his plate. "Look, I'm genuinely glad you're home. I've missed you, and we need you. But I'll be damned if you tell me to kill our father a week after you pull into town because you have a voicemail. You don't even know if he was lucid when he left it."

"That's not what I said." Black and white, the lines were drawn, just like Dad had noted.

"It sure sounds like it." His jaw muscle flexed.

A decade in the army had taught me when to retreat and regroup. This was definitely that moment. "I just want to honor Dad's wishes," I said softly. "Let's drop it."

"And I'm just trying to show him that his good days are worth living for. He's only been diagnosed for two years, and the days he's lucid enough to realize what's going on are devastating for him. He's still dealing. We both are."

And I wasn't? Maybe I'd lost the right when I brought our little brother home in a box.

I started eating to keep my mouth busy, and Xander followed suit.

A few minutes later, Willow walked in. She shed her coat, tossing it to her sister behind the bar, and I stopped chewing. Stopped breathing. Stopped thinking.

Her long-sleeve pink shirt hugged every damn curve she had up top, while her jeans did the job on her bottom a little too well. Her hair fell down her back in soft waves, every color from mahogany to amber catching the light as she moved.

Okay, maybe I was losing my mind, noticing her damned hair. But my hands itched to bury my fingers in it, to wrap it around my palms and tug her closer.

And that smile...

I jerked my gaze back to my plate. *Do not think about her like that.* If I could have flipped myself the bird, I would have. Telling myself not to picture her under me was one thing, and getting my mind to cooperate was quite another.

It was Willow, for God's sake. The same Willow who'd grown up underfoot. The one who'd spent her summers swimming in the hot springs between our houses. The one who'd held ice to my battered twelve-year-old face after I'd won the first fight I'd ever gotten into. The fight she'd tried to stop, putting herself between me and Scott Malone, who'd been picking on her like the spoiled asshat he was. The same Willow who'd let me sleep on her floor a year later, the night Mom died, linking her fingers with mine when she'd heard me crying.

The same Willow who fell for my little brother the summer she'd turned seventeen.

That one fact eclipsed every other detail— She was Sullivan's.

"So are you thinking about coming to the Historical Society meeting? We could sure use your opinions and expertise," Xander said, breaking the silence.

"When have I ever had any expertise you could find helpful?" I countered.

"You're a civil engineer, right?"

"So my degree says." The degree that had taken me eight years to complete, between deployments and ops that gave me a shit ton of real-world experience.

"Then you're pretty much the most useful guy in Alba." He tipped his beer to me like some kind of salute. "Not sure if you've noticed, but we have a few buildings that aren't exactly up to code." He paused. "You know, because they were built in the 1880s?"

Willow took a seat at the bar, and Oscar Hudgens noticed, leaning so far back on his stool that I thought gravity might help me out.

"Cam?" Xander called.

"Yeah." I whipped my attention back to my brother. "I'll be there."

"Good. Oh, look, Jonathan Young just sat down." He nodded toward another table. "Give me a second, would you? I need his help with a council vote."

I nodded. Or something. Alexander disappeared as Oscar stumbled off his barstool, headed toward Willow.

My feet took me across the bar before my head could object.

"Hey, Charity, any chance I can grab the bill before my perfect older brother tries to pay it?" I asked, leaning over the vacant stool next to Willow.

"Cam! I thought that was you! Sure thing—just give me a second to get Jenny." Charity offered me a bright smile.

"Thanks."

She went to find our waitress, and I turned to Willow, who was already watching me.

I held her silent, questioning gaze as the track changed on the jukebox.

"Willow Bradley," Oscar slurred. "You sure are looking— Whoa. Cam?" Oscar's words slurred together.

I pivoted, a wave of pity washing over me. He looked like crap.

"You're home." He swayed toward me.

"Apparently."

"Good." He swung, throwing his weight behind the punch that came surprisingly quick for someone as drunk as he was.

I could have stopped it.

Instead, I let his fist connect.

CHAPTER SIX

Willow

My heart lurched as Oscar swung.

Cam's head snapped to the side.

That dull *thud* of fist meeting face was a sound I'd never wanted to hear again. Ironically, I'd only ever heard it in Camden Daniels's presence.

But usually Cam was the one delivering the hits, not taking them.

"I've been waiting six years to do that," Oscar shouted, jabbing his finger in Cam's direction and swaying.

"And I probably deserved it," Cam admitted as he straightened his posture. "But it's the only one you get." He didn't swipe at his cheek to see if there was blood. He simply stepped to his side, blocking me from Oscar.

Chairs squeaked against the hardwood as figures rose, and I caught a glimpse of Tim Hall barreling toward us, no doubt looking for the first excuse to arrest Cam.

I stood, but Xander got there first.

"Hey, he didn't even throw the punch." Xander blocked Tim's path.

"Oh yeah?" Oscar asked, and I moved to see what was happening. He swung at Cam again, but even as the crowd gasped, Cam grabbed Oscar's fist, stopping the punch before it connected.

Holy moly, Cam was fast.

While Oscar still gawked, I grabbed Cam's free hand. "Come with me."

He looked down at me with an amused smirk.

"Now." I let my glare speak volumes.

His smirk faded, and he followed as I dragged him past the bar and into the back room of Mother Lode, noting Charity's nod toward the floor above us and giving her one of my own. At this moment, Cam needed to be out of sight and out of Tim Hall's mind.

I waved to Marie, the cook, but didn't stop, pulling Cam through the kitchen and storage rooms until we reached the stairs to Charity's place. After climbing them, I unlocked her door with my four-digit code and led Cam into the apartment, shutting the door behind us.

"Rose is asleep upstairs, so don't make a ruckus," I warned him.

"Who the hell still says ruckus?"

I shot him another glare and yanked him through her living room, dining room, and into the kitchen, turning on lights as I went. "Sit," I ordered, pointing to the kitchen table.

He sat.

Okay, that was enough to stun me for a good second or two. I couldn't remember the last time Camden had done anything I'd asked...probably because it had never happened.

"Now what?" he questioned, mocking me with those dark eyes.

I spun, then opened Charity's freezer and pulled out Rose's ice pack. It was a slim unicorn with thin fabric and a glittery mane, sporting an ice pack in the belly. Shutting the freezer door, I turned back to Cam, wincing at the angry red mark blooming on his cheek.

To his credit, Cam didn't complain as I placed the unicorn on the side of his face. "Hold that there."

He complied. "It's not that bad. I turned, so most of the force glanced right off. His ring didn't even cut me."

"How would you know?" I asked, lifting a corner of the unicorn to make sure Oscar hadn't broken Cam's skin with his class ring. "It's not like you paused to look in the mirror."

"I've been in hand-to-hand enough to know when my skin splits," he answered in utter boredom.

"Well, that's comforting," I mumbled, noting that he was right. The skin was intact. "Why didn't you hit him back? No one could have faulted you for it." Okay, that was a lie. If there was fault to be found, Hall would have found it with Cam. Didn't matter that Oscar hit first.

"I'm not giving Tim Hall a reason to run me out of town. It's going to take a hell of a lot more than Oscar throwing a punch to provoke me into a physical fight, especially because I'm not feeling up to manslaughter charges."

I searched his face for any hint that he was kidding and came up empty. "You think you could kill a man with your bare hands?"

His eyebrows rose slightly. "Don't think. I know. I'm not the same kid I was when I left here a decade ago, Willow." There was a wealth of experience in his eyes that I both longed to understand and desperately wanted to ignore. While I'd been away at art school learning about beauty, Cam had been at war.

"That's obvious. The Cam I knew would have thrown the first punch and never looked back." Leaving the rest of us to pick up the inevitable mess.

He brushed his hand over where mine lingered at the unicorn. "I'm still the Cam you knew, just not the one everyone else did. Same Cam, with better decision-making."

The touch had happened so fast, I wondered if I'd imagined it.

Cam cocked his head to the side. "Rose is up."

"What? How do you—" Sure enough, before I could finish my question about his freaky ninja skills, my nine-year-old niece popped her head into the kitchen, sporting a Taylor Swift pajama set.

"Aunt Willow?" she asked, her big brown eyes way too alert

for just waking up. Her chestnut curls were still braided in perfect, smooth piggies, too.

"Hey, Rosie. Sorry we were so loud." I glanced at the clock and read eight thirty. Charity must have just put her to bed before checking on the bar.

Rosie's eyes swung to Cam, a little note of shock widening them. "Oh! Hi! Who are you?" she asked.

"Camden Daniels. Nice to meet you, Rosie." His voice softened, which softened me.

"You too," she replied, looking to me for reassurance.

"Cam has been a friend since we were kids. He grew up next door to your mom and me."

"Like Mayor Daniels?" She snuck another peek at Cam.

"Yep, he's my older brother," Cam replied.

"Oh. I like him!"

"Everyone does."

"We just needed to borrow your unicorn really quick," I told Rose, opening my arms. She walked straight into them, hugging me tight. "Need anything?" I asked before dropping a kiss on the top of her head.

"Nope. Just heard the door beep and thought it was Mom."

"She's still downstairs, but I think she's just checking up on things. She's not working tonight. Want me to get her?"

She shook her head against my chest. "Nope, I'm okay. Love you, Aunt Willow." She gave me an extra-hard squeeze.

"Love you, Rose."

"Thanks for letting me borrow your unicorn," Cam told her, pulling the ice pack from his face.

Rose's nose scrunched. "You're welcome…and you should probably put it back on." She nodded in encouragement. "That's gonna leave a mark," she finished in a tone so like Charity's that I couldn't help but laugh.

"I'll do just that." Cam immediately put the unicorn on his face.

I let her go, and she gave Cam a shy nod before heading back up to her room.

"Charity doesn't bring men here, so you probably gave Rose the shock of her life," I told him, leaning back against the counter. "Even when Gabe comes to get her for visitation, Charity makes him wait downstairs. Not that I blame her. He didn't show back up until Rose was two."

"Is she going to be pissed that you brought a man up?"

"You're hardly a man." I shrugged, then laughed a little at his wounded expression. "I mean, you're...you. You're our friend, not just any man. Besides, Charity gave me the nod to bring you up." I rushed through that last part, hoping to cease my babbling.

"This is why she bought the bar, huh? So they could live above it?" he asked, his eyes sweeping over the hand-drawn pictures taped on the twenty-year-old refrigerator.

"Exactly. She used her inheritance from our grandfather's will. When Rose was born, Charity and Dad weren't exactly speaking. Mom and I supported her when she'd let us, but she wanted to do it on her own. We'd babysit, but she installed the alarm, wired cameras to her cell phone and everything, so she could manage downstairs while Rose slept and still spend her days with her."

"I understand that," he said, looking at the camera in the corner of the kitchen. "Needing to make it on your own."

"You're just as stubborn as she is." I shook my head.

"Well, you know us black sheep. When you reject the path everyone else takes, you have to carve your own."

"Is that what you call it?" I braced my hands on the counter and jumped to sit on the edge.

"What did you use your portion of the inheritance for?" he asked, ignoring my question.

"Why did you reject that path?" I challenged, folding my arms across my chest.

He watched me for a moment, and I held my breath, tension winding in my limbs as he decided whether or not to answer.

Decided which sides of himself he was willing to share with me.

God knew he kept me guessing, shifting our roles so frequently that I never knew our norm. I was never sure if that was to keep me off-balance or because he genuinely never knew, either.

"Charity did it for love. First for Gabe, then Rose. But why did you reject that path?" I asked again.

"The path rejected me," he said quietly. "It didn't want me, so I decided not to want it."

I swallowed the lump in my throat, my mind racing with every possible situation that he could apply that philosophy to and wondering how many times his disdain had masked longing.

"Now you. The inheritance?"

"I went to art school. It took me about six months after Sully died to realize that *I* didn't, and it didn't matter how long I waited here in Alba, he wasn't coming home." I broke eye contact. Would Cam see it as the betrayal my father had? "So the plans we'd made to go away to college together once his three years were up didn't matter anymore. I had to take a really hard look at what I'd thought my future would be without him and ask myself an impossible question."

"How much of that plan reflected your choices and how much belonged to Sullivan?" Cam's question brought my gaze right back to his.

My heart pounded, my tongue heavy and unwilling to say the words I'd never been able to before.

"Yes," I finally admitted, the word taking six long years of guilt with it as it left my lips. "And I realized how much of myself I'd given up in the interest of an easy relationship. And it was easy— with Sullivan, that is. I don't want you to think it wasn't. Or that he wasn't good to me."

"I don't think that."

"Okay. Good." Fingers trembling faintly, I tucked my hair behind my ears. "Because we were happy, and I think I could have been happy following our plan. Going to Boulder. Then maybe law school. Then back here. I could have been happy…," I trailed off in an unconvincing whisper.

"You just wouldn't have been you." The way he watched me sanded away layers of my carefully polished veneer.

"Or maybe that was really me, and this is the alternate reality where everything is messed up."

He stood, filling the room with more than his massive frame. Cam was a presence that walls couldn't contain. I wasn't sure anything could.

"The girl who painted the murals on the hot springs ruins wouldn't have been happy. Maybe content, but not happy. There's a difference, Willow. And I'd like to think that Sullivan would have seen that eventually, and you would have gone to art school anyway."

I shook my head. "Sully never wanted to ruffle feathers. I mean, if Alexander was the good kid, and you were the rebel, then he was the one who wanted to simply exist without conflict. So he would have gone with Dad's plan. He was the easy one, and it was so easy to love him." I'd simply realized in these last years that it wasn't the right love—the consuming, passionate, all-encompassing one in the books and songs I loved. But that truth would never leave my lips. I'd let it fester and rot inside me before admitting something like that.

"It was easy to love him, for all of those reasons and more," Cam agreed. "But that doesn't explain why you had to use your inheritance to go to college."

"My father thought I was still in shock from Sully's death. That I was being irrational and lashing out against what he felt was a logical and acceptable plan. In reality, I was trying to honor my first dream, since I'd lost my last. I was trying to figure out who I was without Sullivan." *And without you.* Not that I hadn't lost Cam years before when he'd shipped off to basic. "Dad refused to pay for it, which was fine. It's his money, after all. But once I saw his decision for what it was—his need to control me because he'd lost that control over Charity—I paid for it myself."

"You carved your own path." He moved closer but didn't crowd me.

"For four years, I did. I learned, and I lived, and I even dated, not that anyone in Alba would believe me." I inhaled deeply, bolstering my courage. "Does that make you hate me?"

"What?"

"That I moved on."

His eyebrows furrowed. "No. Of course not. Why the hell would you even remotely think that?" He moved to lean against the counter next to me, effectively breaking eye contact.

"Xander was disappointed when I told him one Christmas. The look in his eyes... It was like I'd cheated on Sully. And honestly, that first date felt a lot like I had."

"Willow, you can't cheat on someone who's dead." His gaze fell to the floor.

"I know that now. It took a few years for me to really get that, but eventually I did. But every time I came home on break, it felt like I was moving on and the town wasn't. And I get it. I do. Change is literally Alba's worst enemy. The people in this town would still have me wearing widow black if they had their way, weeping at a shrine for Sullivan."

"And yet you came back."

"It's my home." I turned to look at him. "And so did you, I might add." *Why?*

His eyes rose to meet mine, and he shifted the ice pack on his cheek.

"I came home because Dad left me a voicemail saying that Xander wouldn't give him a DNR and he needed my help. Then he shot me, kicked me out, and forgot who I was—all within forty-eight hours—so I'm not really sure which of those he was lucid for."

"Cam," I whispered. The heaviness of what he faced hit my stomach like an anchor. The mere thought of losing my dad and fighting with Charity about it was nauseating.

"But you chose to come back… Why? To settle down and do what? Get married to a man who will never measure up to Saint Sully in Alba's eyes? To be ridiculed when you haven't grieved on their time line and done what they expected? Followed their script?"

"I came home for the same reason you did. Family. And people change. The town will just have to adapt."

"Don't fool yourself, Willow. This town exists for the dead, not the living. When the younger generations leave, they only come back for funerals—their family's or eventually their own. Alba is a huge mausoleum, literally funded by tourists who flock here to see the dead things we refuse to let go. We're all just part of the exhibit. If you're expecting change or acceptance, don't. Survival here depends on our ability not to change, to preserve the past. Change and progress are the two things that will kill this town."

His words stabbed at something deep—a truth I wasn't ready to surrender to.

"That's a really narrow way of looking at our home. And it's ours, just like you said. If you're capable of change, they are, too."

"That's the point." He pushed off the counter and put a few steps of distance between us before turning around. "It doesn't matter who I am now. They won't let me be anyone other than the kid who threw too many punches, broke too many rules, and got Sullivan killed. They can't let me change, the same way they can't let you. It's a matter of self-preservation. And you know it, otherwise you wouldn't live so far up the mountain, where you're all tucked away and safe from prying eyes and judgmental mouths."

"So you're saying that I'm doomed to a life of loneliness? Of becoming the eccentric old hermit lady? Because I'm going to love again, Cam. I'm going to love and get married and have kids. All of it." My eyes narrowed as heat spread in my cheeks.

"No, I'm saying that you would have been happier somewhere else, at least until you knew your man was strong enough to withstand the weight of Sullivan's shadow."

I scoffed, hopped off the counter, and turned toward the door before I said something we'd both regret.

His hand closed around my arm, surprisingly gentle in its strength but enough that I stopped in my tracks. I could have shaken him off, it was that light, but instead I savored the contact.

"I know you're strong enough, Pika. But this town isn't going to be gentle on whoever you deem worthy enough to give your heart unless they decide for you. And I don't see you going for that. You let the town dictate once, and I know you loved him, and he loved you, but can you honestly say you'll let Alba choose for you again? Do you love your comfortable boundaries that much?"

My posture softened, and he let go of my arm. He was right, which only pissed me off even more. Loving Sully had been easy because we'd fit. We'd been supported and encouraged—enabled—by everyone around us.

He placed the unicorn on the kitchen counter. "Thank you for taking care of me. It's been a hell of a long time since anyone's done that. I'm going to head down, hopefully get to pay my bill, and go home."

His broad back filled my vision as he passed me.

How was it possible that no one had cared for him in the past decade?

"You should come to the Historical Society," I blurted.

He paused but didn't turn.

"If you want to help your dad, you're going to have to go against Alexander. You'll need support, and reminding them that you're a son of a founding family will go a long way. You don't have to like the game to play it."

"I'll keep that in mind."

He walked out, and less than a minute later, Charity breezed into the kitchen.

"Camden's sure in a mood," she remarked, grabbing a glass

from the cabinet and apple juice from the refrigerator. "Want some?"

I shook my head. "Camden is always in a mood. Stubborn ass." My voice definitely lacked its usual bite when discussing the middle Daniels.

Her shoulders shook with laughter as she poured her drink.

"How did you two not get together?" I questioned. "You're exactly alike. I always figured you'd end up dating when we were in high school. Both rebels to the core." Not to mention that Charity was timelessly beautiful, where I was cute, maybe passably pretty at best.

She looked at me like I was a class-A moron and put away the juice. "Seriously?" She sipped her juice but peered at me over the glass.

"What? It's not like he's hard to look at, and you graduated the same year." It was a logical conclusion. Hell, maybe they had hooked up once and I'd never known. I rubbed my chest, trying to soothe the ache that surfaced at the thought.

"Oh, Cam was hot, and somehow he's only gotten hotter with age. Have you seen those arms? And the way he caught Oscar's fist? Smokin' hot, baby sis."

Maybe I really didn't want the answer to the question I shouldn't have asked. Nor did I want to see my sister walk through the door I'd stupidly opened. *Stop being selfish.*

"Yeah, so I'm going to head home. Want me to throw Rosie's unicorn in the wash?" I asked.

"I got it." Her mirror-image eyes saw more than I was willing to show.

My feet took me to the door, my sister following behind.

"I love you, Rule Maker," she said, hugging me tight.

"I love you, Rule Breaker," I replied before leaving, wondering for the millionth time if Dad had known who we'd grow up to be when he'd given us those nicknames in elementary school.

And Cam was right. I needed change and progress, but what

I wanted was for the rules to shift. To bend.

He'd always broken them, just like Charity.

I was halfway down the stairs when Charity poked her head out of the door. "Willow."

"Yes?" I turned, wondering what I'd forgotten.

"I never hooked up with Cam for a reason. He only had eyes for one Bradley girl, and it wasn't me." There was zero teasing in her tone or expression.

"Wh-What?" I sputtered. That was definitely not the answer I'd expected.

"Think about it. You're the only girl who's lasted more than five minutes in his orbit. He may have glanced at other girls, but he only saw you."

"No. That's not..." But it was true. Just not in the way she thought. "He sees me like a sister." That was why he'd protected me growing up. Why he walked me to the bus when Scott Malone started teasing me. Why he sat across the aisle on the half-hour ride from Buena Vista back to Alba. Why he did everything until we got older and then he...stopped.

"Because you almost were his sister. But don't be blind, Willow. He looked at you for years. He only stopped when you got together with Sullivan."

That was impossible. "No, you're wrong. Cam never cared that Sully and I started dating. He was barely speaking to me anyway. I annoyed the crap out of him by then."

She rolled her eyes. "Okay. If you say so."

"I do!"

"Yep. Okay. See you tomorrow. Good night!" She shut the door, leaving me gawking up the stairs.

"You're wrong," I muttered, but having the last word didn't make me feel any better.

She was so wrong that it wasn't even funny. I balked the entire drive home, mumbling to myself as I parked in the garage of my house. Charity had zero idea what she was talking about. Cam had been relentlessly apathetic that last year. He hadn't given a crap what I'd done.

I picked up the onyx rook from my desk and rolled it between my fingers.

The path rejected me. It didn't want me, so I decided not to want it.

His earlier words ran on repeat through my brain as I readied for bed.

"You're wrong, Charity," I whispered into the dark. Not because I wanted her to be but because I needed her to. And Cam did, too.

But what if she was right?

CHAPTER SEVEN

Camden

held my breath and turned the key in the ignition. It cranked for a second, then turned over, the Scout's engine roaring to life.

"Yes!" I stood, my fists raised toward the sky in victory.

The 1967 International Harvester Scout hadn't run since before I'd left for basic, even with Uncle Cal's magic touch. It had taken a new alternator, belts, hoses, and more than a few prayers to a God I wasn't sure I believed in, but she was running.

I brought my hand down to the rail that ran across the windshield and nodded to myself, savoring the momentary high of satisfaction. I'd been in Alba a full week and had managed to scrub down the house, change the oil in the Scout and the snowmobile, schedule the roof repair, and stock groceries.

It was the most domestic I'd been since…ever.

Then again, it had only been a week, and I'd already broken my vow to never see Willow again three times. Which was why I'd kept my ass here at the house today. At this point, my well-meant vow to leave her to her happiness was turning into a well-intentioned suggestion.

Now, if only I could stop thinking about her, that would be great.

I jumped down from the Scout, letting her run in the open air to charge her battery. Which reminded me—batteries were next on my checklist.

The power shed door stuck momentarily, but a nudge of my shoulder persuaded it to open. I stepped from the side of the garage into the small room and whistled.

Apparently, Uncle Cal had been going all *Doomsday Preppers* in his last few years. No less than twenty solar batteries sat on their industrial shelves, all wired from the roof's panels to the electrical grid of the house. Three would have kept the house running twenty-four hours a day without hooking up the generator.

Twenty-five was definitely apocalypse compound level: expert.

At this point, he just should have harnessed the creek and put in a micro-hydroelectric system. Those suckers were clean and efficient.

My cell phone buzzed in my back pocket. I reached for it, then swiped it open when I saw Dorothy's name pop up.

"Camden?"

"Hi, Dorothy. Did you get that list of home care providers I left yesterday?" I asked, checking the date on the closest battery.

"You mean the one you left in the mailbox because you were too chicken to come in?"

A smile lifted the corners of my mouth. "Yep, that's the one."

"I did, and I passed it along to Alexander. Now, you asked me to call if he was having a good day, just like I did yesterday and the day before."

Pressure settled in my chest. "And he's having another one today?"

"Well, he knows you're here and remembered kicking you out last week, so I'd say yes."

Silence stretched longer than the half mile between our houses.

"Camden Daniels, are you coming down here?"

My head rolled as my eyes drifted skyward. "Is he going to scream at me from the porch like he did yesterday?"

"Probably."

I could practically see her shrugging from here. "Okay, I'll be there soon."

"I'll let him know."

"I'll get my bulletproof vest."

I hung up the phone, noting that the solar batteries were dated from nine years ago. That gave me another six years, more or less, before they expired.

"You really were prepared for exile, weren't you, Uncle Cal?" I asked aloud.

Depending on anyone else is what will get you, Cam. You have to be self-sufficient in every area of your life.

The advice he'd given me when I was fourteen answered for him.

After hurrying through a shower and parking the Scout back in the protection of the garage, I headed over to Dad's in the Jeep.

Winds had picked up again, making the pine trees sway. Weather must be moving in. Score one for not being on the town's electricity grid.

I pulled through the tree line and stopped in front of Dad's, putting the Jeep into park. Then I mentally strapped on whatever armor I had with a resigned sigh and headed for the door.

I'd no more climbed the steps than Dad burst through the front door, dressed in a flannel shirt and jeans, hair combed, waving his finger at me.

"You're not welcome here, Camden. I told you that yesterday."

I pushed back my instinctive fuck-you response, stopping on the last step. "I'm here to help."

"The hell you are! You ruin everything you help, so excuse me if I don't want it." His eyes were wild with emotion but not dementia.

"You know, you're a lot nicer when you don't know who I am."

"Get off my land before I—"

"Before you what? Shoot me?" I put my hands up. "We've already done that once, so try something a little more creative, would you?"

His eyes flickered with something I was too smart to call regret.

"Look, Dad. I'm here because you asked me to be."

"Bullshit," he spat. "You're the last person I'd ask for help."

I shoved that little insult into the don't-ever-think-about-it pile and gave him a mocking smile. "Well, you did. And maybe when you're done being an asshole, I'll give you the proof."

"Get. Off. My. Land."

"Okay," I agreed and headed back to the Jeep, zipping up my coat as I went.

By the time I opened my tailgate, he'd slammed the front door. "Stubborn ass," I muttered, grabbing my camping chair.

After setting up next to the Jeep, I settled into the chair with my water bottle and the copy of *East of Eden* I'd brought from the house. I cracked the well-loved spine and fell into Steinbeck's description of living between two mountain ranges.

"I told you to get off my land!" Dad shouted from the porch, Dorothy looking on from the doorway.

"I am off your land," I replied, already back in my book.

"I beg your pardon?"

"According to the property survey, this little stretch of land is part of the easement you sold to Uncle Cal so he could access his house." My eyes traced the letters on the page before me, but nothing registered with every other sense concentrating on Dad.

"You... He... Go to hell."

I expected the slam of the door, but it still made me flinch when it happened. An hour later, Dorothy appeared, a steaming cup in her hands.

"To keep you warm. Temps are going to drop soon."

"Thank you," I told her, taking the offered coffee.

"He's..." She rubbed her fingers at the skin between her eyebrows.

"He's him," I offered. "Don't worry. He fathered the only man more stubborn than he is."

She blew out a long, exasperated breath. "Xander said he's not paying for the at-home care. Says it's cheaper and safer to take him down to the home in Buena Vista, where he can get around-the-clock care."

Fuck me, did I have to fight Xander on every front?

"I'll talk to him again," I promised.

She nodded, her lips pressed in a flat line, and gave me a look so full of pity, I almost cringed. "I wish Art didn't let his heart fill with all this misplaced hatred. I know you've never been perfect, Cam, but you don't deserve this."

I glanced toward the east end of the property, where Sullivan lay beneath a stone I'd never seen. "I earned it."

The coffee was hot and bitter, rich with memories of rushed mornings and zipping backpacks.

"Thank you," I told her, handing back the mug after I'd downed its contents.

"You're welcome. He'll come around." She gave me a little nod, then headed back into the house.

I returned to my book until another hour passed and the sun slipped behind the Collegiates, sending shadows across the pages.

His eyes stayed on me, just as they had been for the majority of the time, as I packed up my chair and put it into the Jeep.

"I'll be back tomorrow and the day after that and so forth," I called up to where he watched at the window. "You are the reason I'm here, and I have nothing better to do."

The curtain closed, and I almost laughed at the insults he was no doubt muttering in the house.

"As long as he doesn't get the shotgun," I mumbled.

I began my reading session earlier the next day, not even bothering to knock on the door before setting up in the driveway in front of Dad's house.

The day after, I did the same.

By Wednesday, I thought about bringing a more comfortable chair.

An hour after I opened my book, Dad stood on the front porch, arms folded in front of his chest as he watched me. It was an odd thing, seeing Dad, not knowing who he would really be today.

I put my book in my lap as he came down the steps, his footsteps heavy on the creaking wood.

"You came to help." Condescension clung to every word.

"I came because you asked me to."

His eyes narrowed. "What exactly did I ask you to help with?"

He's probably not even lucid in that message. For the first time, I wondered if Xander was right.

"Death."

Shock flashed across his features, and I cursed inwardly.

"Dorothy made lunch." With those words, he walked back to the house.

"Awesome," I muttered, opening the book again.

"If you're hungry, get in here. She's too old to be hauling your food outside," he called back from the porch.

My eyes shot to his, just to make sure he was actually talking to me.

"I'm not waiting all day," he said, answering my silent question, holding the door.

I lurched to my feet, abandoning the paperback on the canvas chair, and followed him inside.

"Take off your damned shoes," he ordered, and I did just that before joining him in the kitchen, where Dorothy sat at the table with lunch, watching us like hawks.

"Rabbit food," Dad groaned as he sat in front of his salad.

"It's good for you," Dorothy argued.

"Thank you," I told her before digging into the grilled chicken that topped the greens.

"What's your proof?" Dad asked. "You said you had proof."

Guess we weren't beating around the bush.

Still chewing, I put my phone on the table and cued up the voicemail. Then I watched him as it played. As usual, he gave nothing away. Heaven forbid he let anyone know how he was feeling.

The message ended, and I put my phone back in my pocket.

"Where's the rest?" he asked, his eyes boring into mine.

"That's it. You didn't leave another one."

He nodded slowly, then turned his attention to his salad, spearing hunks of cheese with his fork.

"I really don't want to ask this, but Xander brought up a point," I started.

"You played this for your brother?" he snapped.

"I did. I was hoping he'd already given you what you asked for." My entire body felt tense, like I had to balance on the one cleared spot of a minefield. There was nowhere to move without getting blown up.

"Ask your question."

Dorothy raised her eyebrows but didn't say a word.

"Do you remember leaving the message? Is this...really you asking for this?" The stem of the fork bit into my finger, I gripped it so hard.

Dad studied me, his gaze unforgiving and harsh. Then he stabbed more of the cheese, avoiding the lettuce. "No. I don't remember leaving it."

I sagged in my chair. Had I really come all this way—?

"But it's true. I want one. I've been telling him that for a while." He shoved a forkful in his mouth and began chewing.

"I'll talk to Xander again." I didn't mention that my brother had frozen me out since I brought up the DNR in the first place.

His posture softened. "He won't change his mind. Once Xander thinks he's right, that's all there is to it."

"This is your choice to make. Not his." The weight of what it would mean to fight Xander settled on my heart. "If this is what you want, I'll fight for it."

He scoffed. "You willing to take on the town? Because that's Judge Bradley sitting on that bench. Not sure if you remember, but he hates you."

"Don't pull any punches, Dad." I pushed my salad around the bowl as my mind raced.

"You've never been the one who needed me to," he replied.

"And Judge Bradley hardly constitutes taking on the entire town. He's one man." One man who wouldn't bother pissing on me if I were on fire, but still.

"One man who's up for a retention vote this November," Dorothy noted. "He'll take public opinion into account—you can be sure of it."

"How is that fair? He's a judge."

"Since when is politics fair? Don't forget, your own brother is the mayor," she countered.

"Xander isn't corrupt," Dad snapped. "Don't even think about implying that."

"Relax, Art. I'm just saying that Judge Bradley isn't going to forget that it's Mayor Daniels on the other side of that courtroom."

Dad grunted. "That, I believe." He looked to me and shook his head. "Unfortunately, you really are the only person Xander will listen to. If you've already tried and he's denied you, then there's not much else you can do without getting your ass kicked in court." He dropped the fork and leaned back in his chair.

The pros and cons list in my head was pretty much all cons, but I knew one pro could outweigh them all.

"Tell me your reasons. I want to hear them while you're…you." I kept the words soft, but there was no mistaking the demand.

"I'm not trying to off myself, if that's what you're asking. I just don't want to stay any longer than I have to. If the Lord is going to take my mind, then I sure as hell don't want my body to hang around. The last thing I want is to wake up with no idea who or where I am, stuck in a hospital bed with a tube down my throat. I can't imagine a life where anyone wants that…"

Taking on Xander… Dad was right. It would mean taking on the town, and I wasn't exactly the welcomed prodigal son. Judge

Bradley despised me, Xander probably had Milton Sanders on retainer as his attorney already, and there wasn't another lawyer in town. I would be classified as a bigger villain than I already was, the bad seed who came home from war just to kill his dad, against the perfect blond mayor of Alba who was fighting to keep his father alive.

I'd never have peace here.

Maybe that was my penance, living a long, battle-filled life to pay for the one I'd failed to protect.

"I'll do it," I said, looking at Dad. "I'll take it to court. I'll fight for your right to determine your own fate. You deserve that much. But I want two things."

Dad's brows lowered. "Of course you do. What are they?"

"First, I want a truce." I spoke every word clearly and slowly so he couldn't possibly misunderstand.

"A truce."

"I'm well aware that you share the same opinion of me as the rest of the town. I'm not stupid. But as of this moment, we have a truce. You don't ban me from the house. You don't attack me verbally, and you definitely don't shoot me again."

"The house..." He tilted his head.

"I'm still staying at Cal's—at my house. It's time, and I figure that my staying here would only make this harder."

Dad nodded slowly, considering my words. "And second?"

My stomach twisted, but I knew this was my only chance.

"You hate me because I got Sullivan killed."

Dad stiffened, his eyes stricken with pain and anger, but I kept on.

"You've never been willing to hear what happened that day. Not past the choice I made."

A muscle in his jaw flexed.

"When this is over, when I've given you what you want, you'll listen. Maybe you'll hate me even more once you know the truth of it. That's a chance I'm going to have to take. At least I'll know your hatred will be based on fact." It was the most I'd said about Sullivan's death in six years.

I saw the rebellion in Dad—the curl of his fists and the flare of his nostrils as he struggled for control.

"If you deserve to determine your future, then I deserve to explain my past."

His eyes met mine in a clash of will and grief, but finally he nodded. "Fine. But I have one caveat."

"Of course you do." I used his own words on him.

"There are days and moments when I won't be able to keep our truce. I can't remember who I am, let alone who you are. And those days will come when even if I do recognize you, it might not be this version of you I'm seeing." He gestured to my torso.

"Okay. I can handle that." I didn't expect the sadness that engulfed me, clogging my throat as he admitted that he was no longer himself 100 percent of the time. No longer completely sane or dependable. The man who preached that you were only as good as your word was no longer capable of keeping his.

"Then, we have a deal." He thrust out his hand, and I shook it. His grip was firm as always, and it was over in a heartbeat.

"So where would you start this whole battling-the-town thing?" I asked, returning to my salad.

Dad looked to Dorothy, who shook her head, dabbing at her eyes. "I don't know why you're looking at me, Arthur Daniels. I can't remember the last time you took my advice on anything."

"Come on, Dorothy," Dad cajoled.

"You already know what I'm thinking."

"The Historical Society," he guessed.

Every road around here seemed to lead back to that damn organization.

"It's the fastest way to remind this town who he is and where he comes from. Out of the thirty-five voting members, there are only five founders living in Alba, and your boy comes from one." She turned to me. "But you have to start acting like you don't hate everyone and everything this town stands for."

"I can do that." I didn't hate everyone. Just the majority of Alba.

"And cover those up." She motioned toward my tattoos. "Long sleeves for at least a month. You're scaring the little kids."

I laughed, thinking of Rose and her absolute lack of fear as I used her unicorn ice pack. "You mean I'm offending the morning crew at Ivy's."

She scoffed. "Don't underestimate the power of gossiping old women and a morning hair routine."

"And how exactly do you want me to win over the Historical Society when I'm aware that Xander is already using your vote and sitting in your council seat? Plus, they already despise me." Xander and I wouldn't qualify for our own voting memberships until Dad passed on, and even then, I had zero personal property to contribute to the historical district. It was all owned by the mining company.

His eyes narrowed in thought as he looked out the window, over the ridge that led to my house and beyond. "Setting fire to the bunkhouse definitely didn't make you many friends in the society."

My jaw locked.

"You have to give them something they've wanted for years," he finished slowly.

Dorothy's eyes widened. "You said it was too dangerous."

Dad shrugged. "For the majority of the property, it is. But I know it better than anyone else in the county, and the only person who comes a close second is Camden."

I followed his line of sight and felt the blood leave my face. "You can't be serious. That place is a damned disaster."

"It is. But it's the one piece of property they've never been able to access, and you're the only one who can give it to them. That's the crown jewel in their tourist tiara."

"And when Xander blocks that, too? He'll never go for it. He's always said it was too dangerous, and you and I both know that place scares the shit out of him. Always has. I might have been given Uncle Cal's shares in RR, but Xander controls yours." The twists and turns of the Rose Rowan Mine were almost completely impossible to navigate unless you knew it like the back of your hand, and Xander had never bothered to try. It had been my haven. My playground. My first experience with tempting fate.

"You ever read the paperwork when Cal died? Or was that too boring for you?" Dad challenged. "Go home and read the damn file, Camden. Not just the will but the mining company papers. Property sales. All of it. Then offer the mine to the town and trust me."

"You really want me to reopen the mine."

"No, but it's the only way they'll see you as anything other than a dangerous nuisance."

Shit. That mine had been closed to visitors for the last thirty years, and with good reason. Some of the supports dated from the last gasp of the mine in the fifties, but other places were the original 1880 timbers. It was a maze of crumbling floors, cave-ins, bad air, and God only knew what else.

"Do you know how much money it's going to take to restore it?"

"You just let me handle that," Dorothy said with a smile. "I'm expecting a call from the State Historical Fund board, and I might be able to redirect some things."

"This is insane."

"You can design and build things all over Afghanistan and Somalia and wherever else, but you don't think you can do it in your own backyard?" Dad challenged.

"I thought you didn't know where I was?"

His eyes narrowed. "Are you going to do it or not? Because I'm expecting Xander to ship me down to the old folks' home at any minute."

But then it hit me. Opening the mine would kill two birds

with one stone.

"I'll do it."

Hours later, when I'd finished reading all of Uncle Cal's documents, a chill of apprehension raced down my spine.

The town might love me for what I was about to offer, but they could just as easily hate me for what I was about to do to my brother.

CHAPTER EIGHT

Willow

"Every year we petition for caramel corn, and every year you give it to the Halversons," Peter Mayville argued at the wooden podium, facing down the almighty Alba Historical Society Council. The town council might handle the administration of the town, but the real power was held by the council of the Historical Society.

Usually, society meetings were held once a month, but with only seven weeks until the opening of the season, they happened weekly. Attendance skyrocketed, too, as families who didn't winter here came back in preparation for opening weekend. Town Hall, which was pretty much the multipurpose building of modern Alba, was heating up quickly with nearly a hundred bodies straining her capacity.

Every person in this room either owned a building in the ghost town—civic or commercial—which gave them a vote in the society, or their income was directly linked to the money the tourist season brought in.

Gotta love small-town Friday nights.

"Now, Peter, I hear what you're saying. I do. But it's not about us giving them the caramel corn as much as it is them keeping it. It's unfair to take their time-honored tradition when they've perfected it over the last fifty years," Walter Robinson responded, peering over his reading glasses from the center of the horseshoe-shaped dais where the council sat.

I shifted in my folding chair in the back of the room and glanced over this week's agenda. We were twenty minutes into the meeting and still dealing with item number three, where voting members requested changes to their summer business plans. Luckily, I had snacks, because it could get *Survivor* in here real quick, and I had to make it to item seven to present my new Alba logo for the marketing plan.

"He bitches about this every year," Thea muttered next to me. "Get over it, Peter, and be happy with your cotton-candy machine, for God's sake," she called out.

My pretzel went down the wrong pipe, and Thea pounded on my back until I stopped coughing.

"Mrs. Lambert, if you could avoid interjecting commentary," Dad said into his microphone. As a founding member, he had occupied his seat on the council since Grandpa died. Five seats on the council were reserved for the eldest surviving members of the founding families, and the other four were elected annually from the voting members.

Basically, if the founding families wanted something—or didn't—they got their way.

"I'll avoid the commentary if he stops asking for the same thing year after year." Thea folded her arms across her chest.

Oh man, I knew that look, and Dad was not happy.

"Okay, if we can stay on topic," Walter said, leaning forward in his foreman's seat. "Peter, I'm sorry, but we're going to have to decline your request. I know we all believe in capitalism, but it's not in our best interest to compete with each other when it comes to the season, and you know it. Caramel corn is pretty much what keeps Mrs. Halverson's feed store in business. And besides, last time I checked, you were the only vendor allowed to sell sunscreen. Did you want to offer Mrs. Halverson a trade? Her caramel corn for your sunscreen?"

Peter glanced at Mary Murphy, the society's secretary, as she lifted her pen, ready to record. "No." He quickly shook his head. "I'm happy with what I have. Thank you." He took his stack of papers and sat on the edge of the third row.

"Greedy asshat," Thea whispered. "He owns the drugstore. He makes more money than almost anyone else up here during the season."

"Not that your mom doesn't score with her restaurant," I reminded her.

"True, but you don't see her trying to take Jennifer's freaking caramel corn."

"You have a point." I doodled on the notebook I'd brought with me, sketching out an idea for a logo I'd gotten a commission for today. Business was good, and it was even better that I could work remotely.

James Hudgens took the podium and pitched the changes in his summer plan for the old Alba firehouse. How that man had ever produced an ass like Oscar, I'd never know.

A body occupied the seat next to me as I added shading to the design I was tinkering with.

Thea nudged me with her elbow, and I yelped, shooting her a glare.

She raised her eyebrows and glanced pointedly to the seat on my other side.

"He really thinks that Alba FD beer koozies are going to sell?" Cam's voice rippled through me like an avalanche, crumbling what measly defenses I'd tried to construct in the almost week since I'd seen him. Not that I was counting.

I tried to steady my heart with a deep breath, but the darn thing wasn't listening. Apparently I could go six years without seeing him and be fine, but six days turned me into a teenager. Awesome, I actually was counting days.

"It's hard for the guys like James," I told him quietly. "The supplemental fund helps, but you know the owners of the civic buildings don't make much."

"I'm not taking exception to his merchandising, just the merchandise." He shrugged.

Ugh, his profile was annoyingly imperfectly perfect. He knew it, too. Even his eyebrow had an arrogant curve to it. His beard was trimmed close, softening his jawline, but I knew from the way he ran his thumb over it that he'd shave it soon.

I hated that I knew that.

Couldn't he have gotten uglier in the last decade? At least have a receding hairline or something?

"What are you doing here, anyway?"

"I thought you told me to come," he replied, still focused forward.

"Right. And when was the last time you listened to me?"

"Apparently right now." He smirked.

I fought the urge to stick my tongue out at him like we were back in elementary school. Everything had been so orderly two weeks ago, so...safe. Predictable, even. The very reasons I liked Alba no longer existed with Cam in town.

"What's that?" I asked, spying a manila envelope in his hands.

"That's for me to know and you to find out," he replied in a singsong voice.

Apparently I wasn't the only one struggling with acting my age.

"If that's our last request, then I move to enter all summer business plans as final for this season," Dad said.

Cam's jaw clenched.

"Actually, I know there's a matter of business on the agenda being brought by Mrs. Powers later that may affect summer plans, so I'd like to keep this matter open until the end of the meeting," Mary Murphy stated from her council seat, her fingers twisting her single strand of pearls.

"Mrs. Murphy has a seat now, huh?" Cam asked, stating the obvious.

"She was elected about five years ago," Thea replied. "And it's nice to see you, Cam."

"You too, Thea. How's Patrick?" He leaned forward and offered Thea a quick smile.

"Probably bored out of his mind right now." She pointed to where her husband sat two seats down from my dad. "He was elected to the council last year after his dad passed."

Cam's eyes sought out Patrick. "Wow, I didn't recognize him." The light in his eyes died, and he dropped his gaze to the folder in his lap.

"I'm sure he'd love to see you," Thea lied.

"Right. I somehow doubt that." He pushed the sleeves of his shirt up his forearms, then seemed to think twice about it and pulled them back down.

"What's got you nervous?" I asked as Tyler Williamson took the podium to introduce new business.

He finally looked at me, and butterflies shot through my belly. *Don't react. Do. Not. React.* Funny thing about my body: it always betrayed my logical brain when Cam was near.

"I'll tell you later," he promised as Dorothy Powers took the podium, leaving Arthur Daniels next to the seat she'd vacated.

"It's still weird to see Xander in your dad's seat."

As if Xander heard me, he saw Cam in the crowd and forced a fake smile.

Cam gave him a two-fingered wave and looked away quickly. My bewilderment only grew when Art looked back at Cam and gave him a subtle nod.

What the fresh hell was going on?

"As you know..." Dorothy leaned into the microphone, her voice booming through the hall. "One of Alba's own has recently returned to our fair town. I'm excited to say that Camden Daniels would like to submit his summer plan. Now, what he's proposing might not be feasible until the end of the season—"

I blinked. Surely I didn't hear what I thought I did.

"Respectfully, Mrs. Powers, let me stop you there," Dad

interjected. "Only a voting member can propose a summer plan, and seeing as Art is happily still with us, the Daniels family only maintains one voting position in the Historical Society."

"You have a summer plan?" I hissed at Cam, irrationally insulted that he hadn't told me. Having a summer plan implied that he wasn't just home…he really was staying. My heart stuttered, then raced.

Cam ignored me, but he gripped his folder tighter.

Every council member's attention flickered between Dorothy and Cam in obvious, open shock.

"Respectfully," Dorothy replied, saccharine sweet, "I'm well aware of our rules, Mr. Bradley. I've been a voting member for the last twenty-five years. If my memory serves me right, you've been in that seat for the past…seven?"

Dad's mouth twisted, but he didn't open it. Man, was I glad I didn't live at home anymore, because he was going to be livid for days.

"Now, you're right, of course," Dorothy placated him, "but if you'll take a look at these—" She nodded to Mom, who walked up to the dais with a folder and began handing a set of papers to each council member. "You'll see that when Cal Daniels passed away, he left all of his estate to his nephew Camden. He didn't split it between the Daniels boys. He chose Cam as his sole heir, which also transfers his membership seat."

The council buzzed, covering their microphones so we couldn't hear them. People blatantly turned around in their seats to gawk or glare at Cam.

"Milton?" Genevieve asked from her council seat.

Milton Sanders, Alba's only practicing lawyer, seeing as Simon practiced in Buena Vista, stood and made his way to the podium. He ran his hand through his head of thick brown hair as he read over Dorothy's documents.

"He hates me," Cam muttered.

"That won't matter. He's the Historical Society's lawyer," I whispered, which earned me a glare from three of the women sitting ahead of us.

Mrs. Rhodes shook her head at me before turning back around.

Well, that was uncalled for.

"This is Alba. It matters," Cam concluded.

My eyes met those aimed in Cam's direction, staring down each of our townspeople until they looked away. He didn't deserve this kind of treatment.

"Actually, this looks like the boy has a seat," Milton answered.

The buzz in the room grew to a roar.

"We can't leave voting memberships in our wills," Dad countered.

"No, but section seven, paragraph three of our bylaws states that seats pass to our recognized familial heirs, and Cal's will is worded such that it names Camden as his sole, recognized familial heir." Milton shrugged.

"He knew what he was doing," I whispered.

"Always did." Cam kept his eyes locked on the council.

"Then, it's not valid!" Genevieve squawked.

"Well, it seems Judge Bradley accepted the will as valid when Cal died, so…" Milton looked up at Dad, whose face now resembled a tomato. I wasn't sure if it was in embarrassment or anger, but either way, the man was red.

"But he doesn't meet the requirement," Pat interjected from his council seat. "He has to have been a full-time resident of Alba for a year before he can exercise his membership."

Thea crossed her arms. Pat was going to get an earful at home.

Were they all against him?

Heads around us nodded in agreement.

Guess so.

"That would normally be so, but paragraph five states that the residency stipulation is waived upon any return from military service, given that the member does not delay in asking for it." Milton turned to look over the crowd. "Camden? Are you asking for the residency stipulation to be waived?"

"I am." Cam stood, attracting every eye that hadn't been able to see him before.

"Well, as much as I hate to say it, Camden Daniels qualifies for a voting membership seat," Milton told the council. "We now stand at twenty-seven voting members and nine council members."

"And what personal property does he list for inclusion of the historical district?" Xander asked.

My heart sank. Xander was actually speaking out against his brother? Even on our worst days, I'd never stand opposite Charity.

Cam didn't show a single sign that he was surprised. He'd expected Xander's lack of support?

"Come on up here, Cam," Dorothy urged, waving him up.

Cam walked up the center aisle, his head high.

"This is the best Historical Society meeting I've been to in ages," Thea remarked.

That earned a good glare from the three women ahead of us, but I noted that Mrs. Rhodes didn't glare at her. She aimed that sour face right at me. "It's not like he can claim the bunkhouse as his property, now, is it?" she remarked with a hiss. "You barely made it out of that fire alive yourself, Willow Bradley. I would think you'd know better."

My jaw slackened as she turned around with a judgmental shake of her head.

"He didn't—" I started, but Thea put her hand on my leg.

"Don't bother. They'll think what they want to anyway."

"I'm glad you asked, brother," Camden said into the microphone. "I am the owner of the Rose Rowan building on Main Street. Cal bought the property from the mining company and left it to me in that same will."

If my muscles tensed any more, they were going to snap in half.

"Are you serious?" Xander asked as Dad smirked.

"I am," Cam insisted. "And though it is not in any condition to—"

"There's three feet of snow sitting inside that building right now, because it doesn't have a roof," Xander continued.

"Correct, and according to section two, paragraph four of our bylaws, an owner wishing to exercise his vote has two seasons to renovate his property to be considered for the benefit of the Historical Society but may use his status as a voting member immediately."

"What would he want with it, anyway?" Mrs. Rhodes snapped.

"Probably wants to burn the place to the ground," another woman answered. "That boy's never cared about this town." I didn't bother to see who said it, not when it would have taken an act of God to look away from Cam.

"You understand you'll need a restoration expert," Dad fired into his microphone. "A Historical Society–approved expert."

My scalp tingled. Oh God. I wasn't going to have to say it, was I? Surely—

"Well, I'm certainly not volunteering to help him," Genevieve added with her nose in the air. "You've done your fair share of damage to this town, Camden, and I'm not willing to lend my expertise so you can take down the Historical Society. We're all that keeps Alba in business."

A murmur of agreement went through the room.

Crap. I liked my uncomplicated little life. I liked designing logos and such for the Historical Society but not getting pulled in any deeper than I had time for. I liked my boundaries, and I had a feeling I was about to break them all for the boy I'd sworn I'd never give anything else to.

Except that reckless boy was now a man who appeared to be doing his best to prove that he'd changed to a town that didn't want to let him.

"I think that settles it," Dad said. "Doesn't it, Foreman?"

Walter's eyes were heavy as he looked at Cam. "I'm sorry, son, but unless you have a society-approved restoration specialist up your sleeve, I'm bound by the bylaws, even if certain members are just acting out of spite."

Dad smirked.

It was cruel and ugly and sparked something within me too loud to ignore.

I found my feet, my notepad falling to the floor with a *thud* as indignation flooded my cheeks with heat.

"I'll do it," I blurted.

The noise level only increased, so I climbed up on my chair, put two fingers between my lips, and let loose a shrill whistle.

Silence followed, with a whole lot of people staring right at me.

"I said, I'll do it!" Pretty sure everyone down to Buena Vista heard that one.

"Willow Bradley, you get down off that chair!" Dad bellowed.

I did, out of sheer habit. Then I sucked in a deep breath and headed for the aisle, walking down the ominous path to where Cam waited, watching me with a focus so intense, I nearly tripped.

"What are you doing?" he whispered once I reached him.

"You took a bullet for me, so I'm taking one for you. Now move over and let me." I didn't bother to mask my determination as I stared up at him. Who cared what the town thought or how angry my dad was going to be?

Just when I thought Cam wasn't going to relent, he stepped to the side and then stood by mine as I walked up to the podium. My fingers shook as I lowered the microphone.

"I'll be his restoration expert." My voice was a lot steadier than my nerves, thank God. They already saw me as a child; the last thing I needed was to act like one, too.

"Willow, we know your heart is in the right place." Genevieve's voice dripped with sympathy. "After all, Camden is Sullivan's brother, and I know you must feel obligated to help him on Sully's behalf. But, honey, how on earth are you going to be a restoration expert? Don't you draw things on the computer? That's hardly historical, dear."

My resolve hardened from steel to titanium.

"This isn't about Sullivan. This is about Cam. More than that, it's about doing the right thing. Cam has a right, and you're trying to deny it out of sheer pettiness." I shook my head in disgust. "I graduated last year from Rutgers, which is one of the top five art schools in the country," I said, turning my focus to Walter. As foreman, he'd have the power to approve me.

"In graphic design," Dad interjected. "Not the same thing."

I thought of that little onyx rook on my desk. The knight I kept in my nightstand drawer. The other pieces I'd tucked away, all memories from the boy who stood next to me in a man's body.

"I double majored." I addressed Dad, who blanched. "Yes, I have a degree in graphic design, but I also hold one in Art Restoration and Conservation, specializing in the American West." Because I'd known this day would come, eventually, where I'd have to step into Genevieve's shoes if I wanted to ensure our town could survive.

I just figured that would happen in another twenty years, not twenty minutes. Genevieve clutched the arms of her chair like I might hop up there and unseat her from a throne I had zero interest in.

"And you're just now telling me?" Dad seethed, despite the calm, collected tone of his voice. It wasn't at the degree itself. He would have crowed his satisfaction had he been the one to introduce me into the role. He was pissed at the loss of control and my support of Cam.

Cam, who moved a few inches toward me, his arm brushing my shoulder and sending little currents of electricity through my veins.

"Dad, they said it as I walked across the stage at graduation. It was hardly a secret. Mom filmed it and everything." Because he hadn't been there, still holding a grudge because I'd had the nerve to deter from his plan.

The crowd murmured, but I kept my attention on Dad.

"I'm assuming you won't have a problem with your own daughter lending her services to the Historical Society. It would hardly be charitable if I kept my mouth shut and let the town suffer for it." Good thing I'd bought my house this year, or I'd probably be sleeping on Charity's couch tonight. How quickly I disposed of all the goodwill I'd earned since coming home.

If he'd been a tomato before, he was now a giant maroon balloon, ready to pop.

"I'll accept your expertise," Walter declared, and my breath gushed in relief, my posture softening against Cam's. "Camden, I'll also accept the Rose Rowan Mining Company's building as your historical building. Welcome to the society."

"Now, his summer plan," Dorothy leaned over me to say into the microphone, filling my nose with the scent of grape aerosol hairspray.

Battle won—now on to the war. Whatever it was.

"Cannot be put forth at this time." Tim Hall's gaze darted to my dad's furious glare in my direction. "He's a first-year—hell, first-day member. He can't put forth a plan until his second year without a council member willing to sponsor his plan, of course. Rules are rules."

"Certainly one of you will sponsor it." Dorothy raised her eyebrows at the council. "Trust me: you want to know what he's offering."

I would have missed the subtle shake of Cam's head at Dorothy if I hadn't been watching his expression so closely.

Walter looked up and down the dais. As foreman, he couldn't sponsor a plan, and I wasn't sure what other support Cam could count on up there.

"I'll sponsor it." Julie Hall leaned forward, blatantly looking away from her father-in-law's seat. She was the youngest member of the council, having inherited the seat from her mom when a car accident took her last year.

"That's my girl!" Gideon shouted from the second row, causing a few sputtered laughs.

"What is this plan?" Walter asked before any other objections could be raised.

Camden leaned over me to raise the microphone, and I scooted to the left, giving him the podium. When I moved to retreat, Dorothy put her hand on my back, effectively stopping me.

"I'd like to offer the Rose Rowan Mine up for tours."

There was that collective gasp again, and this time it included mine. The Rose Rowan Mine was the one property this council had always salivated over, but Art and Cal had kept it closed for decades.

"I'm sorry, son?" Walter asked for clarification, his eyes wide.

"I would like to open the mine to tours. I'll get started on it right away, but I can't guarantee it will see visitors this summer. Next is probably a more accurate opening."

"How?" Dad barked, clearly torn between his hatred for Cam and his longing for the mine to reopen.

"I figure a giant sign that says 'open' should do the trick."

Great. He'd come this far only to let his mouth ruin the whole darn plan. Go figure, Camden Daniels losing his cool at the last second and letting everything turn to crap.

"Not what I was asking," Dad retorted. "That mine is a mess and in no shape for visitors. We all want it to open, that's no secret, but have you thought this through? Engaged an engineer?"

Funny how the tone changed when something he wanted was on the table.

"Well, I'm a civil engineer, so it's not like I don't have the expertise myself. I've worked on far bigger projects from Afghanistan to Somalia. College degree and everything, since résumés seem to be the order of the day. Figure if the United States government trusts me to design and construct dams, bridges, and buildings, you should, too."

"But the money...?" John Royal questioned.

"The State Historical Fund has offered us a two-hundred-thousand-dollar grant to use as we see fit," Dorothy added. "I confirmed today that we'd be getting it, though I'm jumping about three places ahead on the agenda."

"But that's for the entire district!" Tim Hall blustered. "What about restoring the tannery?"

At least Tim was consistent. He didn't care what Cam had. He just wanted him gone.

"Running tours through the Rose Rowan will easily add another thirty thousand visitors a year, you stubborn fool," Dorothy snapped. "Are you telling me you don't want that? We don't need it? You're willing to punish the townspeople of Alba simply because you don't like Camden Daniels?"

This time, the crowd murmured its assent.

"I'll help with the mine, too," I offered, hoping to turn the tide.

"Well, now, I could certainly—" Genevieve interjected.

"I accept Willow's offer," Cam cut her off.

Cam turned as he looked at every single member of the council until finally reaching his brother.

"But you don't have the authority to open the mine," Xander said, his forehead crinkling. "Not that it's not what the town needs, but you and I both know it's incredibly dangerous down there, which was why it was closed in the first place. Just imagine the liability. One tourist goes wandering, and we're not just a ghost town in name. I'm sorry, Cam, but you just can't make it safe enough. Speaking for Dad's half of the Rose Rowan Mining Company, I can't in good conscience let you do this. Cal may have left you the building on Main Street, but we both own the mining company."

Every seat on the council turned to look at Xander like he'd licked the candy bar they'd been eyeing.

"We can't let our tourists get hurt. That will kill the town faster than anything," he said, and other members nodded. "Cam's only been home a couple weeks. That's not even long enough to assess what the mine needs. I'm thrilled that he's willing to open this avenue for us, but it's really a matter of business to be handled after the season. Not in haste, and not now."

Camden's jaw flexed, and his fingers bit into the podium, turning his knuckles white. "Then, it's a good thing I'm more than qualified to see to both the safety and mechanical restoration of the mine. It will be completely safe in the designated tour paths by the time we open and blocked off in every other area. And as for my ability to speak on behalf of the mining company, why don't you read the first page of the Rose Rowan Mining Company documents I attached?"

All the council members flipped through the stapled pages.

"Are you kidding me?" Xander exclaimed.

"Afraid not, big brother. It was easy to skip over, seeing as the mining company hasn't made a cent in the last seventy years."

Xander shook his head, reading the page over and over.

"What does it say?" someone in the crowd yelled out.

"It says that Uncle Cal was the majority owner in the company. You might be able to exercise Dad's vote, but I still own fifty-five percent of it, and I say we open the mine." Cam didn't smile or look away from his brother.

"Give us a moment," Walter said, then beckoned the other council members. They covered their microphones and moved inward to talk among themselves.

"Look at you, breaking the rules and going against the town," Cam whispered to me.

"More like bending the rules. And why didn't you just come out and say that you wanted to open the mine?" I asked Cam quietly. "They would have rolled over immediately instead of putting you through that."

"I need the mine for leverage, for something way bigger than getting a vote in the Historical Society."

"Your dad?"

He nodded. "My dad. And honestly, I figured if they wouldn't let me into their precious club because of my past, they don't deserve what the mine could mean for their future."

"I get that."

"I didn't know about your degree. Not that part, at least. Thank you for taking my side." He inclined his head but still didn't take his focus off the council.

"Always," I said before I could stop my foolish mouth.

"Not always," he countered with a wry smile.

"Fine, you're right. But I'm taking it now."

"Thank you," he repeated.

"You're welcome." He was right. Once I'd started dating Sullivan, it had been his side I'd taken, not Cam's. The dynamic shifted, as anyone would have expected.

A few more tense moments passed before the council resumed their seats. My fingernails carved half-moons in my palms as I prayed that just once they'd break the rigid mold of their traditions. I didn't even care if it was greed that moved them as long as they moved.

"Camden, the council has agreed to consider your summer plan. We'll need detailed plans on both the Rose Rowan Mine and the restoration of the Rose Rowan building by the March twenty-ninth meeting, so you have two weeks. As long as everything is in order, I don't see why you can't begin working on the mine immediately." Walter grinned.

My hands covered my mouth as shock and joy took turns overwhelming me. For the first time in my memory, the town of Alba cheered for Camden Daniels.

Reopening the mine implied that he was home for good, and while that sent my heart skipping, it also caused my smile to falter. I could only hide my feelings from Cam for so long, and something told me that working with him was only going to hasten the inevitable.

CHAPTER NINE

Camden

"It's seen better days."

I rose from where I was inspecting the pilings on the interior and turned around to see my brother standing in the doorway of the Rose Rowan building. There were only about twenty minutes until Willow would walk into whatever shit storm my brother was here to deliver.

"That could pretty much be the town motto of Alba," I replied.

"And yet here you are, riding in like some white knight, ready to save us all." He folded his arms over his chest but still gave me a million-dollar smile.

"Hardly." The snow crunched beneath my boots as I crossed the fifteen feet to where he stood. "The town is doing just fine. Opening the mine might give it a boost, but that's it. Honestly, I'm shocked you didn't think of it first."

His lips pursed before smoothing. "I knew there was zero chance in hell I was going to get you back here, let alone get you to sign over your half of the mining company. Not to mention find an engineer willing to take it on. That place is a liability nightmare."

More than half of the mining company. Not that I'd say it, of course. He didn't need salt rubbed into an openly raw wound.

"I'm not asking you to sign over your portion. But getting on board with this would go a long way, don't you think? At least politically for you."

"Is that what you're looking for? Political clout? Want to run for office now? Cam, you've been home all of a minute, and suddenly you know best when it comes to Dad, the mine, the needs of the town. What are you doing?"

"The best I can to keep the promise we made."

"What are you talking about?" His hands waved with every word.

"We told Dad he could die in that house. Don't give me that look. We did." I tucked my hands into my pockets to ward off the cold.

"We were kids," he said slowly. "Mom had just died. You were what? Twelve?"

"And you were fourteen," I reminded him.

"And Dad was drunk!" Xander shouted, then took a deep breath, his face turning left, then right, no doubt checking to see if his outburst had been overheard. Not that anyone was listening. This section of Main Street had at least six abandoned buildings that had yet to be restored, and none of the restored buildings was open yet.

"Don't worry—we're alone out here. You don't have to be all shiny perfect. Just be real. Yes, Dad was drunk, but we weren't. He was heartbroken and said that he was going to die in that house, just like she had. And then he turned to us and said, 'You promise me that when I'm old, I can die in this house.' And you promised."

"We didn't know he'd get early-onset Alzheimer's! We didn't know that Sullivan would die or that you wouldn't come home for ten years. Stuff changes, Cam. What the hell does any of this have to do with the mine? Because you and I both know you couldn't give a shit about what happens in Alba."

I took in the roofless building I stood in, from the stacked-timber walls to the glass panels on the north wall that had miraculously survived the last 140 years.

"This is my home. I absolutely care about what happens here. And yeah, I was gone for ten years, and you can judge me for that.

I'm used to it. We didn't know what would happen to Dad or to Mom, or to Sully, for that matter. But it's in our capability to keep Dad in his house. And don't tell me it's too expensive. We both know Dad can afford at-home care."

"You want me to strip Dad's accounts to nothing?" Xander wavered between incredulous and mad. "You realize that's it, right? When he dies, all we have are the mining company and the land. That's it. Dad isn't exactly up to going back to work with the Forest Service."

"It's his money. If home care strips his accounts to zero, then we'll just have to figure it out. Please don't tell me that your argument for putting him in a home is about preserving your inheritance." The words tasted bitter in my mouth.

"He's only fifty-eight. You don't know how many years we'd be signing up for, but he sure as hell doesn't have another thirty years of at-home care in his accounts, Cam. And as for the inheritance? That's easy for you to say. You came home to a house that's already yours. Land that's yours. This building that's yours. You have fifty-five percent of the mining company already and a voting membership in the Historical Society."

"You sit on the damned council!" I snapped. "Do you honestly care if I vote?"

"I don't sit there. Dad does. I only have his seat because he's incapacitated, and you know it. And when he dies, what then?"

"Are you seriously asking me about his seat?" Flames licked up through my lungs, tickling my tongue to say something reckless, to breathe the fire that Xander knew I was capable of. "Do you think I give a shit about who sits on the council?"

"I didn't think you cared about the company or the mine, yet here you are." He gestured to the doorframe with his leather-gloved hands.

"I'm only in this building because I have to get a plan to the council by next week. That's the only way to reopen the mine!" This was a means to an end.

"Why is that so important to you?"

"Because it will pay for Dad's care if you won't!" I shouted, pointing directly at him.

His mouth hung open for a split second before he closed it. "You're reopening the mine to pay for Dad's care?"

Now was definitely not the time to get back into the DNR question. Xander was a politician, but I'd spent the last ten years waging war and building infrastructure. I wasn't showing my hand yet. Not when I couldn't trust him to have a rational conversation about it.

"Yes. I have no control here, Xander. You have it all. You control Dad's care, his finances, his council seat, and his very life. So if money is really the only reason you won't let him stay in the house he was born in, that our mother died in, then I'm alleviating that concern. The money the mine will bring in from tours will more than cover it. Even if I can only give Dad fifty-five percent of the money."

He flinched at that last sentence.

"I just thought you needed a job. Needed income," he admitted quietly.

"Needed income? I've barely spent half of my army pay for the last ten years. I left my job to come here, and I've already had about a dozen offers with different firms making a hell of a lot more than anything the mine could haul in during the season. If I just wanted a job, I'd take one of those offers and cut the amount of shit I'm being given. Do you really think I'm here as a last resort?"

He glanced down at his shiny dress shoes. I bet his toes had to be freezing, and a part of me hoped so. "The thought had occurred to me, yes. Not that I'm not happy you're here."

"You show it so well."

He sighed, looking up like he was praying for patience. Maybe God still listened to him. Good for Xander.

"You went behind my back," he said softly, and a twinge of

hurt echoed through his eyes.

"Coming home?" I clarified. "Because you've been asking me to come back to Alba for the last five years. Hell, you asked me to get out after Sullivan."

"No, with the mine. You could have come to me. We could have pitched it like a team. Instead you left me out and made me look like a fool in front of the council for not knowing what you had planned."

I swallowed the instinctive retort that he was only pissed because the optics hadn't gone his way. But it had to be deeper, didn't it? Sure, he cared about his image way more than I did mine, but it couldn't all be about his reputation.

"I'm sorry," I said, bleeding as much sincerity into my voice as I could so he'd know I was telling the truth. "I was afraid you'd react...well, exactly how you did. After dinner the other night, I didn't trust you to have an open mind. I should have, and I'm sorry."

He stood motionless for an awkward moment, then finally shook his head. "I'd like to think I would have listened and supported you. But maybe you're right. The stuff with Dad the other night put me on the defensive. I don't want to see you as the enemy, Cam. You're the only brother I have."

Left. I'm the only brother you have left.

"I don't want to be your enemy. Ever. I'm just trying to do the best I can for Dad, and if that means pissing you off at times, then I have to be okay with that. But I am sorry that I didn't bring the mine idea to you. It was a dick move."

He shook his head. "You just apologized twice in the last two minutes. I should have recorded it, because I don't think I'll ever hear those words again."

A half smile lifted the corner of my lips. "I'm bound to screw up, but I'm man enough to own it."

"You didn't used to be."

"I didn't use to be a lot of things."

"Okay," he said slowly, as if he'd come to some sort of decision. "I have more than enough on my plate with Dad and running my accounting business—"

"Plus the whole mayor thing," I added.

"I think we both know that running Alba isn't exactly a full-time job. Point is, my hands are full. And I know you technically don't need it, but you have my support for the mine. I still think it's a shit decision that has the potential to get people killed, but I'm trusting your skills. I'm trusting you. So while I'll voice my concerns often and loudly when it's the two of us, I'll back you when it comes to the council."

"Really?" I kept my voice as neutral as possible, not letting hope or disbelief change the tone.

"Really." He shrugged. "If I'd known why you were doing it, I hope I would have been on your side from the get-go."

"But you're on it now."

"I am. And we can talk about at-home care for Dad. Let's have dinner at my place this week. I'll show you the research I have and Dad's finances, and maybe we can figure something out together." The pressed line of his lips told me what his words didn't—he didn't want to give up any control, but he was willing to try.

"I'll bring the food."

"Sounds good. I'll let you get back to your..." He glanced around the building that was way worse off than it had been when we were kids.

"My giant wreck," I offered.

"Your giant wreck," he agreed, then smiled. "Later."

"See ya." I sent him off with a wave.

When his shiny blue truck passed the doorless entry of the mining building, I went back to my inspection, mentally cataloging all the structural problems while replaying the conversation with Xander in my head.

Sullivan would have smoothed everything over effortlessly.

"He's going to kill me when he figures out what I'm really doing. You know that, right?" I said softly. "Sure, there's a slight chance I can win him over, but you know how he is."

I moved to the window frames on the south side of the building, taking a minute to climb over the fractured support beam that had fallen from the ceiling before I'd even left Alba.

"Look at this place," I muttered. "You would have loved it, though, wouldn't you? You would have seen it as an adventure. A way to bring back a slice of our family legacy. I just see a structural nightmare with too many restoration rules to contend with." Dropping to a crouch, I eased my way under another fallen timber to get a better look at the pilings. "I'm going to have to replace almost all of these. Let's just add it to the list, shall we? Fight for Dad, fight the town, figure out what I'm going to do with my life… You would have taken it all in stride with a grin, wouldn't you?"

"Hey," Willow said from behind me.

I stood and smacked my head on the very timber I'd been trying to avoid. "Shit," I cursed and rubbed the top of my head as I ducked and came out.

"Sorry. I was trying not to startle you." She bit her lip and winced from under a green winter hat that brought out the same color in her eyes.

"You failed." Damn, my head hurt. "That's a lie. I should have heard you. I must have been lost in all the amazing restoration we're going to do."

She gave me a small, soft smile. "It's okay. I talk to him, too."

"Who?" I swallowed, hoping she'd say anything other than the truth.

"Sullivan." She walked farther into the building, eyeing the structure with appraisal.

I could almost see the gears turning in her head, and it was fascinating. Her eyes lit with a fire I hadn't seen in years, darting over the walls, the windows, and even the fallen beams. She pulled a tablet from her bag and started to write on it with a stylus. Great, now I was watching the graceful way she moved her hands, even with gloves on.

"He wouldn't have taken it in stride, you know," she said, breaking my stream of thoughts.

"Sullivan?" His laugh came to mind, filling my chest with a bittersweet pressure that I'd become well acquainted with over the last six years. "Yeah, he would have. He would have jumped in with both feet and a grin and made it all look easy."

She snorted. Actually freaking snorted. And what was worse was that I thought it was cute.

Cute like a little sister, I reminded myself.

Yeah, okay, I fired back.

"Sure, he would have jumped in with both feet and a grin and no common sense." She paused, looking over her shoulder at me. "Sully made everything look easy because it was easy for him. It was easy because the town loved him and you loved him. You and Xander tackled anything that was remotely a challenge for him."

I stuck my hands back in my pockets, hoping the feeling would return to them soon. It had to be in the low twenties today. "I don't know if I should be insulted or proud."

"Both." She grinned and turned back to her tablet, scribbling away. "And let's face it. Sully would never have been in your position."

"Because the town would have welcomed him with a smile." I stepped over the support beam and made my way to where she was taking notes.

"Sure, that too," she admitted with a shrug. "But I was thinking more along the lines that he never would have gone against Xander. Sully would have taken Xander's word as gospel and moved on. He never would have stood up like you did—like you're doing." She glanced at me, knocking the breath from my lungs.

Green, gold, blue, and bronze. How was it possible for one person to have all those colors in her eyes?

"Maybe," I conceded once she'd looked away and my brain

started working again. "Or maybe we wouldn't be in this situation in the first place."

"Maybe you would have come home after three years," she said softly, face down in her tablet.

No, I wouldn't have. Not for one very fucked-up reason.

"Maybe you'd be married to Sullivan." I didn't mean to say it.

She tensed but looked up at me after a minute, conflict etched in the lines of her forehead where her hat began.

"Maybe," she whispered.

Maybe not. The unspoken words hung there between us, where they had no right to be.

Because they were a damned lie. I walked away from her, choosing to examine the joints where the south and east walls met.

Of course she would have married Sullivan. They were Alba's golden couple. The outgoing boy and the quiet girl who spoke through her art. The ones who fell in love after living next door to each other for years.

They were the fucking storybook, and I was the fire-breathing dragon. And sure, I'd burned shit to the ground, but never them. Never him.

Never her.

I would have rather died than see any of my shit touch either of them.

Yet somehow, I'd given the order, and Sullivan had died in my arms.

And now I was standing here next to the woman he'd loved. The woman he'd wanted to marry. The woman he'd left behind to go join the army, not because Xander was finishing up his three years but because he thought it was cool that I'd just made it through the Special Forces Qualification Course.

I got to wear a green beret.

Sullivan got to wear his dress blues for eternity.

Willow never got to wear our mother's ring.

I was a grade A asshole for even thinking about Willow or her eyes or how soft her hair was. It was an absolute betrayal of my little brother.

"I have the dimensions on file with the Historical Society, so I think I can get started with this plan. At least the restoration part. You good on structure?"

"Yeah. I have a good enough idea to draft a plan." I fought my instincts to stay there, facing the corner, blocking out everything in the world besides the grain of the wood before me. Instead, I stood and turned to face her.

"Okay." She stayed buried in her tablet. "Then, how about we look at the mine on Wednesday? I have a project I really need to finish up tomorrow."

"Sounds good," I agreed, willing to say anything if it would mean an end to this moment.

"Okay. I'll see you then?" she asked, looking up.

"Yep," I answered with a curt nod.

Her mouth moved like she might say something but then thought better of it. With a forced smile, she said a hurried goodbye and rushed from the building.

When I heard her car leave, I found the strength to move, but instead of leaving, I fell to my knees. Snow melted against the heat of my jeans, quickly soaking the material and hitting my skin with blistering cold.

Still, I kneeled there until my breaths turned even and measured.

Then I looked up through where the roof should have been and stared at the crystal-blue sky.

"I'm sorry," I told him.

And I was.

I just wasn't sure if it was for what I'd already done or what I was scared I had yet to do.

CHAPTER TEN

Willow

"Okay, why are you avoiding me?" Thea questioned.

"I'm not." I hopped on one foot as I tried to get the other through my tights. "If I were avoiding you, I wouldn't have picked up the phone, now, would I?"

"See, I would believe that if I hadn't been calling you for the last three days."

"Have you?" I lost my balance and fell back onto my bed with an *oof*. I gave up trying to balance and put Thea on speakerphone.

"You know I have. Jacob! I swear, if you don't eat your dinner because you're snacking on those cookies... Pat, help me out?" Thea didn't bother muffling the phone. We were way past that stage of friendship.

I worked the black tights up over my legs and stared at my skirt choices.

"Thank you, honey," Thea said. "Okay, sorry. I think I just bought myself about five minutes of quiet."

"No worries." I laughed softly, picturing the chaotic happiness that Jacob brought into Thea's and Pat's lives. "So what's up?"

"You're asking me what's up? You, who outed your second degree in the middle of a Historical Society meeting and then took Camden Daniels's side over your father's? You're asking me what's up?"

"See, this is the reason I didn't answer. I'm not reverting back to high school, Thea. I refuse." The black skirt was safer, and Dad would appreciate that. The shorter red one had been a favorite while I was at school, but it would no doubt lead to a lecture.

"Ha! You *were* avoiding me! And by reverting, you mean when we'd chat for hours about boys? Or just the Daniels boys?"

Guess I walked right into that one.

"I just don't have anything to say about Cam."

"I could say a whole hell of a lot. I mean, it's Camden."

Yep. Right back to high school.

"Yes, it's Camden," I muttered, putting on the black skirt.

"Oh, come on. Is it fun to be around him again? Please give me something. I'm dying here."

"'Fun' isn't the word I'd use for it." I zipped the skirt up the back and headed to my closet, bringing my phone along.

"Exhilarating? Exciting? Heart-pounding? What?"

"You have a very distorted idea of what it's like between us. Try frustrating, confusing, aggravating, and just plain weird." I found my knee-high dress boots and hauled them out. Sure, I'd get some comment about them from Dad or even Mom, but the temps had dropped, and I wasn't going out in heels.

Her sigh was loud and long. "Willow, you have to remember that I was there. You can't fool me. And if you don't want to talk with me about what his return is doing to you, then fine, I know Pat's feelings about him complicate things. Just make sure you're talking to someone. That boy—that man—ties you into knots and always has."

"Can't we just pretend that you weren't there?" I asked softly, then bent to put on the boots.

"No." Her voice dropped in volume. "Because you can't pretend, honey. You spent years shoving those feelings away, and I'm afraid if you do it again, you'll implode."

"I'll be fine." I was always fine. It was the only option.

"Maybe. But last time, you both retreated to your corners. You got together with Sullivan, and Cam pretty much took his ball and went home. Working together on the mine? That's a lot."

"Cam didn't retreat. There was nothing to retreat from. And I loved Sullivan."

"I know you did. I just…"

My breath paused as I waited for her to drop the nuke, to rip apart every ounce of denial I clung to. Having a best friend who knew me since childhood was a pain in the ass sometimes. She never let me forget anything or change the script in my head.

"I'm here if you need anything. That's all," she finished, and I exhaled.

"Thank you. I might take you up on that. Right now, I have to get down to Mom and Dad's for another awkward family dinner."

"Okay. At least your antics will give your sister a break from the Judge Bradley death stare. Give Rosie a kiss for me. Love you."

"Love you," I told her and hung up, pausing for a moment to evaluate my reflection. The black was a good, solid choice.

But the red would put a little more of the heat on me and off Charity.

Red it was.

As awkward went, it wasn't naked-without-my-homework-on-the-first-day-of-school, and that was all I could really say for it.

Thank God Rosie kept up a steady stream of conversation with Mom, because Dad was barely looking at Charity or me.

Mom's usually phenomenal cooking tasted like cardboard, but I just kept chewing, knowing it was more my nerves than her seasoning. Hopefully we could end this super-fun evening with relative quickness. A front had moved in this afternoon, and snow had started falling in a thick blanket as I'd pulled into the driveway.

"Since when did you become persona non grata?" Charity asked under her breath as we sat in the formal dining room. Dad occupied the head of the table and Mom the foot, while Charity and I held down one side and Rose the other. Her multicolored skirt and sequined unicorn top brought desperately needed life to the cherry-wood-and-crystal room.

"Since she decided to choose the Daniels boy over her own family," Dad answered.

"Supersonic ears," Charity whispered.

I tossed her a heavy dose of side-eye before facing my father. "Dad, I didn't choose Cam over you."

"Cam? Oh man, I bet he was hoping it was at least Xander," Charity quipped.

"Charity," Mom warned.

"I like Cam," Rose added. "He's nice."

"You—" Dad's face turned a mottled red as he struggled for control. "You brought that boy around Rose?"

"Noah," Mom chided. "I'd hardly call a twenty-eight-year-old a boy. He's a full-grown man now."

"All the better to cause even more damage," Dad shot back. "What were you thinking, Willow?" He stared at me, fork and knife clutched in his hands like he was going to cut into me instead of his turkey.

"About what?" I asked.

"Are you kidding me?" His voice dropped low.

"She means are you asking about why she took his side—which I would love to know the story behind—or why he was around Rose?" Charity's gaze swung between Mom and me, ignoring my dad completely. "What? Just thought I'd help interpret."

"He used my unicorn," Rose said with a shrug before shoving in a mouthful of mashed potatoes.

"I'm sorry, honey?" Mom questioned.

Rose swallowed and looked at both of my parents, then chose Dad. Girl had guts. "He used my ice pack. The unicorn we keep in the freezer. You know it, Grandpa. You gave it to me when I was little and called it my boo-boo pack."

Because she was so big now. I held my pressed lips between

my teeth to hide my smile and then quickly took a bite of broccoli.

"I do remember it, Rosie." Dad's tone changed to the one he reserved for Rose. The one he used to use when we were small and hadn't disappointed him yet.

"Well, his face had a bump, so Aunt Willow let him borrow it. He didn't even care that it was a girl ice pack or anything. He's pretty big, though. Takes up the whole kitchen."

Someone save me—this was about to get ugly. I swallowed the broccoli, which slid down my throat as smooth as ash.

"You took Camden Daniels into her apartment? Where Rose lives?" Dad growled.

"What do you think he was going to do, Dad? Graffiti the place? Clog the drain and start a flood? He's not a kid anymore," I retorted. "Oscar Hudgens hit him with zero warning, and Tim Hall was coming at him, so I took him upstairs and got him out of the line of fire."

"And you thought the apartment was appropri—"

"That's my apartment," Charity interjected, addressing Dad directly.

Hell had officially frozen over. While she'd always brought Rose around and encouraged their relationship, she'd given up trying with Dad after Rose turned two and now spoke to Dad exactly three times a year.

Happy birthday.

Merry Christmas.

Happy Father's Day.

It was March, and none of those applied.

Mom's fork hit the plate, but neither Charity nor Dad looked away from each other.

"It's my apartment," she continued. "Mine. I own that whole building, and I get to say who goes into my bar. My home, for that matter, too. It's mine. Just like Rose is mine."

Dad put his silverware down with care.

Maybe now was a good time to stand up and twirl around in

my super-short red skirt like a matador with an angry bull.

"I'm sorry that it bothers you that Camden was in my home, but I trust him. I trust Willow."

"Well, I sure don't trust Camden, and I'm not sure I can trust you, either," Dad said, his gaze sliding to me. "Taking his side after everything that boy has done."

"I hardly think petty vandalism and a few fistfights make him untrustworthy."

"You call setting fire to the bunkhouse petty vandalism? That building survived a hundred and thirty years before Cam destroyed it."

"That fire was ruled accidental, and you know it," I snapped.

"You almost died."

Smoke filled my memories, acrid and harsh in my throat. "Cam saved my life."

"After he put it in danger in the first place. It may have been ruled accidental, but we all know what really happened. He set it on fire just because he could. That boy has always been destructive and dangerous."

"He was a kid, Dad. An entire decade has gone by, and he's spent it serving his country and finishing his education. Doesn't that mean anything to you?" I searched my father's face, looking for a drop of compassion, a crack in his steel-enforced moral code.

"It means that the boy who was prone to violence went and found himself a career where he could continue that violence, and they decorated him as a hero for it. People change in very small ways, Willow. We change our decision-making and even our actions, but we don't change who we are here." He tapped his chest.

"A career where he could continue that violence," I repeated. "That's not what you said when Sullivan enlisted. You told him how proud you were, how he was a man to admire for serving his country just like his father and brothers had. Why is Cam's choice any less honorable?" They had made the same decision, so how was it that Sullivan was applauded while Cam had been sneered at?

Dad sucked in a breath, his posture going straighter than the supports on the bench he loved to sit behind. "I thought the military was good for Camden and told Art exactly that. The boy needed some discipline."

"And he's now an engineer, Dad. This town needs him, and yet you tried to run him off, not because it was the rule but because you don't like him." I shook my head. "I've never seen you step outside your little black-and-white code and bring your own bias into a decision like that."

"This town needed Sullivan more. You needed Sullivan more." The skin between his brows wrinkled, and pain filled his eyes for a second before he blinked it away.

I didn't examine the truth or the lie in his statement.

"It's not Cam's fault that Sullivan died." The words fell from my lips as if they'd been doing it for the last six years, though they never had before. Not that I'd ever blamed Cam. I knew better than that. I'd simply never contradicted Dad because he'd never been bold enough to say it in front of me.

There is more beauty in truth. Cam's words from the library, reciting that book, settled on my chest with a warmth I didn't deserve. Shame crept up my neck, hot and uncomfortable. I'd known what my father had thought all these years. I should have said it long before now.

My silence may as well have been an endorsement of Dad's preposterous thought. Of the entire town's.

"He was there. Did you know that?" Dad challenged.

Charity reached into my lap and gripped my hand.

"Yes." It was well known that Cam's unit had rushed to the firefight that took Sullivan.

"He gave an order that got Sullivan killed."

I'd heard that rumor, too.

"It wasn't Cam's bullet that hit Sullivan, Dad."

"He sure as hell didn't save him, did he? If you were in battle with your sister, you would have been right by her side." He left the damning accusation hanging there.

Charity's hand tightened around mine, and I squeezed back.

"I can't answer that, Dad. I've never been to war. Have you?"

He pulled his napkin from his lap and flung it on the table. "Thank you for dinner, sweetheart. I'm going to start on the dishes." He pushed back from the table and stood, taking his plate with him. He seemed to struggle with his thoughts, then brought his eyes to mine. "I saw what Sullivan's death did to you. When you watch the person you love most lose what they love most, then you'll understand. But I pray to God that never happens to you, Willow."

He left the room, taking some but not all of the tension with him.

My eyes swung past Rose, who was chewing slowly with wide eyes, to my mother, who glared at both Charity and me.

"I'm going to help Grandpa," Rose announced, springing from the table, plate in hand.

"Traitor," Charity whispered at her daughter's back with a little smirk.

"Really, girls? You with the whole 'my life, my rules' thing." She pointed at Charity. "And you with…"

"The truth?" I offered.

"You can't make him accept Cam. The day he brought you home with that broken nose, your dad made up his mind about him." Mom shook her head as the sound of the faucet running started from the kitchen. "The fire sealed the deal."

"I was nine and fell in the mine," I argued. "Cam was the one who found me and brought me home after—" I dropped Charity's hand and put my napkin on the table. It didn't matter how many times I went over the events of that day; Dad would always side with Xander and against Cam. "And it was Cam who carried me out of that fire when I lost track of Sully. Cam, Mom, not Sullivan.

And it was almost ten years ago!" Almost ten years since I left the white onyx bishop on Cam's dashboard when he wouldn't let me thank him.

"I know how you feel about him," Mom whispered.

"Well, that makes one of us," I muttered and stood.

"For the love of God, Willow, that skirt can't possibly pass the fingertip test." Mom's lips pursed.

"It doesn't," I assured her, dropping my hands straight down my thighs to show her that it was a few inches shorter than her ridiculous mandate.

"I had a child out of wedlock," Charity blurted, standing next to me.

Mom sighed, waving us off as she stood up. "This is not a competition. Now, both of you get home. The snow's coming down heavy, and it looks like the wet stuff. I'll handle the dishes...and your father."

We kissed her cheeks, and after Charity had Rose buttoned up, we escaped out the garage door. One look at the accumulating snow and Rose's dress shoes, and Charity hefted Rose into her arms.

"Crap, she wasn't kidding," Charity groaned as she trekked through the water-laden snow. We were up to at least five inches already.

"Here." I scrambled, slipping twice as I got ahead of her to open Charity's back door. "In you go, Rosie. Love you." I pressed a quick kiss to her forehead.

"Love you!" she called back.

"I have to stop feeding you so much," Charity complained with a grin as she lifted Rose into the SUV. "Buckle up, buttercup." She shut the door, leaving us standing in the silence that only comes with snowfall. "It used to be easier to carry her."

"She used to be smaller." A wave of gratitude hit me—I'd be around to see her grow again. She'd shot up in the four years I'd been gone. "You spoke to Dad."

"You defied him."

We both nodded and then hugged, holding each other tight.

"I should have said something earlier, about Cam and Sully," I admitted into my sister's hair.

She squeezed me closer. "You did what you could when you could."

"I should have said something earlier about you, too. About you and Rose. I never should have stayed quiet and let him shun you. I was just trying to keep the peace, but it was wrong."

She shook her head against mine. "No. No, Willow." She pulled back, cupping my cheeks in her bare hands. "That was my fight. Not yours. Don't you ever apologize for that. You have always shown up for me. For Rose. And you keeping that peace is what allowed me to bring her around those first years before you went to college. You laid the groundwork for it to keep going once you left. You're the reason we can still have these dinners. The reason I know he loves Rose more than life. You've held your tongue in the moments I couldn't, and that's something to be proud of. Restraint can be so much harder."

I blinked furiously, keeping the burn at bay as snowflakes landed on my eyelashes and Charity's.

"I'm so scared that I let the silence speak for me," I whispered.

"Well, you seem to have found your voice now. Use it for good. You know, the whole 'with great power comes great responsibility' thing."

"I'm not Spider-Man." I laughed.

"You've survived more than anyone I know, then gotten on your feet and started going again. That makes you a hero in my book."

"You've raised a daughter on your own. That makes you mine."

She grinned and shrugged. "I just learned how to tell people no. Something tells me you did, too. Now, go back up the mountain before this gets any worse. The last thing you want is to call Dad to come rescue you if you get stuck. You'll never hear the end of it."

"Truth." We gave each other another squeeze, then piled into our separate cars.

Icy air blasted as I started the engine, and I quickly turned down the vents. After Charity pulled out of the drive, I did the same, following her for a couple hundred yards. The snow fell in thick curtains, working my wiper blades overtime. Visibility was pure crap.

I turned up the road that led to my little outpost, then paused to put my car into four-wheel drive. Spring snow was nothing to mess with. It was heavy, wet, and slick. Great for snowballs and forts but horrible for driving.

My car groaned as we made it up the first ridgeline, skimming the edge of Cam's property at the hot springs. My toes tingled, reminding me that there was nothing hot about this ride. I slammed the heat to full now that the engine was good and warm and adjusted my defrost. I'd grown up on this mountain, and while this was definitely one of my more challenging drives home, it wasn't the worst.

Judah & the Lion came through my stereo, and I turned the volume down as I peaked, knowing that the downhill could be just as challenging with the already packed snow under this mess.

I took it slowly, maintaining traction.

"Shit!" I yelped as a doe ran out in front of me, followed by three of her friends. Fighting the instinct to slam the brakes, I pumped quickly and swerved at the last minute to avoid the fifth deer. Darn straggler.

My back end came around, sending me down the path sideways.

"A little help here," I shouted to whoever might be listening, using every skill I had to get myself out of the slide.

I slid right off the road, and the side of the mountain suddenly felt much more death trap and much less home. If I slid much farther, I'd fall a good three hundred feet and end up in Dad's backyard.

The tires gripped for a millisecond, and I took advantage,

pulling the wheel hard, only to hit a set of boulders even harder.

The impact jerked my entire body, but it was pretty anticlimactic as far as car accidents went.

"Fantastic." I let my head fall against the headrest for a second, hoping the adrenaline would cycle out and calm my racing heart.

The headlights shone but only tracked the snow as it streaked from the sky. If I hadn't known the terrain, I'd have no clue if I were in the field or on the edge of the drop-off before the switchbacks that led to the Rose Rowan Mine.

I put the car into reverse and went nowhere, so I stopped before I spun myself even deeper.

My cell phone had 70 percent battery, and my tank was half full, so at least I had that going for me. It took me a few minutes to get the canvas tow straps I kept in the back seat looped around my waist at one end and tied to my seat at the other. Once I was tethered to the car, I grabbed the bag Dad had preached about carrying since I was little and put on a thick winter hat and spare gloves.

"Seriously, is this karma for sticking up for your brother?" I asked Sullivan. Naturally, he didn't respond. I wasn't nuts.

I mentally prepared myself for this to suck, zipped my coat to my chin, then got out of the car, carrying the bulk of the strap with me and quickly shutting my door to keep the snow out. It was deeper up here, coming almost to the top of my boot.

My very thin, not-snow-friendly boot.

Ignoring the biting cold, I crouched and used my cell phone as a flashlight to inspect the damage.

The front left had taken the impact, leaving me with a flat tire and a busted rim. I cursed softly. Without the snow, it would have been a hell of a spot to change a flat, but with the snow, it was impossible.

I was so freaking screwed.

Keeping one hand on the car, I walked toward the back. I was close to the drop-off. Another twenty feet and I would have seen

Sullivan way sooner than I'd planned on.

I checked to make sure the tailpipe was clear and dug out a space underneath it to keep snow from overtaking it. Then I opened the hatch and retrieved the snow boots I'd left there after taking Rosie sledding last week. I got back into the car and gritted my teeth against the pain that assaulted my feet as heat returned to my toes.

There were not enough swear words in the English language for this moment.

I could call Dad.

He'd be pissed, but he'd come.

As long as the deer didn't ambush him, he'd probably make it. But the snow was deep and only coming faster.

There was no way I was risking Charity up here or asking Pat to leave Thea and Jacob.

I opened the contacts on my phone and scrolled slowly, then paused.

Call him.

I balked at my own inner voice.

"He probably changed his number a dozen times over the years," I muttered. Okay, maybe I was going a little nuts if I was responding to myself.

I tapped his name before I could second-guess myself and prepared to hear the ear-blistering disconnected announcement.

"Willow?" Cam answered.

"Cam." I sagged in my seat as relief hit me smack in the chest.

"What's going on?"

I could almost see his puckered brow from here, that concerned look he got when things went wrong.

"I seem to have gotten myself in a little situation," I said as the wipers slowed. The snow was getting too heavy for them.

"Of course you did. Where are you?"

I cringed but forged ahead, because I didn't want to end up as the headline tomorrow.

"I got into an accident. Right after the first ridge. You know, where it curves instead of going to the springs? Right before the Rose Rowan turn?"

"Send me a GPS pin. I'm on my way."

CHAPTER ELEVEN

Camden

I was going to throttle her. As soon as I found her.

This storm wasn't playing around.

I paused at the ridgeline between our properties and checked the pin she'd sent me with her location against my own. Dropping another fifty feet of elevation should bring her into visibility.

What the hell was she doing out in this? Okay, granted, the weatherman screwed up and said the storm was passing to the north of us, but then again, by saying we weren't getting snow, they had a 50 percent shot at being right. Snow was accumulating fast, and even the Cat wasn't going to be a sure thing pretty soon.

"Just let her be okay," I begged. I hadn't asked if she was injured because it wouldn't have made a difference. I could only get there as fast as possible, and I was already doing that.

I zipped my phone into my pocket and turned the snowmobile down the ridge, giving the Cat some throttle. It was a damn good thing I knew this land like the back of my hand, because visibility was shit, and what I could see hid the dips and rises that could get me into some major trouble.

Not that we weren't already in trouble.

I passed the grouping of pines that marked where the road turned, and a pair of streaming headlights came into view.

"Thank you," I whispered into the gator that covered my mouth, then carefully made my way down the slope.

Damn, she was close to the cliff. I blocked out everything that could have happened and focused on what did as I left the engine to idle and climbed off.

I flung open the passenger door of her 4Runner and ripped at my helmet. "Are you hurt?" I asked before I had it all the way off.

"No," she promised with a shake of her head. "You came all the way in this on the snowmobile?"

"Yeah. I wasn't cutting across the property in the Jeep, and to be honest, I probably wouldn't have made it. I don't know how you made it." Snow hit the exposed back of my neck as I leaned in.

"I didn't. Hence me calling," she admitted with a sheepish crinkle in her nose. "I'm so sorry you had to come."

"I didn't have to, Willow. I chose to." That was partly a lie. Sure, there was some freewill argument to be had, but all my choices when it came to Willow had been made decades ago. She called. I came. It was that simple. And that complicated.

"The front left tire is flat—" she started.

"Doesn't matter. We can't get to it in this anyway. Now, let's go. The snow is only getting deeper." I scanned her frame as I talked, taking in her hat, coat, and gloves, down to— "Holy shit, are you wearing a skirt?"

That crinkle was back. "Well, yes. I was—"

"Again, doesn't matter. Shit. Wait here." I closed the door and pivoted to face the Cat. Unbuckling the saddlebags was a pain with my gloves, but I wasn't risking losing them in this. I'd get frostbite before we could make it back to the house.

I yanked my old set of spare riding pants and sent a quick thank-you Uncle Cal's way for not having cleaned them out of the under-seat storage. Then I snapped the strap and freed the extra helmet I'd brought her and walked back to her door.

"Take these," I said, thrusting the clothes at her with one hand as I slid into her passenger seat and shut the door behind me. "I brought you a helmet, too." Not that I had to say that, since it currently consumed my lap.

"Thank you," she responded, already shucking her boots to shimmy into the snow pants.

"What the hell are you doing out in this?" I questioned, keeping my eyes front and center and not on the slide of her hips as she worked the pants up.

"Vehicular sledding."

I looked her way with a raised eyebrow.

"I was having dinner with my parents, which I was trying to tell you, but you kept cutting me off."

"You should have stayed with your parents."

"Thank you, Captain Obvious." She snapped the pants, then unzipped her skirt and started working it down.

This was definitely not the way I'd ever pictured getting Willow Bradley's skirt off in a car. Not that I'd ever— Okay, yes, I had. A lot.

"Trust me, if I'd realized this was going to happen, I would have gone down the mountain, not up it. But I wasn't staying with Dad. Not with his mood." She cleared the skirt and threw it in the back seat.

"Sorry I cut you off, but I'm worried about getting back and didn't realize you'd need to change."

"You figured I drove around in a snowsuit?" She grinned.

"Something like that." I looked away quickly. The fact that she could find something funny in just about every situation was one of her most attractive qualities, but I didn't have time for that right now. "It's about twenty minutes back to my place." I dropped my gloves on the center console and warmed my hands in front of the vents.

"We're closer to mine," she argued as she braided her hair with quick fingers. Smart girl. The wind would blow it all over the place if she left it loose.

"By maybe thirty feet," I countered. "Besides, I know the terrain back to my place better, and visibility isn't exactly stellar right now." I caught a smirk and pounced before she could speak. "So help me, Willow, if you even suggest that you drive…"

She laughed. "Come on, it was a valid thought."

I knew she was skilled on a Cat, but that didn't mean I was willing to give up control when her life was at stake. Using the time, I fired off a quick group text to Gideon and Xander.

Camden: Willow got stuck. I'm taking her back to my place with the Cat. We're taking the route above the hot springs.

There. Now, if things went royally wrong, they'd know where to look.

Gideon: Power station just failed. Keep her warm. ;)

"What kind of power are you running?" I asked her, shaking my head at Gid's comment.

Her brow puckered. "Town electric."

Xander: Okay. Stay safe. I'm at Dad's, setting up the generator.

Xander: Gideon, shut the hell up. Cam, keep your hands on the throttle.

"I win. Town power is out, and I have a solar bank that can power a space station or a small doomsday cult. We're going to my place. Shut off the car and let's go before we end up here for the night." I handed Willow her helmet, then opened the door and got out, not giving her the chance to argue. We were wasting time we might not have.

My phone buzzed repeatedly as I fastened my own helmet again.

Gideon: I believe that's what I said.

Xander: You're lucky it's snowing.

Gideon: Yeah, yeah. Cam, text when you get there.

Cam: Will do on all accounts.

I zipped my phone into my coat and brushed the snow from the seats of the Cat, grateful that it was a 2-up and not a single.

She trudged over, the snow up to her knees as she buckled her helmet.

I checked it like she was eight again. Old habits and whatnot.

I flipped the buttons on the helmets and then the dash, bringing the headsets online.

"Can you hear me?" I asked.

"Gotcha," she acknowledged.

We climbed on, and Willow reached for the passenger handles as I settled into the driver's seat.

I will never see Willow Bradley again. I was really going to have to modify that fucking vow. Maybe something like *I'll never touch Willow Bradley.*

Yeah, that could work.

I gave the Cat some gas, and we left Willow's 4Runner to the storm, heading back up the ridgeline. My earlier tracks were already gone. GPS told me we'd passed the hot springs down the ridgeline to the east, but I couldn't see shit.

"We're turning down the ridge," I warned her.

"Okay," she responded. "I can't believe how bad it is. I can hardly see you, and you're right in front of me."

I could barely feel her, too. She was leaning back in the passenger seat, no doubt to give me space. We weren't exactly snuggle buddies.

But we were about to be.

"Lean forward and hold on to me," I ordered. It was better for turns and for traversing, and she knew it. At least, I hoped she did.

Her weight settled against me as we started downhill, and her hands clasped first at my waist, then into the fabric of my jacket itself.

I'd never been so glad for a snowstorm to distract me in my entire life.

"You okay?" I asked, using one hand to guide hers to the loops on the bright-orange vest I'd donned in case of emergency. "Is that easier?"

"Yes, thank you." Her grip tightened.

She didn't sound breathless. Nope. She sounded...nervous,

which was understandable. Willow Bradley would never be breathless near me unless she was winded from screaming at me.

We crossed the plain between the ridgelines, the snow coming at us in the headlights like we were at warp speed.

"It's beautiful, in its own little, dangerous way," she remarked, her helmet resting between my spine and right shoulder blade.

"Most everything that can hurt you is."

She sighed softly but didn't reply.

We climbed the last ridge, and I was careful to stick to the path I knew didn't have random boulders that could throw us or a chain.

"I see it!" she exclaimed as we crested the ridge and Elba came into view.

"Almost there," I assured her. We'd made it. Even if the Cat died right now, I could carry her the distance.

I brought us around the back of the house and pulled into the driveway. "You go ahead inside, and I'll pull it in," I told her as I climbed off the Cat.

"You don't need help?" she asked, her gaze obscured by the tinted visors of our helmets.

"No, go get warm." I walked to the garage and punched the code into the panel. The door rose, and Willow slipped inside.

I quickly pulled the Cat into the little bay it called home and closed us in. Then I unfastened my helmet and set it in the metal locker that soon held my coat, snow pants, and boots, too. Willow's coat and boots were already there.

My athletic pants were damp with sweat despite the temperatures outside, and I crossed over to the power shed in my socks. Once I was satisfied that all the batteries were full, I closed it up and headed inside.

Warmth and the smell of something sweet welcomed me as the tension drained from my muscles. I hadn't realized how anxious I'd been until the anxiety left.

She was safe. She was warm. She was here.

Fuck, what if I hadn't come home? I leaned back against the door as the weight of that possibility took me down. If Dad hadn't left that voicemail. If I hadn't acted on it... Where would she be?

"Hey."

My gaze shot up to meet hers as she stood across from me in the entry hall, a steaming cup in her hands. Even though she'd rolled them at the waist several times, my snow pants were huge on her. Her long-sleeve shirt contrasted the ill fit, holding close to her curves, and the tail of her frayed braid fell over her shoulder to end just beneath her breast. Her cheeks and lips were pink from the cold, and her eyes were bright. I'd seen her in almost every way, from tank tops and overalls in the summer to a ball gown on prom night.

She'd never looked more beautiful to me than she did in this moment.

I was so fucked. So. Very. Fucked.

She crossed the floor and held out the mug. "I made you some hot chocolate. I checked the dates and everything."

I reached out and took the mug from her, our fingers brushing in the exchange. It was somehow more intimate than having her arms wrapped around me the entire ride home.

"Thank you," I told her, my voice so rough, I barely recognized it. "I bought it, so it's good. Plus I threw out anything that had been left here."

"I never figured you for a hot chocolate guy."

"I'm a sucker for sweet things," I admitted, letting the mug warm my hand before drinking half of it down.

Her cheeks turned a deeper shade of pink.

"Did you make one for you?" I asked.

She nodded. "It's in the kitchen." When she headed that way, I followed, silently laughing that the bottom of my snow pants dragged on the floor.

Willow was a lot of things. Tall wasn't one of them.

"Why don't you get out of those?" I suggested as she gripped her mug. "You'll warm up a lot faster."

"Only tights, remember?" She cocked her head to the side.

"Right." I had been doing my best to ignore that fact when she'd changed. "Okay, what are you most comfortable in? My pants are going to be huge on you, but you can roll them, or shorts? A hoodie?"

"Yes, please," she responded with a smile. "I'll take whatever you have. I'm not picky."

I excused myself and went through my closet, pulling out pants, shorts, a T-shirt, and a hoodie. Oh, and some thick socks, too. Then I fired off a text message to Gideon and Xander that we'd made it safely before taking a two-minute shower and getting into some clean clothes.

"I'm fine," I heard her saying as I walked down the hallway to the kitchen.

"Mom, just tell him that I'm fine. No, I don't need him to come hook up my generator."

Her back was to me as she stared out the kitchen window.

"Because I know how to hook up my own generator, that's why." She sighed, and her head rolled back a little. "And because I'm at Cam's. I slid off the road, and he came and got me. No, don't tell him that. He's liable to head out with a shotgun and get himself killed in this weather."

Good ol' Judge Bradley. He'd definitely shit bricks if he knew she was about to wear my clothes to bed in my house. A small slice of satisfaction had me smiling when Willow hung up with her mom.

"Here you go." I offered her the clothes. "You can get changed if you want, or take a shower or whatever, and I'll start a fire."

"Thank you." She looked down the hall and hesitated.

"You can use my room if you want. I haven't gone through Cal's yet. Shower is—"

"Connected to the bedroom," she finished with a small smile. "I remember. Be right back."

She disappeared into my bedroom, and I started a fire in the living room fireplace. The solar batteries would hold—I wasn't worried—but there was something to be said for a fire on a night like this. When I carried the last load of wood in from the garage, I found Willow sitting in front of the flames, pulling a tiny brush through her wet hair.

"Let me help," she offered, climbing to her feet. The socks came up to her knees, and she had my athletic shorts rolled a few times, leaving only her knees bare. My hoodie engulfed her, hitting her just below mid-thigh, and she had the sleeves rolled on that, too.

"I've got it," I told her and added the stack to the log rack that sat at the end of the mantel. "Where were you hiding a brush?"

She popped the back, and it compressed into an even tinier rectangle. "I managed to strap my purse on under my coat. Good thing, too, since I have my wallet and all those important things."

"Because you were planning on taking a trip to the store?" I teased as we both sat. She curled her legs under her, and I brought up my knees to brace my elbows as we both stared into the fire.

"I bet you think I'm the biggest damsel ever."

"What?"

"Damsel. You know, 'save me!'" She waved her hands in the air and shook them, still looking into the flames.

"Why would I think you're a damsel?" I questioned.

"You've been home what, two weeks? And now you've had to come to my rescue twice." She shrugged, but I knew she wasn't taking it as casually as she made it seem.

"Okay, well, I've been home more like two and a half weeks, and last time I checked, you've done your fair share of saving me, too."

She shot me a puzzled look.

"You stood up in front of the entire town, and you took my side when you didn't have to. When you knew it was going to cost you. I may have taken a bullet for you, but you took on your dad for me. I'd say that counts us as even for this go-round." A side of my mouth drifted up.

"This go-round?"

"Well, if we were keeping score." I raised my eyebrows. "I can remember a certain episode where you took out my dad's baseball bat and charged Scott Malone to come to my rescue." It was one of my favorite memories of her.

"That hardly counts! You were in a fight with him because of me. Yet another example of you coming to my rescue."

"You were a twelve-year-old girl with a bat. I didn't rescue you; I just gave you time to choose your weapon wisely. Man, you were pissed." I grinned at the memory. The next day I'd broken into her locker and left the knight—the first of our chess pieces.

"Well, yeah, he'd called me an ugly boy and asked why I didn't look more like Charity, and it wasn't the first time. But when he put all that mud in my backpack, I was done." Her cheeks flushed. "Then you flew at him, and what was I supposed to do? Let you take him on? Not with those other boys joining in."

"Exactly. You didn't need saving. You just needed a head start." I laughed.

"Fine, what about that time I got stuck in the pine tree up on your dad's land? You had to climb up for me," she challenged.

"Doesn't count. You were getting the Frisbee I'd thrown, and man, you'd scrambled up there so fast, I didn't even have time to beat you to the tree." I shook my head. "You would have made it if you hadn't gotten your braid caught."

"Fair point. I almost chopped it all off that summer."

"I'm glad you didn't." Shit, I hadn't meant to say that.

Her eyes widened.

I could either back down or own it. What the hell.

"Your hair is beautiful, and I know you like it long. You would have regretted it. Now, when you got gum stuck in it, that's when I thought the scissors were coming out."

She huffed. "I didn't get gum stuck in it. Sullivan dropped it in my hair." Her forehead puckered. "What were we? Ten?"

I nodded. "It was the summer Mom died, so yeah, you were ten."

"She spent an hour getting it out so I wouldn't have to tell my mom," she said softly, a wistful smile sweeping across her face.

"She was pretty amazing like that. Plus, she knew it was my fault, so she was quick to cover for me." I looked up to the picture on the mantel, in which Mom stood smiling with the three of us decked out in ties for her last Mother's Day. Except she hadn't known it was her last.

"How can you possibly blame Sullivan's choice on yourself?" She flat-out glared at me.

"Oh come on, you didn't know?"

"Know what?"

"He only did it because he was mad that we were going out to the hot springs without him. Remember? He didn't finish his chores, so he wasn't allowed to go, and he sure as hell didn't want you going with me." Man, he'd been so jealous, already staking his claim on the girl who hadn't noticed that she was his world.

"Are you serious?" Her nose scrunched. "Oh my God, and you finished his chores while your mom got the gum out," she remembered, looking up at the same picture.

"Yep." Should have seen that as the foreshadowing that it was.

"You were so good to him, Cam. You always put him first, even when I know you missed out on some of the things you wanted." Her eyes met mine, and I knew she wasn't thinking the same thing I was, simply because I'd never told her and she'd never caught on. "That's how I know you never could have set fire to the bunkhouse, you know."

I looked away, scared she'd see right through me to the truth of that day.

"What? Don't think I'm a bored arsonist?" I stared into the fire, remembering the one that had almost consumed her that night. I'd been so damned lucky to find her through the smoke and flames.

"No. I never did. It's not in your nature. Besides, you never would have done anything that put Sully in danger. The torch got knocked over. Accidents happen. I can't believe everyone blamed you, let alone still blames you."

"People need to place blame when things go to shit. Makes them feel like they have control over things they don't. And of course they blamed me." I tossed a smirk at her. "I was there, and therefore it was my fault."

"You were there for me," she said softly. "I lost Sullivan's hand when the beam came down. I thought I was going to…" She paused, taking a deep breath. "I was pretty sure I was hallucinating when I saw you jump the flames, and yet…part of me knew you'd come. Must have been the oxygen deprivation, right?"

"It was just luck that I stumbled onto you." I'd been so fucking scared. Sullivan had come out of the bunkhouse without her, sputtering from the smoke, and my only thought had been to get to Willow.

"It wasn't."

My gaze slowly slid back to hers.

"You weren't in the back like we were, Cam. You weren't finding your way out and happened to come across me. That door led out, and you came through it. You came back in to find me. You saved my life." Her expression softened, and everything in me rebelled. She couldn't look at me like that, like I was some kind of fucking hero for doing the decent thing, the selfish thing when push came to shove.

I hadn't gone after her because it was the right thing to do. I'd gone after her because I couldn't bear the thought of her not existing. I didn't deserve an ounce of her hero worship, not when my motive was pure terror. I wasn't anyone's hero.

"I wasn't there when it mattered." My hands curled into fists. "None of the rest matters when you think about that. I let him down in Afghanistan. I let you down."

She blinked rapidly and looked away for a handful of

heartbeats, but she returned, sadness coming off her in nearly palpable waves. "You didn't let me down," she whispered.

My jaw ticked.

"You didn't," she repeated, leaning toward me but leaving a good foot between us. "It wasn't your fault. Sullivan's death was not your fault."

"You don't know that," I snapped, refusing to even entertain the notion. "You weren't there. You have no clue."

"I do." When others would have flinched and moved away, she stayed, her warmth and compassion holding me captive, torturing me with her sincerity. "I know you. Maybe not as well as I used to, but I know you all the way to your soul, Camden Daniels. If there had been a way to save him, you would have found it. If you could have given your own life for his, you would have. I don't need to have been there to know that." A pair of tears slipped from her eyes, and she quickly swiped at them but still didn't look away.

I wore my grief like armor, a wall I refused to let crumble or weaken.

She wore hers like art, a bold invitation to experience the loss with her, daring you to look away, daring you to forget that he'd lived. He'd loved her.

She'd loved him. How could she not? Everyone did. Sullivan had been charming and funny and made everyone feel like they were important. He was the best of the Daniels boys, and she knew that better than anyone.

"How can you, of all people, possibly forgive me?" I shook my head, trying to dislodge her words. "I sent his squad to hold the line. Even if I didn't know it was his when I relayed that order, I'm the one who got him killed."

"I knew about the order." She swallowed and glanced away before bringing her gaze back to mine. "You didn't know it was him." She stated it as fact rather than questioning me.

I shook my head. "Not until it was already too late." If she knew about the order, did that mean she knew about the choice I'd made, too?

She nodded slowly, as if confirming an idea she hadn't voiced. "I don't forgive you. There's nothing to forgive. You loved Sullivan more than anyone in the world. What happened over there had to have been out of your control, because you would have died with him otherwise. You never would have come home without him." Her voice dropped to a whisper.

"But I did." Somehow my voice made it through the stranglehold of my throat.

"You did." She smiled and swiped away another tear. "So I know there wasn't anything you could have done. I know, Cam. I. Know."

Her words were supposed to bounce off my walls. They were supposed to fall flat with the *I'm so sorry for your loss*es and the *let me know if I can do anything for you*s. Instead those soft, healing words slid right into the mortar of my defenses. Instead of attacking, they simply sat and soaked in.

And when the tension was too much, when it threatened to slice me in half and bleed me out, she didn't push me to accept or even acknowledge her absolution. Instead she leaned back against the couch and simply asked if I still read out loud like I had when we were kids.

So I picked up *East of Eden* from the coffee table, even though I was already halfway through its nearly six hundred pages, and I began at page one.

"The Salinas Valley is in Northern California."

CHAPTER TWELVE

Willow

blinked awake slowly as sunlight streamed in through the picture window, hitting me directly in the face. Sheltering my eyes with a hand, I glanced around the room, the events of last night flooding in.

Right. I was in Cam's living room, stretched out on one of the leather couches with a quilt his mom had made covering me.

He was directly across from me in pretty much the exact same condition on the other couch, but he was still asleep. Both of us had been too stubborn to take his bed, so neither of us had. Taking advantage of this rare moment, I blatantly stared at him, committing every detail to memory.

His lashes rested against his cheeks in thick, dark half-moons. His lips were slightly parted, the full, sculpted lines softening in sleep. He looked a decade younger, relaxed and even content. His tattoos stood out against the white of his T-shirt but blended in with his mom's colorful quilt. Even the ridge in his nose from a break he'd gotten in high school seemed gentler with the giant who wore this body sleeping restfully.

I wanted to paint this moment, to capture this exact feeling as I watched him at peace. A peace I knew would vanish the moment he opened his eyes and the world beat its way in.

Sullivan had been beautiful and charming.

Xander was handsome. Admirable.

But Cam... My heart hurt with how utterly devastating he was. Sure, "gorgeous" was a good word, especially when he opened his eyes, but his appeal was more than that. He was magnetic, which certainly repelled some, but never me. No, he drew me in like gravity, an undeniable, irrefutable force that anchored my world. A decade apart had taught me that I'd never break free of him, not really. It didn't matter where I lived—gravity existed and held my feet to the earth. It didn't matter who I dated—I'd always be drawn to Cam.

Even though he'd never feel the same.

Responsible for me? Yes. He bore that burden by choice. Friendly with me? Sure, when he felt like it. Attracted to me? Eh. Maybe if I ever got out of the sister zone.

But there was one zone I would never get out of—the dead-brother's-girl zone. Nope. That category came with barbed wire, electric fences, and guards called guilt who shot on sight. After last night, I knew I could tell Cam a thousand times that he wasn't responsible for Sullivan's death—it wouldn't matter. Until he forgave himself, there was little I could say about it.

I sighed softly, took one long last look because I knew he couldn't see, and then I quietly left the living room, choosing only the boards I knew from experience wouldn't creak.

There was something to be said for having grown up here, too.

Man, Thea was going to have a field day with this story...if I ever told her. Not that I was hiding it, but she'd want to chat about my feelings. And my feelings were locked up in that whole prickly don't-go-there zone.

I made my way past the dining room and library to the kitchen and surveyed the contents of Cam's fridge.

Bacon. Excellent. Mushrooms. Good. Cheddar. Awesome.

Omelets for breakfast it was.

Once that was decided, I tiptoed down to Cam's bathroom and shamelessly stole the new toothbrush whose mate was already on the counter from the opened pack.

After taking care of all those morning needs and studiously ignoring the mirror, I headed back to the kitchen and started cooking. It was already seven a.m., and knowing Cam, he wouldn't sleep much longer anyway. At least the sun was out and the snow had stopped. Looked like about two, maybe two and a half feet.

I had the bacon fried and crumbled, mushrooms chopped, and eggs whipped when Cam walked in. I dropped a pat of butter in the frying pan and turned to see him watching me.

Oh crap. Sleeping Cam was one thing.

Sleepy Cam was quite another. He cracked a huge yawn, stretching his hands up to the doorframe. His shirt drifted up, revealing so many abs. So. So. So many abs. It was like they'd brought friends along to play or something, because that many ridges couldn't be normal. Nope. He was inhuman.

"Morning, Pika," he said with an easy smile.

And I melted like the butter in the pan. Which was now sizzling.

Also accurate.

Crap.

"I'm making omelets," I said.

"You are," he agreed. "You don't have to, you know. If you give me a second, I'll do it."

"No, I wanted to. Want to," I corrected with a shake of my head. "Mushrooms, bacon, cheddar?"

"Perfect," he answered, but his brow furrowed. "I'll be right back."

He headed toward his bathroom as the smell of burned butter smacked me in the nose.

"Ugh," I groaned, taking the pan off the burner. A tendril of smoke wafted from the pan. Go figure.

Fine. If I was going to be butter, then I was the cold, hard stick in the refrigerator. Yep. Cold and hard. Not soft, not melty, not sizzling, and definitely not burned.

I washed out the pan and set it back on the stove. Then I

started Cam's omelet.

"Please let me help," he said, reappearing in the kitchen, all barefoot and yummy.

"I've got it," I assured him, tending to his breakfast. "Consider it my thank-you for saving me last night." He gave me that weird look again. "What?" I asked.

"I can't remember the last time someone cooked for me," he admitted. "At least not outside a restaurant or something."

"Your girlfriends never make you breakfast?" I could have kicked myself in the face for asking that. My hand clenched the spatula.

"No girlfriends," he said, leaning back against the counter and watching me. "I tend to keep my"—his forehead wrinkled up—"relationships short and breakfast-free."

"Because breakfast equals marriage?" I joked.

"Because letting someone do things for you, letting someone care for you, gives them power. Power's not something I give away."

I stilled.

"What? Does that sound too cold? Too asshole-ish?"

"No," I answered quietly, letting my eyes slowly lift to his. "It sounds lonely."

"Loneliness is a longing, an ache from unmet need for companionship that I don't feel." He shrugged.

"You have needs. You're not a robot." How could he say that?

"Of course I have needs." He smirked. "I'm not a monk."

"That is not what I meant, and you know it." I shook the spatula at him and that stupid little smirk.

"I'll start some toast."

And now my heart was... Nope! I was cold, hard, refrigerator butter.

That Cam was now unwrapping and putting on a butter dish, that was okay. Still cold. Still hard. Still not— "What are you doing?"

He shut the microwave and looked at me with raised eyebrows.

"Relax, Pika. I'm just softening the butter."

My eyes flew wide.

"For toast," he continued slowly. "Okay? Did you have other plans for it?"

"Of course not. It's butter," I said and flipped his omelet to finish it. I cringed when the microwave started. "You know I'm not a little rodent anymore, right?" I quasi-snapped, reaching around him for a plate.

"What?" he questioned, putting bread into the toaster. "Are you okay?"

"I'm fine," I answered quickly, sliding his breakfast onto the plate. "You still call me Pika sometimes." Just like he had since, well, forever.

The microwave beeped, and Cam took out the butter. There was a divot in the center, complete with a little puddle of melted butter. Ugh.

I started my omelet. Maybe once I was fed, I wouldn't be so weirdly emotional. Wanting to first run my fingers along his neck, then strangle him had to be a by-product of being hangry.

"I've always called you Pika."

"Right. But I'm not a bucktoothed little kid with big ears anymore." I evened out the egg and added my fillings.

He laughed, loud and genuine, and my stomach fluttered in hunger pangs. "You think that's why I call you Pika? Is that really what you believe?"

Warmth flushed my cheeks, and I knew it wasn't from the heat of the pan. Great. Now I was turning red.

"Well, yeah. Why else would you call a girl who's basically raised as your little sister a rodent?" I knew it had been a kind of endearment from him. Pet names weren't something that he did, so the fact that I'd had one—and still did—meant something. But Cam had always said he was free to torture me but no one else was allowed to.

It was the same thing he'd said about Sullivan.

I folded my omelet as I heard the first toast pop up. Then the scrape of that softened butter.

"Look at me," he ordered, his voice all gravelly and deep.

I did, arching an eyebrow to hopefully keep him clueless about how absolutely flustered he had me.

"I was five the first time Uncle Cal took me hiking by myself. I'd just done something to piss off my dad, can't even remember what it was now, but Cal told me to get my boots and my jacket, and I did. He'd always taken me with Xander, and Sullivan was still too little, but this time it was just the two of us. He took me up to the boulder slides above this house and told me to sit. So we sat. You're burning your omelet." He pointed to the pan.

"Crap." I flipped it over to the other side and looked at him again, hoping he'd continue, that he wouldn't shut me out and laugh it off.

"So we sat there with the boulders, and I thought he was going to yell at me. Instead, he asked if I wanted to talk about it, and of course I didn't. He didn't make me. He said we could just sit and be still. There was a peace that could come with that if we could master it. And yeah, I'm paraphrasing, because I was five. We sat there so quietly, and this cute little fluffy thing ran out of its hiding place under the boulders and perched on the edge of this rock right next to me."

"A pika," I guessed.

"A pika," he confirmed, turning to grab another plate.

I plated my omelet and moved the pan and spatula to the sink as he buttered the next pieces of toast.

"Uncle Cal told me how rare it was to see one. They usually hide from the bigger predators. He said you have to have three things to see a pika—the right timing, the capability to stay quiet, and the patience to wait."

He was a flurry of activity as he talked, moving plates to the kitchen table, getting silverware, and taking orange juice out of the refrigerator.

"I told him it reminded me of you, all quiet and fluffy and cute." He paused before pressing the first pod into the coffeemaker. "'Not Charity?' he'd asked. You know how they were always shoving us together, hoping we'd be friends."

"You're the same age. My mom and yours used to joke that they'd have to find Xander a good girl for their triple wedding." I rolled my eyes.

Cam scoffed. "Yeah, I was never going to marry Charity. Not in a million years. Not that she's not pretty, or smart, or a friend. She's just..." He paused, his hand on the coffee mug, and my breath held. "Anyway, it stood there—the pika—and it squeaked, and I told Uncle Cal that it was definitely you, because you could get really loud when you were mad."

I smiled, which was probably a little ridiculous, seeing that he was still comparing me to a rodent. But still. A cute, fluffy one.

He stepped forward, and I moved to get out of his way, only to realize I was his way. My back hit the cool granite counter, and I tilted my head to look up—and up—at him. He wasn't touching me or even in my personal space, but it felt like he was everywhere, like he eclipsed the rest of the world behind him.

"So I started calling you Pika. The older I got, the more I learned about them, the more it fit."

"Not because I had really big front teeth."

He shook his head, then slowly took a strand of my braid that had come loose during the night and rubbed it between his thumb and forefinger. "No. Because pikas are elusive. They're only seen when they want to be. They don't hibernate through winter. Instead, they survive under ten or twenty feet of snow, facing each day as it comes."

He moved closer until our bodies brushed but didn't collide. My pulse galloped, racing toward some destination I'd never let myself even contemplate.

"But they can only survive at altitude," he said softly. "They can't endure the heat of the lower elevations. They're made for the mountains. They take the rugged terrain and the cold and the impossible, and they make it home. They survive everything nature says they shouldn't and still stay so soft." He ran his knuckles down the side of my cheek with the last word.

My eyes fluttered shut at the contact. When he reached my jaw, I put my hand over his to hold it there.

A second passed. Two. He didn't move. Neither did I.

I drew in a shaky breath and found the courage to open my eyes, knowing he could be wearing that half smirk, ready with a witty, biting little comment.

Instead, his dark-brown eyes looked just as conflicted as I felt.

"Willow," he whispered, lowering his head inch by slow inch.

"Cam," I replied, refusing to look at those lips descending toward mine for fear I'd break whatever spell we were held in.

"Say no," he pleaded, his words hitting my lips in little huffs of peppermint.

"Yes." It slipped out, that word I'd let dance on the tip of my tongue since I turned sixteen. Maybe even younger, if I was being honest with myself. Maybe even since I understood what that kind of yes meant.

He cursed as my free hand rested on his chest, feeling his heart meet the racing pace of mine.

"Yes, Cam. Yes," I repeated, in case he didn't hear me the first time, knowing full well he did. I'd get him a freaking sign if he needed one.

"Wrong answer," he warned.

A breath later, he kissed me with soft lips that caressed mine gently, almost reverently.

It felt more like a first kiss than my actual first had been. It was the kiss we would have had as much younger, way less experienced teenagers.

Then it happened again and again—light, sipping kisses that had me rising on my toes to get closer to him. He was so tense under my hand, I wondered if he'd snap or shatter.

He pulled back just long enough to look at me, his brow knit together like he was in pain, searching my face for something he didn't name.

I saw the moment he decided. The strain disappeared from his face, and determination took its place.

Then his mouth was on mine, hard and demanding. I parted my lips, and he sank inside to stroke my tongue with his as his hands gripped my hips and lifted.

My fingers threaded into the silk strands of his hair as I kissed him back with everything I had. I wrapped my legs around his waist, locking my ankles like I could hold him prisoner, savoring his groan at the contact.

His kiss held an edge of desperation, and it fueled me, seeking more, faster, deeper. If this was the only time I'd kiss Camden Daniels, then I was going to make damn sure he remembered it, because I would.

We were a mile past electric. Past combustible. Past chemistry or anything that could be explained by science. We simply fit, like two halves of completely different shapes that somehow clicked and became whole and new.

He explored the lines of my mouth, teasing with his tongue, biting gently on my lower lip with sharp teeth. Then, before I could take in a full breath to recover, he was kissing me again, robbing me of every thought besides the absolute wildness he stirred in my veins.

I came alive in his kiss, arching into him, taking as much as he gave and then demanding more. He tasted like peppermint and snowy mornings all tangled together with an edge of fire I knew would burn me if I let him close enough.

He growled my name, and heat answered in my belly as I turned liquid. Whatever he wanted, I'd give him. It was that simple. Because this was Cam.

And he was finally kissing me.

His hands shifted so one arm supported me and the other sent jolts of awareness through every nerve in my body as he trailed his fingers up my spine to cradle the base of my head. Those fingers tightened in a light grip, pulling slightly so my neck arched.

"Cam," I groaned as his lips left mine and sucked a path of kisses down my throat. I was going to die. Right here, right now. There was no way anything got better than this.

His hands gripped me tighter, and—

Ring.

What was...?

Ring.

No cute ringtone for Cam, nope, just the straight-up, jarring blare of an old-school telephone.

He stopped as the third ring sounded, his lips open against the base of my neck. He lifted his glazed eyes to mine on the fourth, then blinked, and just like that, the spell was broken. A flare of panic, of regret widened his eyes.

No. No. No. It was over too soon.

My heart lurched as he set me on the counter, and his arms slackened, letting me go. I fought every instinct to keep him close, to fight his withdrawal, but I uncrossed my ankles, and he literally slipped through my fingers as he retreated.

My body still hummed at a frequency only Cam knew as he reached to adjust a hat he wasn't wearing. As if realizing that, he stared at his empty hands and shook his head.

"Cam," I said, hopping down.

"No." He backed away. "What was I...?"

That hum died a little.

"I can't touch you," he muttered. "Not like that."

"Yes, you can," I assured him. It probably sounded like a plea. Whatever. I didn't care. If it brought him back to my arms, I'd say whatever he needed.

"No," he repeated, looking anywhere but at me. "I can't."

"It was just a kiss." But it wasn't. It was deeper, and we both knew it.

"And what happens when it's more?" he challenged, his eyes clashing with mine for a heartbeat. "Did you feel that?"

"Of course I did, and more is fine! Wonderful, in fact!"

"You. Don't. Mean. That."

"Don't tell me what I mean. I know what I want." I always had. I'd simply been too scared to say it. To reach for it. I'd always known the chances were I could have him like this once but never twice. Even if I let myself slip twice, he never would. And that's what he would see this as. A slip. A mistake.

"Then, you're wrong. There's no way in hell you could want this," he snapped and gestured between us.

"Because you don't? I'm only allowed to want what you do?" I wrapped my arms around my torso, suddenly cold. It was like heat that had been coming off my very skin had simply vanished, leaving me chilled and empty.

"I don't? Are you kidding me right now? You think any of this has to do with what I want?" He shook his head.

"It doesn't?" I sagged against the counter, shriveling a little. It had been about what I wanted. I never gave him the opportunity to say no. Had he really only kissed me because he'd known I'd wanted him to?

No, he wanted me. Any idiot could see that. Athletic pants weren't exactly helpful in the camouflage department.

"Hell no. Willow, I lost any say, any right to even…" His fingers gripped his hair for the longest breath I'd ever held. Then he dropped them to his sides, leaving his hair standing on end.

I took a breath when he did.

"I chose Sullivan's squad," he finally said, rasping the words. "There were two there, and I chose his."

"But you didn't know it was his squad. Making a choice doesn't change that."

That same determination I'd seen earlier flashed in his eyes, but this time it was a warning. "I brought him home in a box. I was with him when he bled out."

"Don't," I whispered. The chill was changing, becoming voracious and numbing. The sensation started at my toes and rose up in waves that fed on my joy, my want, even my stupid longing, then froze them out to nothingness.

"You should know." Pain laced every word, raw and bitter. "It's one thing to think you forgive me, but you should know what he looked like in my arms. How I tried to get the bleeding to stop, but he'd been shot in the neck. Clipped his jugular just enough to make it slower. I couldn't even see where the rest of the blood was going. And the medic was coming, just not fucking fast enough."

Thoughtless. I was empty of everything, even thoughts, as he spewed the story I'd never been told. Never deemed strong enough for the details.

"I ripped off his helmet, and Vasquez—one of my guys—tried to plug the hole in his neck. But Sully's hair...it didn't look as blond as before. It was darker, closer to mine, and I remember thinking that was wrong. That he was supposed to be good, like Xander. He couldn't turn into me. Stupid, right? Because he was turning into nothing right before my eyes, and I could only sit there with his head in my lap."

My lip started to tremble.

"I knew he was going. There was so much blood. They'd never medevac him out fast enough, not while the outpost was still under attack. I took over holding the pressure on the wound and told Vasquez to fire from Sullivan's position. And I told Sully, 'You have to live. You have to. Willow's waiting. Dad's waiting. You gotta hold on.' I knew what it would do to Dad. To Xander...to you."

I swallowed the whimper that came without permission, tears pricking my eyes.

"And..." He looked away, his face contorting into lines of rage and grief and restraint.

"Tell me," I begged in a whisper.

"That's enough. You don't want..." He shook his head.

"Tell me!" I shouted. "Don't you dare hold anything back or hide it from me. I deserve to know!"

His eyes slammed shut for a breath. Two. Three. Then they opened and locked on mine.

"It was hard for him to talk. His airway... It was hard. And when he did, it was between these horrid, gasping breaths. He said, 'Cam. It's really you. Take me home.' He begged me to take him home! And we were sitting there in a filthy combat outpost I didn't even know was his, in the middle of a fucking firefight I'd sent him into, and I couldn't do shit to save my little brother. And when..." Cam sucked in a breath and gripped the back of the kitchen chair like it would anchor him. "When he slipped away, it was Mom's name he called, like he could see her or something. His pulse stopped thrumming against my fingers, and his blue eyes...the pupils... He was just gone. It was two minutes at most. I sat there holding him just like I did that one time he skidded down that last switchback at the ravine and tore his back up when we were kids. Remember?"

"I remember," I whispered. We'd been nine. Sullivan hadn't listened and had run ahead. Cam had been eleven and was blamed. Cursed out by his dad when we got Sullivan back to the house.

"I was covered in his blood, holding onto this husk that used to be Sullivan, so angry, and empty, and even envious. I wanted it to be me."

"Cam, no." I made my legs obey and took a step, but he backed even farther away.

"I begged God to let me trade places. To take me instead of Sullivan, but you know He didn't want anything to do with me. Sully was good and kindhearted and stubborn and didn't have a mean bone in his body. He deserved to live." A tear tracked down Cam's face, disappearing into his beard, and I doubted he even felt it.

"He did." I nodded. "He deserved to live, and he was all those things and more. But, Cam, you deserved to live, too."

"No!" he shouted, throwing his hands out like he'd shake his own head if he could. "Not like he did. Not when he had everyone to come home to."

"So did you!"

"You honestly think anyone would have looked at Sullivan on the day of my funeral and told him that it should have been him in that box?" His eyes narrowed.

"Your dad had no right to say that." I shook my head. My fingertips ached with the need to pull Cam close. To go back to that day and stand beside him instead of across from him. To have said the things I wanted to instead of the things I was supposed to.

"He had every right. Sullivan was dead. I should have saved him. I should have sent the other squad to hold the perimeter. Should have taken his place myself. Realized what combat outpost we'd been called in for. I should have held his wound tighter. Had them transfuse me immediately. I should have shot him in the fucking foot the minute he decided to enlist. There are a million things I could have done and a million things I did do that more than earned me that pine box we buried him in."

"Camden, stop."

"Still think I did everything I could have, Willow? I sat there and let the love of your life bleed out all over me."

"You didn't." The words were as weak as I felt, and the icy hand of fear wrapped around my throat, waiting for Camden to make me clarify that statement.

"I did. And you think you want these hands"—he held them palms out—"on you? The same hands that reached inside Sullivan and felt the life drain out of him?"

"That's not fair."

"News flash. None of this is fair. None of what's happened to you is fair, and you deserve someone better."

My head snapped like I'd been struck. "Better? How can you possibly say that?"

"Jesus, you need more? When he died, I was jealous as hell that he got to see our mom first. She was the only person who loved me just as much as Sully or Xander. I was jealous of my dying brother! And angry. So angry!"

"That's nothing to be ashamed of."

Ring.

"Oh yeah? I was angry at the world. Angry at that asshole with the gun on the other side of the wall. Angry that Dad let him enlist. Angry that Xander sat in a cushy office while I held Sullivan. Angry that you hadn't talked him into staying with you."

I blanched. "I know."

Ring.

"No, you don't. I was most angry at Sullivan, because he had the right I would have died for and never even used it. Because when he passed, it was Mom's name on his lips, when I knew mine would have been yours."

I sucked in air on reflex, but every other muscle in my body stilled. Someone pressed the pause button, and we stood suspended in a moment when not even my heart dared to beat.

Ring.

"What?" Camden shouted into the phone.

My heart pounded. My head felt light, almost detached from my body. I stumbled backward until I felt the counter and then shamelessly used it to keep me upright when my knees threatened to give out.

"When?" His gaze darted to the clock on the wall. "Shit. I'll be there in seven minutes." He hung up and left the kitchen without another word, making a beeline for the garage.

I opened the door that had just slammed in my face and ignored the assault of cold air on my bare knees.

"Cam, what's going on?"

He moved quickly, gearing up to ride.

"Cam!"

He flinched but didn't stop dressing. "My dad's had an accident.

Xander found him in the garage. He must have been trying to leave, because the car was on but the door was shut." Cam shoved his feet into a set of wool socks from the locker and then into his riding boots.

"Oh God. What do you need?"

His eyes jerked up to mine. "What?"

"What do you need me to do? Do you want me to go? Should I call the hospital to send an air ambulance? What?"

He blinked twice. "Medevac is on the way. If I leave now, I should make it to Dad's in time." He stood and zipped up his coat, then reached for his helmet as I grabbed his gloves. "Just stay here. Where I know you're not freezing to death out there." His face disappeared beneath the helmet, and he snapped it on.

I handed him the gloves and grabbed his arm as he turned to leave.

"Be careful," I said clearly, looking at my own eyes reflecting back in the visor. "Camden, I care if you get hurt. So be careful."

He nodded once and left me standing in his socks, his... everything as he took the snowmobile out and headed to his dad's.

I glanced around the garage, my eyes landing on the Bobcat with a very lovely plow attached to the front. At least I wasn't helpless.

Walking into the living room, I saw Cam's wallet on the coffee table and groaned.

Guess it was time to dig myself out.

CHAPTER THIRTEEN

Camden

The mountain flew by in a whir of white snow and blue sky, dotted by pine trees and the skeletons of winterized aspens as I raced down the mountain. Adrenaline pumped through my veins, a familiar and welcome friend. The snow had already crusted, the result of the overnight freeze.

Why didn't I pick up the phone the first time? I could have been there by now, not trying like hell to beat the air ambulance team.

I knew exactly why. Because I'd had my hands full of Willow. The phone had ripped me out of whatever ridiculous daydream I'd been in and dropped me on my ass in the real world.

The world where I would never be able to touch Willow like that again.

The world where Dad left the car running in the garage.

I took the final turn a little too fast and skidded almost to the edge of the drive, just shy of the switchback drop-off. *Pay attention.*

A half minute later, I killed the engine in front of the garage, where Xander hovered over Dad, compressing his chest in rhythmic beats, pausing only to deliver rescue breaths.

I ripped off my helmet and let it fall, already running into the garage. "What are you doing?"

"What does it look like?" Xander asked, up on his knees with his hands locked over Dad's chest.

"Why is he still in here?" God, I could still smell the exhaust even though the truck was clearly off.

"I can't get leverage in that much snow." Xander nodded toward the driveway.

"He can't stay in here." I quickly assessed the garage and moved, spotting a full length of plywood. It came free of the wood stack easily, and I silently thanked my dad for being a type A… whatever he was. It scraped the floor as I slid it toward Dad, then dropped it to cover a section of the concrete.

"Help me," I ordered and crouched facing Dad's head. His weight was inconsequential as I lifted him beneath his arms, and Xander got under his hips. We carried him onto the plywood, then each took an end without discussion and brought him to the fresh air.

The board broke the crust of last night's snow as we knelt on either side of him. When Xander moved to start compressions again, I grabbed his hands. "Wait."

"What?" he snapped.

I rested my fingers on Dad's pulse and felt the beat.

"His heart is beating. You'll do more damage than good if you keep compressions. He's in respiratory failure, not cardiac arrest."

"So breathe."

"Breathe," I confirmed as the distant beat of rotor wings reached my ears. "They're almost here."

Xander tipped Dad's head back and continued rescue breaths as I scrambled to my feet and surveyed the terrain. The flattest area with the fewest trees was directly behind the house. Sure enough, a minute—maybe two—later, the helicopter appeared over the house, blowing a fine layer of snow into the air but not much more.

The snow from last night was too heavy to kick up.

They landed right around where I figured they would, and two EMTs rushed out, only to be immediately slowed as they were faced with snow up to their knees.

"He's this way," I shouted to be heard over the rotors, then led them around the house to the driveway. "He's in respiratory arrest. My brother found him by the steps there, with the garage door cracked but not fully open and the car engine going. He's fifty-eight years old, okay health, but has early-onset Alzheimer's."

"Got it," the guy answered as he and his teammate dropped to examine Dad.

He wasn't breathing. The situation in its entirety hit me. He. Wasn't. Breathing.

He should be dead. How the hell was he alone? How did he have access to the keys?

Xander stumbled over to me, still wearing his riding gear as the paramedics evaluated Dad, one of them already putting a rescue bag over his nose and mouth.

"God, Cam. I just went down to check on John Royal. He's trying to get the power grid back online at Alba Electric." He ran his hands over his hair. "Dad was asleep, and I thought I could make it back before he got up."

He couldn't have called John instead? I kept my mouth shut, though, because I hadn't been here, either. Dad had been alone.

"I should have been here."

"He wasn't going to let you in, and you know it. He wasn't himself last night. Thought I was Cal."

The paramedics moved Dad over to the stretcher.

He still wasn't breathing on his own.

My stomach turned over, chill infusing my flesh instantly. "Oh shit. Xander, this isn't what he wants."

"You don't think I know that? Like he'd ever want to lose his mind to the point that he can't open a garage door?" Xander shook his head.

"No, I mean, he doesn't want to be resuscitated." And I'd helped. I'd fucking helped. I'd been so blinded in my need to save him that I hadn't even paused to remember his wishes.

"Don't start this shit," Xander snapped.

"Xander, they're loading Dad onto that chopper. He's not breathing on his own. You have to speak for him. He trusts you!" I turned, getting in his face. Our heights were comparable, but we both knew I could take him in a fight. Hell, it was the one thing I was good at.

My ability to build shit was always secondary to my capability for destroying it.

"Are you ready for our dad to die?" he challenged as the paramedics started the hike back up to the chopper and we followed.

"Of course not! You think anyone is ready for that?"

"What do you want me to do, Cam? Tell them 'never mind, he wants to die here'?" He gestured to the house.

Shit. Yes. No. I wasn't ready. If Dad died, he'd never know that I hadn't been told it was Sullivan's base. That while I was responsible for Sullivan's death, I hadn't known it when I made the choice. That I'd only recognized Sully seconds before I saw him get hit. I'd never have a chance to repair everything broken about us.

"Yeah, it's not so easy once you're the one making the choices, is it?" Xander shouted. "He has carbon monoxide poisoning. It's not a long-term situation. They just need to get him breathing again, and we'll bring him home. This isn't what Dad meant, if you're so certain he even meant it."

"I'm certain!" We were right under the blades, and the words felt sharper than the metal slicing through the air.

"Sir? We can take one of you with us, but not both!" the paramedic called from the doors.

"I'm coming!" Xander replied and immediately started toward the bird.

I gripped his arm, which earned me a glare.

"For God's sake, Cam, I have to go!"

"I asked him! Last week, we had lunch and I asked him. He meant it, Xander!"

Xander wrenched his arm from my gloved grasp and climbed into the helicopter without another word.

"We're taking him to Salida!" the paramedic said.

I nodded, and he shut the doors. Knowing I needed to move, I turned and made my way back down to the house. Midway there, the helicopter was airborne, flying east down the pass.

Only my heavy breaths and what had to be a bass drum beating in my chest punctuated the silence once I reached the driveway.

The plywood in the center of the snow-covered space was the only evidence of what had just occurred. Xander had resuscitated Dad, and I had helped. Disgust filled my mouth, the taste so bitter that I almost vomited.

Two hours later, I walked into Heart of the Rockies, the closest hospital. It was a Level IV trauma center, so knowing that Dad had been admitted and not transferred was a good omen. That and the fact that he wasn't dead yet were definitely marks in the positive column.

I'd had to call to get that tidbit of information, seeing as I'd found Xander's phone on the garage floor. It had taken me an hour and a half to get the drive plowed with Dad's quad, and I was lucky that the truck had enough gas in it to get down the pass to Salida, since my wallet was currently MIA.

Sure, it would only take a phone call to know that I'd left it at home, but the idea of talking to Willow after everything that had gone down this morning was enough to make me debate switching to the ostrich approach to life.

"ICU?" I asked at the front desk.

She directed me, and I quickly made my way through the sterile halls, my boots leaving muddy footprints on the pristine floors.

I knew mine would have been yours. What the hell had I been thinking to say that to her? Why couldn't I stop it from replaying in my head? With everything going on with Dad, why had my brain decided to cling to that little morning fuckup?

Because you've wanted to say it for the last ten years, you moron. I promptly told my inner idiot to shut the hell up as I arrived at the ICU.

"Arthur Daniels?" I asked the nurse in blue-and-yellow-star scrubs.

"Family?" she questioned, only glancing up at me before continuing to enter data into a computer.

"Son."

"Three sixteen," she responded. "His other son is with him right now. Your brother?"

"That would be Alexander."

She smiled. "Alexander. Got it."

I shook my head and walked in the direction of the rising room numbers. Of course she'd want to know his name. She was young and pretty, and Alexander was a charmer.

I saw his boots in the doorway first; then the rest of him came into view as he leaned against the frame. He'd ditched the riding gear and looked way more responsible in his jeans and sweater than I did in my athletic pants and hoodie. Whatever. Emergencies didn't allow time for fashion.

"Cam," he said in relief, a ghost of a smile appearing. "I'm so sorry. I left my phone—"

I retrieved the device from my pocket and handed it to him.

"Thanks. I'm sorry they couldn't fit both of us. I saw that drive. How long did it take you to get it clear?" He scrolled through his messages, which had to be more than a few dozen, if the way that thing had vibrated was any indicator. It could have gotten a woman off with half as many alerts.

"It's fine. How is he?"

"Docs are with him now," he said, looking back over his shoulder. "We should get an update in a second."

I stepped into the doorway and saw scrubs and white coats

leaned over Dad, obscuring my line of sight as monitors beeped. But that whooshing sound…

Pushing past Xander, I felt the extent of what they'd done punch me in the gut.

I stared in horror as the blue accordion rose and fell, and when the doctors all lifted their heads, Dad's face came into view.

How could he? I swung around, took Xander by the shoulders, and pushed him to the wall opposite Dad's doorway.

"Hey!" one of the docs shouted.

"How could you do that to him? How?" I shouted at my brother as his eyes widened.

"It's okay!" he replied, but not to me. No, his arm half extended at my waist, no doubt holding off the staff that was ready to rip the violent brother off the good one.

"It's not okay," I seethed. "You knew he didn't want that, and you let them put him on a ventilator? He wants a DNR, you asshole!" My fingertips bit into the slight muscle of his shoulders. Feeling the give, I relaxed my grip and took a shaky breath to quell the rage flooding my body. "You knew."

"I'm sorry," an older doctor with perfectly silver hair said calmly, as if he hadn't seen me take Xander to the drywall. "Did you say that Mr. Daniels has a DNR?"

"No," Xander replied just as calmly, not moving an inch. To the outside world, he probably looked like the composed gentleman he was, attempting to divert attention.

But I knew better. He knew he was cornered by a predator—by me—and the minute he moved before explaining himself, I'd put his ass right back on the wall.

"He does not?" the doctor confirmed, flipping through the chart.

"No, he doesn't. You'll have to excuse my brother's outburst. It's been a very emotional day for us both, and my father apparently told Camden that he was thinking about a DNR, but we hadn't ascertained his state of mind when making that request. It's hard to tell with Dad these days. He looks and speaks normally, but he might be in the wrong year or not even have a clue what his own name is."

"Don't apologize for me," I said quietly before turning my attention to the doc. "Dr. Taylor," I addressed him after reading the embroidery on his white coat. "I'm sorry you saw that. I'm Camden Daniels, and my father told me both last week and last month that he wanted a DNR, so I'm just a little furious with my brother for allowing him to be intubated." I tapped into the headspace I used when the mission overruled emotion, the space that had kept me alive for the last decade.

The doctor glanced between us, observing quickly and nodding. "This is a complicated matter, and I can respect that both of you must be at your limit. However, I can't allow that to happen again on my floor. Understand?" Two figures in blue appeared behind the doc. They'd obviously called security.

"Yes, sir," I replied, momentarily kicking myself for allowing my temper to hit so hot. At least I stopped myself from grinning at the guards. As if they could actually physically remove me.

"Good. I wouldn't want to have to ask either or both of you to leave."

"You won't," Xander promised, slipping me a sideways glance that I didn't meet. Fuck him. He let them put a tube down Dad's throat.

"Okay, I'll give you guys two minutes, and then if you'd like to join me in your dad's room, I'll have an update." He waited until we both nodded and then disappeared.

The guards didn't.

"Unbelievable," I seethed.

"I could say the same thing," Xander snapped under his breath. "We're not kids anymore, Cam. I barely kept you out of jail the last time you were here. It took me giving Hudgens ridiculous boardwalk space in the historical district to keep him from pressing charges."

I might not have winced outwardly, but the emotional blow hit its mark. "You could have pressed them, too."

"I would never, and you know it. I love you. You're my little brother. There's nothing I wouldn't do for you. But we're adults now, and I can't shield you from every consequence." His entire posture softened. "Cam, you gotta work with me here."

"You let them put a tube down his throat." I reached for my hat and cursed inwardly yet again when one wasn't there. At least when I was on a mission, the weight of the Kevlar grounded me, took away that one nervous tell I'd never been able to get rid of out of uniform.

"Yeah, I did. It was that or let him die. Don't even say it. I'm well aware that you would have let him die."

"I hope that I would have given him what he wanted, no matter how hard it would have been. But you know what? Up at the house, I helped you. I'm partially responsible for this, and that makes me sicker than anything. I get it, Xander. I do. I don't want to lose Dad. Doesn't matter how mean that asshole is or how deep his loathing of me goes, I want every possible second I can get to turn it around."

"So you agree with me?" Wrinkles appeared in his forehead and at the corners of his eyes.

"No. I don't. I'm saying that emotion can override logic in the moment. I'm saying that you need to take a good long look at the possibility that you're letting your emotional needs trump Dad's God-given right to say what happens to his own body. It's his. Not yours. Not mine."

"He's not capable of deciding anymore, and I'm doing the best I can." His entire face fell, and his mouth twisted.

"I know you are. That's what makes this so damned hard. Now, let's go hear what the doc has to say."

"You're not going to rip the tube out of his throat?" Xander questioned with a sad tone but sarcastic rise of his eyebrows.

"Sure, right after I unplug the ventilator and strike a victory pose. Of course I'm not. I told him I'd help him keep it from happening; we didn't exactly talk about what to do once it was already done."

His hand lifted to my shoulder, but where mine had no doubt left bruises on his skin, his gently grasped mine. "Okay, let's get in there."

We stood side by side at the foot of Dad's bed while Dr. Taylor filled us in. Dad still wasn't breathing on his own, but they'd had success with hyperbaric chambers, so that was the next course of action.

They'd have a full team with him because of the ventilator, but complications were rare as long as they were careful, and the higher oxygen was his best shot.

He'd already had a chest X-ray and EKG, both of which were promising but not stellar. Blood work was on its way back from the lab, since it had been a few hours, and the pulse oxygen wasn't as accurate this far out from the incident.

"Was this suicidal?" Dr. Taylor asked, looking between us. "I need to ask."

"I don't... No. It can't be." Xander shook his head.

"It's not," I answered. "I found the garage door dented. My guess is he tried to back out with the door shut and disengaged it. That's why it wouldn't open with the button." I turned to Xander. "You found him by the steps to the house, right?"

"Yes." He nodded.

"And I'm guessing you had to hand lift that garage door?"

"I did," he confirmed. "That makes sense."

"Not suicidal, Doc. Just demented." I gripped the base of Dad's bed when I saw the soft restraints they'd Velcroed over his forearms, fastening them to the arm rails.

"He's not going to hurt anyone," Xander protested.

"They're more for his personal safety than ours," Dr. Taylor assured us. "We'll bring him back soon."

Xander and I sat in relative silence once they wheeled Dad

out. We stared at each other for an awkward minute before he pulled his phone out and muttered that he had things he needed to check on.

I fired off a text message to Willow. It was less than she deserved but more than I'd thought I was capable of.

Cam: Sorry for running out. Dad has carbon monoxide poisoning. He's in Salida in the ICU. Xander and I are with him.

Partly a lie, since running out was the most self-preservationist thing I could have done, but I'd left her stranded at my house. I tapped the side of my phone, waiting for the three dots to stop on her side and a message to appear.

Willow: I'm so sorry. Just saw Walt and gave him your wallet. I'll make sure he knows. What else can I do for you? Need lunch?

Leave it to Willow to ask how she could help after I pretty much slaughtered her this morning. I looked at the clock. Holy shit, it was already after noon.

Cam: I'm okay. You saw Walter?

Willow: Pretty sure I just said that.

Had Walt gone up to the house? Not likely, given that the power outage had hit the hotel, too.

Cam: Are you still at the house?

Willow: I'm at my house. I live here and all.

Cam: How?

I'd taken the Cat, and there was no way my Jeep was taking on that snow. On the plains, maybe, but not on the mountain.

Willow: A girl's gotta save herself. I'm not a helpless damsel 24-7, you know.

Cam: I'm aware, Pika.

Shit. I'd hit send before my brain caught up. Definitely had not meant to call her that, especially now that she knew why I did.

Which was probably what she was thinking about, considering the fact that she left me on read for a good two minutes. Wasn't I turning out to be a needy little prick?

I knew mine would have been yours.

Maybe she thought I meant if I had been Sullivan, then my last words would have been about her. Not that I'd say them. There was a slight possibility...right?

But what if she knew? What if my lack of self-control let her in on the secret I'd kept as long as I could remember? What if years of keeping my mouth shut had all been for nothing and now she hated me? Or worse, thought I was capable of acting on it? I wasn't capable, and even if I was, the town wouldn't accept it. She'd be miserable either way.

"You okay?" Xander asked.

"What?" My head shot up. "Yeah, why?"

"You look...constipated."

My eyes narrowed a fraction, and he looked away. Then I almost dropped my phone when it alerted me to her text. *Total Green Beret material here.* Good thing I'd gotten out if I was going to turn into a jittery mess over a woman.

Not just any woman, though.

Willow: Thank you for updating me. I was worried about you.

Willow: And your dad, of course.

Willow: I'll check on you later.

Willow: Unless you don't want me to.

Willow: I'm putting my phone away now.

I laughed, which earned me another odd look from Xander. At least I wasn't the only one struggling. Not that I wanted to fluster her, but at least I wasn't solo in the WTF department.

Cam: Okay. I'll talk to you later. Thank you for my omelet.

Willow: You didn't get to eat it.

Cam: The thought meant more than the food.

Three dots blinked for a few minutes, then stopped, but no other text message appeared. I would have traded a year of my life to know what she'd typed and deleted.

• • •

"Hey," Walt called from the doorway in a whisper.

I held up my finger, then checked to make sure Dad was still sleeping and crept past Xander's outstretched legs from where he was passed out on Dad's other side.

"How are you doing?" Walter asked me once I made it into the hallway and shut the door.

"About as well as you'd expect." I ran my hands over my face. How was it only eight p.m.? It felt like it had been years since I'd woken up across from Willow.

"Okay, then how is Art?"

"He's doing better than this morning. Probably needs another couple sessions in the hyperbaric chamber. Still hasn't woken up yet, and he's not capable of breathing on his own. There's some serious lung damage they're hoping to reverse."

"Not capable..." Walt's face fell. "Did Xander put him on a ventilator?"

"Yeah."

Walter's eyes slammed shut, and his mouth flattened as he took a deep breath, then another.

"It's my fault, too," I admitted.

"What?" He visibly startled.

"When I got to the house, I helped drag him out and told Xander to stop chest compressions because his heart was pumping. I told him he only needed rescue breaths." I folded my arms across my chest.

"And you think that led to him being on life support?" he questioned.

"I didn't say anything to Xander until the paramedics already had Dad and were loading him on the chopper. I should have said something from the beginning."

We stepped apart as a medical team came through the hallway, and I saw Simon hovering near the waiting room down the hall. I offered a wave, and he sent one back.

"It's nice to see Simon," I told Walt. The guy looked good.

Happy. Just like his dad.

"He wanted to give us a few minutes before 'barging in,' as he put it," Walt explained, waving to his son. "It's understandable that you told Xander how to save him. Understandable that you helped save him. It would be understandable if you were okay with that ventilator. That's your father in there. No one is going to fault you for wanting him to live." He slung a small duffel bag from his shoulder. "Your girl dropped this off and asked that I bring it for you. Sorry it took so long. Took Royal until this afternoon to get the power back up. I swear that system hasn't been upgraded in the last fifty years. It's a miracle we're not all on nob and tube."

He handed the duffel over, and I took it, recognizing it as one of my lesser-used ones I'd stashed at the top of my closet.

"She's not my girl," I muttered. "Thank you for bringing it to me."

"Willow Bradley has always been your girl, Camden. Doesn't imply any romance." He arched an eyebrow.

"Right." I swung the bag over my shoulder and unzipped it. She sent sneakers and a few sets of fresh clothes that varied from athletic gear to jeans to a pair of pressed khakis and dress shoes. I laughed as I brought out a Ziploc bag full of cookies.

God, she's amazing.

"Yeah, she sure is. Said she owed you or something, since breakfast got ruined?"

Shit, I'd said that out loud.

There was a sparkle he couldn't contain in his eye when I looked up. "I pulled her out of a snowdrift and took her to my house. It's not like that."

"I never said it was," he replied, outright smiling. "I'm also not as blind as the rest of the men in your family." That stare turned pointed.

"Should I be insulted?" I dropped the cookies into the duffel.

"Hardly. You Daniels boys were always a little thick when it came to seeing things you didn't want to. Your mama knew what was what, though. Especially when it came to the Bradley girl."

"Why would you—?"

Chaos broke out behind me.

"Help!" Xander shouted. I was through the door before he finished the word.

Dad thrashed on the bed, his eyes open and wild, panic obvious in every line of his face. Xander was almost on top of him, struggling to keep his arms down.

"Cam! Help, he's trying to rip out the trach!" he shouted.

"Get the doc!" I ordered Walt, then dropped the bag and ran to the other side of Dad. "Dad, stop," I pleaded.

He met my eyes, and his flared with recognition. Then he screamed, a distorted, horrifying, barely audible sound, around the tube that pushed his air.

Seeing Xander losing, I pushed down on Dad's biceps as he flailed, fighting the intubation and arching his neck.

"I'm making it worse!"

"Don't stop! He'll rip it out, and his lungs can't handle it yet!" Xander argued.

Dad slipped free and made contact with Xander's chest, shoving him into the cabinet of medical supplies right behind him.

The strength I'd always been so proud of had now become a liability in a way I'd never imagined.

"Dad! Stop!" I shouted as he reached for the tracheotomy tube. God, he was going to have to go through it all again if he ripped it out. Xander would make them put it back in.

I gripped his wrists in each hand and forced them to the side of his head as the medical team barreled in.

The look in Dad's eyes said it all. I was the enemy who had betrayed him, and in this moment, he was right. It didn't matter if he was lucid in there or if he thought I was fifteen or twenty-eight—I was the bad guy here.

My heart shredded and bled out with each attempt he made to break free, until orders were shouted and a nurse slipped something into his IV line.

Xander came around to my side, since his was occupied by the medical team, and leaned over the bed rails. "Dad, it's okay. It's okay. It's okay," he repeated in a calm tone.

Dad looked at Xander, his eyes softening. Good—the drugs they gave him were taking effect.

Then they came back to me, and all the fires of hell were aimed in my direction until Dad lost consciousness, his body going limp beneath my hands.

"It's okay. He's out," the doc assured me.

I let go of his wrists and blanched at the red marks I'd left on his skin.

Xander reached around me and brought Dad's arm back down to the restraint as the doc did the same on the other side.

"I told you these were for his protection," Dr. Taylor said sternly.

"I'm sorry," I apologized for Xander, knowing full well that he'd been the one to undo the restraints. Most likely while I'd been with Walter.

Xander remained silent.

"Now, my shift is over and I'm going home. Do I need to worry?" Dr. Taylor asked me directly.

"No, sir."

"I won't ask you a third time. I'll simply ban you."

"You won't have to," I promised.

The doc stared me down pretty bravely for a guy I could end in about a heartbeat, then nodded and left, taking all but one nurse with him.

"I'm sorry," Xander said, running his hands over his hair. "I undid them, thinking he looked so uncomfortable, and after I finished the second one, I glanced up, and his eyes were open, and he started thrashing."

The nurse looked up from her chart but didn't say anything.

My chest rose in even breaths, at war with the raging thoughts that circled my brain. I'd just had to hold down my dad for the very thing he'd begged me not to do. I jeopardized what truce we had, assuming he was lucid, and once again was the devil to Xander's perfection.

"This is why he didn't want this," I said softly, menace bleeding into my words despite my attempts to chill. "That right there. Everything that just happened?" I put my hand on Xander's chest and pushed lightly until he moved out of my way. "That's on you."

I didn't pause to comfort him or address his ashy appearance. Nope, I let him stew in the shit he'd caused.

Never again would I be on the wrong side, no matter how legally right. Never again would I let myself get put into that kind of situation. Never again would I let Dad wake up in absolute terror and restraints.

I grabbed my duffel and headed out to the hallway, where Walt waited with tears in his eyes.

"You saw?" I asked.

He nodded.

"I'm going to need Simon's help."

CHAPTER FOURTEEN

Willow

"You know, you could always move back to civilization and come into the office," Matt Wilson cajoled over FaceTime as I walked down Gold Creek Drive, headed for Charity's.

"Yeah, I think not," I declined with a smile. "Remember when we were at Rutgers and I told you I was going back to Alba and staying there?"

He adjusted his tie and laughed. "I remember. You know Vaughn Holdings loved the graphics for the new campaign, right?"

"I do remember hearing that. Good morning, Mrs. Dawson," I said to Genevieve as she came down the sidewalk toward me.

"Willow," she replied, more venom than sugar. "We're all just so excited to see the plans this week. Would be a shame if all that hoopla with Art got in the way, wouldn't it?"

I stilled, looking past Matt's face to Genevieve's... Wait, was she glowering at me? "I'm sorry, you mean his whole just-got-off-life-support hoopla?"

She rolled her eyes. "You'd better talk to your boyfriend, and that's all I'm going to say. But if you think this town is going to sit around and watch poor Art get exploited by that boy, well, that's not going to happen. I've said my piece."

"My boyfriend? Cam?" I guessed. "Because we're not—"

"Oh, don't you play coy. You always were more loyal to those Daniels boys than your own family. But that's all I'm going to say."

She disappeared into her jewelry store, leaving my mouth wide open.

"So, was that really all she was going to say, or is she coming back for an encore?" Matt asked.

"I have no idea. That's Genevieve Dawson for you." I noted several glares as I made my way down the street. What the hell was going on?

"And that's the town you want to live in? Seriously. Come to Denver. You don't get views like this." He turned the phone, showing the skyline of downtown Denver. "Come on, you deserve to sit through the meetings where clients rave about your work."

"This is home, Matt. Where I have my family and friends and views like this." I turned my own camera, shooting him the snowcapped peaks against a crisp blue sky. "You take the credit. It's never been about the applause for me."

"Or is it about the boyfriend?"

The thought of Cam sent a rush of emotion tumbling through me like an uncoordinated circus. "No boyfriend. Look, I have to go. I just got to my sister's place. Send me over the client's wish list, and I'll get started on that new design."

"You got it. Steer clear of the big-haired lady. We need you intact."

"Ha-ha." I hung up with him as I walked into Mother Lode.

Charity was at the tail end of a staff meeting, so I nodded to her and sat at a table. It had been a week since Art's accident. He was off the ventilator and recovering, but I only knew that from a few of Cam's text messages.

I hadn't seen him or heard his voice since he'd hopped on the snowmobile and taken off. I also hadn't said a word about what happened between us. Not to Cam. Not to Thea. Not to Walt when he took me up to the mine, since Cam was on a weird schedule with Xander, both watching over their dad in shifts.

His words were eating me alive.

"What's up?" Charity asked as the last of her staff filtered out.

I looked at my sister and tried to find the words, but instead,

I ended up doing a weird fish-out-of-water thing where basically I just opened and shut my mouth a bunch. Finally, I uttered one word: "Milkshake."

It was our oldest, most sacred ritual.

"Camden Daniels," she guessed with a sigh.

"Basically."

"Well, I have Meredith opening, so I'm free. But you're buying." She took her coat off the rack.

"You sure? I know how busy you get."

"You're my sister. I'm sure. Besides, I owe you for this weekend. Rose's costume looks amazing for the play. Now get off your butt before I make you start scrubbing tables." She nodded, and I moved.

We were seated in the back booth at Bigg's, where Charity made sure no one could hear us, before I said a word.

"Okay, so—"

"Hold up." Charity raised her finger, and sure enough, Tillie Halverson walked over to take our order.

"Hey, Willow! Charity." Tillie's tone didn't mince words.

"It's so nice to see you, Tillie!" Charity responded with an Oscar-worthy smile and nose wrinkle.

"Hmmm," Tillie responded, then took our order. "So is there any truth to the rumors about you and Cam?" she asked me outright once we were finished.

"Rumors?" I asked after nearly sputtering my water all over the table.

"Oh, that you two are hot and heavy, seeing that you're his restoration girl?" Tillie sized me up with a smile.

I had to be seeing things.

"I'm not sure what you mean by hot and heavy, but yes, I'm helping him with the restorations. Cam and I have been friends since I was born, Tillie."

"Of course. Right. Stupid rumors. Especially when you're Sullivan's girl." She flushed, the color reaching her cheeks as she looked at her notepad.

"Except Sullivan's dead." Charity put my thoughts to words with a shrug. "So it really wouldn't matter, would it?"

"Right. Of course. So does that mean Cam's...available?" She drew out that last word so long it may as well have been its own sentence.

"You could probably ask him," I suggested. I was liking Tillie a whole lot less.

"Right! Okay, I'll have these right out!" She flounced away in her fifties skirt, her blond ponytail swishing in time with her hips.

"Usually I worry about Tillie spitting in my food, but I think you may have usurped me in the hated-Bradley-girl hierarchy."

"Everyone is weird today." I swirled my straw through my ice water.

"Normal weird or Alba weird?" Charity asked.

"Over-the-top Alba weird, and Genevieve Dawson was downright mean on the street."

"Okay, well, you're using up your Milkshake on Genevieve Dawson. Start talking." She stared me down.

Calling Milkshake was never to be taken advantage of. It was only for the moments your sister, and only your sister, would do.

I talked.

I started at Cam's arrival, pausing only when Tillie brought us our food. Then I continued.

Charity didn't say a single word, simply sat across from me, eating her burger and fries and sipping on a chocolate shake. There was no judgment in her eyes, like I would have gotten if I'd talked to Mom. No giddy excitement, like I would have received if I were talking to Thea.

She just nodded every now and then, holding up a finger if anyone came close enough to listen, and that gave me the courage to empty it all out. The kiss. Sullivan's death. All of it.

There was a sacred understanding that we were a combination-free vault. Secrets went in. Nothing came out. We were uncrackable.

And when one of us called a Milkshake, the other stopped whatever she was doing, no questions asked.

We'd sipped on Bigg's shakes on our parents' deck the night Charity whispered that she was pregnant.

"And then he said, 'It was Mom's name on his lips, when I knew mine would have been yours,'" I finished.

The straw fell into her shake, but her mouth held the same shape as she stared at me.

"Say something," I urged.

"He seriously said that? Not just all of it but that last sentence?"

I nodded and took a drink of my salted caramel shake. "What do you think he meant? I'm thinking it has to be that if he had been in Sullivan's place, right?" At least that was what I'd told myself just about every hour since he'd dropped that line on me. The rest of the story had been hard to hear, but not the earth-shattering confession he had tried to make it. I knew Cam could never have been responsible for Sullivan's death.

But now I knew just how responsible he actually felt, and that came with the knowledge that he'd use that guilt to freeze me out if I gave him the chance.

"I think he meant exactly that. If he had been the one dying, he would have said your name." She sagged against the seat, like I'd knocked the wind out of her. "Man, I never in a million years thought Camden Daniels had a romantic bone in his body."

"Romantic? No, just logical, because if he'd been Sullivan, then he would have been dating me, and that makes sense." My words slowed, and I drank again, but my milkshake didn't taste quite as sweet with that next sip.

"Wait, what?" she questioned, sitting up straighter. "I think we're crossing wires here, or you're purposefully trying to misunderstand."

"Misunderstand? No. I mean, I guess there was this part of me that always hoped…" I couldn't say the words out loud.

"That you'd end up with Cam?" Charity asked quietly.

I dragged my eyes to hers but couldn't nod. Couldn't breathe. Couldn't answer that basic question, because it would rip apart the very foundations I stood on.

It was okay to be friends with Cam. Okay to be best friends with Cam. Okay to watch movies with him, hike with him, read with him, sit quietly with him while we grew up. Okay to be defended by him and defend him. Okay to sleep next to him the night his mom died and hold his hand during the funeral. We'd been kids.

Maybe it was even okay to kiss him. I was probably one of the only girls in Alba who hadn't kissed him as a teenager.

But it was most definitely not okay to envision any kind of future.

Charity watched me until she sighed and shook her head. "You two are a damned Shakespearean tragedy. It's slightly entertaining yet incredibly painful to watch."

"You're not helping," I accused.

"Short of holding up a mirror, I'm not sure what else you'd like me to do, Willow. That man is in love with you and always has been. And no, before you open that fool mouth, I am not talking about Sullivan. I'm talking about Camden. And no, he doesn't just treat you like the little girl who grew up next door. I grew up next door to them, too. I went swimming and hiking, too. I rode the same school bus and went to the same parties. If you can't accept what he blatantly told you, then you're half the problem, and we're going to need a lot more ice cream." She held up her nearly empty milkshake glass.

"You think that he meant if he were the one dying, and it was his head in Sullivan's lap, that he would have called out for me?" I whispered. Any second now I was going to look down and see a scarlet A on my chest for even thinking it.

"Yes."

"You really think Camden is in love with me?"

"Yes."

My back hit the red vinyl of the booth. "For how long?"

"Since forever."

I scoffed.

"Fine. I knew it the day he carried you home from the mine."

"I was nine."

"Like I said. Forever."

"And you're just now telling me this?" There was no way. Or was there?

"You're just now willing to hear it."

But I wasn't. Not really. "No, he was cruel that last summer. The things he said to me. The way he treated me... That wasn't love."

"No, that was love's ugly second cousin—jealousy."

"If it isn't the Bradley sisters!" We both turned to see Gideon Hall in the center of Bigg's with his arms raised as he walked toward us.

Still reeling from Charity's theory, I barely managed a smile.

"Gid," Charity responded for us.

"Scoot." He sat next to Charity and nudged her over.

"Don't you have better things to do than harass citizens?" She moved even as she chided him. "This isn't high school."

"Thank God, or Julie would be pissed if I were sitting here." He grinned at me. "How are you, Willow?"

"Fine, Gi—" I openly gawked at the door and the man storming through it. "Is that...?"

"Dad," Charity agreed and became preoccupied with her straw as he saw us and stalked over.

But Dad hated Bigg's.

"Willow, I need a word with you."

"Hi, Judge Bradley," Gideon greeted.

"Lieutenant Hall," Dad acknowledged. "Willow, now."

"Okay, what is it?" Suddenly I wondered if Gideon's choice of seat was more to protect than annoy.

"You want to do this here?" he challenged, eyes narrowing on me as his voice dropped in volume.

"Dad, I don't know what this is. Do you want me to step outside with you?" I offered.

"This will be fine. You tell that boy that I saw his motion this morning when I came home from a Buena Vista appearance. I don't know what in the hell you could possibly be thinking to still be helping him with those historic sites after what he's done."

Charity's eyes darted toward the door, but I didn't need her to say a word. I felt everyone's eyes on us.

"Dad, I don't know what you're talking about. I'm guessing it's Cam, but I haven't seen him in a week. What's going on?"

"You haven't seen him?" He loosened his tie slightly but not enough to look unkempt. "Teaching her how to lie?" he asked Charity.

She tilted her head but didn't respond.

Guess we were back to the not-talking thing.

"I'm not lying." Whatever it was had to be huge for my dad to lose his temper in public like this.

"You're not seeing him?"

"Not in the way you're suggesting, no." And bury me in the earth right now, because Tillie Halverson's head popped over the milkshake machine. She had to be standing on the counter to get that view.

"You didn't spend the night with him last week?" he hissed.

My cheeks flamed, both with embarrassment and indignation.

"That's what I thought."

"It wasn't like that," I snapped. But why was I defensive? Even if it had been, I was a grown woman, and he was the one acting like a child. He didn't deserve an explanation, and I certainly didn't owe him one.

"Right. Well, I'll wish you the best of luck getting those plans approved by the Historical Society on Friday. Art has more than a few friends on the council, and none of us is in a hurry to see our friend buried just so Cam can get whatever inheritance he thinks is coming to him."

See Art buried?

"Judge Bradley, you're crossing a pretty clear line," Gideon warned.

Dad looked at Gid's badge, then his eyes. "Maybe if everyone else would stop crossing them, I wouldn't feel like I had to fetch them back across it."

"All the same, you might want to order a shake or something so everyone doesn't think you came in just to yell at your daughters about private legal matters they shouldn't even know about."

Dad's eyes narrowed, but he turned and left without another word, heading toward the counter to do just what Gideon suggested.

"What the hell was that about?" Charity asked.

"Cam had Simon drop a suit today. He's suing Xander for guardianship of their father." He stole a fry from my plate and ate it. "You know how fast word travels around here."

"You knew our dad was coming," I guessed.

"This wasn't the first place he looked," he confirmed. "The whole town is pretty pissed. I had lunch plans here anyway."

"That explains your Genevieve snub," Charity noted, smacking Gid's hand when he reached for one of her fries. "Order your own."

"I will. Just waiting on— There he is." He nodded toward the door.

Camden scanned the room, finding Gideon and then me. His baseball hat rode low on his brow, as did those jeans on his hips. Hips I'd had my thighs wrapped around last week.

And now my face felt like it was on fire.

"Frosty reception," Charity murmured.

That's when I noticed that not a single soul was speaking at any of the twenty tables. They were all watching Cam. "Glaring" was probably the better term.

Cam noticed, too, because his chin rose as he strode across the floor.

Dad moved into his path, and my heart stopped with Cam's

steps as his fist flexed, but he tucked his thumbs into his back pockets. This could go so very wrong, and if Cam's temper got the best of him, he'd never win his suit.

"If you do this, Dad won't forgive you," Charity whispered.

I looked down at her and realized I'd stood. "You're sure about what you said earlier?"

She glanced at Dad and Cam. "Yeah. I am."

"Then I can live with it." Dad raised me to side with what was right, no matter the cost. He just didn't realize he wasn't right this time.

She swallowed, then nodded quickly.

Their words were still muffled as I crossed the checkered diner floor, but the tone was unmistakable. Dad was pissed. Cam was in that scary calm that usually came before he destroyed something.

"Hey, we were waiting for you," I said to Cam as I faced them both. "We're in the back."

Cam's eyes found mine, and if I were anyone else, I would have flinched at what I found there. This wasn't the guy who carried me home on the Cat or the one who kissed me in the kitchen. This was the Cam who killed people, and it finally hit me just how close to the surface that part of him lived, barely leashed. There was a part of him that I wasn't sure cared about anyone or anything—even me.

He expected me to retreat; that's what that little glare meant.

"Saved you a seat right next to me." I held out my hand, palm up, and waited.

The ball was in his court. I refused to look at anyone else or even think of the possible humiliation I'd just opened myself up to. The humiliation Cam would have served me had we still been in that summer before he left for basic. I kept my eyes locked on his and didn't move my hand. Something told me the minute I lost eye contact, he'd blow.

"Willow," Dad warned.

"Cam," I whispered. Every second he waited, my hand felt heavier with potential devastation.

He looked back at my father, and my heart sank.

But his hand took mine and felt lighter than the emptiness I'd been holding, even with its weight.

"Judge Bradley," Cam said quietly in farewell. He moved, putting himself between Dad and me as he started back toward the booth.

"Willow," Dad called, and it wasn't quiet. I paused, knowing the gloves were off.

I looked back anyway.

"What would Sullivan say?"

He hadn't landed a punch—he'd shot directly to the heart, and mine shattered. My breath stuttered, and Cam's hand tightened around mine.

"I don't know, Dad. But I'll be sure to ask him the next time I see him." I faced the booth and put one foot in front of the other until I was seated against the wall with Cam blocking the rest of the diner.

He lifted his arm, then wrapped his hand around my shoulder and pulled me into his side. It wasn't a romantic declaration, though that's probably what everyone assumed. It was full-on structural support.

I concentrated on Cam's scent, all mint and pine, and tried to shove everything else that had just happened in a box to be examined later. Tried but didn't quite succeed. Dad had really just used Sullivan against me. Against Cam.

"What just happened?" Gideon asked.

"Willow excommunicated herself." Charity's eyes glossed over as she offered me a weak, trembling smile. "Are you okay?"

I nodded, the movement jerky.

"Smile," she ordered as her own brightened. "Every tongue in here is going to wag, so don't you dare let Dad win. Not in this. Smile. It's the best armor you've got."

I did, but if Gideon's cringe was any indication, it wasn't successful.

"How long you think your dad can stay pissed about something like that?" Gideon nodded back toward where Dad had declared open war on me, then stole another fry.

"How long will it take him to forgive one of his daughters going against his direct wishes as publicly as possible?" Charity asked.

"Yeah," Gideon clarified.

"She'll let you know when it finally happens." I gave my sister a wry laugh.

"Amen," she agreed, and our laughter turned real.

Cam's arm tightened around me, and I leaned into him.

"It's okay, sis. There's room at the black-sheep table for you. Right, Cam?"

"There's room wherever you want it, Willow." He rested his chin on the top of my head. "Toffee?" He reached for my milkshake and took a sip, startling a little.

"Nope. It's salted caramel. Surprised?"

He looked down at me, and my Cam was back in those deep-brown depths. "Definitely not what I expected to find."

"In a good way?" I whispered so only he could hear it.

His brow knit for a second; then he leaned in and kissed my forehead. "The best way."

Three days later, Cam walked into the Historical Society meeting and took the empty seat next to mine. He'd been back and forth to Salida to watch over his dad and spent the rest of his time designing the rebuilds, and it showed. He looked exhausted.

Other than a short phone conversation, we'd only spoken over text message. I'd basically become a hermit, working nonstop at my house, but the disdainful looks I'd gotten when I walked in told me everyone assumed I was now dating Cam.

I almost laughed at them because even I wasn't assuming that.

In fact, every sign pointed to the opposite.

"We're up in one more agenda item," I told him.

"Okay," he replied, shucking his coat.

"Are you? You are. I didn't even know you owned a tie." But holy crap did he make it look good.

"There's a lot you don't know about me," he teased with a wink.

"Everyone thinks I know everything." I hung on that last word.

"Everyone can mind their own business," Cam said directly to Mrs. Rhodes, who had turned in her seat to blatantly glower.

She wasn't alone. Dad had rotated between ignoring and glaring at me since I sat down, and more than one of the older ladies had muttered that Sullivan would be ashamed.

Yeah, he would have. Of them.

"Our next item of business is reviewing the business plan offered by Camden Daniels," Walt announced from the dais. "Would you like to approach, Cam?"

"Yes, sir," he answered and stood.

"Good luck," I whispered.

He paused in the aisle, file firmly tucked in his right hand, and offered me his left.

"You're just going to piss people off even more if you shove me in their faces," I hissed.

"Come on, Pika. I saved you a seat next to me."

Thea elbowed me in the side.

I took his hand and raised my chin as we walked down the aisle, ignoring the scalding pain from that damned scarlet A branding deeper into my skin with every whisper. Cam was an expert at not caring what people thought—or at least looking like it.

I was a rookie.

Cam went over his plan and answered every question the council threw at him. I counted two or three council members who weren't openly hostile.

Xander remained silent, but that was no surprise. Calm and collected against Cam's rage had always been his MO.

"This looks like a solid plan," Walt finished. "The thought that we could get the mine open to tours as early as August is a huge motivator, too. Shall we vote?"

There was a murmur on the dais, and Walter called the nine-member council to vote.

I held my breath as Mary Murphy counted the ballots.

"Three for aye," she said, her shoulders sagging. "Six for nay."

There was an audible gasp through the hall. Hating Cam was one thing; denying the town much-needed income out of spite was another.

Cam tensed, his grip turning white on the podium.

"Seriously?" Walter questioned, his gaze swinging left and right down the council.

"Vote's been cast," Genevieve said with a fake frown. "It's hard to believe there were six of you who couldn't look past Cam's current legal matters."

Six of you?

Three ayes. That had to be Walt; Gid's wife, Julie; and probably Mary, given her reaction. Or maybe not. No one would go public with their grudge.

Unless we made them.

I tugged on Cam's elbow, and he leaned down.

"Tell Walt that you move to poll the council."

"Why?"

"They secretly voted against you because of the lawsuit. They won't publicly go against the mine. It's literally the reason Alba exists in the first place. Do it," I ordered.

He shot me a look of disbelief but stood tall. "Foreman?"

"Cam?" Walt replied, rubbing the bridge of his nose.

"I move to poll the council."

Walt's eyebrows rose, but he smiled. "What a good idea."

"He can't move to poll the council. He has to have a majority of the eighteen other voting members," Dad interjected, looking straight at Cam when he said it.

"You neglected to mention that," Cam whispered, barely

moving his mouth.

"Whoops. Okay. Just go with it." I turned around and eyed what I could see of the hall.

"Go with what?" he asked.

"Could you move to the left there, Dorothy? Thanks." I climbed up on the folding chair.

"Sweet Lord," Dorothy muttered.

I wobbled when the chair did, but Cam grabbed my waist. Probably not the best imagery, but we were already condemned, so I might as well get the perks. "If you're a voting member, could you stand?"

About ten people did.

"Come on. Stand up. Don't you want to hear which of them is willing to let a personal vendetta against Camden Daniels deny this town the chance to raise our income by fifty percent? You saw the projections. James Hudgens, you have two sons who live in Alba, but you can only leave the historical firehouse to one of them. Don't you want to see if the other can make a living in the season running the tours or shuttling tourists?"

James looked past Oscar's scowl to his younger son, Ian. Then he stood.

"Jennifer Halverson, you make money on one thing. Don't look at me like that—you know it's true. Can you imagine how much more money you'll make for your kids when we have another thirty thousand people come through in the summer?"

She openly glared at Cam but stood.

Funny how moral judgment went out the window when personal finances got involved.

One by one, I called out the remaining five voting members until all seventeen of them stood with Camden as the eighteenth.

"If you'd like to move the council to a verbal poll, please lift your hand and say 'aye,'" I called out.

They unanimously did.

Cam lowered me to the ground, using it as an excuse to whisper

"Thank you" in my hair.

"I just got you here. You have to poll them. You're the one who called for it."

"Great," he muttered.

"They can't answer the poll until you finish calling their name. First and last," I told him.

"How do you even know that?" He looked at me with a combination of awe and confusion.

"Dad," I explained with a shrug. He'd made a game of learning council rules and quizzed us at the dinner table as kids, certain that one of his daughters would take his place as a county judge.

"So call their name really slowly?" Cam asked as Walter urged the crowd to quiet.

"Just keep talking until they're convinced," I suggested. "Go for the throat, because they sure went for yours."

"You want me to change their minds."

"You don't have to do much," I promised. "They're facing a room of angry neighbors, and you only need two to flip. Just remember, founders can outvote them all."

Cam nodded.

"You ready?" Walter asked.

"I am."

"Begin."

"Genevieve, I can't imagine that you would deny all our townspeople the chance at increasing their income. Especially seeing that their income goes back into your jewelry store the rest of the year. My own father bought my mother's engagement ring at Dawson's. You definitely aren't one of those nays, are you, Genevieve Dawson?"

She was redder than her cranberry sweater when he finished. He'd sure chosen to start with a dragon.

"Of course not. I say aye," she finished.

One down.

"Walter Robinson?"

"Aye," Walter voted with a grin.

We only needed three more.

"Julie Hall?"

"Aye," she replied and winked at her husband.

Down to two.

"Mary Murphy?" Cam guessed.

"Aye." She nodded.

He was only going for the ayes, and he needed to flip one more vote.

His eyes landed on Dad, and I stiffened. "Noah, I could come back to Alba as a millionaire with a Nobel Prize and you'd still shut me down, right? How did you vote, Noah Bradley?"

"Nay." Dad leaned back in his chair.

Cam nodded. "That's what I thought."

A murmur went through the crowd. "That was for you," Cam whispered.

He'd turned the tables on my dad and called him out publicly, just like Dad had done to me in the diner. Dad let spite rule over public interest...in an election year.

"Alexander."

I sucked in a breath as Cam addressed his brother.

"You and I have discussed how the proceeds from opening this mine to tours will allow us to generate enough income to keep our father in his own home with proper care. It will let us keep the promise we made to him. Surely you wouldn't vote against keeping our dad in his home, would you, Alexander Daniels?"

Xander didn't look out over the crowd, simply leaned forward and stared right at Cam. "I'll do anything to keep our dad happy and healthy. Aye."

The crowd applauded, and Cam clutched me in a quick hug, but I took one look at Dad and Xander and couldn't help but feel that though we'd gained a win, we'd lost something, too.

CHAPTER FIFTEEN

Camden

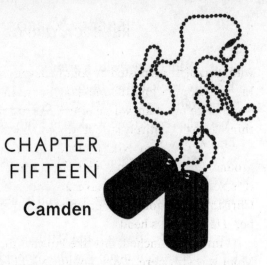

"Take it easy, Dad." Xander tried like hell to ease Dad into his seat in the dining room as I took the one on his left.

"I'm not a child. I can do it." He waved Xander off and stared at the pasta in front of him.

"It's your favorite. Shrimp fettuccine," Xander said with a forced smile.

"I know it's my favorite. What, did you think I forgot or something?" he grumbled but picked up his fork.

Xander and I glanced at each other before starting our own lunch. There was a tentative truce between us for moments like this, but it felt like the Cold War. We put on a good face in front of Dad and built up our arsenals behind the scenes.

"Where's Dorothy? Why aren't we eating in the kitchen?" Dad's brow furrowed.

Xander sighed, so I jumped in.

"Dorothy only comes on Thursdays or whenever she wants to stop by now," I told him again. He'd been home from the hospital for two days, and they hadn't been the best in terms of his memory. "You have a team that comes now, remember?"

"I don't need a team."

"Nikki is with you Monday through Thursdays, and since it's Wednesday, she's here today. You've got Dan and Sandra taking over nights and May taking the other days. I've got a schedule with their pictures posted by your bed, your seat in the living room, the refrigerator, and the message board in the hallway. Do you want me to put it anywhere else?" Not arguing back was my new thing. I wasn't entirely sure it was going well.

"I don't see any Nikki." Dad took a bite and then looked around the dining room. "And why the hell are we in here? I hate this room. Pointless to have an entire room we only use at Christmas, but your mother says that's the way it's supposed to be." He shook his head.

I inwardly flinched, just like I always did when he talked like Mom was still here. "We thought Nikki could use a break, so Xander and I are having lunch with you. And your walker isn't as easy to use in the kitchen, so until you're back to one hundred percent, we thought this would be easier."

He glared at his walker, which rested next to him. "I don't need that damned thing. Or any of this." He ripped the oxygen tube from his nose.

Xander moved, but I stopped him. "Let him eat first."

"Doctor says the oxygen is only for a few more days, Dad. They just want to make sure your lungs are back up to snuff. You gave us quite the scare." Xander's gaze hit the table, and I wondered if he was thinking about the ventilator—the restraints. Because I sure as hell was.

"Fine, then I'll just drive down to Doc Myers and have him clear me, because this is ridiculous." He attacked his pasta like it was personally responsible for the oxygen.

"Dad, Doc Myers died about eight years ago," Xander told him.

Why? I mouthed across the table. There was zero reason to shove it in Dad's face that his mind was going. There were fights you picked and fights you walked away from.

Xander glared in response.

Great. It was childhood all over again.

"Fine, then I'll just drive down—" Dad stood, bracing his hands on the table.

"Dad, no." Xander and I both stood.

"I can go where I damn well please!" He slammed his fist on the bare wood of the table, making the silverware jump.

"You can't." Xander's voice broke.

"Why the hell not? In case you forgot, Alexander, I'm your father. I don't care if you think you're a big man running off to the army because Colorado State rejected you. I'm your father."

I blinked, and my eyes snapped to Xander, who flushed. Colorado State rejected him? That was never the story we were told. He chose to serve his country, chose to be selfless over serving himself. Xander shot me a look, and I lifted my hands like I was under arrest. I wasn't going there.

"Like you aren't going to throw that at me," he snapped.

"Seriously? I wish the worst thing I had going against me was that I didn't get into the college I wanted. I've done far worse."

I knew he was still pissed at me—we were at war, for crying out loud—but at least his posture softened.

"You have no room to talk, Camden. I'm still paying the school for what you did to the bathrooms." Dad swung a finger at me.

I barely stopped a laugh, but when Dad's weight shifted, I moved quickly and caught him.

"Who even does that? Cherry bombs the girls' bathroom. Like you're in some kind of movie or something."

"A thirteen-year-old boy looking for the wrong kind of attention." I helped him back into his seat.

"I swear that stuffy principal charged me double because I laughed," Dad muttered.

My chest constricted. He'd laughed? Really? Because he hadn't been laughing on the way home or when he'd threatened his belt.

Dad picked up his fork again, and we took our seats. I exchanged a tense smile with Xander. See, we could do this. We'd be—

"And where are my car keys?" Dad asked, glaring at Xander.

All that red from Dad's CSU comment drained from his face, leaving my brother instantly pale. "Right. About the keys." He looked to me.

"I took your keys, Dad," I said matter-of-factly and took a bite, forcing myself to chew and swallow. It wasn't the food. The army taught me not to be picky. But I knew how to spot an avalanche, and Dad was ripe for one.

"You what? Whatever for? You can't even drive, Camden."

So about that picking fights thing… This was the one I had to pick.

"I'm twenty-eight, Dad." I swallowed a mouthful of ice water.

"You're… That's not right," he muttered. "You still shouldn't have my keys. Give them back." His blue eyes narrowed on me.

"I can't do that." I wound another piece of fettuccine around my fork, hoping he'd let it go. That he'd forget this as easily as he'd forgotten my age.

"You sure as hell can and will! Those are my keys." He jabbed his fork in my direction, punctuating his words.

"They are," I agreed.

"That's my car!"

"It is."

"Do I have to call Tim Hall? Teach you a lesson about stealing other people's property?" he threatened, leaning forward.

"Dad, you're not safe driving it. I can't give them back to you in order to keep you safe." I spoke slowly, calmly, using every trick I'd learned over the years to talk him down. I'd dealt with warlords less stubborn than my father.

"I'm a better driver than you'll ever be!"

"That might be so," I agreed. "But, Dad, you started the car, ran it into the garage door, then got out to fix it and almost died." My throat closed on the last part, and I had to clear it, then take another swig of my water to ease that lump.

"That's nonsense. I would never hit the garage door." He waved at me, fork still in his hand. "You're lying. You just want to steal my car."

"No, Dad. I have my own car."

"You're thirteen!"

"I'm twenty-eight." I looked to Xander for a little help, but he stared at the table in defeat.

"Cam, you know triggering his emotions is just going to make him spiral," Xander warned.

Thanks for the help. "Dad, you're not safe behind the wheel anymore."

"That's bullshit! You say you're a man?"

"I am," I agreed, even though some days I wasn't quite sure where that line really was anymore, because I sure as hell felt like a child the minute I walked into this house. Hell, even this town.

"Then, you know I need my keys. A man drives! He has control! Who is going to take your mother to the library when it snows? You know she hates that driveway."

Shit, that hurt.

Xander's eyes squeezed shut. Fine, okay, I could be the bad guy. It was pretty much the role I'd been born to play anyway.

"Dad, Mom passed away a long time ago. You don't have to drive her anywhere. Both Xander and I are grown. We can drive you wherever you need. Your nurses can, too. They're extremely capable. Xander and I made sure you have the best people around you. You don't need to worry about driving. Let us make this easier."

"I want my goddamned keys!" The fork flew from his hand, skidding down the honey oak table and landing in Mom's empty chair.

"You. Can't. Have. Them."

He roared in frustration, and my chest clenched like I was a kid.

"Fine, I'll just ask Sullivan to get them. He's the only one of you who ever listens," he grumbled.

That was a fight I refused to have.

We ate the rest of lunch in silence, until Nikki arrived, all smiles in her green scrubs.

"There you are!" She waved to Dad, then turned to Xander and me. "Thanks. It was great to grab lunch with my boyfriend."

"Who are you?" Dad asked.

"Nikki," she answered like it was the first time. It wasn't. "I'm here to spend the day with you. How about we pop this back on"—she looped the oxygen back under his nose—"and get you set up for a little relaxation time? Your boys tell me that you love *Band of Brothers*, so I've got the first episode queued up."

Dad's eyes narrowed as he watched her take his empty dish from the dining room.

"I'm supposed to watch movies with this girl?"

"She's just here to help, Dad."

"She's bossy." He thumbed his oxygen tube.

"So are you," I countered.

"Okay, we're all set. Want to come with me, Art?" Nikki asked.

"Well, I guess you're pretty enough," he commented and stood.

"Dad, you can't call her pretty." I cringed in Nikki's direction. "Sorry."

"No worries. I've been called worse." She shrugged it off.

"Why not? Look at her. Red hair, nice skin. I like pretty girls. We'll get along just fine if you don't talk through the show." Xander moved his walker, and Dad stepped into it, leaning heavily for support.

Nikki smiled and took Dad to the living room as Xander and I carried the remaining dishes to the kitchen.

"So you'll take his keys to save his life, but you're going to take me to court for a DNR so he can end it," Xander accused as I washed what was in the sink.

"Not the same thing," I argued, loading the dishes into the dishwasher.

"Really. Because if you think he's lucid enough to say he wants a DNR, then he should be lucid enough to drive, right?"

I shut the dishwasher and turned to face my brother.

"What? No answers to that?" He shoved his arms through his suit coat and stared me down with an open disdain he'd hidden from our father.

"You still don't see?" I asked quietly. "After everything in the hospital, when he woke up screaming because he didn't know where he was or why there was a tube down his throat. You think he wants to live like that? Tied down with restraints while his own sons hold him prisoner?"

"Twelve days!" Xander snapped. "It was twelve days in the hospital, and now he's home. And half the time, he'll be Dad. So yeah, I'm willing to take those shitty days so we can have the few good ones that we do. Because I love him and I will keep him on this earth as long as I can."

"You'll take the shitty days?" I shook my head. "You didn't take the shitty days, Xander. He did. You watched. At some point you're going to see that this has never been about what you want—what I want. It's about what he wants."

"Yeah, you keep telling yourself that, all the time using our family mine to try and sway public opinion to your side, try to convince everyone that you're some kind of reformed hero. That's all about Dad. Sure. I'm telling you, brother, they'll be grateful for the income, but it won't work to get the people or the judge on your side. I know Alba a little better than you do."

He couldn't have hit the mark any closer yet been further off. I didn't give a fuck if Alba saw me as their tourism savior. I cared that they trusted me enough to give Dad what he wanted.

He left after saying goodbye to Dad and giving me another glare as he walked out the door.

I leaned back against the doorframe to the living room and watched quietly as Dad settled in, his breathing easier now that he wasn't moving as much.

Was this really as good as it was going to get for him? How

could such a beast of a man lose himself to his own mind?

"Hey, Dad, I have to go up to the mine."

"The mine? I know that place better than anyone." He turned his head to reply, looking over the side of the blue recliner he loved.

"Yeah, I know, Dad. I'm getting it ready to reopen for tours, remember?"

His forehead puckered. "Right. That's right. Dangerous place, that mine. You should take me with you. Just in case you get lost. Hate for anything to happen to you or that Bradley girl."

The pressure was back in my chest. He knew. In this moment, he knew what was really happening. He was really here.

"We'll be okay," I promised him. "I won't let anything happen to Willow."

"I know you won't. That girl is wild about you. You know that, right? Everyone knows. It's all they talk about in town." He gave me a soft smile, and that pressure eased to something light and sweet.

"And that's okay with you?" My keys dug into my palm. *Relax. His opinion has never mattered to you before.* Except it always had.

"Of course. You two have been inseparable since you were kids. Figured it would come full circle one of these days. Now, be careful up there. Those train cars will still function on the rails, but you know those tracks stop dead past that first ventilation shaft."

"Yeah, I have your old maps. Don't worry."

"Okay. Have fun. Love you, Sullivan." He gave me another one of those soft smiles and turned back to the television.

There was a two-ton brick on my chest. There had to be, because the air wouldn't come and it fucking hurt. I blinked furiously at the prickling pain in my eyes and laid my head back on the doorframe.

My first breath came in a gasp, filling my lungs but leaving the pain. That was all mine.

"Love you, too, Dad," I responded, because it was what he'd expect.

Because it was the truth.

I walked down the hallway and tapped Sully's picture on the wall. "That one was for you, too."

My phone rang as I climbed into the Jeep, and Willow's name flashed across the screen. I started the engine on the second ring.

On the third, I told myself every single reason I shouldn't pick it up.

On the fourth, I did.

"Hey."

"Hey, yourself. What are you up to?" I could practically see her smile as her voice filled my car, coming through the speakers.

"Just finished lunch with my dad, and I was thinking of heading to the mine. I'm meeting with the contractor tomorrow and wanted to get another look at it." I put the car in gear and headed toward my place.

"I have a better idea," she suggested.

"You sound like you're up to no good." Now my lips were curving, too.

"How about we both skip out on work and you meet me at the hot springs?"

The hot springs. There were ten thousand different reasons I should say no and only one reason why I should go. And damn if that one reason didn't outweigh every other one.

"Cam?" she asked, her voice pitching higher. She was nervous I'd say no.

Probably because she knew I should. This was a bad idea.

"Willow Bradley, are you asking me to play hooky with you?" The Jeep rocked back and forth through a stretch of road where ice had built up in little boulders.

"Maybe. Okay, definitely. Come on. No one else will ever go with me."

"That's because it's covered in snow." I looked up through the windshield and saw brilliant blue skies. At least the weather was good for it.

"Only the outsides. The water is toasty. As you should remember."

A couple of hours with Willow sounded like heaven. We'd had zero time alone together since...well, whatever the hell it was that had happened in the kitchen.

"Come on. Be bad with me."

"Be bad, huh? Let me guess. You're not actually being bad. You have all your work done for the day already."

"Okay, fine. I do. Basically, I'm guilting you into being bad so I can blatantly use you for some fun."

"That's a situation I'm well acquainted with. I'll meet you there in twenty."

There was no way this could possibly end well. But nothing ever did.

CHAPTER SIXTEEN

Camden

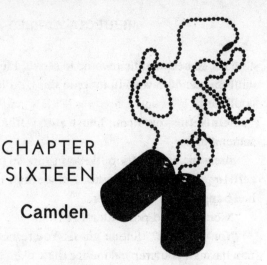

Snow covered every part of the meadow between the ridges, with the exception of the hot springs and the creek that ran beside it, heavy with the beginning of spring thaw.

The contrast of undisturbed snow against the steaming turquoise mineral pool was something I'd never found an equal to. I'd traveled all over the world, seen both the breathtaking and the brutal, but there was nowhere on earth I found as beautiful, hence the tattoo on my arm.

Opening this hot springs up to tourists would have made more than a pretty penny, but our great-grandfathers had agreed to keep it for the private use of the Danielses and Bradleys only. With the exception of a few summer parties when we were in high school, this generation had honored that agreement. Relished it, really.

I parked the Jeep alongside the old bathhouse and got out, hauling my backpack with me. The snow barely gave way under my boots as I trekked above where the bathhouse perched precariously over the north end of the pool and down the other side.

The structure was still sound, as far as an 1880s piece of ruin left to time could be. Dad had reinforced it the summer Xander broke his wrist after we built a tire swing under it, and the supports still looked good.

The tire swing had not survived Xander's misadventure.

Willow's 4Runner crested the ridge from the west, and my

stomach tensed in anticipation. A month. I'd been home a month, and I'd gone from vowing to never see her, to never touching her, to…I didn't even know. She was Willow, and even though I knew this was a shit idea, I couldn't stop myself. I never could when it came to her.

She was the exception to everything.

"Hey!" She grinned as she shut the door to her car, toting her own bag over her shoulder.

"Nice wheel." I pointed to her front left.

"You like that?" She posed like a car model. "It's brand-new from the manufacturer and looks exactly like the other three already installed. But wait, there's more! It comes with four new tires, since its friend on the back right was also flattened while avoiding a deer. All for the price of I-think-I-just-put-Keith-Mayberry's-kid-through-college!" She ended with a flashy grin, and I laughed.

I never knew how she did it, but she could flip my moods with a twist of her lips. Lips I knew the taste and texture of. Lips that had fueled way too many dreams lately. All because I had the self-control of a teenager when she came near.

Or maybe it was because I'd wanted her since I was a teenager.

"Let's get in. It's freezing out here."

She nodded, and we climbed down the stone-ringed embankment until we reached the heavy, flat stones that bordered the north and west ends of the pool. We dropped our bags, and I busied myself with getting my towels out and stripping down, mostly to keep from watching Willow strip down.

I laid out one towel to step on and folded the other for when I got out, then started dropping clothing until I was in nothing but the black swim trunks I'd worn under my pants. "See you in there!" I called out and jumped, careful not to cannonball, because I wasn't fifteen anymore.

The water engulfed me in heat, and I lingered but didn't hit the bottom before I swam back up. I broke the surface, and the drops of water on my face immediately chilled.

"How is it?" Willow asked from the edge.

I turned around and nearly swallowed my tongue.

She stood on the ledge, pulling her long brown hair up into a knot on the top of her head. Words. I didn't have words. "Incredible," maybe. "Beautiful," definitely. "Sexy as hell"? Yeah, we'd go with that, too. Her suit was a two-piece and straight out of a forties pinup fantasy, complete with navy-blue bottoms, gold buttons up her stomach, and a red-and-white-striped top that looped around her neck and tied between her breasts in a bow that I was going to undo with my teeth.

God. Bless. America.

I locked my jaw to keep those teeth exactly where they were.

"Well?" she asked, and it took me a second to remember what she'd asked in the first place.

"It's a balmy one hundred and four degrees, just like every other day of the year." Though I really was wishing it was a hell of a lot colder at this moment.

"Perfect." She sat on the edge of the stone, then lowered herself into the water until it covered her to her neck. Then she moaned. "This feels amazing."

This was the worst idea I'd ever had in my entire life.

Except that it was her idea.

She made her way toward, then past me, stopping at the grouping of shallow stones that made up the east end of the pool. "Come sit," she called out.

"That's probably not the best idea."

"Why?" She tilted her head to the side and leaned back so her weight was braced on her hands.

The water hit her neckline, but it was also crystal clear in that section.

"Trust me. This is close enough."

"So you're going to stay out there in the middle and tread water the entire time we're here?" She disappeared behind a cloud of steam as the breeze shifted, then reappeared.

"Maybe."

"Suit yourself. So you know the entire town thinks we're together, right?" she questioned.

Ah yes, the elephant in the room or, rather, in the hot springs.

"I am aware." I swam a little closer when another wave of steam hid her from me. I might not be able to touch her, not in the way I wanted, but I wasn't going to deny myself the simple pleasure of looking at her.

"Because you keep putting your hands on me when we're in public." She arched an eyebrow in clear challenge.

"Define 'hands on you.'" It was nothing compared to what I wanted to do.

"You put your arm around me at the diner."

"You held out your hand first." I moved through another cloud of steam when I couldn't see her.

"You held my hand at the Historical Society meeting."

"You..." Shit, I had nothing. "You hugged me." There.

"You held on to my waist."

"So you didn't fall off the chair. Do you have any clue how clumsy you get when you're distracted? You get this laser focus on something shiny, and everything else doesn't exist, including your own feet. Trust me—I was saving you from yourself."

"You kissed my forehead." All pretense of play dropped in those hazel eyes.

I'd kissed a hell of a lot more than that in my kitchen. I swallowed and sat on the edge of the ledge that marked the shallow end. "You chose me over your dad."

"You pulled me from my car and carried me home."

I turned to fully face her, the water falling to my stomach. Cold air prickled at my chest, helping to ground me. "That was just being a good neighbor. Plus, the entire town didn't see, so I don't think it counts."

A smile tugged at her lips. "Okay. You took a bullet for me."

"Six," I corrected her, feeling that sliver of terror at the reminder of how close I'd come to losing her. "It was six bullets. Buckshot."

"I thought you were dying," she admitted. "I didn't know about the vest."

"I thought he'd kill you before I could get out there." I ran my hands over my air-cooled face.

"I thought about you before I saw you." She shifted and sat up.

"What?" *Game over.*

"I saw the gun, and your dad was talking about cougars, and I thought about you." She tucked her knees to her chest. "Is that so hard to believe?"

"Yes." Believing in anything earned you a shit ton of disappointment.

"I thought about you every single day, Cam."

Fuck me, the woman wasn't pulling her punches.

I did, too. But I couldn't say those words. Couldn't cross the lines I'd already stumbled across once. That had been passion and need, but to do so here would be choice. An unforgivable choice, and I'd already made one that broke her heart.

"I thought about you when you went to college and when you came home and stopped speaking to me. God, you were so cruel that summer."

"I know." The hurt in her eyes made me close mine.

"Why?"

My heart slammed in my chest, the reason screaming for release. To say the words I hadn't been able to. Because she was everything that was good about Alba—about life, really. And he'd been that good, too.

And they'd been right together.

And I'd never be either of those things.

I looked over at her, and she sighed, realizing I wasn't going to answer her.

"I thought about you when you left for basic, and when Sully told me you'd been selected for Special Forces training, and every day you were in the evaluation process. Every day. I missed you so much that I wasn't sure how people kept breathing with that kind of pain, you know?" She looked up at the sky. "I missed you every day for ten years, Cam."

I knew exactly the kind of pain she meant, because I'd carried it with me, learning to exist around it, to bury it, only to have it resurface time and again. And she was here, within arm's reach, and I still couldn't ease that damned pain. I wouldn't let myself.

"We can't do this," I said softly.

Slowly, she brought her eyes back to meet mine in challenge. "Why?"

"You know why." Logic told me to end it there. To swim over to the other ledge, grab my clothes, and get the hell out before this went anywhere we couldn't come back from. "I should go. I never should have come, and I knew it."

"But you came anyway." She shifted up on her knees, and goose bumps covered her shoulders.

"I have a hard time staying away from you," I admitted. I could offer her the same honesty she gave me. I owed her at least that much. "Always have. Darkness is drawn to the light, right? And there's nothing brighter in this town than you."

She softened at the compliment, and I instantly wanted to take it back. I should be shoving her as far away from me as possible, not saying shit to make her come closer.

"You have a choice. You've always had a choice."

"Not when it came to you. I was never good enough. I'm still not. This"—I gestured between us—"can never happen."

"I decide who's good enough for me, not you," she argued, slipping to the side so we were only a couple of feet apart.

"Then, think again, because all I'm good for is building things and destroying people. I destroyed you once, too."

She flinched.

"I saw your tears, your heartbreak when I brought him home. I know what I did to you."

"Sullivan's death was not your fault," she said in the same tone she'd used when we'd had the same fight in the kitchen. The same fight we'd have forever if I gave in to what I wanted. It didn't matter how many times she said it. Sully's death was on my hands.

"Keep telling yourself that, Willow."

"I'll keep telling you until you believe it," she promised, coming up on her knees and taking my face between her hands. "You told me your ugliest truth that day, but you never let me say mine."

"As if anything you have could compare." The air between us was charged.

"You saw me crying the day of Sullivan's funeral. That's true. I loved him, and I don't regret loving him."

I turned my face, but she followed until her knee brushed my thigh.

"So you saw my grief, but you never stopped to see my relief."

My gaze snapped back to hers.

"I was heartbroken that Sullivan died, but, Cam, the only reason I could breathe was because you survived. I was so ashamed that all I was allowed to feel was the grief when the relief was the bigger emotion." Her shoulders hunched as she looked away.

"What are you saying? You were relieved that Sully died?" I whispered.

"No." She shook her head. "I was relieved that you didn't. And I knew that eventually I'd be okay. I'd heal. And I did. I put myself back together and made myself whole. But I knew that if your places had changed, and we'd buried you, I wouldn't have. I couldn't—I can't—picture my world without you in it somewhere."

"You don't mean that."

"I do."

Was she really telling me that if she had to choose one of us to come home that day, she would have chosen me? That was impossible. Everyone chose Sullivan. My father, Xander, even Willow herself.

How big of an asshole was I that I longed to believe her? That

I wanted to think I was worthy of being someone's first choice?

I wanted to be her first choice.

She came closer until our breaths mingled with the steam rising from the mineral pool.

"Say yes," she begged, turning my words from our first kiss around on me.

But I couldn't. Not when I was only her choice because he couldn't be. As badly as I wanted her, I couldn't be her silver medal. Even when the beating in my chest screamed to take what I could get, the lone scrap of pride I'd held on to all these years couldn't do it.

"No." I moved away from her, sliding back into the pool.

"Why?" she shouted, sitting on the edge of the shallow end. "You fight for your country. For Sullivan. For your dad and even for me. Why can't you let someone fight for you? Why won't you let me fight for you?"

The naked pain in her voice shredded my composure like nothing else could, and my control snapped. "Because I'll only hurt you."

"News flash, we don't have to be together for you to break my heart. Trust me, I've got a few years of evidence to back that up. Try again."

"Because you don't really want me."

"Of all the stupid things to say." She dropped under the water and swam, surfacing past me near the midpoint of the pool, where the steam obscured her again.

"I'm not a replacement for Sullivan!" I shouted at her. At the world. At God. At whoever cared enough to listen.

The breeze carried the steam away just long enough to see her stricken face. "No," she whispered, but it carried. "Sullivan was the replacement for you."

What did she just say? I stopped treading water and immediately sank as she turned her back on me and swam toward the other side.

I dove underwater and shot across the pool, coming up in front of her. We both gasped. Me for air and her with surprise.

"Say it again," I demanded.

"Do you hate me?" She flattened her lips between her teeth as tiny droplets of water slipped down her face. "It would fit, since I hated myself. You were home for the summer after your freshman year of college, and I saw the girls hanging all over you in Julie's hot tub, and you didn't push them away, and it hit me that you never would. Not for me. You didn't see me like that."

But I did. I'd just never acted on it.

"Sullivan found me crying, and he kissed me, and I let him because it dulled the pain. I used him, and he let me, and I grew to love him for it, and eventually for everything else, but I knew I couldn't love him like he loved me. Not when I didn't have a whole heart to give him." Her mouth trembled. "Not so bright and shiny now, am I?"

How could she not see that her vulnerability, her honesty, made her that much brighter?

"Say it again," I repeated, my tone bordering on a plea. I needed to hear it more than I needed my next meal or my next breath. Her words could sustain or destroy me.

She looked away, waging an internal battle I couldn't fight for her. When she brought her eyes back to mine, the fear there was laced with a resolve that had me holding my breath.

"It was always you, Cam." She closed the inches between us, resting her hands on my chest, on the heart she didn't realize only beat because hers did. "I've loved you since forever. I've been in love with you since I was old enough to understand what that meant. No one else ever had a shot of getting close. How could they, when you took my heart with you?"

She loved me. She'd always loved me. She'd wanted me, and I'd been too scared to put myself out there for her, to risk her rejection or her acceptance. I had the strength not to act on my own feelings, but I could never reject hers.

One of my arms wrapped around her waist as I propelled us back to the shallows. Apprehension still lined her forehead, but she laced her fingers behind my neck. When we reached the ledge, I hoisted us up until I sat where I had a few minutes ago, more than ready for a do-over. She didn't look away as I gripped her thighs in my hands and lifted her so she straddled my lap, one knee on each side of my hips.

If she could be brave, then so could I.

"I'll probably never be good enough to believe that you could be mine," I said softly, splaying one of my hands over the bare skin of her back. "I made peace with that years ago. But I've always been yours." Her eyes widened, and I knew I owed her the full truth, the same as she'd given me. "Only yours. Always yours." Holy shit, I'd finally said it.

Her mouth collided with mine, and I lost myself in her. Her hands tunneled through my hair and held me as she poured her love, her joy into a kiss I never could have imagined.

It felt like coming home.

I gripped her hip in one hand and the base of her neck in the other, tilting her head so I could kiss her deeper. Our tongues danced and tangled; our lips caressed and lingered. I kissed her until I knew her mouth as well as I did my own, until she whimpered and rolled her hips over mine.

I kissed her slowly, with tenderness, and then I took her mouth with greed and pure need. Every nerve in my body was alive and tingling, electric with her nearness. Each of my senses filled with her. Just Willow. I was never going to get enough of kissing her. Not if I did it every day for the rest of my life.

When she arched for more, I slowed our pace, sucking on her bottom lip. Her nails bit into my scalp, and I gave her control until her tongue, her teeth, her damned hips had me harder than the ledge we sat on.

It would only take two seconds, the movement of two pieces of fabric, and I could be inside her.

The thought sobered me faster than a bucket of cold water could have. I changed the tone of the kiss, slowing until I pressed my lips against hers softly.

"We have to stop or I'm not going to," I told her as I rested my forehead against hers.

"I'm okay with not stopping." She kissed me again, and we fell back into it, because how the hell could I not? I'd dreamed of kissing Willow for years, almost decades, and she was in my arms. No secrets. No lies. "Not stopping would be awesome."

"I'm not okay with not stopping," I finally managed between kisses.

She startled, looking at me with raised eyebrows and parted lips I immediately wanted back. "What?"

I grinned and stroked my thumb up her jawline. "Contrary to popular belief, sex isn't all a guy wants."

She scoffed. "Really." She wiggled her hips over the evidence that sex was definitely on my mind. "Because I really want you, and it feels like you're in the same boat."

"I didn't say I didn't want you. Because I do. God, I do. But I'm not taking you in the mineral pool. At least not the first time."

"My house is five minutes that way." She nodded toward her car.

I laughed. "I'm not rushing this."

"Can I rush this?" she asked.

"No." There was no force on this earth that could make me take this for granted.

"Because you're scared I'll change my mind? Or because you will?" Her hands slipped to my shoulders, and she started to pull away.

I locked my arms around her waist.

"I saw you that night. When Sullivan kissed you in the gazebo," I admitted.

Her eyes widened, but she stayed silent.

"I saw you leave and knew you were upset, so I went searching for you. If I had to guess, I would say that I was about five minutes too late. Instead of manning up and telling you how I felt, dealing with all the shit we were going to get in town because I'm me and you're you, I watched you kiss my brother. It fucking killed me. That was why I joined the army the next day."

"Oh, Cam." Her fingers soothed the back of my neck.

"I couldn't stay there and watch it happen, even if I thought it was probably what was best for both of you. I was afraid I'd lose it one day and beat the shit out of him—my little brother—for having the only thing I'd ever wanted for myself." I let my thumb graze her lips, and she kissed it lightly. "I was mean to you that summer because I had another month until my basic report date and couldn't let you get any closer than you already were. Couldn't let you see and couldn't take the sight of you with him."

"I'm so sorry," she whispered.

"That's not your fault. It was mine. My point is that five minutes changed the course of our lives. Five fucking minutes and my inability to get out of my own way kept me from kissing you that night. And it wasn't the first night, either."

Her brow wrinkled, and I leaned forward, gently kissing the lines just because I could. Because she loved me.

"By the time you were old enough for kissing, I was a senior in high school, and I didn't want to take the chance that you didn't want me."

"I always wanted you," she argued.

"And I probably knew it, if I'd just thought about it hard enough. But I wasn't just scared that you'd reject me. I was scared that you wouldn't. That I'd hurt you like I did everyone else. That the town would turn on you."

"I don't care about the town's opinion, and you'd never hurt me." She shivered, and I brought us to the edge of the ledge, then lowered us so she was immersed in the water while she wrapped her arms around my neck.

"Hurt you physically? Never. But I wasn't the most trustworthy with your emotions, and the thought of ruining you?" I shook my head. "Besides, I was leaving for college. What was I going to do? Leave you brokenhearted and lonely? How selfish would that have been?"

"I was anyway."

I kissed her lips, letting the touch soften the memories, trying to trust that this was real and not some fucked-up dream I'd wake from. "Our timing was off. It was always off."

She grinned. "You're saying you couldn't find the pika."

I laughed, and it felt great. God, to have her in my arms, to kiss her, to laugh with her. It was beyond my wildest dreams.

"Right. I knew how to sit quietly with you. I knew how to be patient, and that's why I knew the timing wasn't right. Then you were kissing Sullivan, and I realized the time had passed and I hadn't been brave enough to grab it. Five minutes, Willow."

"And this all goes back to you not wanting to take me back to my house because..." She kissed my jaw, and a little of my resolve drifted away with the steam.

"Are you scared you'll change your mind? Or I will? Is that why you're rushing?" I asked.

"No, I'm rushing because I've wanted you for so long that I'm about ready to combust with it, and if we're finally on the same page, I'm done wasting time." She nibbled my ear.

Shit, her reasoning was sound. But so was mine.

"I'm not rushing," I said, tipping her chin up so I could see her eyes. "Because our timing is right for the first time in our lives. I'm not rushing through something I've wanted my whole life just for instant gratification. I'm going to savor every single step I get to take with you. I'm going to date the hell out of you, Willow Bradley."

She grinned. "Dating, huh?"

"Yeah. I've messed up just about everything in my life, but this?" I kissed her gently. "This, I'm going to get right."

So help me God, I was not going to screw this up.

CHAPTER SEVENTEEN

Willow

The doorbell rang, and my heart leaped, just like it had the last three times Cam had picked me up for a date. The last three and a half weeks, he'd taken me to dinner down in Buena Vista and a traveling art show in Salida and held my hand as we hiked the trail that led up to the falls, where I lay with my head in his lap as he read to me.

The snowpack had melted pretty much everywhere but the shaded patches, and I couldn't help but sigh like a lovesick teenage girl when I thought about Cam's defenses melting right along with the snow.

"Got it!" Rose called out, already at the door.

"Hi there, Rose. How's it going?"

Cam's voice slid over me like sun-warmed silk, and I walked out of the kitchen to find him crouched down just inside the living room, talking to my niece.

"Hi." Awesome. My voice was all breathy and awkward.

"Hey, Pika," he replied with a wink.

Hate to break it to Mrs. Barstrom, my freshman biology teacher, but she was wrong. That wink right there was how babies were made.

"So it made me think of you!" Rose finished saying as I shook my head free of the Cam-induced fog. She handed him a black T-shirt with a toothy grin.

"Oh yeah? You really bought it for me?" he asked, holding the T-shirt out in front of him to inspect it. "Wow, that's amazing! Thanks, Rose!"

"You like it?" she asked, hopping on her toes.

"Love it!" He turned it around to show me.

I bit my lip to keep from laughing at the glittery unicorn that adorned the front of the shirt.

"I saw it when I was shopping with Mom, and she said I could get it for you," Rose finished with a nod.

"Well, that was really nice of your mom." Cam stood to his full height and unzipped his black jacket. "You know, I can't remember the last time a girl gave me a present."

That gave me pause. He'd been pretty open about his past over the last few weeks. Of course there had been women, just like I'd dated a handful of guys. And I knew he kept his relationships brief, but none of them had given him a gift?

He dropped his jacket on my couch, and I picked it up, holding it to my chest as he pulled the T-shirt over his long-sleeve Henley and straightened it out.

"What do you think?" he asked Rose, spreading his arms wide.

I buried my nose in his coat to keep my laugh under wraps. It smelled just like him, all mint and pine.

He wasn't fooled, cocking an eyebrow at me as I tried to stop my shoulders from shaking.

"It's perfect," Rose declared.

"I think you chose perfectly. Thank you." He bowed his head to her like he was a knight with a princess, and I fell in love with him all over again.

How easily those words slipped through my mind now that I'd admitted them out loud. I would have thought I'd feel weird or insecure, having said them when Cam hadn't, but instead the words were incredibly freeing.

"Rose, why don't you grab your coat so we can get going?" I suggested.

"Okay!" She bounced down the hallway to the guest room, her braid swinging behind her.

"Thank you for being so easy about this," I said as Cam closed the distance between us.

"It's no problem," he promised, tilting my chin up with his thumb.

"I just promised Charity that she could finally get a weekend with her boyfriend, and then Rose's dad didn't show." I dropped that last part to a whisper so Rose wouldn't hear.

"Willow, it's no problem," he repeated, then brushed a kiss across my lips. "We could probably use a chaperone anyway."

A chaperone was the last thing we needed. What we needed was a week with no phones, no distractions, and a very large bed. Any minute I expected this dream bubble to burst. To wake up and find that we were where we'd been a month ago. Years ago. A decade ago.

And I knew that was exactly why he'd kept his hands PG for the last three weeks. I had to trust this as much as I trusted him.

"I've missed you this week," I admitted, stealing another kiss.

"I'm so sorry. Dad had a rough day on Thursday, and yesterday I got tied up in work."

"You don't have to apologize. I can miss you; that's allowed. It's not like we're back in high school, when I could sneak a peek at you between classes every day."

"Every day?" he asked.

"Every. Day."

He smiled, and I echoed the expression.

"It's okay. You can kiss her," Rose said from the hallway, and I ducked my head, laughing.

"Some chaperone you are," Cam drawled.

"I helped Aunt Willow make lunch!" She lifted the small day pack we'd filled with a picnic this morning.

"Then, I guess we'd better get going so we can eat it, huh?" he asked, crossing over to her and taking the bag from her hands.

She nodded enthusiastically, and we piled into Cam's Jeep once she was all zipped up for the breezy spring weather.

Cam took us out of the driveway and then turned onto the road that led to the mine. "I thought you might want to see the progress before we picnic."

"You thought right," I confirmed.

Five minutes later, we pulled up to the entrance of the mine. Two construction trailers with the contractor's name sat parallel to the road with various pieces of large equipment parked around them, blocking my view of the tunnel I knew lay beyond.

I hopped out of the Jeep and then helped Rose down. "Stay close, okay?"

"You got it," she promised, already staring at the construction equipment.

"Your coat, my dear." I handed Cam's jacket over as we met in front of the Jeep.

"I like the sound of that," he said quietly, taking it.

"My dear?"

He nodded, then slipped the jacket on and zipped it up. I noticed the label and laughed.

"What?" he asked, looking down like he'd spilled something.

"It's silly." I shoved my hands into my purple North Face.

"Oh, now I definitely want to know." He adjusted his hat, pulling the stretchy material down to cover his ears.

I snuck a peek at Rose, who was already examining rocks about twenty feet away. "You call me Pika."

"Right?" He reached over and tugged at my hat, then swept his hand down my unbound hair.

"You know how they like to live with other animals? Well, beneath other animals?" My cheeks heated, and I wished I'd kept it to myself.

His brow furrowed. "Yeah. Sometimes they make burrows under the homes of ones that will alert them to predators."

I nodded and dropped my gaze to the label on his jacket, then ran my fingers over the embroidery. "Marmots."

He looked down where my fingers traced those very letters and laughed. "Guess that's pretty fitting."

When I was sure my face couldn't flush any hotter, he cupped my cheeks in his palms and kissed me with warm, closed lips.

"We have a chaperone," I reminded him but reveled in the contact. It still floored me that I was allowed to kiss Cam whenever I wanted. That he was mine in every sense. Well, at least when we were alone. We hadn't exactly gone outright public, both content to stay in our little happy space.

"A bad one at that," he said with a smile. "Hey, Rose, what do you say we check out your namesake?"

"Can you bring the bag?" she asked, her arms already full of rocks.

"I'll do you one better," he replied. "Wait right there."

A minute later, he returned from the first construction trailer with a canvas backpack. "What do you think?" he asked as he handed it to her.

"Cool! Can you unzip it?"

"You bet." Once they had Rose's rocks secure, he showed me the bag, which had the logo I'd designed for him embroidered across the back.

"Rose Rowan Mine," I read.

"They just came in yesterday. I've also got sample batches of T-shirts, hats, and key chains in the trailer. Told you I loved the design."

We stood there looking at each other with upturned lips. I loved designing it for him. Loved working with him. Loved helping him and confiding in him. Loved everything about every moment I got with him.

"Are you two going to kiss again, or can we go find more rocks?" Rose asked.

Cam took my hand, enveloping my grip in his larger one. "Let's find you some rocks."

We cleared the construction equipment, and the main tunnel appeared. "It's smaller than I remember."

"You were smaller," Cam countered as we approached the wooden platform, where an open-topped train with three cars waited. "Look what I got running this week."

"That's so awesome!" Rose said, racing ahead to the train.

"What she said," I agreed. "Is that...?"

"Completely safe and in park, I promise." He dangled the keys from his finger. "It's the original from the last time the mine ran in the fifties, and I worked with Keith Mayberry to convert it for tours."

"That's great, and I bet Keith really appreciated the business." He was one of the business owners in Alba who didn't own historical property.

"Yeah. He's tracking down another setup just like this one—historically accurate, of course—and then he'll do the same with those. I figured if we've got the grant money, we'd better keep as much of the business in Alba as we can, right? It should benefit the whole town."

I nodded, swallowing back the little lump of emotion in my throat.

"This is amazing!" Rose shouted, already sitting in the car behind the driver's seat.

"Want to go for a ride?" he asked.

"Yes!"

I tensed.

"Relax, Pika," he muttered against my temple. "We'll only go as far back as they've reinforced. I won't let anything happen to her or to you."

My head nodded, but my brain was already down the mine. "How far have they reinforced?"

He heard the catch in my breath and squeezed my hand. "Not that far."

"Okay." I hadn't been more than thirty feet inside the mine since the day I'd been way farther than that.

Cam helped me into the ore cart, which now had cushioned benches and seat belts, and I made sure Rose's was buckled.

"Ta-da!" he said, flourishing a bright-yellow hard hat with Rose's name in big, bold letters above the headlamp.

"That's mine?" she squealed.

"It's no unicorn shirt, but yeah, it's yours." He leaned over the division between cars and put it over her hat. "Can you get it buckled?"

"You bet!" She buckled as Cam handed me a bigger model that read pika.

"Your boyfriend is so awesome!" Rose shouted with her hands in the air.

My eyes popped wide. Oh God. Were we labeled? Was labeling even a thing anymore? Did he think he was my boyfriend?

"Well, it comes with the territory when you have an awesome girlfriend," Cam confirmed. "Buckle up, Miss Bradley," he ordered as he put his own hard hat on.

Dazed, I snapped the helmet in place, then switched on my headlamp and did the same for Rose as Cam started the engine.

Rose's gaze swung back and forth as Cam drove us into the mine, the tunnel beginning a good twenty feet above our heads before sloping down to only five feet or so. The air was musty, thick with moisture and the tang of metal.

It tasted like blood and fear on my tongue, but I watched how excited Rose was, and the panic eased.

We traveled more than a hundred yards before the first antechamber opened up and a wooden platform appeared. Cam put the train into park and killed the engine, leaving the lights on.

"This is as far as the train goes for now," he told Rose. "Do you want to explore a little with me?"

She nodded, then swung her backpack over her shoulders and climbed onto the platform.

"Remember it?" Cam asked me quietly.

I nodded. "How is it that every happy memory I have of playing down here was eclipsed by that one crappy one?"

He traced the bump on my nose with his finger. "We can come back and make an even better memory," he whispered.

"You say no to hot springs, but a dark and creepy mine is on the table?" I teased.

"Eventually everywhere is on the table." His eyes heated.

I did my best to remember that my niece was ten feet away, when all I really wanted was a table. Any table.

"Rocks," I reminded him.

"Right. Okay, Rose, what do you know about the mine?" He turned to where she had leaned close to the chiseled stone wall, examining the rock.

"I know I'm named after it. Well, not it but the lady it was named after. Mom thought it was a pretty name."

"It is a pretty name," he agreed, helping me onto the newly built platform.

It was a good ten feet wide, built according to the specifications I'd given him when we'd discussed this part of the mine.

"They mined mostly gold and silver," Rose told Cam. "The first rush came in the 1880s, but by the Great Depression, they only had a small section of silver, and they stopped mining in the fifties."

"You know that? At nine?" he questioned.

"Every kid born in Alba knows that by the time they're seven." She looked up at him from under her hard hat with an expression that said she wasn't impressed.

"Okay, smarty-pants, do you know where the three tunnels lead?"

She glanced among the three offshoots of the antechamber and shook her head.

"That's the newest tunnel." Cam pointed to the right. "It was constructed in the thirties. Great Depression, just like you said. The one to the left was a 1910 silver find. The one straight ahead is the oldest vein."

"Can we go back there?"

Fearless, that one.

"Not today," he told her. "We haven't cleared all the tunnels yet. There are places the tunnels have caved into the ones under them. Places the air shafts collapsed, so the ventilation isn't good enough for your little lungs. and the sides haven't been reinforced yet like they are here."

"Can I look around here, though?" she pushed.

"If you stay in this chamber and your aunt Willow says it's okay."

Two sets of pleading eyes met mine.

"Promise to stay right here," I ordered, hoping she heard the urgency in my voice.

"I will," she vowed, then scrambled down the stairs and across the tracks to where the space widened a good thirty feet.

"Ready for my surprise?" Cam asked.

"Definitely."

"I think I can have at least one tunnel open for tours by the Fourth of July." His eyes danced.

"Really? That would be amazing! Have you told anyone?" The town was going to flip. As much as they despised Cam, they loved money.

"I wanted to tell you first." His smile blew me away. He was... happy, as much as I hesitated to even think it, and it looked wonderful on him.

"I love you," I whispered.

He kissed me in response, then pulled back with a grin. "Hey, Rose, if you come hang with your aunt Willow, I'll find you something sparkly."

"Deal!" she agreed, already heading back to me, and Cam disappeared off the other end of the platform, his light bobbing down the oldest portion of the tunnel.

"This place is amazing. Pretty sure there's still gold here somewhere."

"Maybe," I muttered, my eyes trained on that light as it got smaller. A few minutes later, it grew larger until Cam came into view.

I let loose a huge sigh of relief.

"You don't like it down here, do you, Aunt Willow?" Rose asked, taking my hand.

"What? No, it's fine. I'm fine," I lied.

"Here you go," Cam said as he handed two sparkling pieces of ore to Rose.

"Is it gold?" she squeaked.

"No. It's pyrite. Fool's gold," he replied.

"Well, it's still pretty." She looked up at him. "You could have pretended it was gold."

"You can pretend it's gold now that you know it's not." He tapped her helmet. "I'm not in the habit of lying to girls."

Her brow wrinkled, but then she nodded. "Pyrite."

"You got it. Now, let's get you ladies out of here." He helped Rose into the train.

"Do you think there's real gold down here?" she asked, buckling her belt.

Cam reached for me, letting his hands linger on my waist once my feet hit the steel bottom of the car. "I think there's a real gold unicorn pin down here somewhere," he told her, looking straight at me.

"Really?"

"Yep. Your aunt lost it when we were kids." His hands flexed on my waist again before he let me go and climbed over into the driver's car.

"You lost a unicorn pin?" Her eyebrows rose in accusation.

"I did. I got lost down here when I was your age, actually." God, she was so young. So small. Had I really been her age?

"You did?"

Cam fired up the engine, and I buckled in. "She did."

"I was exploring with your mom and Xander, and I got

separated somehow. I don't remember a lot of that part, but I slipped and fell down one of those shafts." I motioned toward the older tunnel as Cam drove us around the circular track that would bring us back to daylight.

"Were you scared?"

"Terrified. But Cam found me. It felt like I'd been gone for days, but really it was only a few hours."

She nodded slowly, thinking over what I'd said. "And you left your pin?"

"It got ripped off my shirt when I fell, I think."

We were quiet as the train sped up, and I breathed a heck of a lot easier once the sun hit my face.

"How about I keep your helmet on my desk so you have it whenever you want to visit?" Cam offered.

Rose debated for a moment but eventually agreed. "I can come back, right?"

"Whenever you want," he promised. "I mean, as long as you're with an adult." He shot me a sorry look.

"Deal." She handed it over. I did the same, then walked toward the Jeep with her as Cam took the hard hats back to his office.

"What's that?" she asked, pointing down the hill to the charred, overgrown remains of the bunkhouse.

"That was the bunkhouse," I told her. "It's where the unmarried miners slept."

"It doesn't look like the other buildings," she noted. "Even the roofless ones."

"It burned down."

"When?"

"When we were teenagers," Cam replied, coming up behind us. "We had a really big party one night, and it caught fire. Guess what?"

"What?" she asked him with big eyes.

"I carried your aunt out of that, too." He nodded seriously, tucking me into his side.

She looked from us to the ruins and back with a shake of her head.

"What?" I questioned.

She sighed and headed toward the Jeep. "You guys get in a lot of trouble. Mom would have grounded me if I'd been in the middle of any of that."

I didn't bother telling her that her mom had been at the fire, too.

Cam's phone rang, and he let go of me to answer it as we walked behind Rose. "What's up?" He halted, so I did, too. "Are you serious? Have you tried Walt's cell? Okay, I'm on my way." He hung up and cursed softly.

"What's going on?"

"Can we make a pit stop at Dad's? Apparently Walt busted him from at-home-care jail a few hours ago, and Xander is losing his mind."

"Absolutely."

We pulled into the Danielses' driveway about ten minutes later to find Xander yelling at Walt on the porch.

"At least they're back," I offered.

"Right," he replied, killing the engine and getting out.

I checked to make sure the keys weren't in the ignition and the e-brake was on. "Wait here," I told Rose.

"Where are you going?"

"To make sure Camden doesn't get in any more trouble your mom would ground him for." I jumped down from the Jeep and headed up the stairs.

"What the hell were you thinking?" Xander yelled.

"That my best friend asked me to take him out, so I did." Walt crossed his arms calmly over his chest.

Mr. Daniels sighed and moved to do the same, but he winced instead and put his arms at his sides. Cam's attention focused on his dad.

"And you were okay with this?" Xander questioned, but I kept my eyes on Mr. Daniels, noting the way he shifted his weight.

"Well, he was on the approved list you left me, Mr. Daniels," May explained. At least according to the schedule Cam had tacked on his fridge, it should be May.

"Well, he's not anymore! How could you not tell anyone where you were going? Not pick up your phone?"

Mr. Daniels moved again, the same wince puckering his expression for a second.

He was in pain.

"Alexander, I don't answer to you. You're not my mother," Walt stated.

Xander ripped at his tie to loosen it. He couldn't have looked more different from Cam's casual ruggedness in that moment.

"Enough, you two," Cam growled. "Dad, what the hell did you do? You're hurt."

Art's chin rose at the same moment Walt sighed. "Look, he wanted to."

"Wanted to what?" Xander snapped.

Art unzipped his jacket and let it fall to the wooden porch. "My name is Arthur Daniels. I'm fifty-eight years old, and I have early-onset Alzheimer's," he said to Xander as he started unbuttoning his long-sleeve flanncl shirt. "This here is Walter Robinson, who's been my best friend since we were kids. That's the babysitter you hired—I don't remember her name because I just don't care. Sorry, but it's true." He glanced at May and back to Xander. "You're Alexander, my oldest son. That's Camden, my second son. And that's—" He saw me and paused, surprise flaring in his eyes. "That's Willow Bradley—"

Don't say it. Don't say it. Don't say it.

"Sullivan's girl."

FML.

Cam stiffened next to me, his jaw flexing. I brushed the back of my hand along his. Now wasn't the time or place, but I'd back whatever he decided.

"And you can control just about everything in my life, Alexander, but I'm lucid as you are today, and guess what?" He pulled back the sides of his shirt, and my mouth dropped open.

Under a layer of shiny plastic wrap were large, bloodied, and raised black letters that read do not resuscitate.

"You took him for a tattoo?" Xander shouted at Walt.

Walt shrugged. "When your best friend asks you for ink, you go for ink. Art, I'll see you later."

Art nodded at his friend and began buttoning his shirt.

"Don't you have anything to say about this?" Xander asked.

"As first pieces go, Dad, that's a pretty bold one," Cam told his dad. "Make sure you're keeping it clean. Did they give you anything for it?"

"Are you serious?" Xander fired back.

Art lifted a small brown bag from the deck. "Got the instructions and everything."

"Okay, then I think we're done here." Cam turned to face me. "Willow?"

I nodded and felt Cam's hand on the small of my back as I walked down the steps.

"That's really all you have to say about this?" Xander challenged.

Cam paused, then laced his fingers with mine.

My breath hitched, and he squeezed me reassuringly.

"No," Cam replied over his shoulder. "Willow isn't Sullivan's girl. She's mine. Nice ink, Dad. Call me if you need any help."

I looked back to see Xander's eyes narrow and Art's jaw drop as he saw our clasped hands. "It was nice to see you," I said in farewell.

They didn't respond.

"Well, that was a way to go public," I told Cam as he walked me to my door.

"Seemed like a good day for bold statements." He opened the Jeep and kissed me in full sight of the porch before helping me up into the lifted monster.

"Did you keep Camden out of trouble?" Rose asked from the back seat as Cam walked to his side.

"I'm not sure," I said slowly.

Cam climbed into his seat and gave a little wave to his dad and brother as he fired the engine to life. "Well, I'm starving, ladies. How about that picnic?"

Picnic? He'd just handed the town gossips enough fodder to keep them fed for the rest of the summer.

CHAPTER
EIGHTEEN

Camden

"Cam." Willow moaned my name as I set my lips to the tender strip of skin under her jaw. I'd only meant to kiss her quickly, but one hadn't been enough.

One was never enough lately. I lived in a perpetual state of wanting Willow.

Her fingers threaded through my hair, her nails lightly scraping my scalp as she tugged, sending a shock wave of electricity down my spine. I gave in to her demand, and she arched under me as I settled between her thighs.

This was where I wanted to live, to exist—in these moments where nothing outside these walls could touch what we were building inside them. Where we always should have been.

My hand gripped her hip, then slid up her waist and over her ribs, committing her curves to memory as I brought my mouth back to hers. I kissed her slowly, like we had all the time in the world, because we did. I wasn't going anywhere—not when I had her.

I lost myself in her, drawing out every sigh, every demand for more, fighting the primal need to have her in every possible way. She broke our kiss only to reach between us and pull the hem of her shirt over her head.

"Willow," I warned, keeping my eyes on hers.

"Cam." She dared me with those hazel eyes, then stripped the shirt from her arms and threw it to the floor beside her couch.

"You're killing me here," I growled, hoping for a little mercy.

"Good," she whispered before taking my lower lip between her teeth and biting gently.

God, I could feel the lace of her bra through my shirt. "Do you have any fucking clue how hard it is to keep my hands off you?"

She gripped my hand in hers and put it on her breast. "Let me help you out."

My hips instinctually rolled against hers, and I groaned at the feel of her filling my palm perfectly. Everything about Willow fit almost too well, too perfectly. My thumb grazed her nipple, and she gasped. I should have stopped us, should have reminded her that we had somewhere to be. Instead I made her gasp again.

"Please," she whispered against my lips. I loved that sound.

The strands of my self-control frayed. It had been almost six weeks of dates and working together, of dinners and lunches, of good-night kisses that lasted until both our lips were swollen and aching. Three weeks since I took her up to the mine. I could have lied and said I wasn't counting, but I was. Counting and savoring every single minute, and yeah, waiting for the other shoe to drop. For something—anything—to be wrong between us. Instead, everything with Willow was the easiest kind of perfect I could have hoped for.

Which was why it would hurt even more if this fell apart. If she decided she couldn't handle the scorn of the town she loved— and she shouldn't have to. I could do everything right for the rest of my life, and it wouldn't balance out my past in Alba's eyes.

One day, Willow would realize that, too, and she'd be forced to choose. Really choose. Not just get carried away in the hot springs by a decade of longing. She'd have to choose between me and her reputation—the flying gossip and the palpable scorn. I'd bear it all for her if I could, but that wasn't an option.

There was a reason we hadn't gone out together in Alba much.

First, I didn't want that shit to touch her. Ever.

Second, I didn't have a great track record of being chosen.

"What are you waiting for?" she asked.

"You." I brushed her hair from her face. "Always you."

"If I stripped off all my clothes, would it potentially move you in the direction of using this incredible body?" She ran her hands down my back, and I groaned.

"If you stripped off all your clothes, there's zero chance in hell we'd make it to opening day." Even the best intentions had limits.

"Opening... Oh crap!" Her eyes darted to the wall. "Cam, we're late!"

"Well, yeah." I dipped my head and kissed her.

She laughed and pushed at my shoulders.

"What happened to you stripping off your clothes?" I teased.

"It's opening day, that's what!"

"So you only want me when it's convenient to you?" I let my mouth drop in mock indignation.

"Are you saying that if I choose to forgo opening day, you'll take me to bed?" Her eyes danced with pure mischief.

"No."

"Ugh!" She shoved at my shoulders again, and I let her up, laughing as she sent me to the floor.

I landed on my back, thank God, so the part of me that definitely didn't want to go to opening day wasn't massacred.

Willow slid off the couch and straddled me. "You have the self-control of a saint," she muttered as she reached past my shoulder to grab her shirt, which put those glorious breasts right in my face. Pale-lavender lace and creamy skin filled my vision.

"Don't be so sure about that." My mouth watered, and that praised and cursed control snapped. The skin of her back was softer than satin as my hands splayed to hold her in place. Then I took her nipple between my lips and sucked her through the lace of her bra.

She whimpered, and the sound drove me right to the edge. I scraped her with my teeth and groaned when she rocked her hips against me in response. The denim between us did nothing to mask the friction or the heat.

My hands moved from her back to the rounded curve of her ass. Screw opening day. I was staying right here. There were plenty of ways to satisfy her without—

"We really have to go," she outright whined and sat up, taking her breasts with her. "I swear, Cam, if I couldn't feel how much you want me right now, I'd seriously think I don't do it for you." She tugged her shirt on and pulled her hair free of the neckline.

"Trust me," I told her, switching my grip to her hips. "You do it for me. You more than do it for me. You're it for me."

"Don't even think about getting all sweet with me, Camden Daniels. You have me wound tighter than a freaking…" Her forehead wrinkled. "I don't even know. Pick something that gets wound up."

I couldn't contain the laughter that sputtered from my lips, and her eyes narrowed as she climbed off me.

"It's a good thing I love you," she mumbled as she grabbed her shoes and put them on. The words sank a little deeper into me, just like they did every time she said them. If I wasn't careful, one day I'd start depending on them—on her. "What? Why are you looking at me like that?"

I rose and stretched, noting with more than a little satisfaction that her eyes went straight to the strip of skin I'd exposed while doing so. "Two reasons, really," I explained, walking to her hall closet to grab her jacket.

"Which would be?" She followed me.

I ignored the screaming protest in my dick that I was once again choosing not to take what she was offering and pulled her jacket from its hanger. Then I turned to face an equally frustrated Willow.

"First, I've never been with someone who I could kiss and laugh with in the same thirty seconds. I like it."

Her expression softened, and a ghost of a smile lifted the

corners of her lips.

"And second—" I handed Willow her jacket. "Your shirt is on inside out."

She looked down and let loose an exasperated sigh before turning away and walking down the hall.

"Where are you going?"

"To my bedroom. Show's over for you, buddy."

That only got me laughing again as I let my head bang back against the closet door.

Fifteen minutes later, I parked the Jeep in the owners-only lot just above Main Street.

"There must be a thousand people," Willow said as she jumped down from the Jeep.

"Let's hope. It's one of the three busiest weekends, right?" At least if nothing had changed in the decade I'd been gone. The dirt road that served as Alba's main source of income was a kaleidoscope of colors as tourists wandered.

"Yep. Mother's Day, Fourth of July, and Labor Day. Just like clockwork." She held out her hand, and I took it. "You ready?"

"As I'll ever be." We walked through the parking lot, then took the flight of steps down to Main Street. I was never a big fan of opening day—or the season, really. Not that I didn't understand the purpose. Alba only existed because people thought our ghost town was worth visiting.

I'd just never quite gotten what was so interesting about relics from our past when we could be building the future. Alba was in desperate need of updates.

"What are you thinking?" Willow asked as we reached the bottom step, coming out behind the surveyor's office.

"That I should talk to John Royal about installing micro-hydroelectric intakes along the creek. They're small and ridiculously effective, especially since the creek never freezes entirely. It would be a hell of a lot more dependable in the winter months than the ancient system we have going right now. I've thought about putting one up at my place, but it makes more sense to start in town."

She paused, looking at me with something a lot like wonder.

"What?" I asked, stilling.

"What else?" Her forehead puckered. "What would you change in the town? And no, I didn't open the door for you to go off on the gossip habits. You know what I mean. What would you modernize?"

"The bridge," I answered without a second thought. "It needs to be reinforced or completely rebuilt. Not this year but soon, with the influx of traffic we'll be expecting when the mine opens." I shrugged.

"And?" she prompted, tucking her hair behind her ears.

"We need greenhouses. There's at least a month up here when some people can't get down the pass. Mount Princeton has a ton of greenhouses, and they're only a thousand feet beneath us. I don't see why we couldn't have a little self-sustainability. I actually started one yesterday at my place."

Her smile was shy, like she knew a secret I didn't.

"What are you thinking?" I asked. "It's only fair, since I answered."

"That you said *we*. You're settling in, and it's pretty incredible to watch, especially for someone who hated growing up here." She squeezed my hand.

I quickly bent and brushed a kiss across her forehead. "I didn't hate everything about growing up here."

"I love you," she whispered.

My hands cupped her face, and I swallowed the words that seemed to live on the tip of my tongue. "I have no clue why, but I'm incredibly thankful."

"There you are!"

I dropped my hands and stepped away from Willow as Thea called out to us, coming around the building with her son.

Willow gave me a questioning glance but turned on a smile

for Thea. "Hey! Hi, Jacob!" She dropped down to his eye level. "Already into the caramel corn?"

"Yep! Want some?" he asked, his voice high and bright.

"That's super nice of you to share, but no, thank you. You can gobble it all." She ruffled his light hair and stood. "How is it going at your place?"

"I checked in with Pat about an hour ago, and he said it's booming as usual. Having the only saloon is a definite advantage. I'm just taking this guy home for a nap." She nudged Jacob, who pouted up at her.

"Sawyer doesn't have to nap!"

"Well, I'm not Sawyer's mommy," Thea replied with a patient smile.

"Speaking of Sawyer, is Gideon around?" I asked.

"He's over with James and Sawyer at the blacksmith's. It's good to see you outside the Historical Society, Cam." She arched an eyebrow over a less-patient smile. "Maybe you could bring my best friend around every once in a while?"

I winced. "Point taken."

"Good. It's not like everyone doesn't know that you're together. And I'm super happy for you, of course," she added at Willow. "It's about darn time, if you ask me."

Willow wrapped her arm around my waist, and I lifted mine over her shoulder. "We've just been…" She looked up at me, and the skin between her eyebrows crinkled. "I don't know."

"Not in Alba," I stated bluntly. "I think you might be the only person happy for us, and Willow doesn't need to take any crap for it." Score a point for me—I remembered not to swear in front of Jacob.

Jacob, who was a mirror image of Pat, who hated me for bringing his best friend home in a box.

"I'm not worried," Willow promised, leaning into me.

"That makes one of us."

Thea's gaze bounced between us. "Well, you're never going

to get past the gossip if you don't get through it first. And the Cam I knew never gave a fig what people said."

"Still don't. I only care when Willow's involved."

Her lips flattened, and she shot a frustrated look at Willow. "Good luck with that one. Call me later?"

Willow agreed, and the two embraced before Thea took Jacob up the stairs to the parking lot on the hill above.

"You got grouchy fast," Willow chastised.

I shoved my hands in my pockets. "It's just easier when we're at home."

Her eyes narrowed. "Or when we're in Salida? Or Buena Vista? Or hiking? Or anywhere but Alba?"

"Pretty much."

"You know what would make you way less grouchy?" She slid her arm through mine, openly defying my attempt to pull away.

"Going home?" We took the wooden path that led behind the buildings and turned between the surveyor's office and the bank.

"Sex."

I shook my head, but I laughed when I did it.

We walked into the crowd of tourists and fell into the current of traffic flowing up the wooden boardwalk that served as a sidewalk.

"You know, you've held my hand in public before."

"We weren't together." Because somehow that was different.

"Why would that matter?"

"It was one thing to mock everyone who can't keep their thoughts to themselves, but it's another to open you up to scrutiny when we're actually in a relationship."

"You know what makes relationships better?" she teased.

"Don't start with me, Willow Bradley."

"Can I finish with you?" She grinned up at me, happily tucked into my arm as we walked. "No? Later, then."

We were in the full view of Alba. Lightning didn't strike me dead. No one whispered or glared. The world didn't stop turning.

Because it was the season and we were mixed in with a thousand tourists who didn't give a shit who we were. We had the kind of freedom that only the anonymity of a crowd could give.

I pressed a kiss to the top of her head.

"Willow!"

So much for being anonymous.

Willow's mom stood on the front steps of the original city hall and leaned over the railing to wave.

"Why don't you go ahead—"

Willow's arm locked on mine. "And go to see Mom with you?" She finished my sentence and shot me a look that dared me to correct her.

"Yeah, that's exactly what I meant."

"No need to be sarcastic," she chided. "If you can handle the Taliban, you can definitely hold your own against my mother."

Given the way Mrs. Bradley was looking at me, I wasn't so sure. Oh, she liked me all right. She just wasn't sure she liked me with her daughter.

"Should have worn my Kevlar."

Willow bumped me with her hip as we climbed the steps.

"I'm so glad you're here. Your father had to step out for a second, and I could sure use your help. Hi, Camden." She turned to me with a smile that actually reached her eyes. "Have you—?"

"Cam!" A figure darted from the doorway and crashed into my stomach.

My arm automatically wrapped around Rose. "How's it going, Rosie?"

"I'm bored. Our building is boring." She looked up at me with an expression so like Willow's that I couldn't help but grin.

"It's not boring!" Mrs. Bradley argued. "It's historic and important."

"And boring," Charity added as she walked onto the porch.

"Will you take me to yours?" Rose asked. "Mom said I couldn't go until you got here. She thinks the crowd will swallow me."

"If your mom's cool with it, I'll take you." I looked over at Charity.

She had a silent discussion with her daughter that included a lot of eyebrow raising and narrowing of eyes. "Fine. Just don't be a pest to Cam. Promise?"

"Promise!" Rose nodded.

"Go ahead," Willow urged. "I'll meet you up there as soon as I can." She leaned up, and I bent to kiss her out of habit. "Be good," she whispered against my lips.

"I'm not the one with self-control issues," I teased.

She scoffed but was smiling when she walked into the building.

"Mrs. Bradley." I nodded to her mom.

"She's happy."

"Yes, ma'am."

"Keep her that way." Her gaze hardened for a second in motherly warning, and a pang of longing for my mother hit me.

"Yes, ma'am."

Satisfied, she told Rose to be good, then joined her daughter.

"You survived," Charity noted, lightly punching my shoulder.

"The battle. The war remains to be seen." I scooped Rose up in my arms and sat her on my shoulders. "Now, the crowd can't swallow you."

Rose's nose scrunched as she grinned. "See, Mom?"

"I see. You take care of my girl, Cam." She pointed a finger at me.

"You take care of mine, Charity," I countered as I turned... and barely swallowed a swear word.

Judge Bradley glared up at me from the bottom step. "Put my granddaughter down."

CHAPTER NINETEEN

Camden

"Hi, Grandpa!" Rose waved, swaying on my shoulders.

"Rosie," he replied with a softer smile toward her. "Put her—"

Charity stepped to my side, earning an icy glower from her father. She didn't speak, simply tilted her head.

"I'm going to Cam's building!" Rose informed him.

"The assayer's office," I added, in case he thought she meant the yet-to-be-repaired mining building.

His attention went to Rose, skipping right over me. "Have fun, sweetheart." Then he sidestepped and walked up the stairs, passing Charity without a word.

Charity gave my arm a reassuring pat in farewell, and I carried Rose out into the crowd.

"What's wrong?" Rose asked as she leaned over.

"You Bradley girls are trouble," I complained with an exaggerated shake of my head, adjusting my grip on her legs.

"Technically, I'm a Maylard."

"Yeah, yeah." I crossed Main Street, taking deep breaths when the crowd pushed in.

"I can see everything from up here! You okay?" Rose asked.

"Yep. I just don't like crowds." Especially ones I couldn't control or observe.

"I don't like snakes."

"Oh yeah?" I held her tighter to keep people from bumping into her.

"They move without legs. It's weird."

"Good point."

The crowd eased at the boardwalk, and I quickly climbed the steps into the assayer's office. About a dozen tourists filled the space, some sorting through the raised wooden bins of ore and others waiting their turn to have their finds assessed.

"When we open the mine, they can get ore up there, too," I told Rose as we passed through two of the lines, heading for the wooden rail that separated public from preserved space.

"Really? That will be so cool!"

"Hey, Reece." I waved to the Acosta kid I'd hired to hold down one of the tables.

"Hey, Mr. Daniels." The kid nodded and turned his attention back to the tourist he was helping.

Xander didn't bother looking up from the table he was helping at.

I put Rose down when I saw Dad pacing the length of the glass wall that kept the final fifteen feet of the office perfectly preserved. He tugged at the costume he'd worn to every opening day since I could remember and muttered something about ore, and I looked to his nurse. "May, how is he today?"

"He's a little confused," she admitted from behind the table in the corner.

"Hey, is this the mine?" Rose asked, pointing to the glass on the table that covered a copy of the Rose Rowan's layout.

"That's the Rose Rowan," Dad told her. "You should know that. Everyone knows that. Everyone wants her."

My gaze shot to Xander, who had turned to look at Dad. Our eyes met, and the worry I saw there overpowered my anger at our current legal situation. "I've got him," I promised.

He nodded, then turned back to helping tourists. Good thing I'd hired summer help, because there was no chance Xander and

I were manning this thing all summer, and Dad was in no shape to do it.

"I know it's the Rose Rowan," Rose countered. "That's what I said. I'm named after the mine."

"Are you?" he asked, running his thumbs down the inside of his suspenders. The motion was so familiar that it was hard to believe he wasn't fully lucid. Even on his worst days, he still found small ways to shine through the Alzheimer's.

"I am," Rose told him. "This is the oldest tunnel." She pointed to the layout.

Dad leaned over the table. "Sure is."

"My aunt got lost down here." She pointed again.

He looked at her with obvious strain. "Your aunt?"

"Yep. Aunt Willow. She said Cam brought her out." She pointed at me.

Dad turned his head and gave me a once-over. "You broke her nose."

"I did not break her nose," I argued. "She fell before I could find her." For fuck's sake, was I condemned to having the same twenty-year-old argument with my father for the rest of his life?

His eyes narrowed. "You were covered in her blood."

"Well, yeah. I carried her." She'd kept her forehead tucked against my neck the whole way out.

"She let you." He said it slowly, like he was piecing the memory together.

"She did." In fact, it had taken a very angry Judge Bradley to pry her loose.

"Then, you didn't break her nose," he decided and turned back to the map.

I blinked, speechless.

"They kiss a lot," Rose said with a shrug, like that explained it.

Dad shifted so he could sit at the table and glare at me simultaneously. "She's Sullivan's girl."

I ignored the ugliness that curdled in my stomach and forced a soft smile to my mouth. "Not anymore, Dad."

His forehead crinkled.

"So do you think this is where she fell?" Rose asked, leaning onto the table so far that she might as well have lay on it.

Dad still stared at me, searching for answers I couldn't give him because I didn't know what year he thought it was.

"Mr. Daniels?" Rose asked. "Do you not remember?"

He turned back to Rose. "Of course I remember. I know this mine better than anyone." He pored over the map.

"Cam knows it pretty well," Rose countered and looked at me.

Trouble, I mouthed at her, and she giggled.

"Because I taught him," Dad muttered. "Cam was the only one who listened. Tried with Alexander..." His finger trailed along the path. "I always figured it was around here, but Willow never could describe it. She ran off from Alexander, you know. He'd walked with both those Bradley girls, and Willow just took off looking for gold." He pulled a lump of ore from his pocket. "See, gold."

Rose picked it up and examined it carefully. "That's pyrite."

Dad grinned. "So it is. Do you want to see where I found it?"

She nodded enthusiastically, and just like that, I was no longer her favorite Daniels.

"Camden?" May asked. "Do you think you could grab a bottle of water from the general store? I forgot to bring some for your father, and he needs to take his medication."

"Go ahead. I'll keep my eye on them," Xander promised, motioning to Rose.

"Rosie, you okay if I step out?"

"Yep," she answered, too busy listening to whatever story my dad was telling to pay me any mind.

"She won Dad over," Xander said as I passed him to open the gate in the heavy wooden railing.

"She's a Bradley girl," I explained with a shrug.

"I'm a Maylard!" she called out.

"See what I mean?" We both laughed, and for that moment, we were normal. Dad wasn't sick. Xander and I weren't headed to court to decide our father's future in a month. We were just brothers.

I got the hell out of there before I did something to wreck the moment.

Young's General Store was crowded with tourists shopping for vintage-style candy and goods, and I had to pause more than once as I made my way toward the back.

"Cam, go on in," Jonathan Young called over the crowd when he saw me, and he motioned toward the door only locals were allowed to go through.

I didn't miss the disapproving shake of his head, but I tried to ignore it. He was probably still pissed about the time I replaced all his jelly beans with the Bertie Bott's ones that gambled with taste buds.

Not that I blamed him. I was an asshole as a teenager.

I opened the door and found the back room already teeming with locals looking for a break. The space was small, probably only twenty by twenty, but it housed two stocked refrigerators, a microwave, and doors to the only plumbed bathrooms allowed in the historical district.

I heard my name muttered a few times and simply waved, heading straight for the refrigerator.

"How's your face?" Oscar taunted from the couch he sat on, his arm wrapped around Tillie.

"How's your hand?" I countered as I pulled a six-pack of water from the top shelf of the fridge.

"You think you're a badass, huh?" he asked, coming to his feet.

"Now, Oscar, we don't want trouble in here," Milton Sanders lectured, wiping sweat from beneath his newsboy cap. "Why don't you head back to your dad's?"

"I'm not the one with the infamous temper, am I, Cam?" Oscar poked with a lopsided grin.

"You need to find a hobby, Oscar. I'm not available for a playdate." I set the water on the counter and slid my wallet from my pocket, pulling a ten from the back section.

Oscar snorted. "Find a hobby?"

"Yeah, you know. Something to do besides drink at one o'clock in the afternoon." I dropped the ten into the plastic slot that covered the gallon jar the Youngs kept back here for this kind of stuff.

"I was looking for some*one* to do, but then you started screwing Willow Bradley and threw that plan to hell."

I stilled with my hand on the water, keeping my back turned to Oscar. My senses focused in a way I knew all too well.

"Cam," Milton warned softly. "Walk away."

I sucked air in through my nose slowly, willing the rising rage to ebb. I wasn't seventeen anymore. I couldn't beat the shit out of everyone who offended me or Willow. Willow. She wouldn't want me to kill the asshat running his mouth behind me.

If I could repeat that about a million times, I might be able to calm the fuck down.

"Oh, come on, Milt. He can't be that offended at the truth," Oscar slurred, his voice coming closer.

"Don't, Oscar," I warned, catching his reflection in the microwave door.

"Come on, man," another voice joined in, but I didn't turn. If I set eyes on Oscar, I was going to kill him with my bare hands.

The back door opened and shut.

"What? Don't you think it's fucked up that he shows up after ten years and acts like he's God's gift? Telling Xander what to do with Art, when he's been the one taking care of him all these years. It's bullshit."

The water bottle crinkled in my grip.

"Sit your drunk ass down or take it home, Oscar," Gideon warned, and the water bottle bounced back to its original shape.

"Cam, you good?"

"I'm good." I put the waters under my arm and tucked my wallet away, more than ready to get out of there.

"You're just defending him because he's your best friend," Oscar argued.

I pivoted toward the door, catching Gid's nod in the same direction. I couldn't have agreed more.

"He doesn't need defending. You need to stop acting like an asshole."

"I'm leaving," I told Gid as the door opened again. Perfect timing to get the hell out.

"Hey, Cam? Tell me, when you're screwing Willow, does she say your name? Or does she close her eyes and call out for Sullivan?"

The water hit the floor as Gideon shouted my name.

"Is Xander next—?" Oscar's grin disappeared behind my fist before he could finish.

He went down, and I followed, my fist connecting with his face again. Then again.

"Cam! No!"

Her voice broke through when everyone else had faded into a blur. I halted my fist halfway to Oscar's bloodied face.

"Damn it, Cam," Gideon swore as he hauled me off Oscar, because I let him.

My chest heaved as I surveyed the damage. One beaten and sputtering Oscar. At least six wide-eyed locals gawking at me in fear like the monster I was. The monster I'd nurtured and honed over the last ten years to ensure my survival.

"You good?" Gideon asked me quietly, but his grip had already gone slack. We both knew there was jack shit he could do if I decided to go at Oscar again.

I nodded, then curved the brim of my ball cap.

"Dude, he beat your ass and didn't even lose his hat."

I ignored the comment and turned toward the door, where

Willow stood, her eyes sad with shit I didn't even want to think about.

"Did you see that, Hall? You'd better arrest him for assault!" Oscar slurred.

Gideon's jaw locked, and he looked at me with barely veiled anger. "See what, Oscar? You making an ass out of yourself and taunting this town's only war hero at the expense of Judge Bradley's own daughter?"

I picked up the water and moved toward the door.

"Cam," Willow whispered, reaching for my hand.

The hand currently covered in Oscar's blood because I still couldn't control my damned temper. The hand I'd had on her an hour ago. I yanked it away so the blood couldn't touch her, and she flinched.

Now I'd fucked that up, too.

I walked past her and chose the second door, the one that led to the back boardwalk instead of Main Street.

Crisp air hit my face, and I sucked it in, willing it to wash away the last ten minutes of my life. Hell, the last ten years.

"Cam," Willow called softly as she shut the door behind her. "Are you okay?"

I scoffed, then laughed with sick sarcasm. "Am I okay?" I turned to face her. "I could have killed him without so much as breaking a sweat, Willow. I might have if you hadn't been there."

"But you didn't." She walked forward, and I backed away, shaking my head.

"Don't."

"You didn't kill him. And he more than deserved getting punched in the face for what he said." She wrapped her arms around her middle.

"You heard it." Chalk another mark up on the things-I've-done-to-hurt-Willow board.

"He hit you with your worst fear, and I know how protective you are of me. Of course you're going to hit him back."

"Will you just stop?" I shouted.

She didn't flinch or run, simply stood there and looked at me, accepting everything she shouldn't.

"Stop defending me. Stop acting like the shit I've done is okay. Stop making excuses for me."

"I love you." Instead of running like any sane person would, she took a step forward.

"You shouldn't! I just gave you another reason not to." Because it didn't matter that she was the very air in my lungs—at some point I was going to break her, despite my best intentions.

"But I do! I always have, and you know it. You can't change my feelings because you're uncomfortable. I'm not going to stand by and watch you self-destruct. I did it once, and I've never forgiven myself. Don't ask me to do it again." The wood beneath her feet creaked as she took another step toward me.

"Did it ever occur to you that I'm not capable of being saved? That ship sailed a decade ago. Hell, probably before then, if you ask my dad. Maybe you should listen to Oscar and go for Xander. He never makes a mistake. Never hurts someone he loves. I'll inevitably ruin you. You get that, don't you? What if the next time... God, what if I hurt you?"

"You won't." She still came forward.

I put up my hand, showing her the blood that filled the cracks of my knuckles. "This is all I have to give you, Willow. Hands that were made to rip the world apart and come stained with more blood than you'll ever know, because I'll never tell you the full extent of what I've done in the years I was gone." That was a burden I'd never make her bear.

"Those same hands hold me. They build bridges and dams and restore old, broken mines. I'm not scared of your hands, Cam. I know what's in your heart."

But she didn't. Because I hadn't told her, hadn't shown her the violence I was capable of, and I never would. That little show with Oscar? It was nothing. And what he'd said about her? That was only the beginning if she stayed with me.

It was the last gift I could give her—my silence and the freedom to walk away. "You know what I've allowed you to see. The guy you've been with for the last six weeks—"

"I know who you are! Don't you dare insult me like that." She marched right up to me and stared me down from nearly a foot below me.

"For once in your life, Pika, err on the side of self-preservation. Stop standing in front of loaded guns." I held the water out to her, and she took it, still glowering at me. "I don't want to scare Rose with the blood. Please take this to my father."

"Camden," she begged, but I had absolutely nothing left to give her.

I yanked my keys out of my pocket and put them on top of the water so she wouldn't be stranded.

Then I walked right by her and didn't stop.

She didn't call after me.

Maybe she was finally learning.

CHAPTER TWENTY

Willow

handed the water to May and then took the empty chair at the table where Art sat, teaching Rose about the mine.

Numb. I felt…numb. Which was better than the gut-wrenching pain I'd felt watching Cam rip himself apart for something anyone in his position would have done.

I doubted my own father would have stood there and listened to someone say anything like that about my mother. Maybe he wouldn't have been as lethally accurate, but he also hadn't been trained Special Forces.

"Mr. Daniels, it's time to take some medication," May cajoled.

"No."

She sighed. "He's having an off day," she explained with a flat smile.

Xander looked back, and his eyes softened in concern. "You all right, Willow?"

I shook my head slowly.

His mouth tightened. "Camden?"

I didn't have to confirm what we both already knew.

He sighed and asked the woman he was helping if she wouldn't mind waiting a minute before he walked over to me. "He's… I don't even know."

"He's Cam," I said in explanation.

"He's Cam," Xander agreed. "Look, he's always been hard.

But I never worried about him, not in the way other people did. I never thought he was a lost cause or anything." He dropped down and took my hand. "I'm not going to lie. I was pretty pissed when I heard you two were together. I love you like a little sister, and you've already been through so much. Just seems unfair for you to sign up for more."

"He won't hurt me." Now if only I could get him to believe that. But how could I, when the rest of the world was telling him differently?

"Not intentionally," he agreed. "I always knew Cam loved the deepest out of all of us. He's willing to fight me for what he thinks is right so that I don't do what he's afraid I won't forgive myself for. He would have killed for Sullivan—that's how much he loved our brother." Xander squeezed my hand gently. "And he's always been willing to die for you, Willow. The mine, the fire…always."

My eyes jerked to his. They were the same shade and shape Sullivan's had been, but it didn't hit me in the gut the way it used to.

"I'm torn," he admitted. "Because I love you enough to beg you to get away from him. But I love him enough to beg you not to leave him. Not to give up on him. Because I honestly think you're the one person who can rebuild him—or break him. He's way past ever listening to me."

"I'll never give up on him, Xander. I love him. I've always loved Camden." I loaded each word so he understood the full value of what I was telling him.

His eyes squeezed shut, and he sucked in an audible breath. The way he nodded slowly told me that he got the message. When he opened his eyes, they were clear of the condemnation I'd expected. After all, he'd loved Sullivan more than Cam, and we both knew it.

He simply squeezed my hand and pressed his lips in a thin line as he nodded again. "I'm so sorry, and selfishly, I'm so glad. He's his own worst enemy. You know that, right?"

"Yeah."

"Okay." He stood and let go of my hand. "Hey, Rose, why don't you come and sit with me for a second so my dad will take his medication? I think you might just be too smart for him to walk away from." He held his hand out to Rose, and she came around the table to take it. "Come on. I'll teach you how to judge some ore."

I sat, my eyes unfocused on the map of the mine, while May managed to coax Arthur into taking his medication. The carbon monoxide poisoning had weakened his heart, giving his sons yet another reason to worry about his health.

Eventually, he sat next to me, his finger tracing the paths in the mine. I saw pieces of Cam in him, but only small ones. The shape of his nose. The narrowing of his eyes in focus.

So much of Cam was his mom. Especially his heart.

Art looked up and smiled at where Xander sat with Rose. "He's a good one, Alexander. Always the first to help."

"So is Cam," I said softly.

Art's eyebrows furrowed as he glanced my way and then back down to the mine.

"Why?" The question slipped free before I could stop myself.

Art's hand stilled on the map, but he didn't look my way.

"Why couldn't you just love him the way you love Xander? The way you loved Sullivan? He was just as worthy, even if he wasn't perfect."

The shop behind us was packed with the hum of tourists, and Art was so quiet that I wondered if he'd even heard me.

"There's a balance," he finally said, his voice low.

"What?"

"Good. Evil. Right. Wrong. Karma. It's as old as the first brothers in the Bible. Whatever you want to call it, the universe keeps us in balance." He trailed his finger down the oldest tunnel in the mine, searching for something I couldn't see.

"And you think Cam..." I shook my head. What was I even

thinking, asking a man whose mind had long since quit being dependable.

"Xander was born all sunshine and smiles. He was perfect. Lillian was so happy. And I knew that if we had another one, balance might not be on our side. It wasn't for my parents." He leaned over the table, following the 1880 tunnel down to the lower levels, where the tunnels wound back on each other.

"Cal?" It was widely known that there was no love lost between the brothers.

He nodded. "Cal. But then Camden was born. And he was beautiful. Loud and demanding and full of life. Always looking around, even as a newborn. And Lillian… She…became so unhappy. Cried all the time. Wouldn't get out of bed. Couldn't stand the sight of him. Of any of us. And I knew that Cam was the balance. He was the cost of the happiness Xander brought."

A weight settled on my chest as my stomach hit the ground. "Depression," I whispered so softly that I knew he couldn't have heard me.

"She just disappeared into herself, and Cam screamed his head off. Took forever for her to come back to me, and when she did, and Sullivan was born…" He paused, narrowing his eyes again at a ventilation shaft before shaking his head and continuing to trace the 1880 tunnel. "When Sullivan was born, I knew that the balance had been tipped again. That we'd have to pay. You can't have that much good in your life and not pay for it. That's not how it works. Everything has a price, Hope; you know that. You've seen it, too."

I blinked rapidly. He thought I was my mother.

"And Lillian saw it, too. The balance. The way Cam just…" He shook his head. "That's why she loved him more than the others. Felt like she had to make it up to him."

"She tried to make up for you not loving him," I argued.

"Too much bad in that boy. Too much violence."

"He wasn't." I pleaded for his understanding in a hushed whisper. "Not as a kid. I was there."

"Then the balance righted itself. Took Lillian right out of my hands. But I still had those two good boys." A tear slipped down his cheek, and guilt racked me with nausea. What kind of monster was I to bully a sick man? "So Cam took Sullivan."

The guilt vanished.

"No," I said firmly enough that he looked over at me. "Cam loved Sullivan. He protected him. He would never have hurt him. It wasn't his fault. Cam. Loved. Sullivan."

He tilted his head. "I never said he didn't. Too much love can kill someone just as easily as too little." He turned his attention back to the map.

"He was just a kid. Just a little boy. He wasn't bad. He still isn't."

Art followed another ventilation shaft until it bottomed out, then traced it back to another section. I reached across the table and stilled his hand.

"He isn't bad. He isn't some kind of universal weight to balance out your blessings, Art. He is the blessing. He's kind, and loyal, and protective, and smart. And he wears unicorn shirts for little girls, and rescues bigger ones from snowbanks, and takes on the only brother he has left so you can have what you want."

Art didn't yank his hand away from mine as he watched me through his peripherals.

"He carried me out of that mine—"

"You let him," he said with a tilt to his head.

"Without hesitation."

"He didn't break your nose," he stated.

"Of course not. He's good, Mr. Daniels. He's the best man I know, and you…" My breath shook as I exhaled. "You ruined him. And I don't know if I can fix the parts you broke. He won't let anyone in. And I have to get through to him, because he's just so…" The words clogged my throat, threatening to choke me. "He's so very lonely."

"All great and precious things are lonely." Art turned and

slowly brought his eyes to mine. I didn't see Sully or Xander in those depths, even though they were identical. I didn't even see Mr. Daniels.

My hand fell away from his, and he went back to tracing the paths in the mine, muttering about the passages he'd sealed to keep the boys from suffocating in the bad air.

All great and precious things are lonely.

I'd heard those words before. Just a couple of weeks ago.

I walked over to Xander, feeling a decade older than when I'd woken up this morning. "Hey, Rosie, you ready to go?"

"If Mayor Daniels doesn't need my help," she replied.

"I'm good to go, Rose. Thank you for helping. Oh, wait, I could definitely use another pencil if you wouldn't mind grabbing one for me?"

"No problem!" She scrambled from her seat beside him and headed for the bin of supplies, pausing to grab her jacket.

"Whatever my dad said to you, don't stress. He's having an off day. He might be himself from forty years ago or Napoleon." He took advantage of the lull in tourists and leaned back in his chair, obviously weary from the day.

"Yeah, I think he just quoted a book at me." And that wasn't even half of it.

Xander startled. "Really? He's more of a TV guy. Used to make fun of Cam for always carrying books around. I think that's why he started hanging out at Cal's. Weird." His brow knit together.

"He's definitely not himself." At least for all the mutterings about balance, he hadn't pointed a shotgun at me, so it could have been worse.

"Take it with a grain of salt," he replied with a shrug.

"Here you go!" Rosie popped into the space between us and put a handful of pencils on the table. Among the yellow No. 2s, she'd added two of her own unicorn pencils.

"Thanks, Rose. I really appreciate it." Xander gave her a smile as another tourist stepped up with a handful of ore.

I helped Rosie with her jacket, and she paused at the gate, watching Xander for a moment before we melted into the crowd. Preoccupied with my own thoughts, I didn't notice she'd gone quiet until we reached Town Hall, where tourists examined original documents and photographs.

"Hey, what's up?" I asked just inside the door.

Her lips pursed, but she eventually shook her head. "Nothing big. I did an experiment. We just learned about hypotuses last week."

"Hypotheses?" I asked.

She nodded. "My experiment failed. I need a new hypothesis." She carefully pronounced the last word.

"Do you want to tell me what it was?" I didn't want to pry if she was still working things out in her head. I hated when people did that to me.

"Not yet. I'm going to try again." Her chin rose, and she hugged me before running back to her mother.

Dad stood with a group of fanny pack–wearing travelers, showing off his prized possession: a full wall of original pictures pieced together to show Alba from the mountain above.

He was in his glory here, where history didn't change and the present didn't matter. The conversation didn't stop as Dad lifted Rose into his arms so she could see the top picture. Then Rose jumped in, showing the group where the schoolhouse was.

"And that's the Rose Rowan Mine! I'm named after it, and my aunt's boyfriend is going to have it open for tours soon! But not the bunkhouse. That burned down."

Dad and I locked eyes. He looked away first. He hadn't spoken to me since the diner, when I'd chosen Cam.

Rose tapped at Dad's chest, and he grinned at her before nodding and putting her on her feet. She raced over to Charity, and I slipped into the space the tourists had occupied a moment ago.

On Dad's etched, formal name tag that labeled him a council

member of the Historical Society, there was a sparkly unicorn sticker covering his title.

He looked at it when he caught me staring and smiled in Rose's direction. "She still thinks everything glitters."

"And you don't correct her," I noted, wondering when the first time he'd done so with me was. When was the first time I'd stepped off his approved path to follow my own?

"Why would I? It's a rare gift to see the hidden beauty in things. That kind of optimism is something to be treasured. You have that same spark in your soul, Willow." He glanced to Charity and back to me, a lingering sadness in his eyes that I felt spill over into me. "At least Rose still lets me protect her."

"Maybe I still see the hidden beauty you stopped looking for."

His lips flattened, and he struggled to swallow. "I wish that were the case, sweetheart. I really do."

Charity paused in her presentation of the original town charter, looking over at us with concern. At what point had they said the words they couldn't come back from? Had they ever been spoken? Or was the silence the true cost of cowardice on both their parts? Of unwillingness to see the other's point of view?

Was I standing on that precipice with my father? Or was I already over the edge?

Another group wandered toward us, and I took blatant advantage of his aversion to public scenes, throwing my arms around him.

He wasn't perfect. He was flawed and stubborn and too stuck in his ways to accept the change that was inevitable. But never once had he loved me more than Charity or vice versa. "I love you, Dad. I'm so sorry I can't be what you want me to be. But I love you."

I pulled back before he had a chance to react and walked away before I could judge him for what might linger on his face.

As I walked out the door, I heard him laugh. "Yes, I'm the head unicorn in charge around here."

Opening day was still in full swing when I left. Part of me felt a little guilty for ducking out early, but when push came to shove, I had somewhere more important to be, and after asking around, I realized Cam hadn't returned.

I took his Jeep to my house and was back in it five minutes later, headed across the ridgeline to Cam's.

The sun was just starting to set as I parked in the driveway. I walked into the house and called his name, but there was no answer. What was the right thing to do here? Take his Jeep to my house? Leave it here and walk home? Stay until he returned? Would it do more harm than good to shove myself into the spaces he'd clearly said he didn't want me in?

I hung his keys on the hook by the door and debated calling him. Maybe he'd decline, but maybe he'd pick up. My feet carried me to the library, where the dying afternoon light threw bursts of sun and shade on one of the walls and on the land outside the picture windows.

I ran my fingers across the empty chessboard, remembering all the times Xander tried to teach Cam and me to play, lecturing us for hours about the logic of it all while Cam argued that there was zero logic—it was all about emotion, protecting one piece you valued above the others. Then I smiled, remembering the moment we decided to steal the pieces so Xander would stop nagging us.

Something about what Art said kept tickling my brain, and I picked up Cam's copy of *East of Eden* from where he'd left it on the side table when he'd finished reading it to me.

I thumbed through the well-loved pages, hearing Cam's voice recite the story of generations of brothers who had been shaped by their fathers' expectations and biases. It was no wonder he loved it so much. Page after page was highlighted or annotated, the scrawling script changing from pencil to pen in places, from the penmanship of a child to that of a man.

There it was. My finger ran down the words as I spoke aloud. *"I said that word carried a man's greatness if he wanted to take advantage of it.*"

"*I remember Sam Hamilton felt good about it.*"

"*It set him free,*" said Lee. "*It gave him the right to be a man, separate from every other man.*"

"*That's lonely.*"

"*All great and precious things are lonely.*"

I looked up as the sun glinted on the greenhouse Cam had mentioned he was building, and the man himself stepped through the glass door, wiping sweat from his brow with the sleeve of his shirt. His ball cap was on backward, his T-shirt as dirty and stained as his jeans, and yet he'd never looked so beautiful to me as he did in that moment, this incredible man fighting to make things grow in the most inhospitable terrain possible.

Just like his mother had.

I read the final part of the text, since Cam had highlighted only that portion.

"*What is the word again?*"

"*Timshel—thou mayest.*"

I closed the book and held it to my chest. He'd thought that part was important enough to remember—the concept that maybe he, too, could choose to be what he wanted and not what he'd been told to be.

But he'd skipped over the words that ripped at me as I stood there, watching him secure another panel to the building, still fighting to make his world a little better on a day when he didn't think he deserved it.

Maybe it was a different kind of choice—to shove everyone away—but it was also my choice to let him. Or, rather, not to let him.

I watched him for another few minutes, planning my course, strategizing my next steps, until I knew he'd have to come in soon from lack of sunlight. Then I walked over to the desk, took out a piece of notebook paper, and tore it in a strip.

Then I fought.

CHAPTER TWENTY-ONE

Camden

Gravel crunched beneath someone's steps as I locked in another panel to the greenhouse. I didn't need to look to know who it was, since there was only one person brave enough to come after me on a day like today.

I secured the panel and turned around to see Willow twenty feet away, her hair rippling to the side with the mountain breeze. How the hell was I going to find the strength to let her go? She deserved so much better than the rumors and the comments—than me.

She didn't say a word as she walked forward to the table I was using during construction, and she came no farther after she put something on top of the plans. Then she walked back to the house.

I stared at the small object she'd delivered like it was a bomb and waited for the damn thing to go off. She hadn't shoved it at me or forced me into a conversation. She'd given me the choice, which was what had me reaching for it.

I unrolled the long scroll of paper and barely caught the white onyx rook piece as it fell free from the center of its wrapping.

It was the partner to the black one I'd given her the night Charity had announced her pregnancy. Not that I'd actually given it to her, since I hadn't been speaking to her at the time. I'd left it on her windowsill, telling her silently that no matter what I'd said or done over that shitty summer, she could still depend on me.

Even if no one else could.

She wasn't going to back down or let my words from this afternoon end what we'd barely begun. My shoulders drooped in simultaneous relief and outright despair. No matter how many times I told her that I'd eventually ruin her, she wouldn't believe me—or worse, she didn't care.

She was choosing me.

Against my better judgment, I stretched the paper out and read what she'd printed on it.

"I believe a strong woman may be stronger than a man, particularly if she happens to have love in her heart. I guess a loving woman is indestructible."

I knew I'd find her in the library. With the book. Where we'd spent countless hours as children, silent companions while we both ran from whatever drove us there in the first place. Her need to paint, to create in a family that only valued an analytical mind, and my need to live in someone else's world for a few hours.

I'd known by the time I was ten that the only world I wanted to live in was hers. To see the world in colors and light the way she did, to witness the way her hands created beauty from nothingness, knowing it was a direct representation of her own soul. And when she'd chosen Sullivan...rather, when I thought she had, I'd chosen to blend that part of her with me, to take her with me in the only way I could. I learned to build new, beautiful things in the midst of poverty and war. I gave in to my inevitable nature when the mission called for it and never thought twice about ending the life of someone who could eventually be a threat to this country—to Willow. But I lived for the months where our assignment was supportive rather than destructive in nature.

I built temporary bridges to transport military equipment. But I also built permanent ones to transport food and people. I set off bombs in buildings where terrorists met and then built a school to educate the little sister who'd watched her bigger one killed for daring to crack a book. I was forever paying the debt for the lives

I'd taken, trying to balance out the weight so my handbasket to hell didn't sink quite so fast.

But today, when Oscar had thrown Sullivan at me like that—at Willow—I'd realized the balance might never tip in my favor, and I wasn't sure that was something I could let Willow pay for.

I rolled up the greenhouse plans and secured them in the waterproof bin beneath the table in case weather moved in. Then, with the rook biting into my palm, I walked back to the house, where I knew she'd be waiting, because I'd fallen for a woman who might just be as stubborn as I was.

A quick kick, and I dropped my muddy boots in the laundry room and stripped out of my clothes, throwing all but my boxers into the washer and pressing start. Beauty of a tankless water heater? I could shower at the same time and give myself another few minutes of buffer before I went to battle.

I glanced her way as I passed the library, only to see her sitting at the easel, sketching something, oblivious, or at least acting like she was.

Five minutes later, I toweled off my hair, dressed, and headed into the library, where she still sat at the easel.

"That's where I found the sketch," I said, breaking the silence but raising the tension.

She put the pencil down and pivoted on the stool to face me. She'd hung her jacket next to mine by the door and was still wearing the same shirt she'd put on inside out this morning.

This morning felt like a decade ago.

"I wondered," she admitted. "I recognized it when I saw your arm."

I crossed my arms and leaned against the doorframe. "You didn't say anything."

"Yeah, not sure if you've caught on, but we tend to leave a lot of things unsaid. We should probably work on that."

My jaw flexed as I searched for the words I owed her. "I'm sorry you saw that today."

"Which part? Oscar being an ass or you losing your temper?"

"Yes."

A wry smile fleeted across her lips. "You don't owe me an apology for either."

"Willow, those kinds of comments aren't going to stop. Not around here. Not if you stay with me."

"Okay." She shrugged, and little seeds of frustration took root in my stomach.

"It's not okay. I know how much this town means to you—"

"Don't act like it means nothing to you. Not with all your talk of greenhouses and electric systems. You're just as invested in the future here as I am. Otherwise I'd suggest we move to where it would be easy to be together." She braced her hands on either side of her hips, gripping the stool, but she didn't close herself off from me. "We have roots here. We've both chosen to live here, so don't pretend this town doesn't mean anything."

"I won't deny that, but I've never given a shit what anyone said about me."

"What's your next issue? This one is a dead horse. People are going to talk, Cam. There's literally nothing else to do here besides prep for the season and make babies. I dated Sully. Now I'm dating you. So go ahead and make peace with whatever kind of derogatory comments people are going to come up with, because we can't change what people think."

"Yes, we can. You can walk away from this. Right here. Right now." My entire body tensed, waiting for her to do just that.

"No."

"No?"

"No. Do you know why you won't sleep with me?" she asked, leaning forward and pinning me with her stare.

"Are you serious right now? You want to talk about sex?"

"Kind of. Just bear with me here. You're afraid that jumping into this"—she motioned between us—"will give me regrets later on that you're not prepared to cope with."

"Considering I pretty much said that—"

"And if that were the truth, it would be super sweet, but since you're lying to yourself—"

"Lying to myself?" I came off the doorframe but halted at the desk.

"Shhh, my turn. You can talk in a minute." She held her finger up to her lips.

My eyes widened.

"You think you won't sleep with me because it gives me less to cry about when you break my heart. Which, logically, looking at the bullshit you pulled today—"

"I apologized—" I flattened my palms on the surface of the desk.

"I'm not talking about you punching Oscar. I couldn't care less about that. Now, shush, really. It's not nice to interrupt."

My jaw dropped.

"I'm talking about that crap when you walked away from me. When you stood there spewing out all that self-loathing bullshit and then once again made the decision for me that I was better off without you."

I snapped my mouth shut.

"Right. So yeah, I guess that could give a girl a little insecurity complex if I didn't know you so well. But guess what, Cam? I do. If you wanted someone who was going to run every time you lost your temper or got into a pissing contest with Oscar Hudgens, I can name at least three girls in town who would gladly drive up. But you want me." She cocked an eyebrow and dared me to deny it.

I didn't.

She rose from the stool, barefoot and 100 percent comfortable in my house—my life. "You won't sleep with me because you're scared. Not me. You."

I was about ten seconds from clearing this desk and showing her exactly how not scared I was.

She stopped so the desk was between us. "You're scared that you'll take that step and open yourself up, and no, I don't just mean physically."

My jaw flexed, but I kept silent as those little seeds of frustration grew into a giant fireball of...I didn't even know, but it wasn't pleasant.

"You're scared that eventually I'll see something I don't like about you and I'll walk out. Or that I can't take the gossip and I'll leave you. The distance you force between us is all on you, Cam. Not me. You're not scared of hurting me. You'd die before you let that happen, and we both know it. You're scared I'll hurt you."

I felt the blood drain from my face.

"Yeah. Thought so."

"You should walk out," I managed to say through the sawdust in my mouth.

"And you should really stop saying that. I'm standing right here, Cam. There's nothing you can say to convince me that I should go. Don't give me your self-righteous crap about hurting me, because you won't."

"My temper—"

"Has never been violent in the direction of any woman I've ever known. Unless you're keeping a secret I don't know about."

"Of course not," I snapped.

"You're scared because you're in love with me." She looked me straight in the eye, unflinching and unapologetic.

"I never said that." My hands slid to grip the edge of the desk.

"You don't have to. You've always been bigger on actions than words. I don't need you to say it. What I need is for you to realize that my love isn't going to change or lessen because someone makes a comment or you have a bad day. I love you unconditionally, Camden. At your worst? I love you. At your best? Yep, still love you. And until you can accept that, I'll be right here proving it to you. Choosing you."

Emotion clogged my throat, and I couldn't swallow past it, no matter how many times I tried.

"I'm not going anywhere," she promised. "I'm yours. Now. Always."

Her words didn't chip at my defenses or break them down. They seeped inside the walls I'd had since…*forever* and transformed concrete and mortar into color and light. Into the very thing she was.

"And if that's not enough," she started and then shook her head. "If you decide to walk away, I'll still love you, just like I did the first time, even if you don't want me any—"

I didn't know when I started moving, but I silenced her with my mouth, pouring everything I couldn't say into the kiss. A cry of relief escaped her lips, and I took that, too, slanting over her to kiss her deeper, hold her closer. I needed her as close as the laws of physics would allow, and even then I'd find a way to break a few.

"Cam," she sighed.

"Shh. My turn now. I'll never walk away," I promised, holding her face in my hands. "I'll never not want you. Wanting you is all I've ever known. You're in my blood, my bones, my soul." My hands dropped to her ass, and I lifted her until she was eye level. "There is no me without you. I've known that since we were kids in this room."

Her lips parted at the same time as she wrapped her legs around my waist, locking her ankles. "We're not kids anymore." She skimmed her fingers down my face.

"Thank God for that." I was done holding back. Done trying to convince her she'd be better off with someone else. For better or worse, she was mine.

Now I just had to make sure she never regretted her choice.

I kissed her, and she arched into me, sending the kiss spiraling into pure heat and need as her fingers laced behind my neck.

It was a good thing I knew this house like the back of my hand, because I didn't break our kiss as I walked us out of the library, down the hallway, and into my room. I paused inside the door to flip on the lights. There was zero chance I was missing any part of this in the darkness.

Willow grabbed the hem of her shirt and tugged it over her head for the second time today. This time, I looked my fill, taking in the sweet curve of her breasts against the lavender lace and the freckle that sat between them.

"Beautiful," I murmured just before I set my lips to that spot and worked my way up to her neck.

Her moan went straight through my bloodstream like a hit of adrenaline. I pinned her against the wall as she worked my shirt free, and then it joined hers on the ground.

"Beautiful," she echoed as her fingertips traced the ink on my chest.

My pulse pounded, demanding I move, but I stood still, letting her explore, nearly coming out of my skin with each movement of her hands over my tattoos.

Finally, she brought her eyes to mine and smiled. My control snapped, and I buried a hand in her hair as I took her mouth again. The kiss turned primal, and my world narrowed to the feel of her lips against mine, her tongue and teeth driving me mad.

When her hips rolled, I hissed and rocked back against her until the layers between us were too much to stand.

Four steps and I had her laid out on my bed, her flawless skin the ultimate contrast to the dark bedding. My eyes locked with hers as I reached for the button on her jeans, and at her enthusiastic nod, I flicked the button free and peeled the fabric down her legs.

"Yours too," she ordered, leaning up on her elbows.

I grinned, only too happy to oblige.

My pants hit the floor, and I nearly lost it when she licked her lips. I was going to eat her alive, to devour her so completely, so thoroughly, that she'd never look at me again without remembering exactly what I could do to her—do for her.

Her skin was satin fire as I slid over her, and when she raised her knees, I fell into the vee of her thighs with a groan.

Her hands were in my hair, at my back, touching and stroking everywhere she could reach as our mouths met in a kiss hotter than the last one, only to escalate when we'd break apart and come together again.

Her bra hit the floor, and I abandoned her mouth to kiss a path down her chest. She cried out my name when I took one peak in my mouth and rolled the other between my fingers.

I blocked out every demand my body made, every ache and urge, and concentrated on her, building her pleasure while I learned the curves of her body, the spots that made her wiggle in laughter and the ones that made her gasp and moan. When I reached the hollow of her hips, I hooked my thumbs into the lace bands of her underwear and raised my head to make sure she was with me.

"Yes." She answered the wordless question and lifted her hips so I could slide the scrap of lace down her thighs, where I paused to press a kiss that earned me a soft whimper and a roll of her hips.

When she was completely, gloriously naked, I let my eyes rake over her, marveling that she was mine, that this would be the first time I'd make love to her, but it wouldn't be the last.

I was going to make love to this woman for the rest of my life.

"I don't have words for how exquisite you are," I told her, sending my hands up her thighs. Her skin was so damned soft, so sensitive.

"I think those words work just fine." Her breaths came faster as I reached higher until I skimmed the apex of her thighs. "What are you doing to me?" Her hips undulated, seeking friction, and I gave it to her with my thumb and fingers, rising over her to capture her next moan with a kiss.

"I haven't even started yet," I promised against her lips. "I'm going to keep you in this bed all weekend, until I've kissed every inch of you. Until I know exactly what you like and how much you can take." I pressed in on her clit, and she cried out.

"Off." Her fingers yanked at my boxers.

I rolled and did as she asked, then broke open the new box of condoms in my nightstand.

She took the foil from my hand and then gripped the back of my neck to pull my mouth to hers. This time, when I settled between her thighs, there was nothing in between us.

The feeling was almost too much to take, knowing I was finally where I'd always fantasized about being. But she was better than any fantasy I'd ever come up with. Her skin was softer, her kisses hotter, her need elevating my own until we were lost in the kind of connection I'd never believed existed.

I stroked her until she rippled under my fingers, until her nails bit little half-moons into my shoulders and her thighs locked.

She was so damn close, her breath ragged as she urged me back to her mouth.

"With you," she demanded. "The first one, I want—" She gasped, her eyes flying wide as I stretched her with my fingers.

I groaned at the silk-and-velvet feel of her, at the thought of sinking inside her. If I wasn't careful, I'd be done for before I even got there. "It's not one or the other," I managed to say. "You're not limited on orgasms." In fact, I planned on giving her as many as she could possibly stand.

Her hand wrapped around my length, and I stilled as pleasure shot up my spine, so sweet, I could taste it on my tongue.

"With you," she repeated, then ripped open the foil packet and rolled the condom over me.

She kissed me, testing her teeth on my bottom lip, and I took my fingers from her core only to stroke her to a fever pitch, until her hips pressed into my hand and her back arched.

"Cam!" she begged, her eyes finding mine. The pure need I saw there was my undoing. She looked exactly how I felt—desperate and on edge.

"I'm with you," I promised and lined myself up with her entrance.

"Please." Her knees rose on either side of my hips, and I threaded my fingers through the hair at the nape of her neck to cradle her head.

Staring into her hazel eyes, watching for any sign of discomfort, I thrust gently, easing inside her, grinding my teeth at the utter ecstasy flooding every cell in my body.

Our breaths mingled as I slowly joined us with rolling thrusts, sliding deeper and deeper until she had every inch of me, never once breaking her gaze. Her lower lip quivered, and I took it between mine, kissing her as she adjusted around me.

"Are you okay?" My muscles trembled with the effort it took to keep still when every instinct demanded I move.

"God, yes," she promised, her arms holding me, her hands splayed over my back. "I'm perfect."

"Yeah, you are." Keeping my weight on my forearms so I didn't crush her slight frame, I rolled my hips once, and her mouth opened with the sweetest moan I'd ever heard in my life.

Everything about her was the best, the sweetest, the most intense, and I knew it wasn't just our off-the-charts chemistry or the realization of a dream. It was because my body and my heart both belonged to this woman, and the overwhelming emotion only drove the physical sensation higher.

"I love you." The confession spilled from my lips, melting the last barrier between us.

Her eyes widened in surprise, as if she hadn't already told me that tonight. "I love you, Camden," she echoed, then kissed me as I began to move, rocking within her at a slow, deep pace, drawing out every sliver of pleasure that I could, using my body to love her in a way I never had with any other woman.

Tongues twined and bodies joined, we took each other to the brink, and when she hovered at the precipice with stuttered breaths, when sweat beaded on my skin and hers and my muscles tensed so hard, I thought they might snap, I slid my thumb between us and stroked her past the edge, until she screamed and pulled me over with her name on my lips in an explosion so shattering, I knew she'd irrevocably changed me.

My chest still heaving, I cradled her to my body and rolled to the side as we struggled to recover. I lazily trailed my fingers down her arm as she kissed my chest, then my jaw.

"You're sure about that whole love thing, right?" she teased. "Because I'm pretty sure you just ruined me for anyone else."

I chuckled, reveling again that laughter came so easily with Willow. "Yeah, I'm sure. And good, because I'm never letting you out of this bed."

"Ever?"

"Nope."

"I'm okay with this plan." She turned her head and found my forearm, then kissed the tattoo of her sketch. "What about food?"

"I guess I'll have to cook for you so you can keep up your strength." I brushed my lips across her forehead. How had I lived this long without feeling this? Without her in my arms?

"Say it again," she whispered.

I lifted my head so I could see her eyes. "I love you, Willow."

Her smile was the sexiest thing I'd ever seen. "Yeah?"

"Yeah."

"That's nice, but I meant the cooking thing. I mean, that's enough to turn a girl on." She said it with such seriousness that I couldn't help but bust out laughing.

"Forget cooking," I promised against her mouth. "I'll just eat you."

"Promise?"

I didn't bother responding verbally. After all, she already knew I was bigger on action than words.

CHAPTER TWENTY-TWO

Willow

"Hey, Willow," Tillie said as she glanced up from the notepad she held. "Hey, Thea."

"Hi, Tillie," we greeted almost in unison as we held down a booth at Bigg's for lunch.

"You two know what you want?"

"Actually, we're waiting for one other person," Thea answered.

Tillie looked at me. "Oh?"

"Wait, he's here! Hey, babe." Thea tilted her cheek for her husband's kiss before he slid into the booth next to her.

Tillie's smile drooped, and I almost laughed. Man, she had it bad for Cam, and Cam only had it bad for me. The thought had me smiling from ear to ear. It felt a hair shy of criminal to be this happy.

We ordered quickly—it wasn't like the menu changed often— and Tillie took off to put in our orders.

"So Cam isn't joining us?" Pat asked slowly, his arm wrapped around Thea's shoulders.

Danger, Will Robinson.

"No," I replied with a soft smile, because I couldn't help but smile when I thought about him. "He has the psych eval for his dad's case right now, and then he has to get up to the mine." And I had this lunch, and maybe this lunch only, to get Pat on Cam's side so we could start swaying public opinion. We being myself,

Thea, and Charity, since Cam refused to play politics.

In an election year in Alba, public opinion was everything.

June twentieth had been circled on my calendar since Cam told me he'd been given a court date a few weeks ago. We were two weeks away, and the tension among the locals was about as thick as it could get.

The tourists, of course, couldn't have cared less. They came in waves, trickling in on weekdays like this, only to hit us by a thousand or more a day on the weekend. Business was good.

"How's that going?" Pat asked, his smile tight.

"The case, the mine, or Cam?" This had the potential to get super awkward super fast.

"Uhhh—" Pat suddenly found his napkin incredibly interesting.

"Oh, stop it," Thea chided but tugged his tie playfully. "Come on, Pat. That's still Willow."

Pat rolled his eyes but finally met mine. "I'm sorry. It's just... odd."

"The case, the mine, or Cam?" I teased him with a repeat.

"All of it," he answered truthfully, then let out an *oof* as Thea elbowed him. "What? We've been friends for long enough to tell her the truth, honey."

"We have," I agreed as Tillie appeared with our drinks.

We all thanked her, but she only responded directly to Pat as she moved to another table.

"Well, then truthfully, I have a hard time with the guy. You know that." He shrugged in apology.

"He's still pissed that Cam wouldn't let him into the hot springs party his freshman year," Thea jibed.

Pat side-eyed his wife. "That's not it. Look, Willow, you've been put through more than your fair share, and I just don't want to see you get hurt."

"And I appreciate the concern." I swirled my straw around the ice cubes in my lemonade, making them clink. "But Cam isn't going to hurt me."

His eyebrows shot up, and he leaned forward. "You've only been together for, what? A couple months? Cam isn't known for being easy on anyone or anything."

I folded my hands on the table and looked him straight in the eye. "You were Sullivan's best friend, so I get the protective bit, and I'll let that one slide. That one, Pat."

He opened his mouth like he wanted to say more but then shut it instead.

"I love Cam. Cam loves me. He has never once hurt me, unless you're thinking about the summer he may have bruised my feelings."

Pat's mouth set in a way that told me that was exactly what he'd been thinking about.

"Trust me, I bruised his deeper. There's a hell of a lot of backstory you're not privy to, and no, I'm not going to tell you, because it's none of your business."

"Never once hurt you? He saved you from the fire he started." He said it gently, so I didn't kick him under the table.

"That was ruled accidental," Thea hissed.

"Sure, as in he accidentally knocked over a tiki torch while he was accidentally slipping it to Olivia Maxfield," he countered.

Yeah, I wasn't about to go there.

"Regardless of how that fire started, it was Sullivan who left me in the bunkhouse and Cam who ran in to get me out."

Pat startled, and I almost did, too. I'd never once laid blame at Sully's feet for leaving me there.

"I never thought of it like that." He glanced away. "God, you must have been so pissed at Sully."

"Not really," I answered honestly. "I was terrified for a minute, and the smoke was so thick…" I trailed off, feeling the heat of the flames ghost over my skin and dry out my mouth. "And honestly, if we hadn't been asleep in that back room, we would have gotten out sooner. Sullivan would have gotten us out."

"But he only got himself out." Pat ran his hands over his red hair. "And you didn't beat the shit out of him after? I mean, I don't even remember you being angry. You just said something about getting separated, not him leaving you."

I looked at Thea, and she lifted her eyebrows. There had been only one person truly privy to my feelings back then, and true to the code, she'd never spilled—even to her husband.

"Honestly, the support beam came crashing down between us, and when he saw that I was on the other side, he said he would go for help. I hit the floor to get to the good air. I saw Sully's feet make it to the door, and yeah, I was a little...disappointed. But I also knew Cam would come for me, even if it was only for Sully's benefit. Deep down, I knew."

Pat blinked. "Willow, I love you. You know that. But you simply knew that the biggest asshole in Alba was going to risk his life to come help you? Cam never helped anyone...back then," he amended with a tilt of his head.

"I knew." My shoulders lifted in a shrug. "There are three things you can count on when it comes to Cam." I held my fingers up as I began to list them. "One, his family is first. He always cleaned up Sullivan's messes so nothing bad ever stuck to him."

"Hey," he snapped; then his focus went hazy for a second, as if he was thinking. "Huh. Okay, I'll give you that one."

"Two, he'll self-destruct at the first opportunity. And three, he shows up for me. I didn't always see it back then, but it's true. There was no chance that he wasn't coming in after me if he knew I was in there."

Pat leaned back, absorbing what I said.

"Cam has saved my life four times and has always been there when I've needed him."

"Okay, but just think about this for a second, please, and don't hate me for asking. Did you ever stop to think that the only reason you were in danger in the first place—at least as a kid—was because you were around Cam?"

I waited his requested second only because he was married

to my best friend and I'd loved his. "No, Pat. I get that you might not understand this, but I'm his, he's mine, and that's not going to change. Ever. And I guess you have to choose between joining the rest of the old Alba gossips at the barbershop or opening your mind about Cam. Remember just how much Sullivan loved him. And no, he didn't get Sully killed. By the time Cam got there, he'd already been shot. That"—I held up two fingers—"is now two, because that's none of your business, either, but I know how much you miss Sully."

Pat swallowed, and after what might have been the longest minute of my life, he finally nodded. "How's the mine coming along?"

Thea visibly relaxed.

I took the olive branch and ran. "Good. They're on track to have the 1880 tunnel open all the way to the third ventilation shaft by the Fourth of July. Cam figured that one would be the biggest draw. The rest of that tunnel and the other two will have to wait for next season."

"That's incredible. The Historical Society council was thrilled when they heard there would be a soft opening this year."

"By *thrilled*, he means the clapping exceeding golf level," Thea added as Tillie arrived with the food.

She juggled the plates with a dexterity I envied, then looked at me after setting my burger and fries in front of me. "You sure like the burgers and fries, huh, Willow?"

"Yep." I reached for the ketchup. There was zero chance I was letting her get under my skin.

"I was just thinking it must be hard to stay in shape, seeing as you sit all day with your art stuff, right?" Her smile was faker than her eyelashes. "It must add up quick."

"Oh, don't worry about Willow." Thea chuckled. "She gets plenty of workout time. At night. At Cam's. You know...with Cam."

My teeth sank into my bottom lip to keep a straight face, but Pat didn't bother hiding his sputtering laugh. Progress. A few weeks ago, he would have seethed at Thea's implications.

Tillie gave Thea a look that could have curdled milk.

"True," I jumped in for fear that Tillie would come across the table at my friend. "And in fact, I was heading up to see him after this. Would you mind putting in an order now so it will be hot when we're ready?"

Still glaring at Thea, Tillie took out her notepad and pen. "What would he like?"

"Let's do a double-bacon cheeseburger, medium, with avocado, ketchup, lettuce, and tomato. Oh, and a salted caramel shake, too. That would be great!" I smiled up at her.

She clicked her tongue. "You sure about that last one? I'm pretty sure Cam likes chocolate fudge shakes."

"Oh, he does," I assured her. "That's for me. I have to stock up on my calories so I can burn them off later, right?"

"Right." She spun and left.

"And the case?" Pat asked, clearly making an effort.

"Not sure. Art is pretty adamant about getting the DNR." I started in on my food.

"On the days he's lucid?" Pat doctored his own burger with mustard, but his tone told me he'd definitely been hanging out at the barbershop.

"Yes, Pat. On the days he's lucid. He called Cam and asked for his help, which is the whole reason Cam moved back. Plus, after his hospitalization, he's pretty determined."

Pat chewed slowly and nodded.

"He even went with Walt to get a DNR tattoo across his chest," Thea added. "Xander flipped his lid."

Pat seemed to mull it over. "He did say something about it not being legally recognized," he admitted. "That it was more his dad having a hard time coping with ending up on that ventilator than actually wanting the DNR."

"Trust me, babe. If a man gets that tattooed on his chest, he's serious." Thea popped a fry into her mouth and nodded.

"But still, Xander's been taking care of him for years. This whole mess feels like Cam wants..." Pat sighed at his burger. "I can't even say it."

"Wants what?" I prompted.

"Wants his dad to die," he finished in a whisper. "Everyone knows they don't get along, and it just feels...wrong. He's only fifty-eight."

Holy crap, this was what we were up against. Alba seriously thought Cam just wanted to get rid of Arthur because they didn't like each other?

"You're right. Art's only fifty-eight, Pat. That's only thirty years older than we are right now, and he's asking to determine what happens to his own body. He's asking Cam to go against everyone in this town, including his own brother, because he wants a say in whether or not he ends up strapped to a hospital bed on a ventilator again. And if he didn't have Alzheimer's, no one would think twice about what he's asking. You can get a DNR today if you want one, but he can't, because fifty percent of the time he can't depend on his brain. So what, the other days—when he can—those don't matter?"

"They should," he muttered.

"Yeah, they should. But everyone is making this about Cam and Xander, not Art. And trust me, if Cam wanted Arthur to die, fighting a legal battle to then wait it out doesn't really strike me as his style."

The bell rang as the door opened, and I saw Simon enter in my peripherals.

I jumped out of the booth, and he sighed as he saw me. Oh no. That was a sad sigh. "Simon, is everything okay? I thought you were supposed to be with Art and the doc for the eval."

"I'm glad I ran into you. Art isn't lucid today." He shook his head slowly.

My stomach sank. "How not lucid? Like it's 1998? Or—"

"Or the psychologist was a claim jumper coming to take the

Rose Rowan?" he offered, wincing.

"Oh."

"Oh." He nodded.

"But it took weeks to get in with that guy. What does this do to the case?" Cam was going to be devastated.

"He said he has one opening the week before court, so we're taking it. But if the same thing happens, then Cam's at a real disadvantage."

He'd lose.

"Okay. Thanks. Did you want to come join us?" I motioned back to the table and saw Tillie drop off Cam's food.

"No, I'm grabbing a shake to go. Thanks for the offer, though."

We said our goodbyes, and I slid into the booth so I could get money from my purse.

"Everything okay?" Thea asked.

"Just stuff with Art's case." I took out a twenty and put it on the table. "I'd better go find Cam."

"Okay, honey."

"Wait," Pat said as I slid toward the end of the booth. He took a deep breath, then another, and finally looked over at me. "Yesterday, at the Historical Society council meeting, some people were talking."

Since there were only nine council members, that narrowed it down.

"They were all getting coffee. The meeting hadn't started. And someone brought up Art and the case, and of course Xander was pretty mum about it. He's never going to shit-talk Cam in front of other people. But one member may have suggested that it was impossible not to take into account the history and character of the person bringing the lawsuit."

I stilled. "My dad?"

"No." Pat emphatically shook his head. "But your dad agreed. And then said it's not just the past that a judge would have to take into account in that hypothetical situation but the current decisions that person makes."

My chest tightened.

"And after someone mentioned a certain fight that happened a few weeks ago on opening day..." Shit. "Well, another member asked—"

"Oh my God, Pat, spit it out. We all know who's on the damned council," Thea hissed.

Pat leaned forward, bracing his elbows on the table. "Hall asked your dad if he'd hold it against Cam that he was dating you. Except he didn't use the word...'date.'"

I cringed. "He said no, right? Please tell me he said no."

"He said that dating you didn't exactly show the kind of sound judgment he'd need to win the case. Especially given that Cam is prone to violence around you."

My blood turned to ice, then flash-boiled. "He said what?"

"Shh!" Pat looked to see that no one heard me. "They can't know I told you. We have a what-happens-in-Vegas disclosure. I'll lose my council seat."

Cam was going to lose his case...because of me.

"I have to go." I grabbed Cam's burger and my shake, then paused at the foot of the table. "Thank you, Pat. Both of you."

Rage and disbelief spun in my brain like a pinwheel, the emotions overlapping each other. I put Cam's lunch on the passenger seat and my milkshake in the cupholder. Then I stared out the windshield with my hands on the steering wheel.

I could break up with Cam. That was obviously what Dad wanted. But maybe it was deeper than that. Maybe he honestly thought that being with me showed a lack of character. Why? Because I was his dead brother's ex-girlfriend? Heck, that would have been the simplest label to slap on us.

The thought of losing Cam shredded my soul.

There was no chance he'd let me go, anyway. Or would he? If being with me meant seeing his dad on a ventilator, would he let me walk away? Would I even want him to? This was Art, not some hypothetical dilemma.

Cam loved me.

I'm not going anywhere. I'd promised him. I'd bullied my way into his heart, and now it was going to cost him the very thing he'd come back here for.

I yanked my phone out of my purse.

Willow: Where are you right now?

I held my breath as the three dots coursed across the screen.

Cam: Just got to the mine. Dad's appointment cut short because his brain no-showed.

Willow: I'm on my way.

Cam: Everything okay?

Willow: Physically, yeah. I'll be there in fifteen.

I made it in ten, my 4Runner skidding to a halt in the newly packed gravel lot in front of the construction trailers.

I grabbed everything and skirted around the construction crew as they moved steel beams meant for the tunnels. I made it through the door to Cam's trailer as a small group of workers came out, only a couple of whom I recognized, since I mostly worked with the foremen when it came to preservation.

Seeing Cam for the first time every day still took my breath away. He stood at his drafting table, turned so I could only see a portion of his profile, his shirtsleeves pushed up and his pants hanging on sculpted hips, but even with all that physical beauty, it was his focus that I found enthralling.

I loved him so much that I wasn't sure there was enough space in this trailer—in the world—for it. How was I supposed to give him up? How could I live with myself if I didn't? It had taken years and war and more than a little fate to get us here. This wasn't even in the same realm as fair.

"You'll need to move this beam here," Cam told two of the foremen as he pointed to the blueprints. "These right here are the old load-bearing timbers, and we need to see if we can basically take the load off at this point and this one, so we can maintain the structural integrity of the tunnel without losing that historical piece."

"And if we can't keep that beam?" The foreman pointed to the original one, and my stomach clenched. There were so many sacrifices to be made, and every piece of history that went hurt my heart a little more.

"Safety first. But I know we can keep it, so don't shortcut it for ease." Cam looked up and paused when he saw me. "Everybody out."

The foremen glanced between us and then did exactly as he ordered.

"Lunch?" I asked, lifting the takeout container with a trembling hand.

"What's wrong?" He didn't so much as glance toward the food.

How was I going to say this to him? How could I possibly explain the cost of loving me? I couldn't imagine not having Cam, not after all these years we'd wasted. But I also couldn't condemn Arthur to treatments he didn't want.

"You eat, and I'll talk." I set the food down on the small table and motioned to one of the two folding chairs.

His eyes narrowed, but he sat. I slid the burger over to him, and he opened the takeout container. Only then did he look to see what I brought him.

"Bigg's?" A smile ghosted his lips.

"Just the way you like it." My heart pounded as I took the seat opposite his and moved the shake to his side, too. "The shake is the way I like it, though."

"Willow, you're killing me." He swallowed, watching me with enough intensity to kick my heart rate even higher. "Tell me what's wrong."

"I know. Just…give me a second." The words I knew had to be said filled my mouth, heavy on my tongue, and my stomach twisted—just like it had right before my car crashed—trying to keep them in.

"Are you pregnant?" he asked, leaning toward me with so much love and concern in his eyes that I almost wished I were. "Because if you are, don't worry. I don't know a lot about babies, but I'll learn. And Rose seems to like me well enough, so there's hope our kid would—"

"My father basically told Tim Hall that you'd lose your dad's case if you're dating me." And I word-vomited all over the place. Awesome. My nails bit into my palms where they rested on my lap.

Cam blinked twice, then sat back in his chair. "So you're not pregnant? Because I had the rest of that whole speech planned out. Well, not planned well, since I only had about ten minutes of my brain running amok, but still, it was pretty good." The corner of his mouth lifted.

"No. I'm on birth control, remember?"

"Right. Yeah. Weird, that's where my first thought went when you texted." He lifted the burger and took a bite, groaning in appreciation as I gawked at him. After swallowing, he looked over the massive thing that would have taken me at least three meals to devour. "This is amazing. Thank you."

The man took another bite.

"Cam, did you hear what I just said to you?" Since he was still chewing, I continued. "You're going to lose your dad's case because my dad is pissed that you're dating me."

He set the burger back in its box. "Pika, I'm going to lose my dad's case because Judge Bradley doesn't think I'm capable of being responsible for a puppy, let alone my father's care. The fact that I love you is the icing on an already burned cake."

It didn't matter that he'd told me every day for the last few weeks that he loved me—it still hit me in the heart like it was the first time.

"I...I..." No matter how hard I tried, words wouldn't form.

"I am, you know—capable of taking care of a puppy. I was thinking maybe one of those English bulldogs with all the wrinkles, but I figured I'd ask what you thought first." He took a sip of the shake and grinned.

"What I thought?" Was he utterly and completely mad? I'd just dropped a bomb, and he was thinking about babies and puppies?

"I thought you'd appreciate input." He shrugged. "After all, I figured we'd end up living together and eventually married—when you're ready, of course, if that's something you'd be interested in." He waved his hand like it was all a given. Like we weren't cursed. "So if you hate bulldogs, then we'd have to pick another breed. They've got great temperaments, though. Excellent with kids. When we have them." He tilted his head. "If you want to have them, that is. The marriage thing might not be your style, either. I'm pretty much at your mercy with those." He took another bite of his burger.

My eyes darted around the room, making sure I hadn't stepped into the twilight zone. Once I was sure that this wasn't some really messed-up dream, I pinned him with a stare. "So you don't think we should break up so you have a shot at winning this case? Because that's where I was kind of headed with it." I finished that last part so slowly, it almost felt like a completely different sentence.

He paused mid-chew.

"I mean, that's his best shot, right? If we break up? If my dad sees you're putting Art's interests before your own? That's what makes the most sense." Now the words came fast enough to set their own speed record.

Cam finished chewing and swallowed, abandoning the rest of the burger in its box. "Is that what you want? To…" He shook his head.

"No," I admitted in a whisper. "But isn't this where I'm supposed to leave for your own good? Take the martyrdom road to help your dad and then hope that later, once this is all settled, we can be together?"

"Come here." He shifted and pushed his chair back from the table.

I stood, my knees and resolve shaking as I took the few steps that separated us to stand between his knees.

"Do you love me?" he asked, looking up at me from under dark lashes.

"More than anything in this world." I ran my fingers through his hair, more for my comfort than his.

"Okay." He took my hips and guided me until I sat across his thighs, facing him. "Then, this is where you do that. Where you love me. That's all I need."

I melted, deflated, lost all the tension in my muscles as my fear vanished, but the worry set in. "But what about your dad?"

He ran his knuckles down my cheek. "I can only tackle one problem at a time, Pika. My first priority is and will always be you. This, what we have, isn't something I'm willing to risk."

I leaned into his touch. "I don't want to lose you."

"Then don't." His voice rumbled so low, I felt it in my palm where it lay against his chest.

"Will you hate me if you lose this case?" My darkest fear slipped out on a whisper.

"I will love you for the rest of my life, no matter what happens. None of this is your fault. Do you understand?"

I didn't nod because I couldn't lie. I was the reason my dad hated him. Being with Cam was only going to hurt him in the end. "I'm too selfish to let you go."

"Thank God, because I'm not sure I'd know how to let you. I'm so damned glad you came to me instead of making the decision alone." The relief in his eyes punched me in the stomach. I'd almost done it. Almost walked away.

"We're partners, right?"

"Right."

"You're not going to go yell at my dad right now, are you? Because you're not supposed to know, and if you tell him, then Pat loses his council seat...if they figure out he's the one who told me, since they have an NDA about council meetings or something."

Cam stiffened beneath me, and not in a good way.

"This happened at a council meeting?" he growled.

I nodded.

"You have to be kidding me."

"Promise me you won't go yell at my dad. You know it will just give him more ammunition against you, and I worked really hard to get Pat on your side."

His jaw flexed, and he sucked in three breaths and let them out slowly before he relaxed. "You got Pat Lambert on my side?"

"I'm quite the politician." I shrugged.

His lips lifted in what was almost a smile. "Okay. I'll be good. I promise that I will not yell at your dad."

"Thank you." My forehead fell to rest against his. "I never wanted to complicate your life, Cam."

He kissed me slowly, with a lazy thoroughness that had my hands gripping his shirt in fists before he was done.

"You're not a complication in my life, Willow. You're the reason."

CHAPTER TWENTY-THREE

Camden

I waited a full week to visit the barbershop. My hair had grown since I'd moved home three months ago, and it was time to get it trimmed back into shape.

At least that was my excuse.

Earl McGinty had his scissors close enough to my ear that I could hear the individual strands of my hair being cut. I knew better than to move a muscle.

His hands moved quickly, the product of decades of experience and expertise. When I wasn't watching him in the giant mirrors that lined the wall, I had my eye on the four men who sat in the black chairs behind me, sipping their coffee and shooting me looks that said they weren't certain exactly how they felt about me.

"Don't pay them any mind," Earl said as he caught me looking. "You know how old men like to share the news."

I scoffed. "You're sixty, Earl. Not sure that qualifies as old."

"Well, Tyler back there was born old, and Nick has to be pushing eighty-five."

"Eighty-four!" Nick argued.

"And nothing's wrong with his hearing," Earl said a little louder over his shoulder.

The men chuckled. I wasn't stupid. The power of Alba rested in those seats and had for the last fifty years. Maybe not Xander at this time in the morning, but two members of the town council were already here, and there was little doubt in my mind that the other three would join them in the next hour.

"Since when did John Royal step down from the town council?" I asked loud enough for the men in the back to hear.

"Since he got elected to the Historical Society council," Nick answered. "You know we try not to mix the two. Business and government shouldn't be shaking hands."

"Xander sits on both."

Earl moved to my other side and whistled low.

"Well, now, that couldn't be helped." Tyler Williamson set his coffee down on the small table next to him and stared at me openly. "He's mayor by his own right."

The men nodded in support.

"And sits on the Historical Society council as your father's proxy," he finished.

The nodding continued.

"You gunning for that Historical Society council seat?" Paul Warten asked from his chair next to Tyler.

Every single one of those men leaned forward, and Earl lifted his shears from my head.

"No, sir, I'm not. I wouldn't presume to know enough about the workings of the historical district to even think about it. I've got more than enough on my plate with getting the Rose Rowan up and running, then the mining company building."

One by one, they relaxed, satisfied with my reply.

Earl started cutting again, shooting me a look that said I'd just escaped the guillotine.

"So that's not what this whole mess with Art is about?" Nick questioned over his coffee, acting like he didn't care. The grip he had on that cup said otherwise.

"No, sir. My dad called and asked me to help him take back a little control over his advanced directive. I'm here for his health-care rights, not his council seat. Xander's welcome to it."

Earl lifted a side of his mouth in a slight smirk and kept cutting.

"And Willow? Did you come back for her, too?" Tyler asked.

I tensed, and Earl immediately lifted the shears again. "Well," he started, then glanced up at the clock. "I have a feeling you'll know the answer to that in about five minutes." He caught my eye in the mirror and lowered his voice. "You sure you know what you're getting yourself into here, Cam?"

"I'm sure." I was, and as long as I kept my temper in check, this would all be fine.

"Good morning, gentlemen," Owen McGinty said as he walked in from the back of the barbershop. "I'll take whoever's next." His smile died when none of them took the offer.

"They're waiting for the show to start, Owen," Earl told him with raised eyebrows.

"Show?" He paled when he spotted me. "Hey, Camden, how's it going?"

"Can't complain," I replied, careful not to move as Earl finished me up. "How are Lisa and the kids?"

"Good, good," he answered carefully. The heir to the barbershop empire was about ten years older than me and clearly knew what was up when he started watching the clock.

"Grab me a towel, would you, Owen?" Earl asked his son.

Two minutes later, my hair was done, and Owen handed Earl the hot towel with a warning look.

"I know what I'm doing, son," Earl promised, then reclined my chair so I was nearly horizontal.

"Three minutes," Nick noted, and the rest mumbled their agreement.

"It's not an easy thing you're doing here," Earl said loudly enough for everyone in the shop to hear. "Taking on a brother isn't something I'd ever want my boys to do." He shot a look at Owen. "But I'd hope that my boys would agree to give me the respect of choosing my own path. No one should be forced to surrender control of their own body."

The men muttered in agreement, and I found my chest heavy

with an emotion I was scared to call pride.

"I saw that tattoo, Cam. You're doing the right thing." Earl passed his judgment with a smile. "Now, we'll see if you live through the next few minutes." He wrapped the towel around my face, both softening my week's worth of beard growth and disguising my face. "Don't breathe a word until I tap your foot. Understand?"

I nodded, then resigned myself to breathing in the hot, humid air for the next few minutes.

Right on time, the bell rang as the front door opened.

"Morning, Judge," Earl called out in greeting.

"Morning, Earl. The usual, please. Oh, you men haven't been tended to yet?" Noah Bradley's voice was muffled with the towel so close to my ears, but I made him out just fine.

"Oh, no, you first," Tyler insisted.

I could only imagine the nods of the other men.

"Here you go, Judge. Let's get you softened up. Don't you worry, Owen will catch up with the boys between the tourists who filter in," Earl added, and I knew he'd just given me a cover without technically lying.

"Tourists first" was the rule of law in Alba, and while most of the commercial establishments that locals frequented weren't often sought out by tourists, we deferred to them—and their money—whenever they stumbled into any of the nonhistorical sites.

"Good weather today, Judge," Nick said, breaking the silence.

"So I heard. Highs in the low seventies. Nice and warm for this time of year."

The towel on my face was cool by the time I heard Earl start on the judge.

"Hold up, Judge. I'm not liking the feel of this blade. Let me get you a fresh one," Earl said, then bumped my foot as he walked by.

Showtime.

I sat up, then handed my towel to Owen, who muttered, "The

windows are really expensive."

"Relax," I whispered. *Throw one guy through a window, and you'll still be getting shit for it six years later.*

Then I stood, noting that Willow's dad was reclined the same way I had been, and leaned against the counter directly in front of his chair.

"Hello there, Mr. Bradley," I said, low and smooth.

His eyes flew open, and he sat up slowly, glaring at me with half his face shaved and the other half covered in a thick lather. "Camden."

"So, I need to talk to you."

"This is highly improper." He swung his feet over the side of the chair. "You can't ambush the judge who's about to decide on your case next week."

"Oh, you're completely right. I don't even want to talk about the case. That's a line I wouldn't cross." I tucked my thumbs in the front pockets of my jeans, my casual Rose Rowan Henley a direct contrast to his starched shirt and tie. "I need to talk to Noah Bradley, my girlfriend's dad, not Judge Bradley. Figure you'd feel better having witnesses than any implication of impropriety. I know how much public opinion matters in an election year."

His face paled to a shade just a bit darker than the shaving cream, and he started to get out of the chair, only to catch his reflection in the mirror and think better of it. God only knew the last time the man had actually shaved his own face. "What do you want, Camden?"

"I'm in love with your daughter." The entire shop went so silent, I could hear the beat of my own heart. "I have been since I was about eleven years old, but to be fair, I was probably sixteen when I figured it out."

"Is that what you call it? Love?" His jaw flexed. "Because as I recall, you were eleven when you broke her nose and tried to pass it off as a fall."

Icy rage frosted my nerve endings in what I knew was

preparation for a battle I couldn't let happen. Instead of sinking into that calm, deadly space, I forced a smile to my face. "You see, Mr. Bradley, I promised the woman I love that I wouldn't yell at her dad. I've never broken a promise to Willow, and I'm not going to let you goad me into breaking one now. So I'll simply say that Xander came out of the tunnel that day with Charity, screaming that he'd lost Willow. I took his headlamp and went after her, just like I've always done and will always do."

He seethed but didn't move.

"I found her by the grace of God. Or, since you think I'm evil, maybe it was a deal with the Devil. Either way, I didn't care. My soul in exchange for her life is a trade I'll make any day."

His eyes narrowed.

"When I found her at the bottom of a ventilation shaft that I still can't find on a map, she had a busted nose, bloodied lip, and skinned...everything. I put the headlamp on her so she could see in case anything happened to me, and then I pushed her up thirty feet of that shaft, give or take an almost-twelve-year-old's memory. She cried the entire way, and a couple times it was for you."

He flinched.

"Once we got to the top of the shaft, I took the headlamp back so I didn't trip on my face. Then I picked her up in my arms, and I didn't put her down again until I found you."

Two lines appeared vertically in his forehead. "Xander said you wouldn't let him help you. That you slowed everyone down getting her the help she needed."

"He's right. And he had just turned fourteen, so he probably could have gotten her out of the mine faster once we got up the shaft. But he wasn't in the mine, Mr. Bradley. He was waiting at the entrance with Charity and Sullivan, and since he'd already lost her once that day, I wasn't about to hand her over to anyone besides you."

He stared me down, still not believing.

"You took Sullivan with you to the hospital and sent me home."

"They were friends. You were—"

"Her soul mate. But that's okay. I forgave you for that a long time ago."

Two figures approached the door, and Owen flipped the sign from open to closed. First time for everything.

"How can you even say that? She was Sullivan's. She's only with you now because she sees something of him in you. You think she's in love with you? She's not. She's in love with that part of Sullivan you represent, and it will eventually destroy her."

If I hadn't been so certain of Willow's love, I would have lost it right then. Instead, I focused on the warmth in my chest that grew every time I thought about her.

"You're wrong, but it's not my place to talk about Willow's feelings. I can only speak to what she's told me and how I feel about your daughter. I'm not here to argue about Sullivan. I loved him more than you ever could have and will carry his loss with me every day for the rest of my life."

"At least he deserved her," he threw in my face, his voice rising. "He never got her hurt. Never got into fistfights. Never covered his body in tattoos or set fire to a damned building! And he sure as hell asked my permission when he wanted to date Willow. He came to me like a man, his intentions clear and his heart honest, because he knew she was the kind of girl who respected that tradition!" He jabbed his finger in my direction.

I shifted, bracing my hands on the counter and squeezing the top. "I'm not even sure where to start with that. I guess at the beginning. I have never hurt Willow intentionally, and the only wounds I've inflicted on her were emotional and due to my supreme idiocy when I was nineteen."

His eyes flared in surprise for a millisecond, but it was there.

"I got into my share of fistfights, and I'd say probably half of them were defending Willow. Scott Malone was an asshole, and when he got tired of bullying her, Oscar stepped in. This"—I pointed to the tattoo of the hot springs on my arm—"is a sketch

Willow did the summer before I left for basic training. I had it done the week before I reported, and yes, it hurt like a bitch until it healed.

"As for the fire? Accidents happen, and you have no idea how terrified I was when I heard she was still inside. I'll never forgive myself for how long it took me to get to her." It always came back to that fucking fire.

"What, you're not going to throw in that you carried her out then, too?" he challenged.

"You already knew that." I shrugged. "As for the last part? I'm not Sullivan. He was a better boy than I was, and he never got to grow into manhood, but I bet if he hadn't died that day?" I paused, taking a second to swallow the memories. "He would have been a far better man than I am. There's no doubt."

"At least we agree on that," he snapped. "Now, are you done?"

"No. Because here's the thing—Sullivan was wrong. He never should have asked your permission."

A collective murmur in the background reminded me that we had an audience.

"I'm sorry?" Mr. Bradley asked, his eyebrows rising.

"I didn't ask your permission to date your daughter because it's not up to you. What happens between Willow and me requires the consent of two people: Willow"—I held up one finger and then the second—"and me. You're not in that equation."

"I'm her father!"

"Yeah, you are, which is why we're having this conversation. She loves you, and the rift between you two is ripping her apart."

"She knows how to repair it." His voice dropped to a hiss.

"By choosing you over me."

He raised a single eyebrow, confirming my statement.

"If you continue that ultimatum, you will lose her." I said it softly, making the guys in the back lean forward.

"Hardly. She knows I'd do anything to protect her, even fight her for her."

"She will choose me, Mr. Bradley. And sure, partly it's because she loves me as much as I love her. But mostly, it's because I won't ever make her choose."

His features slackened.

"I don't need to control her to love her. I don't conquer my own fears that way, and I'm so sorry if you do. I only came to tell you that she loves you and she misses you. And I hope you come to your senses soon, because there's nothing on earth that would make me walk away from Willow. I'm hers until she decides otherwise, not you."

Anger sparked in his eyes, and the color not only returned to his cheeks but flared.

"I'm glad we could have this conversation." I pushed off the counter and headed toward the door, only to pause and look back at him, my thoughts tripping over something he'd said. "If you want my intentions, here they are. I'm going to marry your daughter. Then I'm going to spend every day of my life making her as happy as possible. But when I ask her to be my wife, you won't know. I won't ask your permission because she's not a piece of property, and I won't respect your tradition because you don't respect that it's really her choice. And if she says yes, you'll only know if she tells you. You'll only know if we get married if she chooses to invite you. You'll only know if we have a child if she deems you worthy to know, worthy of being in her life."

He turned a mottled shade of red, and I knew I'd passed the do-not-cross line a while back, but I couldn't bring myself to care.

"You've raised two amazing, independent, intelligent women, one of whom owns my soul. Two women you should be incredibly proud of. I just wish you would be."

Owen held the door open for me as I walked out of the barbershop, giving me a smile and a nod in farewell.

Then I drove straight to Willow's house, interrupted her work like the selfish bastard I was, and made love to her until the ugliness of the morning faded into nothing but love and bliss.

CHAPTER TWENTY-FOUR

Willow

The little brick building that served as both the Town Hall and Alba's municipal court was packed to the brim with just about every local who wasn't tending their shop in the historic district.

Xander already had the home-field advantage, seeing as his office was right across the hall, and he looked more than comfortable in his suit across the aisle, sitting with Milton Sanders, his attorney.

I sat on the bench behind Cam and Simon, who had their heads together in a conversation I couldn't hear, even four feet away.

"I've never seen so many people here," Charity noted as she slid in next to me. She was dressed similarly to me, wearing a simple sheath dress and pearls, just like our mother, who scooted in next to Charity.

"Or heard so many," Mom added. "They've got Scott Malone turning people away at the door."

We weren't exactly built or staffed for such a public case, considering that we had an active courthouse only because Dad was willing to split his time between here and Salida. No other judge was volunteering to come up the pass.

"Of course Genevieve is sitting behind Xander," Charity said with a shake of her head.

"But Pat, Gideon, and John are behind us," Mom reported after a quick glance over her shoulder.

"Good morning, ladies." Walt slid in behind us with Dorothy Powers.

"They didn't sequester you?" Mom asked with raised brows.

"Nope. Deposition yesterday," Dorothy replied. "Art is finishing up with that psychologist, and then he'll be in, too."

"Again?" Charity questioned.

"They're hoping he'll be lucid enough to testify." I kept my eyes forward and saw Simon shake his head. Cam didn't look pleased at whatever that was the answer to. "He wasn't all there the first time the doc interviewed him, but he was pretty lucid at last week's appointment. Why don't you guys come up here?" I looked back over my shoulder for the first time and saw they were closing the doors.

"I make him nervous." Walt nodded toward his son with pride shining in his eyes.

Scott Malone let Art in, and Dorothy walked back to guide him up the aisle, where he eventually sat next to Cam, much to the muttering of the other side of the courtroom. I committed the image to memory, knowing I might not ever see Art take Cam's side against Xander ever again.

The doors reopened, and Julie Hall hurried down the aisle with a manila envelope. She handed it to Cam, who tensed as he thanked her, then put it into the file he had in front of him without opening it.

That certainly got my curiosity piqued.

Peter Mayville, our bailiff, entered the front of the court, and Mary Murphy came in directly after to take her spot at the recorder's desk. We were ready to start.

My heart slammed against my ribs at the thought of what was coming. How could I ever forgive my father for ruling against Cam in this? Against Art?

Cam looked back at me and winked.

I love you, I mouthed.

I love you, he echoed before turning back around.

"You two are nauseating," Charity mumbled. "Not that I'm not happy you finally pulled your heads out of your asses, because that had to be the longest slow burn I've ever seen in my life."

"Charity! Language!" Mom snapped.

She merely rolled her eyes.

"You act like you're the only person who knew what was going on," Mom mumbled. "Who do you think distracted your dad while Willow snuck out to rescue all of Cam's stuff that night? Huh?"

We both slowly turned our heads to look at her with wide eyes.

"You did what?" Dad asked as he slid in next to me.

"Nothing you need to worry about," she told him with a wifely smile that said he was better off not knowing.

"You talking about those boxes full of Cam's things she had stacked in her closet for years?" he asked.

We all gawked at him.

"You knew?" I asked.

His jaw flexed twice. "I'm stubborn, Willow. Not stupid."

I blinked, and then it hit me. "Wait, what are you doing—?"

"All rise!" Peter Mayville called out, and we did so. "The Alba Municipal Court is now in session, the Honorable Judge Deborah Wilson presiding."

My gaze snapped to my father, who stood, chin raised over an expertly knotted tie, as he watched someone else take his seat at the bench.

"You may be seated," a feminine voice declared.

I was all too happy to, considering I already felt like I'd been knocked on my ass.

Peter announced the case, but all I heard was a buzzing in my head. "Dad?" I whispered, unable to look anywhere else.

He gave me a tight-lipped smile but didn't speak.

"Good morning, all three Mr. Danielses," Judge Wilson greeted the men facing her, and I took her in for the first time. She was about the same age as Dad, with classically beautiful Korean features and an equally classic French twist in her hair.

"Your Honor, if I may." Milton Sanders stood. "We were told this case would be heard by Judge Bradley." His voice pitched higher than usual as he finished.

I felt the weight of a thousand stares in our direction.

"Yes," Judge Wilson responded with a smile. "I apologize for the confusion and the last-minute switch. Judge Bradley informed me he needed to recuse himself and asked if I would mind driving up to hear the case rather than going through a reschedule so close to the date. Since I had an opening, I agreed."

Milton paled. "Thank you for the explanation, Your Honor. Could you tell us when the request was made?"

"Last night. Apparently, his daughter is in a relationship with one of the parties, and he felt he couldn't be impartial." She adjusted her thin-framed glasses. "The docket has been updated online, naturally."

"Of course, Your Honor." He leaned down and conferred with Xander as the courtroom buzzed with muffled commentary. "Your Honor, my client would like to request a continuance."

"On what grounds?" she asked.

"On the grounds that this last-minute change has left us at a disadvantage and we'll need extra time to prepare." Milton sounded rockier than his reasoning.

"Your request is denied. An impartial judge is an impartial judge, and I assure you that I couldn't care less about where Judge Bradley is seated. Also, the court psychologist has assured me that Arthur Daniels is capable of testimony today, and that's not something I'm willing to risk losing, given his diagnosis. We'll proceed as planned."

Milton's shoulders sagged as he sat.

"Mr. Robinson, since your client has moved to change the guardianship of Arthur Daniels, the floor is yours," Judge Wilson stated.

As Simon stood to give his opening, I looked at Dad. "You

recused yourself?" Emotion tangled my tongue and clogged my throat.

His eyes met mine, softening exponentially. "I'm stubborn, Willow. Not stupid," he repeated with a wry smile. "I've presided over thousands of cases, and none of them—including this one—is worth losing my daughter over." He looked around my head. "Either of my daughters."

"Thank you," I whispered.

"Just remember that I'm sitting with you, Willow. You and Charity and your mother. Not him." He nodded toward Cam. "You."

"That's more than enough." I smiled slowly, and when I turned to watch Simon start his delivery, I caught Charity nodding at Dad.

Both sides delivered an opening, stating their cases as to why Art's guardian should be their client. Both stood firmly on their stance with the DNR.

Cam was first on the stand.

He answered Simon's questions easily, telling the judge about the voicemail that had brought him home and what it had been like to see Art on the respirator after he'd been poisoned by carbon monoxide.

"He did well," Dad whispered as Milton rose to question Cam. "Strong, clear voice, sound reasoning, and no ill will harbored toward Xander. Very well."

"If you ever decide to give up the bench, you could always go for a career in courtroom commentating," I whispered.

He shot me a look that said he'd rather die.

Milton started in hard on Cam, asking about his estrangement with Art over the last decade. He then moved on to his return to Alba and painted a picture of Cam being an unstable drifter who couldn't be depended on to stick around.

"On the contrary," Cam argued. "I own property in Alba, have a voting membership in the Historical Society, and have two properties included in the district, one of which is projected to increase the income of the town by fifty percent. I'm in a committed relationship and recently offered my civil-engineering skills to the town's electric company to upgrade Alba's energy supply. The fact that I served in the military—as both my brothers also did— doesn't make me a nomad."

Milton flushed, and I almost fist pumped.

"What financial gain do you stand to receive in the event of Arthur Daniels's death?" Milton asked, flipping through his file.

"I don't understand the question," Cam stated, his posture straight and his face relaxed.

"I mean that you're pushing hard for a do-not-resuscitate order for a fifty-eight-year-old man. Isn't it true that you stand to gain fifty percent of Arthur's considerable land and financial holdings when he passes?" Milton's insinuation sent a murmur through the crowd.

Judge Wilson looked over her glasses at Cam.

"I don't stand to gain anything," Cam stated.

"I'm sorry, but that's just not true. His will states that you three receive equal shares, and since Sullivan has passed on, that leaves you and Xander at fifty percent."

Cam blinked and looked at Simon.

"Your Honor, it appears Mr. Sanders is working off an older copy of Mr. Daniels's will. If I could supply both him and the court with the valid copy?" Simon offered.

"Please do," she responded.

Simon handed out the wills. "As you can see, this will is dated from five years ago, making it newer and therefore valid."

"You prepared it!" Milton snapped. "How convenient."

"It's a small town, Your Honor." Simon didn't spare a glance for Milton. "It was actually my first document post–law school and was accepted by Judge Bradley."

Judge Wilson flipped through the document. "This appears to be the valid will, Mr. Sanders."

"As you can see, after the death of my younger brother, my father took me out of his will. Everything goes to Xander." Cam stared at his brother.

Alexander was visibly shaken, his attention darting among Art, Cam, and the document in his hands.

"He didn't know?" I asked.

"He didn't," Dad confirmed.

Milton gathered his thoughts quickly and conferred with Xander. Then he turned back to Cam. "Can you tell me about the bunkhouse fire?"

"Objection!" Simon snapped. "Immaterial!"

The crowd's mutterings exploded.

"Order!" Judge Wilson demanded. "Keep it up, and we'll close the courtroom."

"Your Honor, this goes to the heart of his character."

"How can something that happened almost a decade ago comment on his character?"

"Hey, your client is the one who brought up the properties in the Historical Society. The fact that there was a third, potentially profitable property matters when looking to his future."

"I'll allow it," Judge Wilson ruled.

"What can you tell me about the bunkhouse fire?" Milton poked the bear.

Cam's eyes flashed with indignation. "Our family owns what was the Rose Rowan bunkhouse. It burned down nine years ago. The summer I was nineteen."

"Were you responsible for this catastrophic loss of a priceless historical site?"

"The fire was ruled accidental." Cam's voice hardened.

"And there was no mention of you in that report? Because I have it right here if you'd like to read it." Milton sifted through his file.

Cam locked eyes with Xander.

"Mr. Daniels?" Milton prompted.

A look of utter betrayal passed over Cam's features, and my heart sank.

"Mr. Daniels." Judge Wilson's voice brought Cam's focus back to Milton.

"The report says that though the fire was ruled accidental, it was caused by my negligence." Cam's jaw flexed.

"And do you agree with that report?" Milton asked.

"Since I'm the one who admitted to it, it would be hard not to, wouldn't you say?" Cam snapped.

"If you could simply answer the question." Milton tilted his head slightly.

"I agree with it."

Milton declared that he had no further questions, and Simon jumped on the chance to redirect. "Camden, how many years did you serve in the United States Army?"

"Nine."

"And during that time, you served in the Special Forces and managed to get your degree in engineering?"

"I did."

"Would you say that you had upward potential in income and rank?"

"I would. I've already had four job offers for more than six figures a year."

"And yet you gave that all up for an income far less than that. Why?" Simon prompted.

"Because my father asked for my help."

"And for the record, could you tell the court which medals you earned during your service?"

Cam tensed and glanced at Xander. "I have a few."

"Let me be specific. Is it correct that you not only have a Purple Heart but a Bronze Star for heroic actions in combat that not only saved lives but earned you a bullet in the upper arm?"

My jaw dropped an inch. His upper arm? Both were covered in tattoos. He'd been wounded? Awarded one of the army's highest honors?

"My record will confirm that," Cam said slowly, looking away.

"But you've never told anyone?" Simon asked.

"I got a scratch because I did the right thing in a firefight. That's not something that should be bragged about. It should simply be assumed that anyone would do the right thing in that situation, not rewarded."

"I understand. Last question. When were you given this citation?"

Cam's eyes unfocused. "Two years and three months ago."

"Sounds like that's a much better example of your character than an accident from a decade ago." Simon shrugged.

"Objection!" Milton shouted.

"Withdrawn."

Cam stepped down, his eyes searching mine as he took his seat. There were apologies written in his pressed lips, and I smiled softly at him, forgiving that which needed no explanation.

"How did he do?" I asked Dad when Cam sat down.

"Strong finish," he whispered, "but the fire? That made the whole thing a draw."

I just wasn't sure a draw was enough to beat Xander. It was hard to compete with flawless.

CHAPTER TWENTY-FIVE

Camden

I couldn't bring myself to look at Xander. Not during his perfect testimony of his perfect life with his perfect choices and perfectly planned future. Not when he'd just thrown the fire in my face.

He used it against me, then testified that I was a great brother and son, just misguided about what was best for Dad. After all, I'd been gone for a decade, between that first year in college and the years in the military, so how could I really understand the level of care he needed? Being back for the last three and a half months couldn't possibly give me a good enough perspective to judge my dad's intentions, even though my heart was in the right place.

I had never hated my brother. Maybe I'd been a little jealous that he was the assigned angel of the family, but I'd never wished him ill.

Right now, I wanted to throw him through the gas station window again, especially since he brought that moment up, too. Even with the context Simon added, I came off like an asshole.

The doc was next, who went over Dad's Alzheimer's diagnosis, his level of dementia, and his ability to make decisions. It was his opinion that while able to make decisions about his daily routine and care, he was unable to understand the impact of long-term decisions on more than half of his days.

The more the doctor talked, the more agitated Dad became,

shifting in his seat and shaking his head.

"Are you sure you want your dad up there?" Simon asked me quietly.

Of course I wasn't sure. The further we got into the hearing, the less I was certain about anything, including my brother's morals.

"The doc says he's lucid enough today, or at least he was at this morning's interview. It's his life. You ask him." If Xander was hell-bent on keeping Dad from making life decisions, then I could at least give him this choice.

A few minutes later, Simon leaned in. "He says he wants to."

"Then, let him. At least he never set anything on fire." This might be the only chance he had to say exactly what he wanted to Xander, and the witnesses would hold him socially accountable.

Once the doc stepped down and Dad was headed up to the stand, I looked back at Willow.

She gave me a reassuring smile—not that everything would be okay but that she would be there even if it wasn't. I couldn't return the expression, and hers softened in understanding.

Being up there on the stand, having my military record brought out like that, only served to remind me that even though we knew each other on a cellular level, we hadn't caught up on all the details of the years we'd spent apart. But we'd have time for that…at least if the envelope Julie had given me decided so.

I wasn't looking. Not until after this was over.

Simon questioned Dad, and he did surprisingly well. His answers were clear and concise, and he actually came off as perfectly lucid. We couldn't have hoped for a better day to do this.

"Art, tell me: are you certain about wanting a do-not-resuscitate order?" Simon asked.

"Since I had it tattooed across my chest, I'd say I'm very certain," Dad insisted. "This isn't your choice, Alexander." Dad turned to stare at my brother, and my stomach clenched. "I'm not a child. I am a man who deserves the dignity of controlling what happens to his body."

"Objection," Milton called out.

"You know it's wrong," Dad continued, and now my stomach twisted with nausea. "I taught you better than to tie another person down and force things into their body that they don't want. That's what you did to me!"

The crowd behind began to speak at the same time.

"Objection!" Milton shouted.

Shit. He was going off the rails.

"No further questions," Simon finished, then sat down next to me. "Well, if nothing else, the entire town will be talking about that for a while."

My muscles locked as Milton approached my father. He started easy, laying the foundation that, in every other matter besides that of his DNR, Xander was an excellent guardian in his opinion. And the DNR wasn't a matter of malice or negligence but opinion.

That's where he lost Dad.

"I do think it's malicious to directly ignore someone's wishes about his own body," Dad argued.

"I agree," Milton said. "But are you sure they're your wishes?"

"I am." Dad nodded.

"Today, you are. But what about tomorrow? Next year? Your memory isn't always supporting you, Art, is it?"

Dad's forehead puckered. "Some days it's...faulty."

"Like the day you shot Camden?"

My eyes slid shut as the muttering of the crowd washed over me.

"I..." He shook his head. "I don't remember much about that." His confession was quiet.

"It was Alexander who wrestled the gun away so you didn't kill his little brother a few months ago. Is that true?"

Dad looked down, his gaze darting back and forth, fighting to remember. "That's what I've been told."

"You don't remember that moment?"

"Not as clearly as I'd like," Dad admitted.

"Okay, for the sake of establishing your memory loss, can you tell me how your son, Sullivan, died?"

I almost came out of my skin.

"Objection!" Simon shouted. "Immaterial. We already have his diagnosis on file."

"It goes to suitability of the guardian, Your Honor." Milton looked at the judge like he was requesting a transcript from his last college, not ripping apart my father.

"You're on a short leash, Mr. Sanders," Judge Wilson warned.

"Yes, Your Honor. Art, do you remember how Sully died?"

My hands clenched into fists beneath the table, and I savored the bite of pain from my nails, using it to ground and focus me.

"Sully..." Dad looked away.

I knew that look. We were about to lose him. "You have to stop this," I whispered.

"I can't." Simon sighed. "I'm so sorry. I never thought Xander would use Sully."

"Sullivan died in Afghanistan, right?" Milton pushed.

"That's right," Dad confirmed, nodding but still focused on the floor. "Afghanistan. He was shot."

"In the neck, right?"

I was going to rip Milton's head from his fucking shoulders.

"Right. His neck." Dad started subtly rocking.

"Another one of your sons was with him. Do you remember?"

Dad slowly looked over to me, his eyes full of agonizing grief, and my throat closed. "Cam. Cam was with him."

"Is it true that Camden ordered Sullivan's squad into the firefight that took his life?"

"Yes."

Left. I'd chosen the man standing to my left instead of my right. One choice made in a flash of a second. It had been the flap of the butterfly's wings that began the hurricane. And we were all still drowning.

"That must be hard, knowing that Cam didn't bring your Sully home safe." Milton's voice dripped with pity.

Dad's face crumpled, and I found it hard to draw a breath.

"Objection!"

"Isn't it true that you blame Cam for Sullivan's death?"

"Leading the witness!"

"I... Yes. He gave the order. You gave the order." Dad looked toward me, his eyes glazing over.

How could I argue with the truth?

"Withdrawn." Milton immediately put out his hand to Simon, like he was the one who needed to calm down. "Art, can you tell me what you had for breakfast this morning?"

"What?"

My heart fell to the floor.

"Breakfast? Or dinner last night? Or maybe what you watched on TV? Can you tell me any of that?" Milton asked softly, like he actually cared.

"I'm... Eggs?" he guessed.

"It was French toast, according to your home nursing staff. Can you tell me the date?"

Dad swayed. "It's June. I know it's June."

"June what? Fifteenth? Seventh? Twenty-eighth?"

"It's June!" Dad shouted.

My eyes pricked, and I blinked back the moisture that welled, watching my father dissolve.

"But what day in June?"

"I don't know!"

"I understand, Art. Can you tell me the names of your home-nursing staff?" Milton didn't even give Dad a chance to recover.

"There are a few," Dad replied, looking so lost that my instincts screamed to get him down from the stand.

"But who are they?"

"I don't...I don't know."

"You don't know the people who are currently responsible for your around-the-clock care?" Milton questioned.

"No! I don't! They're people in my house. They're always there. They never leave me alone anymore!" His voice broke and took my spirit with it.

"That's okay, Art. Let's try one last thing. Camden says that he was brought home by a voicemail you left. Do you remember that?"

Dad's eyes brightened. "Yes. I remember the voicemail. I asked him to come home and help me. Xander wouldn't let me have a DNR."

"That's right. Do you know when you left the voicemail?"

Shit. I felt the blood drain from my face.

"I…" Dad looked at me helplessly.

I wanted the last twenty minutes back. I wanted to tell Simon, *No, don't put him on the stand*. Not because he didn't deserve to say his piece but because he didn't deserve what Milton was doing to him right now.

"Look at me, Mr. Daniels," Milton ordered softly, like he was talking to a child and not a grown-ass man who had raised three sons and buried one of them, plus his wife and brother. "Do you remember when you left the message?"

"It was this year. I know that." Dad nodded. "I know it. I know it. This year. This year. I know it."

"Mr. Daniels, do you remember leaving that message at all?"

"This year. Had to be."

"Mr. Daniels?"

"Objection. Your Honor, this is…" Simon just shook his head. Cruel. It was cruel.

"This is your last question, Mr. Sanders. We're not here to torture those who need our protection," Judge Wilson warned.

"Yes, Your Honor. Art?"

"What?" Dad whispered.

"Do you remember leaving Cam that voicemail?"

"No."

"So everything we've done here, from Cam giving up his career to this very hearing, was all started over something you can't even remember?"

"Mr. Sanders, that's enough," Judge Wilson ordered.

"I'm finished," Milton promised and took his seat.

Dad's gaze darted around the room to the ceiling and the floor, never settling on any one person or thing.

"Your Honor, may I help my dad down?" I asked, knowing it wasn't my place to speak and risking it anyway.

"Yes, Mr. Daniels," she agreed, her voice softer than before.

The court was silent until my chair shrieked across the polished floor as I pushed back from the table. I approached Dad with shaky knees, my eyes filling with tears I couldn't shed. Not here. Not like this.

"Dad, let me help you," I said as I stood next to the witness stand.

"I don't… Why…?" He finally looked at me. "Why am I here? I want to go home."

"Yeah, Dad, we'll get you there, I promise. Come on down." I held out my hand, but he refused to take it and instead stumbled from the stand.

"No. I'm okay. Don't touch me. I'm fine!" He walked past me, gaining his balance as he went.

"Walt?" I called out as Simon opened the gate that separated the spectators from this hellhole.

"I got him," Walt promised as Nikki walked with him to help.

"You," Dad whispered, turning to me at the threshold.

"It's me, Dad. Cam. I'm right here."

His eyes turned cold. "You killed my Sullivan." The whisper was barely loud enough for me to hear, but I did, and it cut me to the fucking core.

"Come on, Art. Let's get you home." Walt put his arm around his best friend and walked him from the courtroom. I stumbled into my seat as the volume of the crowd reached new heights.

Logic told me otherwise, but the rending in my chest overpowered it. I'd lost every member of my family. Sullivan and Mom to death. Dad to Alzheimer's. Alexander to his own warped sense of good and evil.

The judge called for order as I felt hands on my shoulders. I turned and found Willow leaning over the railing.

"I love you," she promised, her hazel eyes red and her cheeks blotchy. "I love you." Her thumbs swiped at my face. "Do you understand me, Camden Daniels? I know your truth. I love you, and I have always loved you. First and always. You."

"Order!" the judge demanded again, and the noise started to die down.

I kept my focus on Willow, anchoring myself in her eyes and slowly settling my boiling emotions into a soft simmer.

"Willow," I whispered.

She let go of my face only to push something into my hand. "I'll be right here. I'm not going anywhere." Then she sat back in her seat, where her father put his arm around her. Her father, who had recused himself because I was hers. He looked at me with pursed lips and sorrowful eyes.

The crowd quieted, and I opened my palm to see what she'd given me.

It was the white onyx queen. The most versatile piece on the board. The protector of the king. I forced deep and even breaths through my lungs.

A soft sob reached my ears, and I turned to see Xander's head in his hands, his shoulders shaking as he cried. As Simon and Milton both gave their closings, I stared at Xander. It took until the end of Milton's speech for my brother to look at me.

When he did, he flinched.

I let it show—my anger, my loathing, and my utter disgust. When Judge Wilson dismissed us until her ruling, the crowd emptied out into the hallway.

"I'll be there in just a second," I promised Willow.

She nodded, squeezing my hand as she passed by on her way to where her family waited.

I finally opened the envelope Julie left.

With shaking hands, I read the three sheets she'd included and felt simultaneous relief and sorrow. Deep, gut-wrenching sorrow.

"You okay?" Simon asked.

"No. None of it is okay." I slid the papers back into their envelope, then walked over to my older brother, my idol, the perfect example of love and forgiveness, and openly glared at him as he rose to leave.

"Cam," Simon warned.

"I need a minute with my brother." I kept my eyes on Xander.

"Alexander?" Milton probed.

"It's fine. I'll meet you out there," Xander replied.

The courtroom cleared out until it was only us standing between the tables we'd gone to war at.

"No matter what happens, what she rules, I will never forgive you for what just happened. I'm ashamed of you, and Sullivan would be, too. How could you use him like that? Use the fire?"

Xander shook his head at me in confusion. "Forgive me? You're the one who keeps trying to kill Dad even though the doctors have said he's not mentally capable of making that choice. And you want to blame this on me? I have no choice but to stick to the decisions he made before he lost his mind, because that man we saw up on the stand is no longer our father!"

"He's still Dad! He doesn't want tubes and ventilators! He wants the dignity of making that choice, and you can't even give him that? You have to shred what's left of his pride in front of the entire town?" My voice rose.

"You made me do it!" Xander shouted. "Do you think I wanted this? Any of this? I don't! I said, 'Hey, Dad, you need a medical power of attorney, just in case you need someone to sign for a surgery or something.' Do you know when that was?" He shook with anger. "It was five years ago, after Sully died! I never saw this coming! I never wanted this!" He motioned to the courtroom. "Never wanted to be responsible for his care, for making decisions that would mean his life or death over and over and over. But that's what happened, because you were too busy being a hero to bring your ass home! But they don't give you medals when you stay home, do they?"

His voice echoed in the empty room, and I began to understand. I'd been so focused on the house of cards crumbling at the top that I hadn't stopped to look at the foundation. Xander was never going to let me win, because that's how he saw this.

"You honestly don't think he deserves to choose what happens to him," I stated softly.

"He's not capable of choosing. I have to choose for him. I have to step up, just like always, because you want to take the easy way out. So fine, I have, and I will, and every choice I make for him will be with his life and health in mind. I'm keeping our dad alive as long as I can, Cam. That's what a son does for his father."

"Yeah? And what would a brother do for a brother?"

"What do you mean?" Xander asked. "I would fight for you, too."

God, I hoped not.

"I'll keep that in mind," I told him, then left the courtroom without another backward glance. Simon led me to a quiet room, where I sat with Willow, her hand steady in mine, her head on my shoulder.

"I told your father on opening day that you were lonely," she told me.

I turned my head, and she lifted hers.

"He replied that all great and precious things are lonely."

My brows knit together, and she nodded. That line... Holy shit. The same man who'd mocked me for always having my nose in a book as a kid took the time to read the one I'd declared my favorite, and not just once, but enough to recall that line.

I kissed her forehead with gratitude and held her against my side as we waited for the judge to decide Dad's fate.

"This case is definitely not an easy one," Judge Wilson told us four hours later. The room held its breath.

"Mr. Daniels," she said to me. "Your love for your father is obvious. The dedication you've shown by moving home and seeing this through is admirable. I truly think you are acting in what you feel is his best interest, and I would have done exactly the same had it been my father who called."

I nodded as nausea turned my stomach into a cesspool of bile and hope.

"But in order for me to change the current guardianship, your brother has to be proven negligent, and he's not. He's stable, with a proven history of caring for your father. I cannot find legal grounds to grant you guardianship, no matter how much I would like to."

That pit in my stomach filled with dread and defeat as the sour taste of despair hit my tongue.

"Mr. Daniels," she addressed my brother. "You have done an excellent job of caring for your father's body. I understand the strain you must be under. Being a parental caregiver isn't easy. You deserve to keep your guardianship based on your history. However, I would urge you to listen to your father. Though legally, he cannot be deemed competent enough for me to order a DNR on his behalf, I sincerely hope you change your mind.

"The ability to control what happens to our flesh and to choose our future is the core of our personhood. Free will is the most precious of our possessions, and to lose it is a tragedy to which there is no equal. But the compassion we show to those who lack that control—both the very young who have yet to claim it and the very old who face its loss—that is the essence of our humanity. While I don't think you lack compassion, I do think you lack empathy for your father's plight, and I hope you find it before he's made to suffer again.

"I find in favor of the defendant, who will retain guardianship of Arthur Daniels." The gavel hit the bench.

Dad no longer had a say in the rest of his life.

CHAPTER
TWENTY-SIX

Willow

"So how did you choose?" I asked Rose, who had just finished telling me about the love triangle she'd found herself in the middle of. Apparently where you sat at her school's lunch table was the step before an engagement ring, and while she always sat next to Addison, her best friend, her other side was the hottest commodity at Alba Elementary.

"I haven't yet, but I have a plan," she told me as we made our way through the crowd that had gathered for the ribbon-cutting at the mine. It was hard to believe it was already the Fourth of July, and even more unbelievable that Cam had made enough progress for this soft opening. We still had a few hours to go, but locals and tourists alike had made their way up to the Rose Rowan already.

"What is this plan?" Cam asked, sneaking up behind us.

"Hi, Cam!" Rose's smile was instant and bright.

"Hi, Rosie." Cam picked her up in a hug before kissing me quickly.

"Rose apparently has to choose between two boys," I told him as he took my hand in his.

"What? I thought boys had germs and stuff at your age."

Rose flat-out rolled her eyes at him. "There they are." She not-so-subtly pointed to two boys who stood near the punch table.

"Wait, this showdown is happening here?" Where was her

mother when I needed her? I rose on my tiptoes to see if Charity stood out in the crowd, but it was too thick to find anyone who wasn't as tall as Cam.

Speaking of tall, there was Alexander, having his picture taken over by the podium. Now I was the one rolling my eyes.

"It's not a showdown. It will be easy, see?" She slipped her Rose Rowan backpack from her shoulder and pulled out two glittery unicorn pins. "I've been conducting an experiment, and now it's time to test out my hypoth..." Her forehead puckered.

"Hypothesis," I offered.

"Yep!" She grinned and put her pack back on.

"Do you want to explain?" I asked, noting that one of the boys was shorter with glasses and the classic underdog haircut, while the other could have modeled for *Fourth Grade Weekly* or whatever.

"Later," she promised.

"Need some muscle?" Cam offered, eyeing the boys.

"I can take care of myself, but thank you!" she called over her shoulder as she walked toward the boys.

"I don't know how I feel about this," I muttered.

"Ditto," he agreed, squeezing my hand.

We watched as Rose presented the boys with the pins.

"I wish we could hear what they're saying."

"If I'd known, I would have wired up a mic." His eyes narrowed, and he leaned forward like he could wish himself into supersonic hearing.

The taller boy took the pin and forced a smile, then slipped it into the front pocket of his jeans. The shorter one grinned at Rose and then stuck it to the front of his *Star Wars* shirt.

Rose smiled at the shorter boy, said something that made him grin even wider, then ran back over to us.

My heart melted into a puddle of goo as I realized what she'd done and what the man I loved had inadvertently done for her.

"It worked!" she said, her eyes shining with the wisdom of childhood.

"What worked?" Cam asked, his gaze darting back to the boys.

"My experiment!" She raised her hands in victory.

"Well, I think it's about to get interesting," I said as I spied the taller boy coming over. He fumbled with the pin but eventually got the back through his polo and fastened it.

"Rose!" he called, waving enthusiastically. "Look!" He pointed to the pin.

She sighed and shook her head. "I'm sorry, Drake, but it's too late."

"And way too early," Cam muttered, earning him a poke with my elbow.

"But I like it! I really do!" he proclaimed with big blue eyes.

"No you don't." She shook her head emphatically. "You just want me to think you like it. There's a difference."

"Burn," Cam drawled.

"No one says that anymore," Rose lectured him, but she did it with a smile.

"Fine," Drake snapped, ripping the pin from his shirt and leaving a hole in the fabric. "Keep your stupid unicorn. I don't want it anyway." He thrust it at Rose, and when she didn't take it back, Cam reached over and took it for her.

The boy looked up and up, and when he finally met Cam's eyes, his widened. Then he ran.

"Thank you for proving my hypothesis!" Rose shouted after him.

"That's the word! Good job!" I told her with a high five.

Cam had already fastened the pin above the Rose Rowan logo on the button-down shirt he wore. I had zero doubt the white fabric would be stained with dirt by the end of the first train run, but I loved that he had the sleeves rolled up, not caring what anyone thought of his tattoos.

"Camden, the newspaper is here all the way from Denver. They're hoping to get an interview with you and Xander and maybe your dad?" Walt asked with more than a little hesitation. "It's understandable if you want to say no or if you'd like to use his camera to violently bash your brother over the head."

A smile ghosted Cam's lips, and he sighed. "It's okay, Walt. It's good for the mine, and with the cost of at-home care, I'll take all the free publicity I can get."

"Don't have too much fun," I told him.

He kissed me as a reply. He was doing that more often, too—kissing me in public, ignoring what anyone thought about him or us. It wasn't an act of rebellion like it would have been when he was younger. Now it was because he genuinely didn't care what anyone thought and knew I didn't, either.

We were happy, and that made all the difference.

"I should have brought one for you, too," Rose mumbled.

"I don't need one," I assured her, spying Charity standing with her boyfriend. "You already know I don't care what people think about me."

Her eyes widened. "You get it."

"Cam? The ice pack?" I asked.

"First, you have to answer a question." She pinned me with her stare as people moved around us, heading for the buffet or the display of historical pictures.

"Okay?"

"Your unicorn pin. Who gave it to you? You know, the one you lost in the mine?" She tilted her head toward the Rose Rowan.

"Cam. He bought two at the Mother's Day shop at school that year. One for me and one for his mom." Lillian had been buried with hers.

She frowned. "I bet you really miss it."

"The pin? Well, of course it would be nice to have it, but I made peace with losing it a long time ago." Seeing how sad that seemed to make her, I pushed forward. "But you know, the mine is opening today! There's always the chance that someone finds it. Who knows! I don't remember where I was, but Cam has the 1880 tunnel ready for exploration, so any one of these thousand tourists might stumble onto it."

"But what if one of them thinks it's treasure and keeps it?" she demanded.

"I can't really control that." I kept my voice soft, trying to soothe her.

"Why didn't you look for it?"

"I was too scared," I admitted. "Even now, the mine scares me at times. Reminds me of being trapped and lost and hurt."

"Still?" she whispered.

"Yep. Sometimes fears don't die just because you get bigger. They just get bigger, too." I shrugged.

She nodded, as if mulling something over in her head. "I'm going to go find Mom, okay?"

"Sure thing. She's right there." I pointed to the lone grove of aspen trees, and she hugged me before taking off.

I made my rounds, stopping to talk with Dad and John Royal before getting called over to Mom and the Ivy's crew. They all wanted to know how Cam was after that horrid display Milton Sanders had put on.

None of them mentioned that he'd done so at Xander's request. In that regard, he'd come out of last month's hearing squeaky-clean. Sure, it was sad that he wouldn't give Art the DNR, but if the doctors and the judge said Art didn't know what he was asking for, then really, he was just a son defending his father's life.

After about twenty-five minutes of that crap, I made my excuses and snuck out of their gossipy clutches, with Mom mouthing, *Run*.

I chatted with Julie Hall and flipped off Oscar Hudgens when he walked by, then took Julie and her boys over with Thea and Jacob to see the trains, telling them all about the history of the ore carts.

"Willow, will you ask Rose if she wants to grab lunch now or after the ceremony?" Charity asked, walking over with her boyfriend.

I noted with a smile that she'd finally brought him out in public and that the Salida resident was wearing a unicorn pin.

"What? You ask her," I teased. "Hi, I'm Willow," I introduced myself.

"Travis." He smiled as he shook my hand. "It's nice to finally meet you."

"Same here."

"Yes, yes, now you know each other. Willow, seriously, grab Rose for me." She looked over at the train and waved to Thea and Julie.

I blinked in confusion. "Rose is with you."

Charity moved her sunglasses to the top of her head. "No. She was with me. She said you needed her for some kind of ore hunt with the kids and ran off to find you."

Dread filled every cell in my body, and the noise of the crowd faded in my head, only to be replaced by a roaring in my ears. "When?"

"It must have been an hour ago." Her eyes flew impossibly wide. "Willow, where is Rose?"

"I don't know," I whispered, my head swiveling left to right, searching for her familiar braid.

"Well, when is the ore hunt? Maybe she's setting up for it?" Travis asked.

"There's no ore hunt." I looked Charity square in the eye. "I never asked her to help me with it because it doesn't exist."

"Oh God." She pushed past me and ran for the reconstructed gatehouse that served as a ticket booth and launchpad for the train.

"She never lies," I told Travis. "Something is wrong."

"Excuse me," Charity said into the microphone, and her voice blared across the crowd through the speakers Cam and his team had rigged for the event. "Has anyone seen Rose Maylard?"

The crowd murmured, but no one threw up a hand or answered.

"Rose?" Charity shouted into the microphone, the panic in her voice grating on my heart like nails on a chalkboard.

I scanned the crowd again, then looked at the trains…and past the trains.

"Oh no." My heart sank. "Tell Charity to wait here," I ordered Travis. Then I ran into the crowd, pushing my way through the thickest parts until I reached the construction trailers that had been moved to the far end of the cleared space to accommodate the crowd.

I took the stairs two at a time and flung the door open. Everything looked the same at first glance. But there, above Cam's desk. No. There sat Cam's hard hat and my hard hat, but Rose's was missing.

I barely felt the ground under my feet as I sprinted from the trailer, jumping the stairs and racing through the crowd, which was now thickest at the steps that led up to the gatehouse.

"Move," I ordered as someone blocked my path.

"I'm sorry, ma'am, but only—"

"Shut the hell up and move, Scott!" I screamed at the man who'd been the biggest bully in my class.

"Willow, sorry, I didn't see you."

I shoved my way past him and ran up the stairs, where Charity stood under my father's arm. Mom and Travis watched nervously while Cam and Gideon conferred with Xander and Tim Hall.

"Cam!"

He looked over at me and immediately came my way.

"I know where she is."

"Where?" Tim Hall demanded, but Cam just watched me, steady and calm.

"Her hard hat is gone," I told him.

His eyes flared wide, and he pivoted to look down the long black tunnel of the mine. "Why would she?"

"She said something about me having that pin. The one I lost that day. And she was really upset that someone might find it before I did." My knees weakened. "Cam, I think she's looking for the ventilation shaft I fell down."

He glanced back at the mine, and when everyone burst into questions and demands, he was already gone, already mentally down that shaft.

"What do we do?" Dad asked Tim Hall.

"We get search parties going," Tim answered.

"How far was the shaft, Willow?" Charity grabbed my arms. "What do you remember?"

"You were there!" My voice pitched high. "You were with me until you weren't!"

"I was eleven," she whispered. "All I remember was walking so far, and then...it was dark, the batteries died on the lamp—at least that's what we thought—so we put our hands on the wall of the tunnel and started walking back out. When the headlamp turned back on, you were gone. It was just us. I was eleven, Willow. I don't remember the rest until Cam found us near the entrance."

"I was nine," I whispered.

The same age as Rose.

"Everyone get in the trailer," Cam ordered. "Gideon, you start rounding up volunteers to search."

"How far was that drop?" Dad asked Cam as we walked to the trailer, the crowd parting as we approached. "The shaft you pushed Willow up?"

"At least fifty feet," he replied. "I don't know how she survived it."

"You did, too," I told him as he took my hand.

"I had a headlamp and could more or less skid my way to the bottom. It was a miracle that all you did was break your nose."

We filed into the trailer, and Cam pulled the blueprints of the Rose Rowan onto the drafting table. "We figured the shaft had to be one of these two." He pointed to the longest ventilation shafts the mine had. They traversed three levels of the mine. "Xander, what do you remember?"

Xander shook his head as he studied the blueprints. "God, it was so long ago."

"You were fourteen!" Charity cried. "That's older than the rest of us. You have to remember!"

"I can find her," Art said as he walked into the trailer with Walt and Nikki at his heels.

"Dad, not now," Xander said gently.

"Tim, get ten search parties of five together if you can. That's how many hard hats and lamps we have on hand." Cam looked at the police captain. "Now, Tim!"

Tim nodded and left.

"I can find her!" Art declared again.

"Dad, what do you mean?" Cam asked, moving Travis out of the way so Art could come closer.

"No one knows that mine like I do. I think I know where she is." Art looked at the blueprints. "It's not on the map. Not this one, at least."

"Dad, we don't have time for this. Why don't you go with Nikki?" Xander urged.

Art ignored him and pointed to the blueprints. "It should be right there. I know I've seen it there on another set." His forehead puckered. "It's where the 1880s meets the 1930s."

"Dad, those tunnels don't intersect," Xander argued.

"Be quiet. You never wanted to listen to me about the mine when you were younger. I don't know why you'd start now." He swiveled to look at Cam. "I can find her. Take me."

"No way!" Xander shouted.

"Take me," Art demanded, not even bothering to look at Xander.

"You know what putting him under emotional strain does! He'll lose it down there, and then you'll both die." Xander folded his arms across his chest.

"Camden, I'm her best hope. There are only four people who have been there." His brow wrinkled. "Five, when you count Willow."

Me. Xander. Charity. Cam. Who was the fifth?

"I'll go," I said, already moving to grab my hard hat and Cam's.

"You're terrified of the mine," Charity countered, tears silently running down her face.

"I'm the one who fell down it in the first place," I told her. "Cam and I are the only ones who have actually been there."

"I've been there, too. That's what I'm saying," Art interjected.

"Right. And Art." Which made sense, seeing as he was the expert on the damned mine. "Charity, you have to stay here in case another party brings her back, in case they find her before we do."

"Are you sure, Pika?" Cam asked.

"I'm sure." I handed his hard hat to him, then put mine on the desk and began to braid my hair.

"Take me, Cam. I'm the best chance you have at finding that little girl alive." Art moved directly in front of Cam.

"You can't even be sure Rose can find that ventilation shaft! If you couldn't find it again, then how can she? It was a miracle you stumbled onto Willow back then!" Xander argued.

"I told her how to get there," Art admitted. "It wasn't on the map I had, either, but I showed her where it should be."

"It wasn't on the map because it's not there. He's not going. I forbid it. I'm his guardian." Xander's voice rose with each word. "You can't take him down there!"

Cam locked eyes with his dad for a long minute, then nodded before stepping up to Xander. There was no physical comparison between the two, and Xander knew it, but Cam had never used it to his advantage before. "Stop me."

Ten minutes later, Cam, Art, Gideon, Dad, and I piled into the train. Cam drove us into the mine, speeding faster than we had when Rose had been with us. I kept my eyes peeled for her pale-pink jacket and yellow helmet but came up empty.

We sliced through the stale air of the tunnel, and I gawked at the difference now that it was lit. We passed the first antechamber we'd stopped at, then made our way past two ventilation shafts and several displays Cam had set up with historically accurate mining equipment.

We finally stopped, and I marveled that we'd managed to walk this far in all those years ago, if this was really where I'd fallen.

Cam showed Dad how to work the train so he could take it back for more search parties. "You're sure about this?" Cam asked me, his hands cupping my face.

"You won't let anything happen to me," I answered. "And I won't let anything happen to you."

He leaned his hat against mine and took a deep breath. "Just promise me you'll stay close. I almost lost you once in here, and that's not going to happen again."

"I promise."

He nodded, but I knew he wasn't happy about me being down here. Well, that made three of us, if the way my dad was staring at me was any indication.

"It's okay, Dad. Go."

"I love you. Your coat is too big. Are you going to be warm enough?"

"I love you, too. And I'm fine. It's Cam's." I didn't bother arguing the logic of his statement.

He turned to look at Camden. "You brought her out of this mine once, and I expect you to do it again. Do you understand me? You bring her and Rose out."

"What changed your mind?" Cam asked, hefting his pack over his shoulders.

"When did I realize you didn't break her nose?" Dad asked.

Cam nodded.

"First I pulled her X-rays when you started dating. The break was too symmetrical. Like she'd literally fallen flat on her face or walked into the wall. Then I realized I didn't need the damned

X-rays. Willow is a smart girl, and she would have kicked your ass if you'd hurt her."

Cam nodded again, but a smile lifted his lips. He didn't demand an apology for the last twenty years of my dad being an ass to him; he simply accepted that Dad knew he was wrong.

I took his hand, and we waved to Dad as he took the track switch and headed back to the mine's entrance.

The lights were on, but the smells, the sounds... They were all the same.

"Breathe in through your nose and out through your mouth," Cam suggested gently as we started walking.

"This way," Art said at a random offshoot.

"Dad..." Cam said. "I don't remember coming this way or taking any downhill path until I found that shaft."

"That's because you took the long way. I told your little Rose how to find the shortcut." He sounded like he was slipping into an episode, but his eyes were clear and certain.

"What shortcut?"

"It was a ventilation shaft. What did you think it was ventilating? Look, you can trust me or not. I'm telling you it's this way." Art turned and started walking.

"This should be a great story to tell at my funeral," Gideon muttered.

"Okay, I guess we'll trust you," Cam said, then took my hand and followed his dad.

"How far do you think it is?" Gideon asked.

"Probably ten minutes if you stop whining and start walking," Art chided.

Cam smiled and shot Gid a knowing look over his shoulder.

The tunnel narrowed, and we passed the demarcation line of where it had been reinforced. The lighting ended, leaving us with only our headlamps as the tunnel began a steep descent into the mountain. The beams that supported the sides and roof were mostly intact, but there were a couple I had to climb over.

"Here's where it starts to get sporty," Art said with a grin.

Starts? I sucked a deep breath in through my nose and out through my mouth, then trudged on into my personal hell, praying we'd find Rose in time...or at all.

CHAPTER TWENTY-SEVEN

Camden

We trudged down a tunnel so narrow, I could have touched both sides if I stretched my arms wide. The grade was steep, and bits of loose gravel slid where we stepped, but at least the floor was dry.

"Dad, are you sure this is the way?" I asked, my fear growing every minute that his mind would slip.

"I'm as sure as I can be. I know today is July fourth, you're Camden, and you're holding on pretty damn tight to Willow Bradley, so I'm lucid, if that's what you're asking." He didn't even look back, just kept moving down the dirt-covered floor.

Willow tightened her grip on my hand, but the tunnel became too narrow to walk side by side, and she had to fall behind me. I hated not being able to see her, but I wasn't going to let her walk across any ground my weight hadn't tested this far into the mine.

The air stirred from ahead, and Dad's light bounced as he nodded. "See?" He pointed to the tunnel that appeared on our right as the path leveled out and widened into another large chamber. "This is an offshoot of one of the 1930s."

"It's not on any of the maps," I said to myself as I took in the expansive tunnel and its sturdy beams. To the left were dozens of smaller chambers, some with wooden half walls, trimmed and topped with vertical iron bars and swinging doors made of the same, and some barren, left from exploratory blasts.

"I know it's on at least one map," Dad replied. "I just can't remember where it is." He touched his forehead. "I thought I gave it to you, but that can't be right."

Apprehension landed in my stomach like a brick. "Dad, are you okay?"

"Yeah. Of course. I'm fine." But the lines in his forehead told me otherwise.

"How deep do you think we are?" Gideon asked.

"Sublevel three," Dad declared, his headlamp illuminating the expanse of wall that was dotted with mined alcoves stretching as far as the light could reach on either side as the chamber narrowed to two tunnels that ran to either side. "Found a vein down here that wasn't worth much, but something was better than nothing. But the miners needed air."

His headlamp shone right, then left. Where the hell did we go from here?

"Them and me both," Gideon said, walking past my dad and following the curve of the tunnel.

"Are you okay?" I asked Willow, noting that the rise and fall of her chest had increased.

"I just want to start screaming her name."

"I'd hold off on that," Gideon said, shining his light on a rubble pile in the back left of the chamber. "The entire thing is caved in over there."

"Been like that for years," Dad muttered. "Don't just stand there—start looking. Don't go moving rocks around or causing another cave-in."

"Left or right?" Gideon asked.

My throat tightened.

"Doesn't matter," Dad stated, his headlamp swaying as he shook his head. "It's a fifty-fifty shot. Pick one and start looking."

"It matters," I countered as Willow slipped her hand into mine.

"Split up but stay in this section," Dad ordered. "We can search twice as fast."

Left or right? There was no obvious choice as I looked both ways. It was a coin-flip dilemma.

"Left," Willow said, her lamp shining on the barred chambers.

"You sure?" I asked.

"Left," she repeated, quieter this time.

"We'll take the right," Dad announced and walked off with Gideon on his heels.

The first alcove was empty, save a wooden desk and a flat, raised surface that must have served as some kind of bed.

"Cam," Willow whispered as her hands ran over the iron bars. "I remember this."

"You're sure?" I asked, but the way her face drained of blood told me she was certain.

She nodded. "The shadows from the bars, then darkness. Charity shrieking. Xander saying to keep calm...then I fell..." Her voice trailed off as she left the chamber, and I followed her into the next one, this one lined with shelves and an array of dust-covered canned goods. "I hit so hard. God, it still smells the same down here. It's not this one," Willow declared, and I got the hell out of her way as she pushed by me. "Or this one," she said at the next and the next.

"We found the shaft!" Gideon called out loud enough to make me cringe. Did I think shouting would bring a cave-in? No. Was I sure? Also no.

Still, relief barreled through me. But...wait. Wouldn't Rose have called out if she'd heard them? God, what if she wasn't even here? There were miles and miles of tunnels in this place. What if she'd stumbled into bad air?

"Stop," Willow whispered, stepping farther into the chamber.

"Willow, they found it." I held out my hand, already focused on heading toward Gid and Dad.

"It's a door." She looked over her shoulder. "Cam, it's a door!"

Ignoring the logic in my brain screaming at me to get to the shaft with Dad, I moved farther back into the chamber to see

Willow tug open a rusted iron door. It swung clear of the floor, and my heart stopped as she stepped through the doorway.

"Rose!" Willow cried.

I jumped over a fallen beam and caught the heavy door before it shut.

"It won't open from this side!" Rose wailed, and I nearly let go out of sheer surprise and knee-weakening relief.

She stood at the ledge, her back to the ventilation shaft, looking at us with wide eyes and tearstained cheeks. She was alive. She was okay.

"Rose, step away from the edge," Willow said softly. "Come here." She held out her arms, and my heart rate dropped with each step Rose took from the shaft.

"I'm so sorry," Rose cried as she reached Willow and collapsed against her aunt. "I just wanted to find your pin."

"It's okay," Willow promised as she held her tight, resting her chin on the top of Rose's head. "It's okay."

"I couldn't find it. I did all of this, and it's still not here."

"Rose?" Gideon called from across the shaft. There was another entrance at this level?

"We've got her!" I confirmed. "Come on, ladies. Let's get you out of here." The need to get them as far away from that damned shaft as possible clawed at my gut.

Willow clasped Rose's hand and then gently pushed her ahead, toward where the tunnel narrowed to the door.

"Hi, Cam," Rose said softly as she squeezed by me.

"Hey, Rosie." I wanted to scoop her up, but I wasn't going to let go of the door and have it close on Willow.

A shaky, trembling smile graced her lips as she passed me next, kissing my cheek. "Thank you," she whispered.

"Nothing to thank me for," I replied, then let the door swing shut once she was through. It met the frame in a heavy slam of metal.

Then I grabbed Rose and hugged her. "You scared us."

Her tiny shoulders heaved. "I'm so sorry. The door shut behind me, and there's no handle."

There were about thirty ways I wanted to yell at her for scaring us, for coming down here in the first place, for listening to the ravings of a man who'd already lost his mind—even if he'd actually known what he was talking about in this instance. But her mother could do that as soon as we got her back to the surface. I just needed to feel her breathe for a second.

"You're okay," I promised, but I wasn't sure if it was to the little girl in my arms or to myself.

She nodded against my neck.

I looked at Willow, but her eyes were on the door, two lines forming between her eyebrows. "Pika?"

"I can't remember, but I know I was here." She'd been the same size as Rose but alone for so many more hours. Broken, bleeding, and so cold, her skin had felt like ice against mine.

"Give me just a second," I said to her and carried Rose out to where Gideon and Dad had just made it to the chamber. "Keep her," I told Gid, handing Rose over, then went back to Willow.

She stood with the door open, her headlamp illuminating the tunnel beyond. "I want to see it. Is that weird?"

"Understandable." There was a hook on the wall, and when I took the door from Willow and pushed it wide, the iron slipped into the ring on the door, holding it open. "I'll go with you."

"Thank you."

I took her hand and stepped through the door first, keeping contact as she followed behind. The tunnel widened and opened onto a small ledge that looked over the ten-foot-wide ventilation shaft, and Willow stepped up beside me.

"You know when you go somewhere as an adult, and you say, 'It felt so much bigger as a child'?" she asked.

"This does not," I said, looking up and up at the fifty feet or so to the next sublevel. It wasn't vertical, thank God, or we both would have died, but the incline was steep enough that I wondered at my own bravery back then.

"No, it's just as awful as I remember." She stepped closer to the edge and looked down, focusing on the jagged outcropping I'd found her on about ten feet below us. "Cam, I didn't fall the whole way." She looked up the shaft at the tiny pinpoint of light that marked the surface. "That's why I didn't break more."

Like her neck.

"You fell from here." I put it together, watching one of the small rocks just past my feet give in to gravity and fall. It smacked the outcropping, then fell into the blackness. I tugged Willow's hand and pulled her back a step. This thing was anything but stable.

"But you didn't. You came all the way down." She looked up again, shaking her head. "How did you do it? Get down here and get us both out?"

"Sheer willpower." I clutched her hand even tighter.

"You're incredible. Do you know that?"

I nudged her hard hat up so the beam didn't hit me straight in the eye. "Not really."

"Desperation and love make ordinary people do heroic things," Dad said from behind us, moving to stand next to Willow at the edge of the unstable ledge. "You were never ordinary, and you had both." He stated it like a fact, not a compliment, then glanced at me before surveying the space.

"I didn't see this ledge," I admitted. "Or the one across the way. We climbed all the way up for nothing."

"This one wouldn't have done you much good, seeing as the door can't be opened from this side." Dad thumbed back toward the door. "And the other opening is small, too. As dark as it is in here, you wouldn't have seen it. We've got three headlamps, Camden, one of which is brighter than twenty of what we had back then."

I kicked myself for not being more observant, for putting her through more than I had to when she was already so hurt.

"Stop," Dad snapped, seeing my guilt. "You focused on the light and started climbing, just like anyone else would have."

"You saved me." Willow smiled up at me.

"Hey, isn't that—?" The ledge gave way under Dad.

"Art!" Willow screamed, grabbing for Dad as rocks crashed to the unknown bottom below.

"No!" The sound ripped from my throat.

She fell to the side, slamming her hip against the ground, and slid toward the edge as if dragged. I lunged behind her, landing on my hands and feet before hitting my stomach, then locked my arm around her waist to hold her back. I swung her legs, bringing her feet back toward the door and the more stable portion of the ledge.

"Cam!" she shrieked. "He's too heavy!"

I crawled forward to see that she had Dad's hand, and it was twisting her arm at an angle that was going to snap it quickly.

"Dad!" I reached for him, following the line of Willow's arm.

"Let me go. Don't let her fall with me!" he called up.

Willow cried out.

I felt the killing calm come over me and welcomed it like a long-lost friend.

"I've got you." I gripped his wrist with my left hand and immediately felt some of the strain lift from Willow's arm. Then I reached around the back of Willow's hand, her knuckles white from trying to keep Dad from falling. "Let go, Pika, so I can get two hands on him. You can't lift him out at that angle. Let go." I kept my voice soft even as my heart slammed against my chest.

"Cam?" she asked, still holding on to him.

"I promise I've got him."

She released her hand, and Dad swung to the left before I could get his hand with my right. "Got you! Willow, get Gid."

She scrambled for the door.

"Let me go," Dad ordered.

"You have no idea how deep that goes, Dad. Just hold on."

Rocks crumbled from the area Willow had just vacated.

"Camden."

My eyes met his, and it struck me how calm he was. How I'd been cursing the parts of me that were like him, only to be grateful for them later on.

"Gideon is coming, and we'll pull you up. I just don't have the leverage," I told him. "You're not slipping, and I'm strong enough to hold you." Thank God he had on a fleece jacket. My hands would have slid right off his skin.

"The ledge is going to go. Do not do this."

"The ledge is fine," I shouted. "Gideon!" Where was he?

"I love you, Camden. And I know I was shit at showing it. But you were just so much like me. Sully and Xander, they were your mom, but you…in everything but looks, you were me. And Cal… he was the lovable one. The good one."

Another section of rock gave way, and I heard footsteps hurrying toward us.

"Dad, you can tell me all about it later."

"Let me go."

I sucked in a breath, finally understanding what he was saying. "No, Dad. No."

"I'm not taking you with me."

"Holy shit," Gideon shouted, hitting his stomach and sliding up next to me.

"Gid's here, Dad. We can pull you out."

He stayed silent, but his expressions flickered so fast that I couldn't tell what he was feeling or thinking. Sadness? Anger? Acceptance? Even happiness?

"Just reach up with your other hand."

Gideon leaned forward as far as he dared and lowered his hand.

"Dad?" I begged. "I can't do this for you. It's your choice."

Gideon's gaze snapped toward me and then back to Dad before managing to lower his hand another inch.

"You have to choose, Dad."

This was it: the moment he'd wanted. The decision was his. Another section of the ledge collapsed, ending right before my arm started, but I still didn't look away from those eyes. Sullivan's eyes.

His lips pursed, and his brow furrowed. Then he roared and swung up with his left hand. Gideon caught it, and we both immediately lifted, scraping Dad's arms, then his chest and stomach on the edge of the ledge as we pulled him back onto the solid surface. Once he got to his knees, he fell forward, and we all rushed for the door, where Willow waited.

Dad looked back at me and gave me a singular, knowing nod, and I knew that was all he'd ever have to say about what just happened.

"I think this belongs to you, young lady," he said, pressing something into Willow's palm before walking through the door.

"I need a beer," Gideon muttered, following Dad.

I grabbed Willow to me, holding her against my chest, not caring that her helmet dug into the layers of my jacket to press the skin beneath. "I love you."

"I love you," she repeated, her hands clutching the fabric at my back.

"Let's get you out of here." I could go the rest of my life and never see this portion of the mine again. That would be fine by me. She nodded, and we walked back into the chamber.

"Look what your dad found." She held up her unicorn pin. It was a tiny thing, barely the size of a quarter.

"Look at that." I brushed my thumb over her palm, but when I looked up, she was focused on something to her right. The door. "What is it?"

She tucked the pin in her pocket and turned to face the heavy iron mass. Then she brought her hand down from her chin, as if she were measuring something, and when she reached mid-chest, she moved her hand to the same level on the door.

"Cam," she whispered.

There were two darker spots in the rust. Blood.

Rage swept over me, holding hands with a knowledge I never wanted. And it all made sense. All of that day, those that came before, and the ones that followed.

Our eyes locked, hers wide with shock, and I shut the door, letting it close with a satisfying slam.

I knew where that fucking map was.

CHAPTER
TWENTY-EIGHT

Willow

Cam was nearly silent as we made our way out of the mine. He reminded me of a caged tiger, prowling the edges of his bars, waiting to be unleashed. I kept Rose's hand in mine and tried not to think about what we'd found and what we'd almost lost.

Gideon checked for cell reception as we climbed sublevels, and it didn't surprise me that there was none to be found this far underground.

Art was showing signs of sundowning, and I knew we needed to get him out of the mine before he couldn't remember why he was here. I needed to get out of this mine before I couldn't forget.

We reached the main 1880 tunnel, and I almost let myself relax. Even if we all collapsed here, someone would find us. The distance the train had covered in five minutes took twenty to walk. We reached the first chamber, where the tunnels split in three directions, and my dad shouted, running for us with a search party on his heels.

"Grandpa!" Rose dropped my hand and ran for him. He fell to his knees and threw his arms around her, his shoulders shaking. "I'm okay," she promised.

Exhaustion slammed into me, and my steps slowed as I neared them. "We found her—"

Dad gripped my coat and pulled. I slipped to the ground, and he wrapped his arm around my back. His breaths were ragged, and I laid my head on his shoulder as he regained his composure.

"Thank you."

I didn't need to look to know that he spoke to Cam.

"I didn't have to carry her this time," Cam replied, and I smiled despite the weariness creeping into my bones.

When Dad felt together enough to rise, we piled into the train. Art drove after telling Cam he damn well knew what he was doing. Dad sat across from me with Rose tucked under his arm, and I rested my head on Cam's chest.

"I'm so tired," I told him as the train took off.

"Adrenaline letdown." He pressed a kiss against my forehead.

"Same with you?" I asked as the train sped toward the light and fresh, clean air.

"I'm not done yet." His muscles were coiled with tension, but he still held me gently as we came to a stop at the gatehouse.

Xander stood at the structure, giving an interview to some news channel, and I wondered how much time had passed. The crowd erupted when they saw us, and Charity sprinted from the side of the tunnel, sobbing wordlessly as she ran for her daughter.

Dad lifted Rose over the side of the car, and Charity enveloped her in her arms.

"Thank you!" she cried at Dad, then pulled back from Rose long enough to examine her face.

"Thank Cam," Dad answered.

But Cam wasn't watching the reunion. His eyes were narrowed on Xander, malice pouring off him in waves.

"Cam," I whispered.

He dropped his eyes to mine, and they didn't soften, but he gently stroked the bridge of my nose with his fingertip, then looked at my father.

"I make no excuses for what's about to happen."

That was our only warning. He climbed from the train onto the platform and charged at Xander.

"There you are, Cam! I was just giving an update!" I heard Xander's voice despite the thirty feet that separated us. Then I heard his breath expel in a gush as Cam pinned him to the side of the building.

"Cam!" Gideon shouted, racing after him.

I scrambled to the deck and ran.

"How could you?" Cam screamed. "How the hell could you do that to her? She was nine, you asshole! Nine! And you shoved her into that tunnel and slammed the door on her goddamned face!"

I skidded to a halt, realizing that Cam had figured it out, too. He'd been so silent on the trek back here that I wondered if he'd come to the same conclusion I had when I saw the bloodstains. My bloodstains.

"What?" Gideon questioned, voicing pretty much everyone's exact thought.

"I don't know what you're talking about," Xander countered, putting his hands against the rock, showing the world that he wasn't the aggressor here.

"I'm talking about you killing your headlamp and shoving Willow into that damned tunnel. You're the one who broke her nose! Why? Why would you do that? Why would you leave her there?"

"You have no proof! You sound as crazy as Dad!" Xander's eyes bugged out.

"I remember," I said loud enough for Xander to hear. His eyes snapped to mine. "The headlamp died, and you said to keep our hands on the wall. But then there was a rush of air, and you pushed me. I stumbled back, and when I tried to run forward to get back to where we'd been, you slammed the door. I woke up on the ground, and when I backed away, I didn't see the ledge in the dark and tumbled right over it." Where I then lay for hours until Cam found me, not remembering exactly what brought me there in the first place.

Xander shook his head. "No, Willow, you must be confused."

Cam pressed his forearm across Xander's throat. "Try again."

Gideon stepped forward, but his father stopped him, putting a hand on his shoulder.

"I'm not," I snapped. "I didn't remember until I saw the blood. It's still on the door, Xander."

He blanched. "I was coming back for you!" His eyes swung to Cam's. "I was going back for her. I thought if she was missing for a few hours, and I found her..." He shook his head. "I was fourteen! I was a stupid kid!"

"She was nine!" Cam shouted, shoving Xander harder against the frame. "Nine! And you left her there bleeding and hurt so you could go back and rescue her? Are you fucking kidding me?"

"She was fine! See, she's fine!"

"Because I found her! Because I slid down fifty feet of a mine shaft and then pushed her up every foot of it to get her out. She's fine because of me!" Veins bulged in Cam's neck, and for the first time, I worried that he might really kill Xander.

"I would have found her if you hadn't ripped the headlamp off my head and run!" Xander shouted. "You ruined it. You ruin everything."

Cam pushed off Xander, putting a foot of space between them, and Gideon relaxed next to me. "This is what you really are? Under all the polish and the PR, you're just a pile of shit." Cam shook his head. "I thought you were the best of us. You were the golden boy. You were going to change the world, Xander. That's why I took the fall for you that night when you set the bunkhouse on fire."

There was a collective gasp, and my heart broke. The very thing he'd been condemned for in this town hadn't even been his sin. He'd taken it from his brother.

"That's not—"

"Shut up! I saw you! I couldn't figure out what you were doing with the hose from the mine's water tank until I saw you throw the torch."

My head felt light, and I swayed on my feet.

"No one was in there! Everyone was outside at the bonfire." His eyes darted toward me. "At least they were supposed to be."

"So, what? You were just going to put the fire out and call yourself a hero?" Cam shouted. "Instead you sat there. Holy shit. You watched Sully crawl out. You watched me go in. You stood there the whole time, didn't you?"

Xander swallowed. "Look, it caught so much faster than it was supposed to."

"You let me take the blame for it! You watched them pin it on me, and then you used it against me in Dad's case." Cam shook his head. "What the hell is wrong with you?"

Don't hit him. Don't hit him. He wouldn't get away with it, not with the crowd and the cameras.

"Like you'd understand!" Xander shouted. "You, who can't stay out of trouble. You, who gets into fistfights defending her!" He pointed at me. "And who manages to carry her out of a mine covered in blood. And who rips apart the entire town for fun but then emerges from a burning barn with Willow in your arms. It was all so easy for you to be larger than life! And I did everything I could to be good. That's what I was supposed to be, but it was never enough. I was never good enough. And you come home a decade later, covered in your army medals, and think you can rescue her again, rescue Dad, now rescue Rose? Hell, rescue this whole damned town!"

The realization that began that day at the courthouse came full circle. It was all about perception for him. He had been so consumed with trying to look like a hero that he forgot to be one.

Cam shook his head and took another step back. "News flash, Xander. I didn't want any of it. I only wanted her."

"I just wanted one medal. One moment."

"I would trade every medal on that uniform to have Sullivan back."

Xander's head snapped to the side as a fist slammed into it, but it wasn't Cam standing above him as he slid against the wall. It was my dad.

Gideon and Tim sprang into action, one cuffing Xander and one cuffing my dad.

"Alexander Daniels, you're under arrest for arson," Gideon growled and guided Xander by the neck down the steps.

"Gid!" I shouted, and he looked back. "You might want to take his mic off."

Xander's head snapped up to look out over the crowd of a thousand people who'd heard it all go down over the speakers. Gid unsnapped the tiny mic from the front of Xander's shirt and tossed it to the reporter after nodding his thanks to me.

"I don't want to do this, Noah," Tim Hall said quietly. "But the damned cameras are on us."

"The law is black and white," Dad answered Tim while he looked at me. "And it was worth it."

"Noah Bradley, you're under arrest for assault." He finished his Miranda rights as Mom trailed after him.

"I'll get the bail money!"

Cam wrapped his arm around me, and I melted against his chest. "Take me home?"

"Gladly." He kissed the top of my head.

"I guess we put on quite a show for the tourists," Dorothy Powers said, her arm looped through Art's. "Let's get you home, Arthur."

Art looked at Cam, and I knew the lucidity he'd had in the mine was fading fast. "The map," he said quietly.

"It's framed above Xander's bed," Cam explained.

His eyes drifted toward mine. "Balance." Then he walked off with Dorothy, looking like he'd aged ten years in the past hour.

"Should we open the mine?" John Royal asked, gesturing out at the tourists.

Cam groaned.

"Tourists first," I whispered, looking out over the crowd. He'd done this—made it possible for Alba to not just continue surviving but thrive. All because he'd been unafraid to stand alone and fight for what he knew was right, even if everyone else screamed that it was wrong.

"I guess we'll open her up." Then he kissed me in front of everyone, and the crowd roared.

"We don't need to put on that good of a show," Dorothy muttered.

"That was just for fun," Cam replied, smiling down at me.

He'd never been the one to care how things looked, and I couldn't have loved him any more for it.

CHAPTER
TWENTY-NINE

Camden

The aspens' leaves danced shadows across the gravestones as I stood and faced my little brother for the first time in six years.

"It's not like I need to fill you in," I told him as I brushed fallen leaves from the top of the gray marble. "I've always felt like you hung around. Hell, I talk to you enough. Of course, I'm hoping you don't hang around too often, given..." Given the fact that I had Willow in my bed every night. "But I hope you'd be happy for us, and even if you aren't, I'm just going to pretend that you are, because even you being pissed at me couldn't keep me away from her."

"Nikki told me you were out here."

I glanced over my shoulder to see Dad coming up the slight incline, his nurse staying back a few dozen feet to give us some privacy.

"You look good," I told him as he came to stand next to me, directly in front of Mom's stone.

"It's my mind that's going, son, not my face." He smirked before stepping forward to brush his hand over Mom's name. "I'm glad she wasn't here for this part, though. No one should have to watch the person they love disappear right in front of them."

I looked him over, doing a quick assessment. He wore the new Rose Rowan shirt I'd dropped off for him last week, his hair was combed, and he looked, well, like him.

"Nikki also said that the last few times you've stopped over, I haven't recognized you." Dad crouched and brushed the leaves from Mom's stone.

"But you do today?" I asked slowly.

He sighed and stood, wiping his hands off on his jeans and glancing toward Uncle Cal's stone a little past Mom's. "I'm enough of myself to recognize that I'm not always myself."

"And everything that happened a couple weeks ago?" I probed.

"I know your brother is out on bail, if that's what you're asking," he grumbled. "He really left Willow in the mine when you were kids?"

"Yeah." I beat back the anger that welled up every time I thought about it.

"And he set fire to the bunkhouse?"

"He did."

Dad turned to face me. "And you took the blame."

"My reasons seemed sound back then." I looked away. We'd come a long way since I'd returned home, but this was still awkward as hell.

"I swear, you always cared too little about what other people thought, and Xander cared too much." He shook his head. "There was a girl in the mine..."

"Rose," I supplied.

"Right. She okay?"

"She is. Grounded, I believe, but physically fine. You saved her. We never could have found her without you."

He grunted a reply that I couldn't interpret.

"I'm sorry I couldn't do more for you," I said softly, spitting it out before I lost whatever time I had with him.

His gaze jerked toward mine. "More what?"

Shit.

"The DNR," I reminded him. "The judge denied us. Do you remember?"

His brow furrowed. "I remember Walt telling me the judge's

decision. But I know you did what you could. You opened the mine, for Christ's sake. Took on Judge Bradley and won him over, from what I remember."

"It wasn't enough." I shifted my weight and crossed my arms over my chest.

"Cam, you can't control the choices other people make. You do the best you can, and then it's out of your hands."

My gaze drifted to Sullivan's stone.

"And what happens when you make the wrong choice?" I arched my neck slightly to ease the tightening sensation in my throat. "What happens when you're standing in the mine and you have to choose left or right in a split second with no way to justify your choice?"

"You went left and found the girl. Why are you beating yourself up? It worked out in the end."

Willow chose left. I followed her.

"I made a decision just like that. Two men stepped forward, I pointed to the guy on the left, and Sullivan died."

Dad sucked in a breath. "Camden…"

"I want you to know what happened that day, but not for the reasons you think. I'm starting to realize you can't give me absolution, if that's what you're worried about. What I need you to know is that while I'm responsible for Sully's death, I didn't know it was his squad leader I chose." I closed my eyes against the barrage of imagery in my head. Sullivan's smile, his laugh, his eyes going vacant as he bled out. "I didn't know." My voice dropped to a whisper.

For a long moment, the only sounds were the rustling leaves above us and the faint whirl of the wind.

"We made a deal when you came back."

My eyes flew open at Dad's comment, and my stomach clenched. "We did, but I'm not holding you to it. I want you to listen, but I won't force you." As much as I knew I deserved to be heard, my father deserved to make his own choice in the matter.

Sullivan was his son.

"Tell me what happened."

With Sullivan only a few feet away, I did.

"We got the call that an outpost was in serious danger of being overrun, and we went. We landed under heavy fire, and it was a shit show on the ground. A new company had just rotated in the month before, and from what we'd seen from the air, they were vastly outnumbered. Our team split to accomplish different objectives. Once my commander relayed what we'd seen to that company's commander, I was ordered to take a squad with another operator—they couldn't spare a whole platoon—to reinforce the section of the perimeter we'd seen was about to fall. I'm talking minutes, not hours."

The smell of gunfire filled my nose, and even though I told myself it was all in my head, my heart rate picked up.

"Two squad leaders answered their captain's request. They stepped forward, and I pointed to the guy on the left and told him we needed to move." I'd gone over the memory so many times in my head, and yet I still found myself searching for any sign that I'd missed Sullivan at that point. "He pulled his guys off the line, and we ran."

I glanced Dad's way to see that he was focused on Sullivan's stone but appeared to be listening, so I forged ahead.

"I go over it in my head a lot," I admitted. "More than the psych guys would want, at least. That moment, had I picked the sergeant on the right, Sullivan wouldn't have been shot."

Dad flinched.

"The next opportunity I had was when we ran. I let their sergeant lead the way because he knew the outpost better, of course, but I kept up with him step for step as his men followed and Vasquez brought up the rear. If we'd traded places, maybe I would have recognized the way he ran." I cleared my throat as it tightened again. "We spread out along the wall and began returning fire." I skipped over the details. "A few minutes later, I heard

Vasquez call for a medic. I can still hear him calling, to be completely honest. I don't even know why I looked, but I did."

I turned my head and waited until my dad's eyes met mine.

"It was Sullivan. He was standing there with those wide eyes of his, holding on to his neck while blood..." I closed my eyes and took another deep breath. "I screamed his name and ran as fast as I could, but I barely made it there in time to catch him as he fell. Ten feet. That's all that had separated us. Ten fucking feet."

"Was it quick?" Dad asked, his voice thick.

"Just a couple minutes."

"And he wasn't alone?" The last word broke.

"I was with him the entire time. He knew it was me. There was nothing I could do." I made the realization as the words slipped free. "I've spent six years reliving those moments, and once he'd been shot, there really was nothing I could do but stay with him. And I did. I stayed with him through transport and through Dover and didn't leave his side until we laid him next to Mom."

Tears blurred my vision, but I saw Dad swipe at his face.

"I loved Sullivan, Dad. I would have traded places with him in a heartbeat. God knows I did my best to join him in the years that followed. I never would have chosen his squad if I'd known. Hell, I would have sat on his stubborn ass in the middle of that outpost, far from the wall. I made the choices that killed him, but I didn't know. I didn't know."

I couldn't say how long we stood there, but the afternoon sun had shifted by the time Dad spoke.

"You might not want my absolution, Camden, but you have it."

My knees weakened, and I swayed.

"Were you a part of his death? Yes, but only in the way a cog moves the hands of the clock." His jaw ticked as his gaze met mine briefly. "The truth is that while it was easier to levy the blame on you, we all made choices that led to his death. I let him enlist—not that I could have stopped him. I think about that every day. That boy worshipped the ground you walked on. He wanted to be just like you. Even fell for the same girl."

"He would have been better for her," I admitted.

"Maybe," Dad admitted with a nod. "But maybe not. And you'll be better to her. You tend to safeguard something once you realize how precious it is."

"I will." Losing Willow wasn't an option, and maybe I didn't deserve her, but I was sure as hell going to earn her every day.

"Your mother told me once, 'You're free to make your own choices, but you're not free from the consequences of that choice.'" His lips curved slightly before falling again. "Sullivan made his choice. Xander did, too. We all do. Every day. You're no different. You have to love your choices, Camden, no matter what they are, because you have the freedom to choose." He looked me in the eye. "Don't waste them, either, because you never know when it's the last one you'll get to make. It goes faster than you think."

He turned and headed down the hill.

"Dad!" I called out. "One thing has been bugging me."

"What is that?" He paused but didn't turn.

"The door in the mine. What was it there for?"

He shrugged. "Who knows. Your great-grandfather wasn't exactly all there in the head."

I huffed a small laugh and watched him walk away. We might not be a sitcom family, but at least he wasn't shooting at me anymore.

My phone buzzed as I headed toward my Jeep, and I checked it with a grin.

Willow: Finishing up a design and then headed to your place.

Cam: Sounds perfect. I just need to run an errand. I'll meet you there.

Willow: Love you.

I grinned. That right there was what my choices—the good and the bad—had earned me.

Cam: Love you.

I slipped my phone back into my pocket and climbed into the

Jeep. There was one more choice to be made today, and it was Xander's.

Ten minutes later, I rang the doorbell at my brother's house. It was one of the newest buildings in Alba, go figure, all sparkling new, and the setting sun bounced off the gleaming windows, picture-perfect.

"Cam." He answered the door, looking like nothing had changed. Like he wasn't out on bail or facing ten years in prison if he didn't plead it down. "Come here to gloat? I just saw the follow-up on Rose's rescue on CNN if you want to revel in your glory."

"You still don't get it." The manila envelope crinkled in my hands, and I was glad I'd only brought copies.

"What do you want?"

"About Dad—" I shifted my weight, at a loss on how to broach the topic.

"I'm still his guardian unless you want to take me to court again. Then again, now that this has happened to me, maybe you'll get guardianship this time."

I didn't state the obvious—that he'd done it to himself.

"Dad doesn't want to die. You know that, right? He just wants the choice. To him, that's what makes life worth the living. Choice."

Xander crossed his arms over his chest. "Well, I choose that he lives. And if you think that's selfish, then I don't care. I don't want to lose my dad. I'm not going to be the son who lets it happen."

"What if it were you?" I asked quietly. His eyes narrowed, and I continued. "What if you were the one who couldn't make your own choice?"

"I don't have to think about that. I'm thirty-one years old." He shrugged.

"But if you did," I pushed. "What would you want?"

"Are you asking if I'd want a DNR?"

"I'm asking you to think about it," I said slowly, clutching the envelope, "because one day you might not have the choice. The ironic thing about you fighting Dad for his right to his own body is that you never stopped to ask yourself about the genetics."

Xander froze.

"I did." I shrugged. "When I realized that Willow was it for me, that I wanted marriage and kids and the whole domestic package, I started reading. Guess what, Xander? Dad's form of Alzheimer's is genetic. It's a presenilin-one mutation."

The color drained from his face. "So that means we could have it."

"Sullivan did," I announced, handing him the envelope. He refused to take it. "I got the results for all three of us the day of the hearing."

"How?" He looked at the envelope like it would grow teeth and bite him, which was the most logical reaction I'd seen him have in a while.

"Mom kept all our baby teeth in those little memory boxes in her closet. Gross but useful."

"You did this without my permission." He glared at me, but there was fear in his eyes, stark and sharp.

"I did. But the lab doesn't know that. The results are in there. Patients S, C, and A. Totally anonymous." I waved the results again. "Don't you want to know?"

"I don't know." He stared at the envelope.

"I could tell you. I read it."

His eyes jerked back to mine, wide and furious. "Don't."

"Why? Don't like to have your choices taken?" I asked. "I can make you feel better. I don't have it."

His lips pursed. "How does that make me feel better?"

"Other than knowing your little brother won't be taken by early-onset Alzheimer's?" I chided. "It should comfort you because no matter what that envelope says, I won't be you. I'll listen to you. I'll give you the choices you won't give Dad, because I don't give a shit what people say or how I look to the world. I know who I am. I've made peace with my choices."

I thrust the envelope at his chest, and he slowly took it.

"Make peace with yours, Xander." His body tensed as I nodded, then turned around and headed back to my Jeep.

"You're not going to tell me as some kind of punishment?" he called after me.

"It's not my job to punish you, Xander. Not in anger. Not in jealousy. Not...ever. Read it. Don't read it. That's your choice, not mine."

I already knew what it said.

A week later, Dad's guardianship documents arrived at the mine. Xander signed everything over to me, so we just needed an appointment with the judge to make it official.

At the bottom of the stack was a signed do-not-resuscitate order.

Thirty minutes after telling Dad, who thanked me and promptly hung up, I pulled into my driveway, smiling at the fact that the lights were on, which meant Willow was already here.

"Honey, I'm home," I called out as I walked in.

"In the library!" she answered.

I left the pizza I'd brought for dinner on the kitchen table and walked in to see her sketching at the easel. Her hands moved gracefully over Rose's face, adding details as she tilted her head this way and that.

"How was your day?" she asked, setting the pencil down and walking over to loop her arms around my neck.

"I don't have the Alzheimer's gene."

"Okay?" Her brows lowered in confusion.

"I had the test run because Dad's is genetic. I don't have it." I wrapped my arms around her waist, still surprised all these months later that I got to do it.

"Oh, good." She leaned up and kissed me. "That's a load off."

"Wait, you've thought about it?" I pulled back just enough to look in her eyes.

"I figured if you wanted to get tested, you would, and if you didn't, that was okay, too." She shrugged.

"And if I had it?" My heart clenched at the thought of not recognizing her one day.

"Then, we'd make the best of the years we had."

I lifted her in my arms and walked to the armchair, adjusting her so she straddled my lap. "But now you have me for a lot of years."

"Seems like it," she noted with a grin, throwing my very words back at me. "Did I mention that Walt called about you taking your dad's seat on the Historical Society council?" she asked with a scrunched nose.

"No." I shook my head.

"No, I didn't tell you, or no, you don't want it?"

I groaned, letting my head fall back against the couch. "Can no just be the universal answer?"

"Not if you want to do some good." She kissed my nose.

"You're my good." I settled my hands on her hips and tugged her closer.

Life was built from our choices. Mine hadn't always been good, but not all had been bad. And I couldn't bring myself to regret a single one of them, especially not the one in my arms.

I kissed her deep and long, vowing to make every single one of those years worth everything that had happened to bring us here.

For more of Cam and Willow's story, including a
free epilogue, visit Rebeccayarros.com

ACKNOWLEDGMENTS

First and foremost, thank you to my Heavenly Father for blessing me beyond all measure.

Thank you to my husband, Jason, for being my person. For always choosing us. You are the best choice I've ever made, and I love you beyond all measure. Thank you to my children, who roll with the deadlines, the signings, and the curveballs we're tossed. To my sister, Kate, because we finally get to raise our kids together. To my mom for teaching me that a woman's place is wherever she wants it to be. To my best friend, Emily Byer, for being my vault for the last twenty-plus years.

Thank you to my dad for inspiring so much of this book and my life. For your love and overwhelming grace caring for Grandpa as he slipped away into Alzheimer's. For raising me as a military brat and then a miner's daughter. For your incredible love of mining history and your willingness to share your library. For always keeping your office in my toy room and interjecting your own story lines when you thought my dolls might end up with the wrong guys. Thank you for raising a dreamer. You are the standard to which I hold all men.

Thank you to my team at Entangled and Macmillan. To Liz Pelletier not only for editing but urging me to write this book. I'm incredibly grateful for your overwhelming support. To Heather and Jessica for answering endless streams of emails. To my phenomenal agent, Louise Fury, for pretty much nodding when I tell her that I'd like to be a woodland fairy and then somehow making it happen. To Karen, for always picking up the phone.

Thank you to my wifeys, our unholy trinity, Gina Maxwell and Cindi Madsen, who hold my sanity in their capable hands and keep me at the keys. To Jay Crownover for being my safe place and the wolf to my rabbit. To Shelby and Mel for putting up with my unicorn brain. Thank you to Linda Russell for chasing the squirrels, bringing the bobby pins, and holding me together on days I'm ready to fall apart. To Jen Wolfel and Cassie Schlenk for reading this as I wrote it and cheering me on with enough enthusiasm to power a small city. To every blogger and reader who has taken a chance on me over the years. To my reader group, The Flygirls, for bringing me joy every day.

Lastly, because you're my beginning and end, thank you again to my Jason. You're the reason my heroes are so swoony. Here's to retirement and s'mores in the living room.

Turn the page to start reading
Full Measures, *Rebecca Yarros's*
Goodreads Choice–nominated bestseller.

CHAPTER ONE

Who the hell would be pounding on the door at 7:05 a.m.? Three tiny knocks on my bedroom door echoed the harsher ones downstairs. Mom was going to chew their butts for interrupting her morning routine.

"Come in!" I called out, scanning through my iPod's playlist before pressing sync. Music made running more tolerable. Barely. Running was hellish, but I'd already calculated how far I had to go to compensate for the Christmas fudge I'd be scarfing down during the rest of my visit home. The thermometer outside said thirteen degrees, and human ice sculptures were overrated, so Colorado at Christmas meant it would be treadmill city. *Yay, me.*

Gus's strawberry-blond curls popped through the small opening of the door, my lab goggles from Chem 101 perched on his forehead. They gave his seven-year-old, puckered-up-in-frustration face a more mad scientist vibe. "What's up, buddy?" I asked.

"Ember? Can you answer the door?" he begged.

I turned down the music coming from my laptop. "The door?"

He nodded, nearly losing the goggles. My lips twitched, fighting the smile that spread across my face while I tried not to laugh.

"I'm supposed to go to hockey, and Mom won't answer the door for carpool," he said.

I put on my best serious face as I glanced back at the clock. "Okay, Gus, but it's only seven, and I don't think you have hockey until the afternoon. Mom never forgets a practice." I'd inherited my type-A nature from somewhere.

He let out an exasperated sigh. "But what if it's *early*?"

"Six hours early?"

"Well, yeah!" He gave me a wide-eyed stare declaring me the most oblivious sister *ever*.

"Okay, buddy." I caved like always. The way he'd cried when I left for college last year pretty much gave the kid free reign over my soul. Gus was the only person I didn't mind going off schedule for.

I checked Skype one more time before closing my laptop, hoping I'd see Dad pop online. He'd been gone three months, two weeks, and six days. Not that I was counting. "He'll call today," Gus promised, hugging my side. "He has to. It's a rule or something. They always get to call for their kid's birthday."

I forced out a smile and hugged his scrawny body. It didn't matter that I turned twenty today, I just wanted to hear from Dad. The knocks sounded again. "Mom!" I called out. "Door!" I grabbed a hair tie off my desk and held it in my teeth while I gathered my long hair back in a pre-run ponytail.

"I told you," he mumbled into my side. "She won't answer. It's like she wants me to miss hockey, and you know that means I'll suck forever! I don't want Coach Walker to think I suck!"

"Don't say suck." I kissed the top of his head. He smelled like his orange, Spiderman-labeled shampoo and sunshine. "Let's go see."

He thrust his arms out in victory and raced down the hallway ahead of me, taking the back stairs closest to my room. He slid through the kitchen in his socks, and I snagged a bottle of water from the fridge on my way. The knocks sounded again, and Mom still didn't answer. She must have run off for errands with April or something, though seven in the morning was way too early for my younger sister.

I passed through the dining room, twisted open the top on the bottle, and walked into the living room, opposite the foyer. Two shadows stood outside the door, poised to knock again.

"Just a minute!" I called out, hopping over the Lego star destroyer Gus had abandoned in the middle of the floor. Stepping on a Lego was a special degree of hell that only someone with a little brother could really understand.

"Don't answer it." Mom's strangled whisper came from the front staircase, which stopped only a few feet from the front door.

"Mom?" I came around the steps and found her huddled in on herself, rocking back and forth. Her hands covered her hair, strands of dark auburn the exact same shade as mine weaving through her fingers where she tugged. Something was wrong. "Mom, who's here?"

"No, no, no, no, no," she mumbled, refusing to lift her head from her knees.

I drew back and took a look at Gus with raised eyebrows. He shrugged in response with a see-I-told-you-so look. "Where's April?" I asked him.

"Sleeping." Of course. At seventeen, all April did was sleep, sneak out, and sleep again.

"Right." Another three knocks sounded. They were brisk, efficient, and accompanied by a soft male voice.

"Mrs. Howard?" His voice was distorted through the door, but through the center glass panel, I saw that he'd leaned in. "Please, ma'am."

Mom raised her head and met my eyes. They were dead, as though someone had sucked the life from them, and her mouth hung slack. This was not my Stepford-perfect mother.

"What's going on?" April asked with a massive yawn, dropping to sit on the top step in her pajamas, her bright red hair a messy tangle from sleep.

I shook my head and turned to the door. The knob was warm in my hand. They taught us in elementary school never to open a warm door during a fire. *Why did I think of that?* I glanced back at Mom and made my choice. Ignoring her plea, I opened the door in slow motion.

Two army officers in Dress Blue uniform consumed our stoop, their hats in their hands. My stomach lurched. *No. No. No.*

She knew. That's why Mom hadn't opened the door. She knew.

Tears stung my eyes, burning my nose before the men could even get a word out. My water bottle slipped from my hand, bursting open on the doorframe and pouring water over their shined shoes. The younger of the two soldiers started to speak, and I put my finger up, silencing him before I softly shut the door.

My breath expelled in a quiet sob, and I rested my head against the warm door. I had opened the door to a fire, and it was poised to decimate my family. I sucked in a shaky breath and put a bright smile on my face as I turned to Gus. "Hey, buddy." I stroked my hands over his beautiful, innocent little head. I couldn't stop what was coming, but I could spare him this. "My iPhone is on my nightstand." *In the room furthest from the front door.* "Why don't you head up to my room and play Angry Birds for a bit? It's not hockey, just grown-up stuff, okay? Play until I come get you."

His eyes lit up, and I forced my smile harder. How long would it be until I saw that in his eyes again? "Cool!" he shouted and raced up the front steps, passing April on his way. "See, Ember lets me play with *her* phone!" he teased as his footsteps raced toward my room.

"What is going on?" April demanded. I ignored her and turned to Mom.

I dropped to my knees on the step beneath hers and brushed back her hair. "It's time to let them in, Mom. We're all here." I gave a distorted smile through the blur my vision had become.

She didn't respond. It took a minute before I realized she

wasn't going to. She just wasn't…here. April scooted down the steps, sitting next to Mom. I opened the door again and nearly lost it at the pity in the younger soldier's eyes. The older one began to speak. "June Howard?"

I shook my head. "Ember—December Howard. My mother," I choked out and gestured behind me, "is June." I stood next to her and reached through the banister railing to rest my hand on her back.

He could be wounded. Just wounded. They came to the door for serious wounds. Yeah, just wounded. We could handle that.

The soldiers nodded. "I am Captain Vincent and this is Lieutenant Morgan. May we come in?"

I nodded. He wore the same patch on his shoulder as my father. They stepped in, their wet shoes squeaking on the tiles of the entry hall, and shut the door behind them. "June Howard, wife of Lieutenant Colonel Justin Howard?" he asked. She nodded weakly, but kept her eyes trained on the rug while Captain Vincent ended my world.

"The Secretary of the Army has asked me to express his deep regret that your husband, Justin, was killed in action in Kandahar, Afghanistan, earlier this morning, the nineteenth of December. He was killed by small arms fire in a Green on Blue incident in the hospital, which is still under investigation. The Secretary extends his deepest sympathy to you and your family in your tragic loss."

My hands slid to the railing to keep me upright, and my eyes closed as tears raced down my face. I knew the regs. Twenty years as an army brat had taught me they had to notify us within a certain number of hours of identifying him. Hours. He'd been alive *hours* ago. I couldn't breathe, couldn't drag the air into my lungs in a world that didn't have my father in it anymore. It wasn't possible. Everything dropped from under me, and unmatched pain tore through every cell in my body, erupting in a sob I couldn't keep contained. April's scream split the air, ripping through me.

God, it hurt. It hurt.

"Ma'am?" the young lieutenant asked. "Is there someone we can call for you? Casualty Assistance should be here soon, but until then?"

Casualty. My father had been killed. Dead. Green on Blue. He'd been shot by someone in an Afghani uniform. My father was a doctor. A doctor! *Who the hell shoots a doctor?* They had to be wrong. Did Dad even carry a weapon?

"Ma'am?"

Why wasn't Mom answering?

She remained silent, her eyes trained on the pattern of the carpet runner on the stairs, refusing to answer.

Unable to answer.

Something shifted in me; the weight of responsibility settled on my shoulders, dislodging some of the pain so I could breathe. I had to be the adult right now because no one else here could. "I'll take care of her until Casualty Assistance arrives," I managed to say with a shaky voice, speaking over April's shrieks.

"You're sure?" Captain Vincent asked, concern etching his unfamiliar features.

I nodded. "They keep a binder, just in case this—" I shoved my knuckles into my mouth, biting down as hard as I could to stop the wail desperate to emerge. I steadied myself again, sucking in air. Why was it so damn hard to breathe? "In case this happens—happened." Dad was a believer that nothing bad happened to prepared people. He'd hate to know he'd been wrong.

The captain nodded. He pulled out a form and had me verify that the information in Dad's handwriting was correct. This was our address, our phone number. Those were our names and dates of birth. The lieutenant startled. "Happy birthday, December," he whispered.

Captain Vincent sent him a silent glare. "We are so very sorry for your loss. Casualty Assistance will be here within the hour, and the care team is ready if that's okay with you." I agreed. I knew the drill, and what Mom needed.

The door shut behind them, leaving our world shattered.

For the next hour, Mom sat silently on the stairs while April wailed on my shoulder. This wasn't real. It couldn't be. I couldn't hold her tight enough to make it stop. The care team arrived around the same time April's cries softened to sniffles. I waved them inside. Armed with sympathetic eyes and casserole schedules, the three women from the family readiness group of Dad's unit took over the tasks that hadn't been done yet. The breakfast dishes were cleared, laundry put in place, the cereal Gus had spilled earlier on the kitchen floor swept. I knew they were here to help—they would smooth things over until Grams could get here—but I couldn't help but feel invaded, taken over like we were somehow unable to care for ourselves.

Who was I kidding? Mom was still huddled on the stairs. We couldn't care for ourselves. One of the care team members took Gus a snack and assured me he was still engrossed in Angry Birds. I couldn't tell him. I couldn't do it.

The casualty assistance officer knocked quietly an hour later, and I opened the door. April walked Mom to the couch and sat her down, bracing her with pillows to keep her upright. Her eyes changed focus from the carpet runner to the blank screen of the television deep within the recesses of the armoire. She refused to look at any of us. I'm not sure she was capable of understanding what had truly happened. Then again, I'm not sure I was capable of understanding what had really happened, either, but I didn't have the luxury of going catatonic.

"My name is Captain Adam Wilson," he introduced himself. He wore Dress Blues just like the notification officers had, but he seemed uncomfortable in the role he had been assigned to play. I knew I would be. His frame nearly filled the loveseat across from the couch my mother sat upon, and he dragged the coffee table toward him, softly scraping the carpet. "Did you want someone to take notes?" He glanced at Mom. "For when she's feeling up to it?"

"I've got it," a woman from the team said softly, pen and notebook ready.

Captain Wilson gathered a stack of papers from his leather briefcase, and tugged at his tie, making a minor adjustment. "There's another child, correct?" He shuffled through a few of his papers until he selected a form. "August Howard?"

"Gus is upstairs," I answered, taking the seat on the other side of Mom, closest to Captain Wilson. I clutched the black binder I'd gotten out of Mom's office. It was the very last item in the filing cabinet, just like Dad had told me before he left. "I haven't told him yet."

"Would you like me to?" Captain Wilson asked softly. I briefly considered it. Mom was in no state to discuss it with him, and Captain Wilson had probably been trained to deliver information like that. I couldn't do it though, let a stranger alter the universe of my little brother.

"No. I'll do it myself."

April began crying again, but Mom sat as still as ever, vacant, not really here with us. "I want to give him as long as possible before I have to. His world is still normal. He doesn't know that nothing will ever be the same for him." I bit back my own sob. "He's seven years old and everything he knows just ended. So I think I'll give him just another few minutes." *Before I tear him to pieces*. My skin flushed as new tears came to the surface. I supposed that was the way things would go for a while. I needed to get better at pushing them back.

Captain Wilson cleared his throat and nodded his head. "I can understand that." He explained his role to us, that he would be our guide to Dad's casualty process. He would help us through the paperwork, the ceremony, the things no one saw coming. In a way, he was our handler, sent here to be a buffer between our grief and the United States Army. I was thankful for him just as much as I hated his sheer existence.

He would be with us until we told him we no longer needed him.

After he finished his explanation, the barrage of questions began. April excused herself, saying she had to lie down. There was no doubt in my mind that within a few minutes, this would all go public on Facebook. April was never one to suffer in silence.

The questions started, and I opened the black binder. Dad's handwriting was scrawled all over the pages of his will, his life insurance policy, and his last wishes, all the paperwork carefully organized for this exact moment. Did we know where he wanted to be buried? What kind of casket he wanted? Was there anyone we wanted with us? Was the bank account correct for the life insurance money to be deposited? Did we want to fly to Dover to meet his remains while the army prepared him for burial?

Dover. It was like crossing the army's version of the river Styx.

Mom remained silent, staring at that blank television as I found the answers to what he asked. No question pulled her from her stupor, no tug of her hand, no whisper of her name could bring her back to where I was desperate for her to be. It was becoming blatantly obvious that I was alone. "Is there someone we can call to help make these decisions with your mother?" His mouth tightened as he slipped a discreet glance toward my mother. I was unsure how many shocked widows he'd seen in his career, but Mom was my first.

Grams was a day away. Because she was Dad's mom, I knew the army had officially notified her, just as we had been. No doubt she was already on her way, but until she got here, there was no one else. Mom's parents were dead. Her brother had never been around much in our lives, and I couldn't see a good reason to bring him in now. "There's just me," I replied. "I'll take responsibility for the decisions until she can."

"Ember?" Gus's small voice came from the steps where he stood. "What's going on?"

I placed Mom's hand back in her lap. It wasn't like she noticed I was holding it anyway. After the deepest breath ever taken, I walked over to my little brother. I sat down next to him on the steps and repeated everything we knew in seven-year-old terms, which wasn't anything really. But I had to repeat the one thing we knew for certain. "Daddy isn't coming home, Gus."

Little blue eyes filled with tears, and his lower lip began to quiver. "Did the bad guys get him?"

"Yes, baby." I pulled him into my arms and held him, rocking him back and forth like I had when he was an infant, our parents' miracle baby. I brushed his hair back over his forehead and kissed him.

"But it's your birthday." His warm tears soaked through my running shirt and immediately chilled as I held him as tightly as possible. I would have done anything to take away this pain, to unsay what I knew had to be said. But I couldn't take the bullet from Dad.

Gus cried himself out while Captain Wilson sat, patiently observing my mother and her nonresponse. I wondered how long it would be until words like "medicate" and "psychologist" were brought up. My mother was the strongest person I knew, but she'd always stood on the foundation that was my father.

Once the last of his little sobs shook his body, I asked him what he needed, if there was anything I could do to make this better for him. "I want you to have cake and ice cream." He lifted his head off my chest and squeezed my hand. "I want it to be your birthday."

Panic welled within me, my heart rate accelerating, tears pricking my eyes. Something fierce and terrible clawed at my insides, demanding release, demanding acknowledgment, demanding to be felt. I grimaced more than smiled and nodded my head exuberantly, cupping Gus's sweet face. I turned my attention to Captain Wilson. "Can we take a ten minute break?"

The captain nodded slowly, as though he sensed I was close to losing it, his one stable person in a house of grieving women and children. "Is there anything you need?"

"Could you please call my Grams and check on her? She lost

her husband in Vietnam…" It was all I could force out. I inched closer to the inevitable scream that welled up within my body.

"I can do that."

I kissed Gus's forehead, grabbed my keys, and ran out the door before I didn't have the strength to stand any longer. I flung myself into the driver's seat of my Volkswagen Jetta, my high school graduation present from my parents. Dad wanted me in something safe so I could make it home on weekends from the University of Colorado at Boulder. Too bad he wasn't as protected in Afghanistan.

I forced the key into the ignition, cranked the engine, and backed out of the driveway too quickly. I tore down the hill, taking the curves, heedless with my safety for the first time since I got my driver's license. In front of the grocery store, the stoplight turned red, and I became aware of the chill seeping into me, making my fingers tingle. The car read seventeen degrees outside, and I was still dressed for treadmill running. I hadn't grabbed my coat. I parked the Jetta and walked into the grocery store, thankful for the numbing sensation in my arms and heart.

I found the bakery section and crossed my arms. Cake. Gus wanted a cake, so I would get him one. Chocolate. Vanilla. Strawberry. Whipped icing. Buttercream icing. There were too many choices. It was just a damned cake! Why did I need that many choices? Who cared? I grabbed the one nearest to me and headed for the ice cream section where I snatched a quart of chocolate chip cookie dough on autopilot.

I was halfway to the checkout counter when I ran into a small family. They were average: mom, dad, one boy, one girl. They laughed as they decided what movie to rent for that night, and the little girl won, asking for *The Santa Clause*. How was it possible these people were having such a normal day, such a normal conversation? Didn't they understand the world had just ended?

"You know, they'll write on that for you if you want his name on it." The masculine voice broke me from my train of thought, and I looked up into a somewhat familiar set of brown eyes underneath a worn CU hat. I knew him, but couldn't remember how. He was achingly familiar. Of course I would take note of a guy as hot as this one. But in a university with forty thousand other students, there was always someone who looked familiar, and there were very few who I could actually name, or even remember the details of how we'd met. With a face and body like that, I should have remembered this guy, even this shell-shocked.

The guy was waiting for me to say something.

"Oh, yeah, the cake." My thoughts were fuzzy, and I was desperately holding on to what I had left of them. I nodded my head and muttered thanks as I headed back to the bakery. My feet moved of their own accord, thank God.

The heavyset woman behind the counter reached out to take the cake and I handed it over. "Could you write 'happy birthday' on this?"

"Sure can, honey. Whose special day is it?"

Special day? This was a day from hell. I stood there at the counter of the grocery store, with a cake I didn't even care about, and realized this was unequivocally the worst day of my life. Maybe there should have been some comfort in that, knowing if this was the worst day, there was nowhere to go but up. But what if it really wasn't the worst day? What if tomorrow was just waiting around the corner, ready to pounce and bring me to a new low?

"Miss?" My eyes focused back on the baker's face. "Whose name would you like on the cake?"

"December."

"Yes, ma'am, it is December, but whose name would you like on the cake?"

The same griefy-panic threatened to well up again in me, choking my throat. "It's mine. My name is December."

A string of giggles erupted from the baker. "But, ma'am, these are Teenage Mutant Ninja Turtles. It's a boy's cake!"

Something snapped inside me. The dam broke, the river raged, whatever pun came to mind. "I don't care what kind of cake it is!"

"But surely you'd be happier—"

I'd had it. "No, I wouldn't be happier. Do you know what would make me happy? I would like to go back to bed, and for none of this to have happened. I don't want to be standing in the middle of this grocery store, buying a stupid cake so my little brother can pretend that our dad isn't dead! So, no, I don't care what kind of cake it is, Ninja Turtles or Barbie or Sponge Bob freaking Square Pants!"

The woman's lip began to tremble, and tears formed in her eyes. "Happy...Birthday...December," she said as she slowly dragged the icing bag across the green and blue cake, inscribing my name. She handed the cake back over with shaking hands and I accepted it with a thankful nod.

I turned to see the CU guy with his hand in mid-reach for a pack of blueberry muffins, but his eyes were locked on me, wide with shock.

I couldn't blame him; I was shocked at my outburst, too, appalled that I'd lost it in the middle of the grocery store.

Tears streamed down my face unnoticed as I stood at the register, waiting for the young girl to ring up my cake and ice cream. "Thirty-two nineteen," she told me. I reached for my back pocket, where I normally kept my tiny wallet, but found only the smooth spandex of my running shorts.

"Shit," I whispered, closing my eyes in defeat. No coat. No wallet. Great planning.

"I got this." The brown-eyed guy slid a fifty dollar bill across the conveyor belt to the clerk. I hadn't even noticed he'd been behind me.

I turned to look back up at him, stunned at how tall he was. I only reached his collarbone. The sudden turn made me sway, and he reached out to steady me, his strong hands gently supporting my arms. "Thank you." I dragged the backs of my hands over my cheeks, wiping away what tears I could, and handed him back his change. There was something so familiar about him... What was it?

"Do you need me?" he asked softly, as the clerk rang up his Vitamin Water.

"What?" I had zero clue what he was talking about.

He flushed. "Do you need me to carry that out? I mean, it looks kind of heavy," he finished slowly, like he couldn't believe he'd said it, either.

"It's a cake." He had to be the hottest awkward guy I'd ever met.

"Right." He grabbed his bag and shook his head like he was trying to clear it. "Would you at least let me drive you home?"

Wow, did he choose the wrong day to try to pick me up. "I don't even know you. I hardly think that's appropriate."

A soft smile slid across his face. "You're December Howard and I'm Josh Walker. I graduated three years ahead of you."

Josh Walker. Holy shit. High school. Memories crashed through me, but that Josh Walker couldn't possibly be the one standing in front of me. No, that one had been a tattooed, motorcycle-driving, cheerleader magnet, not this clean-cut all-American nice guy. "Josh Walker. Right. I used to have a picture of you taped on my closet door from when you guys won state." Shit. Why did I say that? His eyebrows raised in surprise, and I mentally added *or still do, but whatever.* "If I remember correctly, you had your head stuck too far up your hockey helmet to notice any underclassmen." But I had noticed him, along with every other girl in school. My eyes narrowed as I assessed the lean cut of his face, only made more angular and freaking hot by quasi-adulthood. "And you had a lot more hair."

His devastating grin cut through the fog of my brain, distracting me from the pain for a blissful moment. How did a hockey player have such straight teeth?

"See, I'm not a stranger." He handed me my cake, and his smile vanished, replaced by a flash of...pain or pity? "Ember, I'm sorry about your dad. Please let me drive you home. You're not in any shape to drive."

I shook my head, tearing my gaze from his sympathetic one. For an instant, I had nearly forgotten. Guilt overran me. I'd just let a pretty face distract me from…everything, and it all came rushing back, shredding into me. What was I doing even thinking about him? I had a boyfriend, and a dead father, and no time for this. Dead. I squeezed my eyes shut against the pain.

"Ember?"

"I need to do it. I need to know I can." I thanked him again for paying and headed back into reality.

I slid onto the frozen leather seat in my car and sat in stunned silence for a moment. How could something as simple as seeing Josh Walker again right a little piece of my soul when the rest had been flipped so wrong? The cold of the seat seeped through my running capris, forcing out the warm thoughts of Josh. The cake on my front seat mocked me with silly, happy, martial-arts turtles. Gus would love it. If Gus *could* love it. God, what was he going to do without Dad? What were any of us going to do? Panic welled up in my chest, catching in my throat before exploding in a cry that sounded nothing like me. How was I supposed to take care of Mom without Dad? How was I going to do any of this when I wanted to curl up and deny it all?

My composure crumpled, and I sobbed against my steering wheel for exactly five minutes. Then I sat up, dried my tears, and stopped crying. I couldn't afford to cry or break down anymore. I had to take care of my family.